COURTNEY
CRUMRIN AND THE COVEN
OF MYSTICS™

COURTNEY CRUMRIN AND THE COVEN OF MYSTICS

By Ted Naifeh

Design by
Ted Naifeh
& Steven Birch @ Servo

Edited by
Joe Nozmack & James Lucas Jones

Series edited by
James Lucas Jones

Published by Oni Press, Inc.
Joe Nozemack, publisher
Jamie S. Rich, editor in chief
James Lucas Jones, associate editor

This collects issues 1-4 of the Oni Press
comics series *Courtney Crumrin & the Coven of Mystics.*

ONI PRESS, INC.
6336 SE Milwaukie Avenue, PMB 30
Portland, OR 97202
USA

www.onipress.com
www.tednaifeh.com

First edition: September 2003
ISBN 1929998-59-7

1 3 5 7 9 10 8 6 4 2
PRINTED IN CANADA.

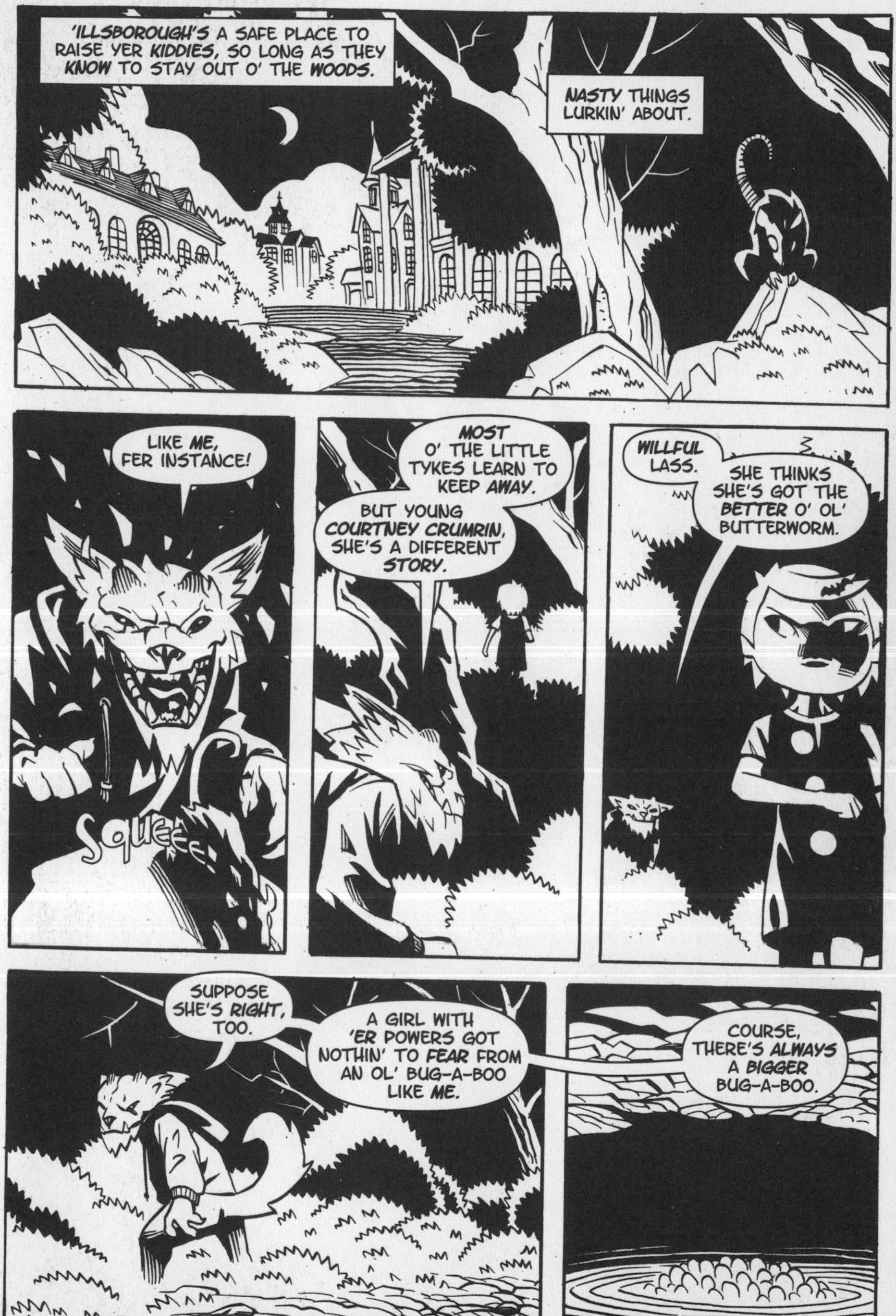
'ILLSBOROUGH'S A SAFE PLACE TO RAISE YER KIDDIES, SO LONG AS THEY KNOW TO STAY OUT O' THE WOODS.
NASTY THINGS LURKIN' ABOUT.
LIKE ME, FER INSTANCE!
SQUEEE
MOST O' THE LITTLE TYKES LEARN TO KEEP AWAY.
BUT YOUNG COURTNEY CRUMRIN, SHE'S A DIFFERENT STORY.
WILLFUL LASS.
SHE THINKS SHE'S GOT THE BETTER O' OL' BUTTERWORM.
SUPPOSE SHE'S RIGHT, TOO.
A GIRL WITH 'ER POWERS GOT NOTHIN' TO FEAR FROM AN OL' BUG-A-BOO LIKE ME.
COURSE, THERE'S ALWAYS A BIGGER BUG-A-BOO.

CHAPTER ONE

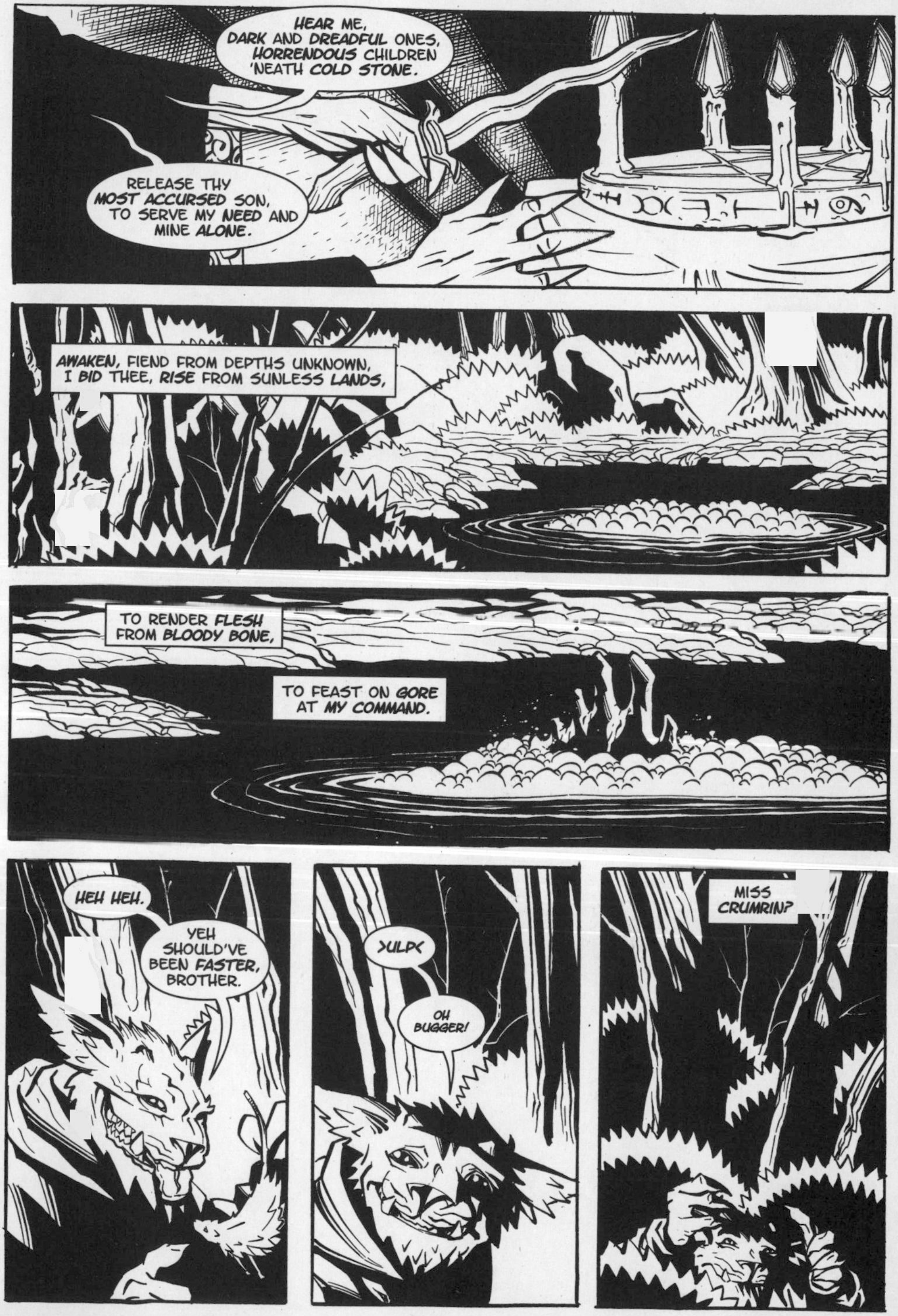
HEAR ME, DARK AND DREADFUL ONES, HORRENDOUS CHILDREN 'NEATH COLD STONE.
RELEASE THY MOST ACCURSED SON, TO SERVE MY NEED AND MINE ALONE.
AWAKEN, FIEND FROM DEPTHS UNKNOWN, I BID THEE, RISE FROM SUNLESS LANDS,
TO RENDER FLESH FROM BLOODY BONE,
TO FEAST ON GORE AT MY COMMAND.
HEH HEH.
YEH SHOULD'VE BEEN FASTER, BROTHER.
>ULP<
OH BUGGER!
MISS CRUMRIN?

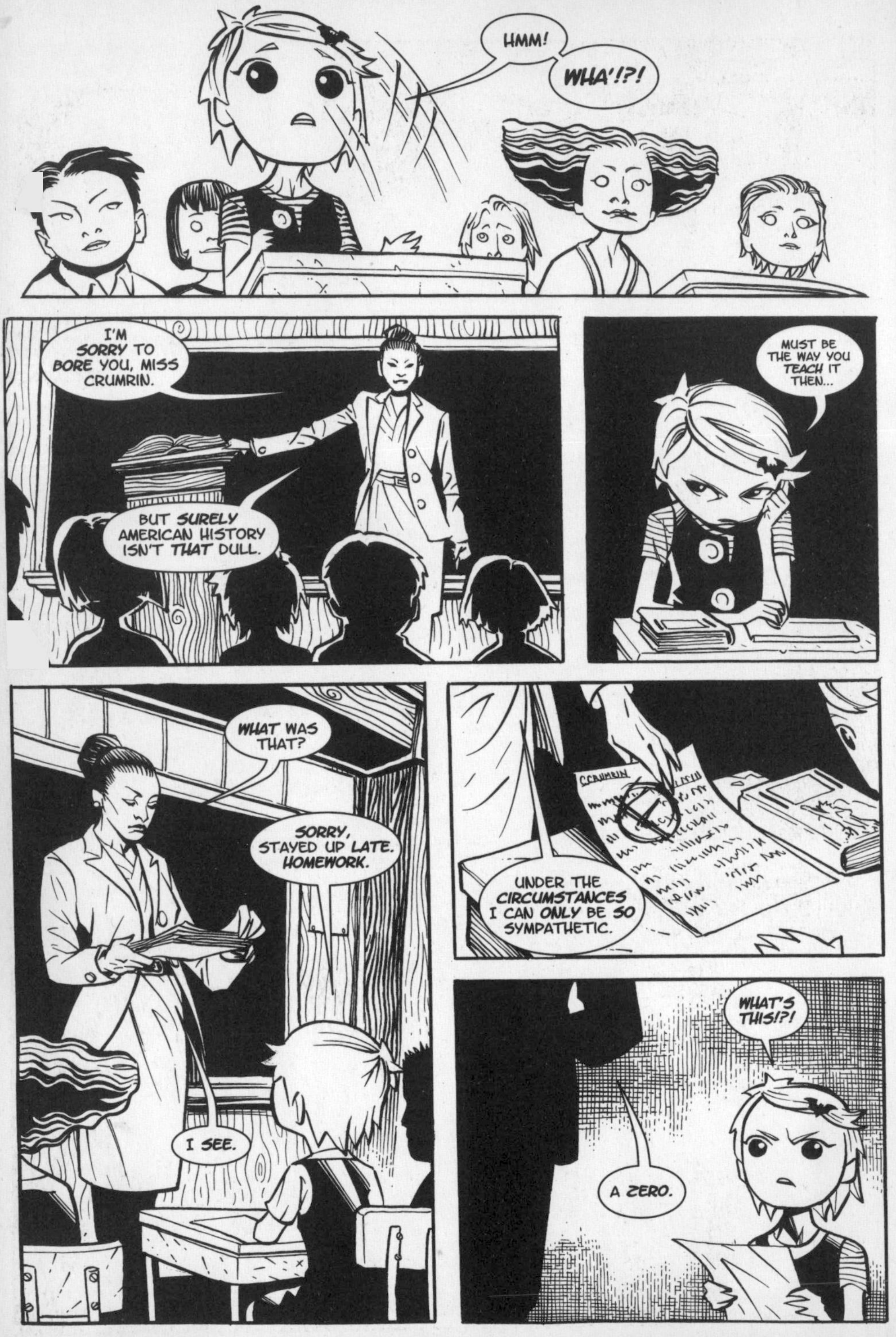
HMM!
WHA'!?!
I'M SORRY TO BORE YOU, MISS CRUMRIN.
BUT SURELY AMERICAN HISTORY ISN'T THAT DULL.
MUST BE THE WAY YOU TEACH IT THEN...
WHAT WAS THAT?
SORRY, STAYED UP LATE. HOMEWORK.
I SEE.
CCRUMRIN
UNDER THE CIRCUMSTANCES I CAN ONLY BE SO SYMPATHETIC.
WHAT'S THIS!?!
A ZERO.

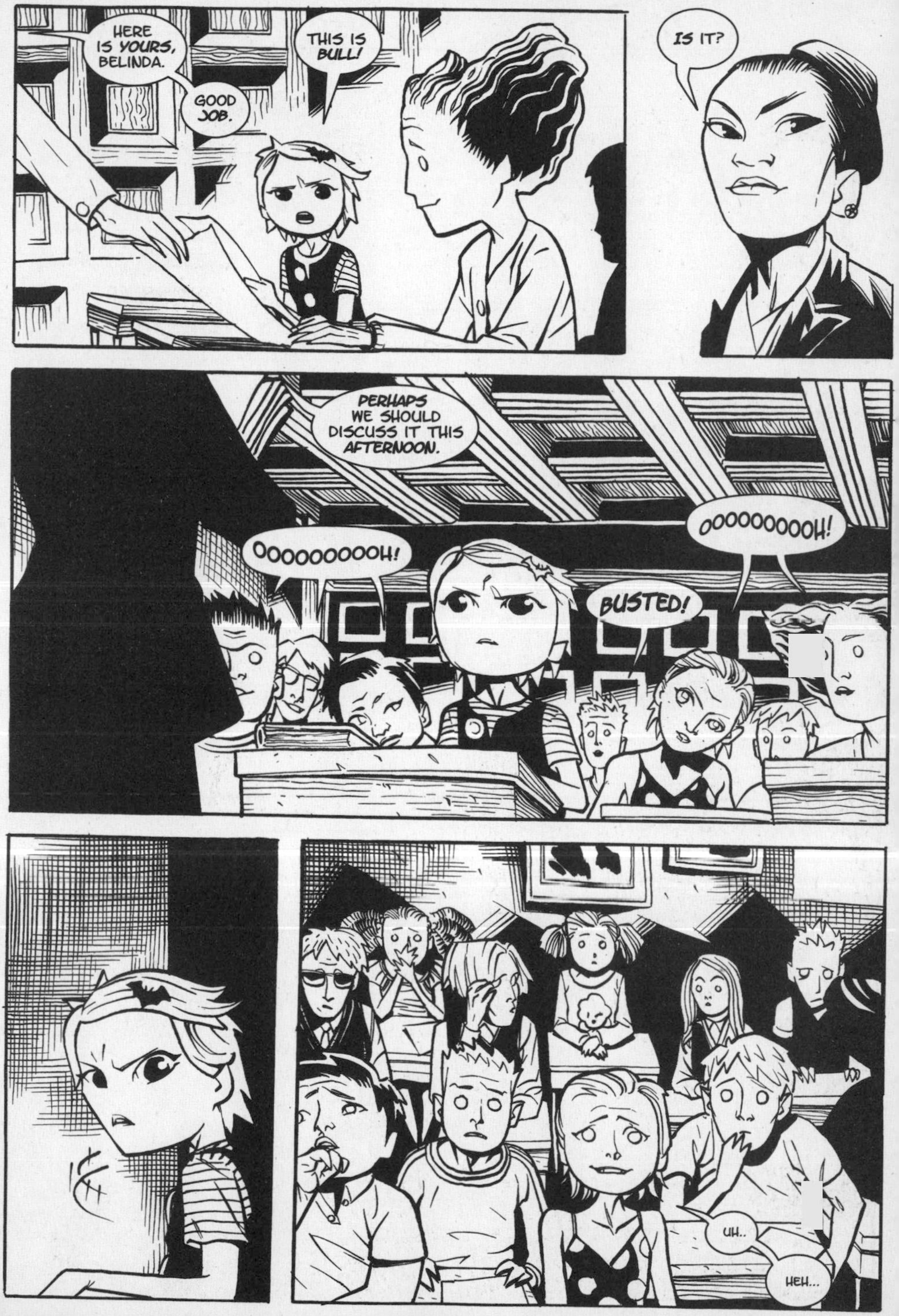
HERE IS YOURS, BELINDA.
GOOD JOB.
THIS IS BULL!
IS IT?
PERHAPS WE SHOULD DISCUSS IT THIS AFTERNOON.
OOOOOOOOOH!
BUSTED!
OOOOOOOOOH!
UH..
HEH...

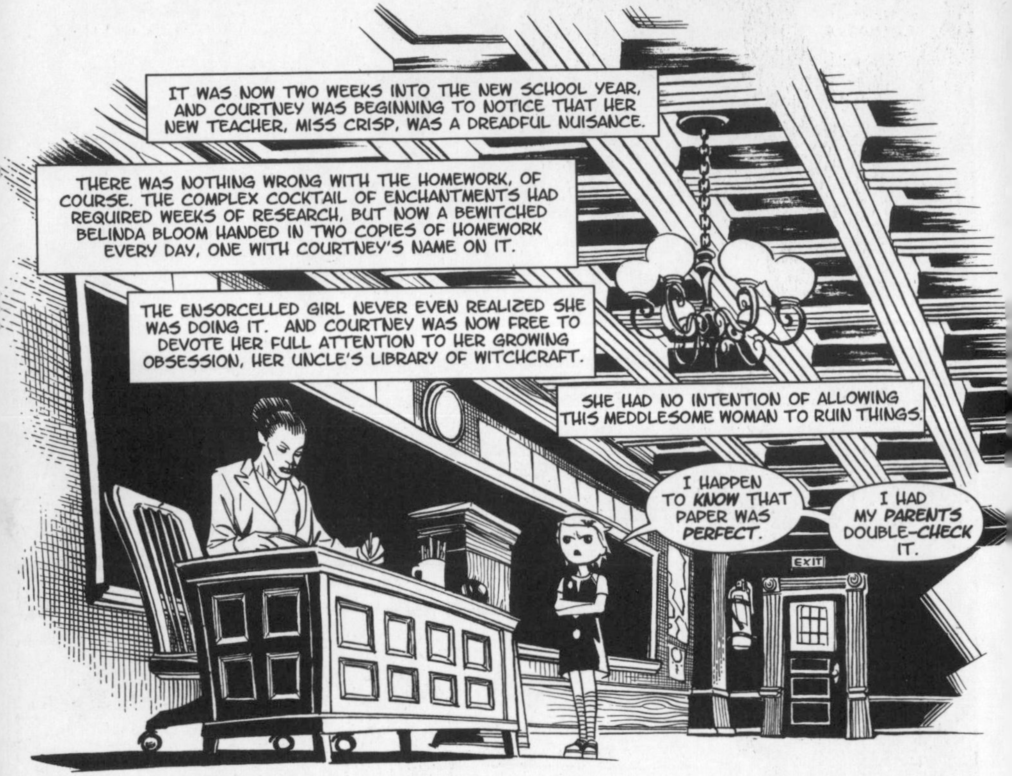
IT WAS NOW TWO WEEKS INTO THE NEW SCHOOL YEAR, AND COURTNEY WAS BEGINNING TO NOTICE THAT HER NEW TEACHER, MISS CRISP, WAS A DREADFUL NUISANCE.
THERE WAS NOTHING WRONG WITH THE HOMEWORK, OF COURSE. THE COMPLEX COCKTAIL OF ENCHANTMENTS HAD REQUIRED WEEKS OF RESEARCH, BUT NOW A BEWITCHED BELINDA BLOOM HANDED IN TWO COPIES OF HOMEWORK EVERY DAY, ONE WITH COURTNEY'S NAME ON IT.
THE ENSORCELLED GIRL NEVER EVEN REALIZED SHE WAS DOING IT. AND COURTNEY WAS NOW FREE TO DEVOTE HER FULL ATTENTION TO HER GROWING OBSESSION, HER UNCLE'S LIBRARY OF WITCHCRAFT.
SHE HAD NO INTENTION OF ALLOWING THIS MEDDLESOME WOMAN TO RUIN THINGS.
I HAPPEN TO KNOW THAT PAPER WAS PERFECT.
I HAD MY PARENTS DOUBLE-CHECK IT.
EXIT

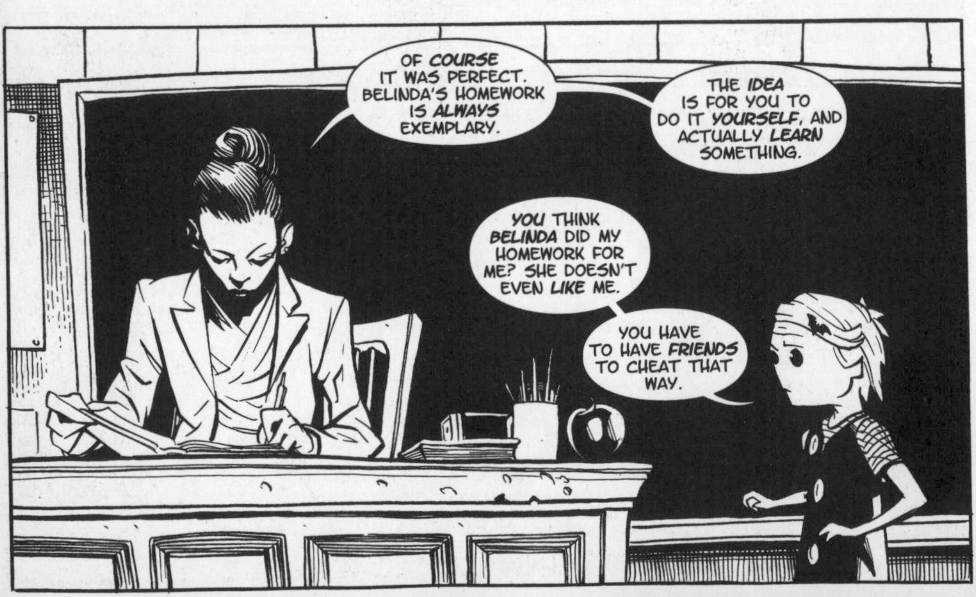
OF COURSE IT WAS PERFECT. BELINDA'S HOMEWORK IS ALWAYS EXEMPLARY.
THE IDEA IS FOR YOU TO DO IT YOURSELF, AND ACTUALLY LEARN SOMETHING.
YOU THINK BELINDA DID MY HOMEWORK FOR ME? SHE DOESN'T EVEN LIKE ME.
YOU HAVE TO HAVE FRIENDS TO CHEAT THAT WAY.

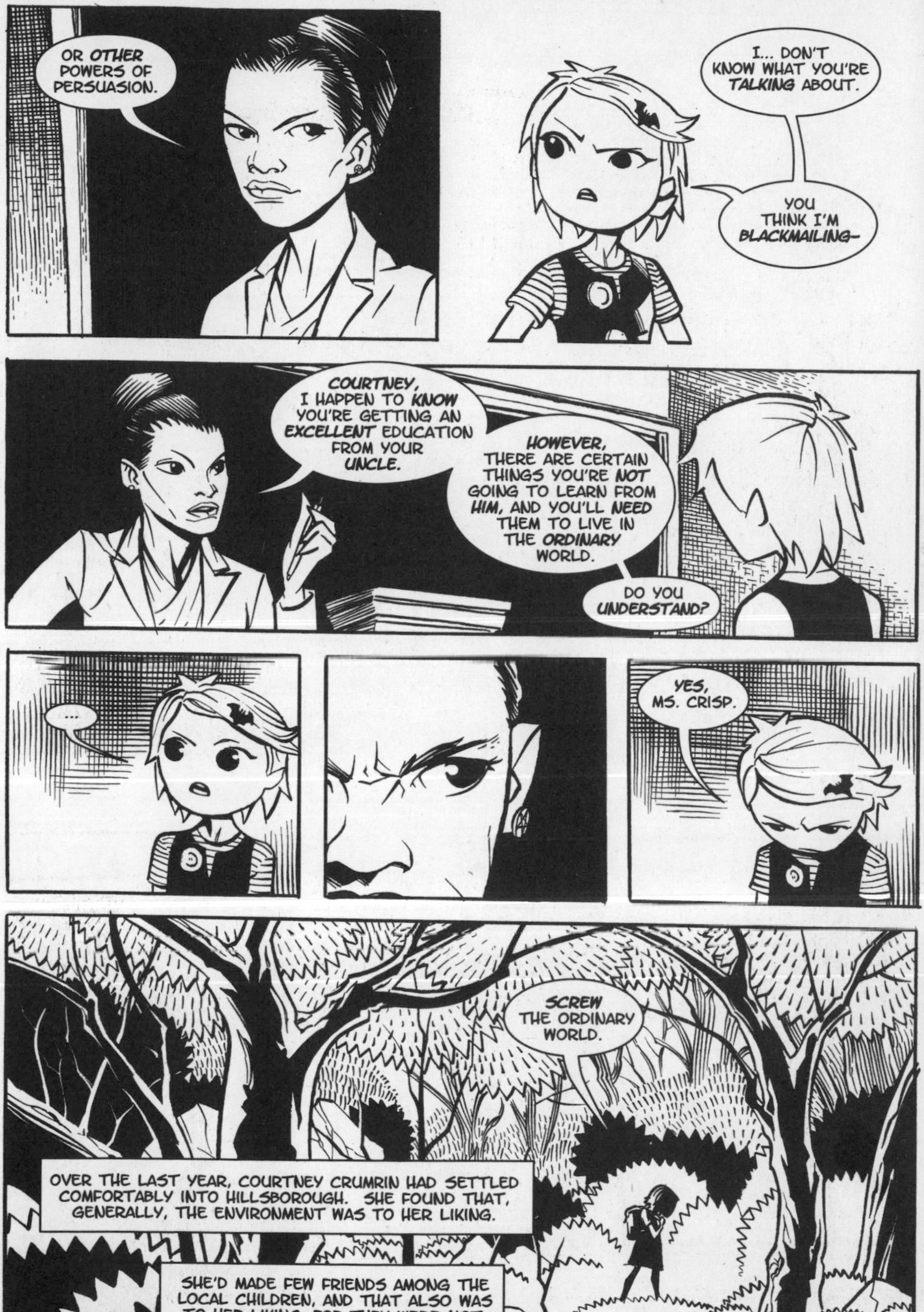
OR OTHER POWERS OF PERSUASION.
I... DON'T KNOW WHAT YOU'RE TALKING ABOUT.
YOU THINK I'M BLACKMAILING-
COURTNEY, I HAPPEN TO KNOW YOU'RE GETTING AN EXCELLENT EDUCATION FROM YOUR UNCLE.
HOWEVER, THERE ARE CERTAIN THINGS YOU'RE NOT GOING TO LEARN FROM HIM, AND YOU'LL NEED THEM TO LIVE IN THE ORDINARY WORLD.
DO YOU UNDERSTAND?
...
YES, MS. CRISP.
SCREW THE ORDINARY WORLD.
OVER THE LAST YEAR, COURTNEY CRUMRIN HAD SETTLED COMFORTABLY INTO HILLSBOROUGH. SHE FOUND THAT, GENERALLY, THE ENVIRONMENT WAS TO HER LIKING.
SHE'D MADE FEW FRIENDS AMONG THE LOCAL CHILDREN, AND THAT ALSO WAS TO HER LIKING, FOR THEY WERE NOT.

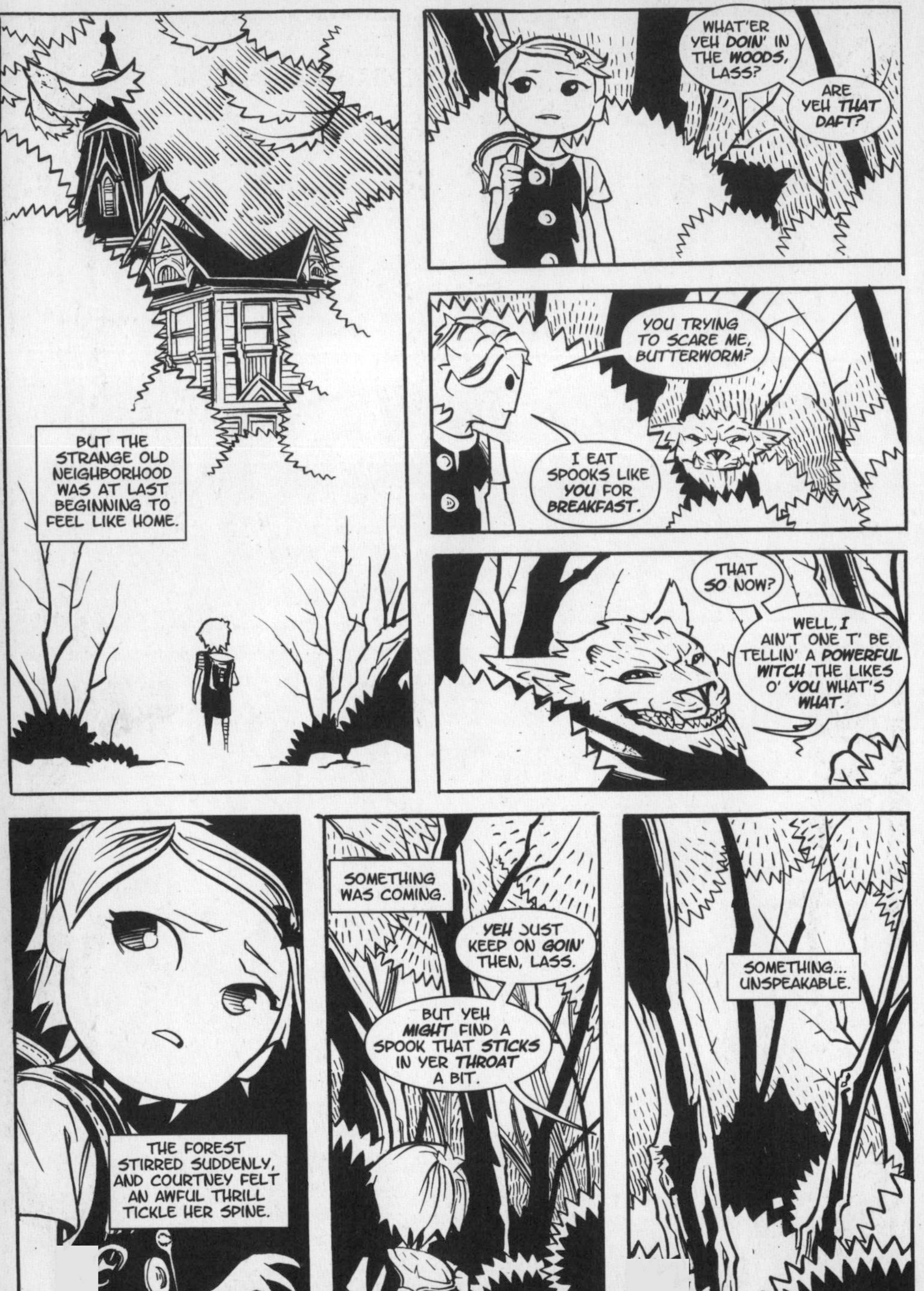
BUT THE STRANGE OLD NEIGHBORHOOD WAS AT LAST BEGINNING TO FEEL LIKE HOME.
WHAT'ER YEH DOIN' IN THE WOODS, LASS?
ARE YEH THAT DAFT?
YOU TRYING TO SCARE ME, BUTTERWORM?
I EAT SPOOKS LIKE YOU FOR BREAKFAST.
THAT SO NOW?
WELL, I AIN'T ONE T' BE TELLIN' A POWERFUL WITCH THE LIKES O' YOU WHAT'S WHAT.
THE FOREST STIRRED SUDDENLY, AND COURTNEY FELT AN AWFUL THRILL TICKLE HER SPINE.
SOMETHING WAS COMING.
YEH JUST KEEP ON GOIN' THEN, LASS.
BUT YEH MIGHT FIND A SPOOK THAT STICKS IN YER THROAT A BIT.
SOMETHING... UNSPEAKABLE.

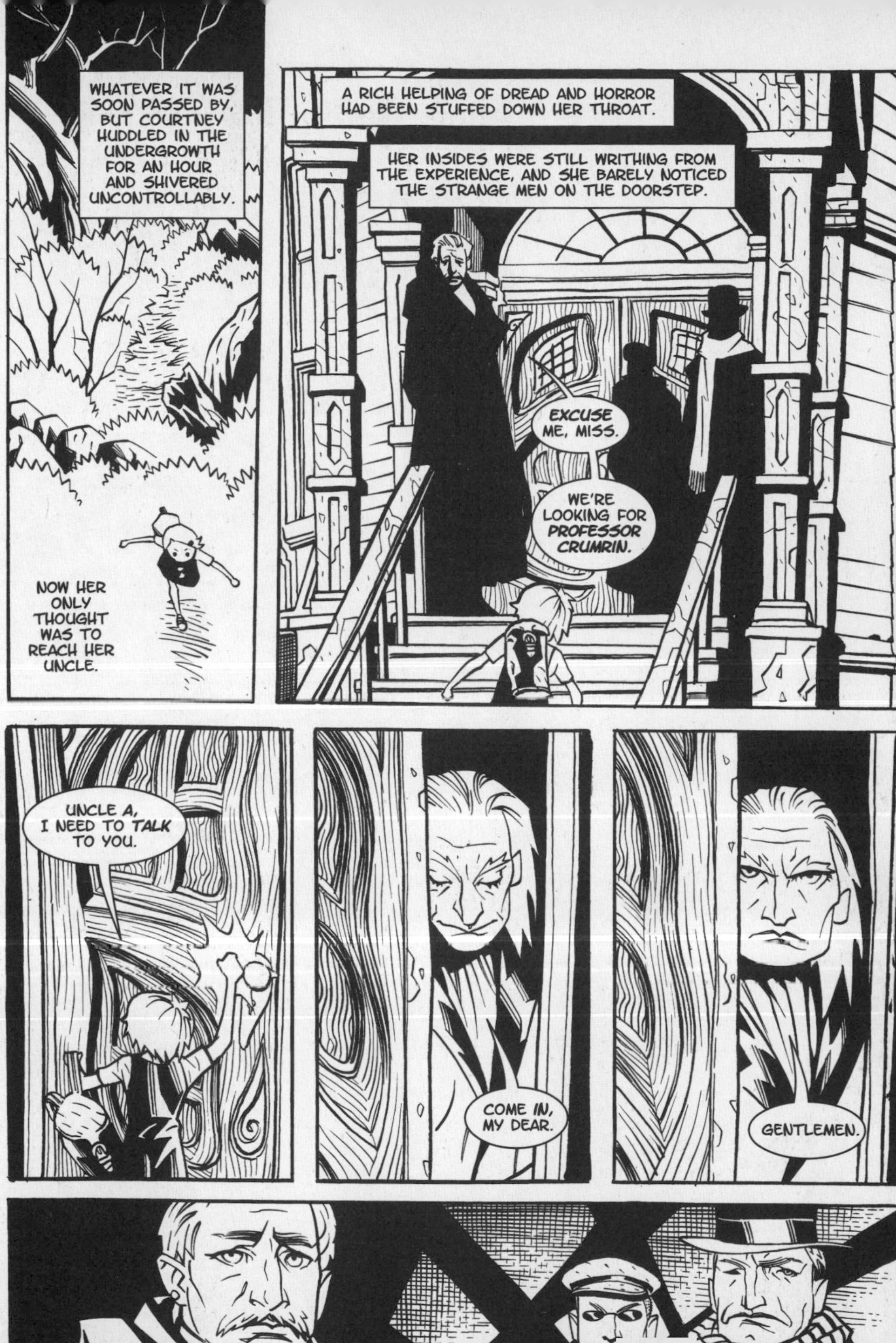
WHATEVER IT WAS SOON PASSED BY, BUT COURTNEY HUDDLED IN THE UNDERGROWTH FOR AN HOUR AND SHIVERED UNCONTROLLABLY.
NOW HER ONLY THOUGHT WAS TO REACH HER UNCLE.
A RICH HELPING OF DREAD AND HORROR HAD BEEN STUFFED DOWN HER THROAT.
HER INSIDES WERE STILL WRITHING FROM THE EXPERIENCE, AND SHE BARELY NOTICED THE STRANGE MEN ON THE DOORSTEP.
EXCUSE ME, MISS.
WE'RE LOOKING FOR PROFESSOR CRUMRIN.
UNCLE A, I NEED TO TALK TO YOU.
COME IN, MY DEAR.
GENTLEMEN.

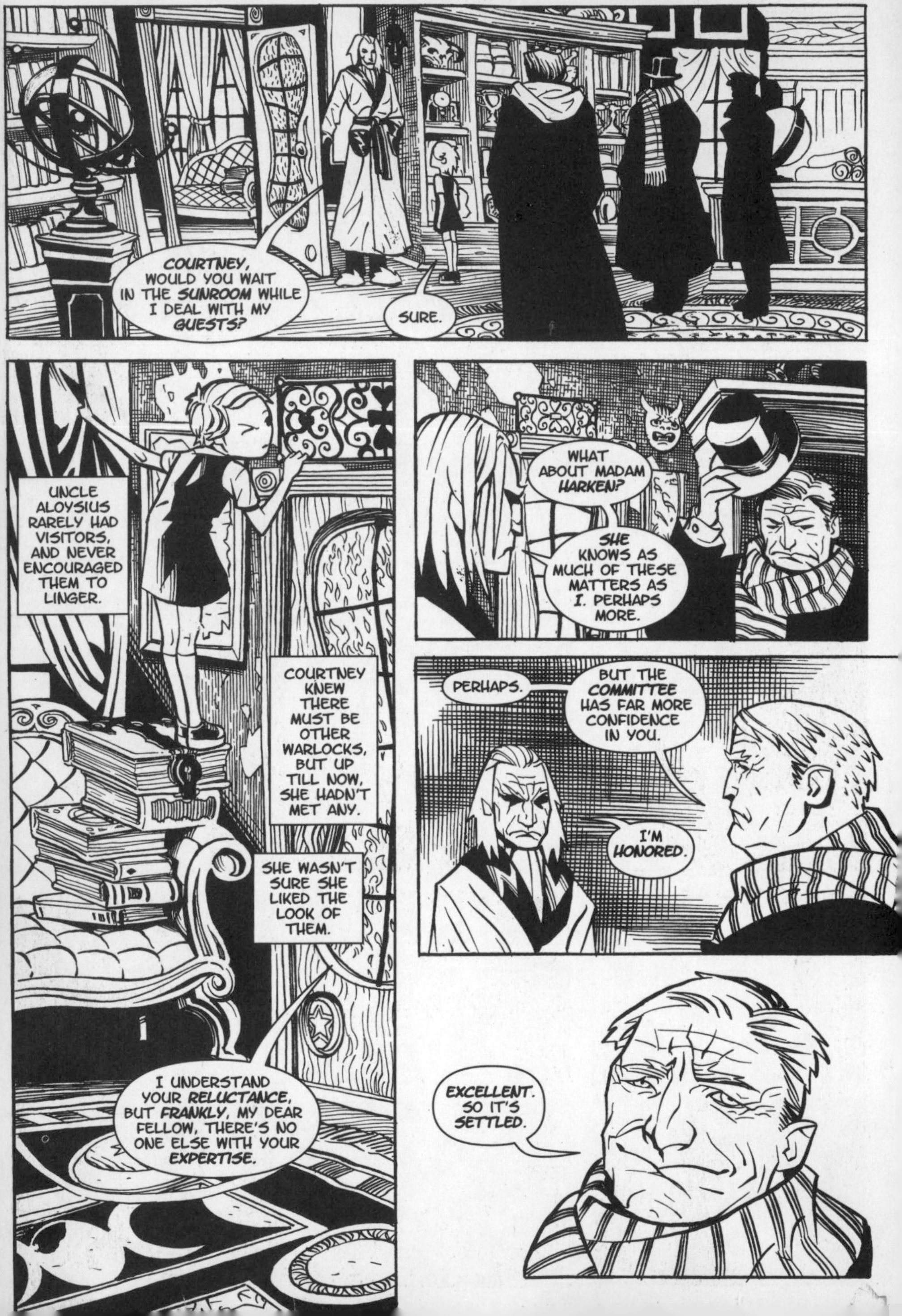
COURTNEY, WOULD YOU WAIT IN THE SUNROOM WHILE I DEAL WITH MY GUESTS?
SURE.
UNCLE ALOYSIUS RARELY HAD VISITORS, AND NEVER ENCOURAGED THEM TO LINGER.
COURTNEY KNEW THERE MUST BE OTHER WARLOCKS, BUT UP TILL NOW, SHE HADN'T MET ANY.
SHE WASN'T SURE SHE LIKED THE LOOK OF THEM.
I UNDERSTAND YOUR RELUCTANCE, BUT FRANKLY, MY DEAR FELLOW, THERE'S NO ONE ELSE WITH YOUR EXPERTISE.
WHAT ABOUT MADAM HARKEN?
SHE KNOWS AS MUCH OF THESE MATTERS AS I. PERHAPS MORE.
PERHAPS.
BUT THE COMMITTEE HAS FAR MORE CONFIDENCE IN YOU.
I'M HONORED.
EXCELLENT. SO IT'S SETTLED.

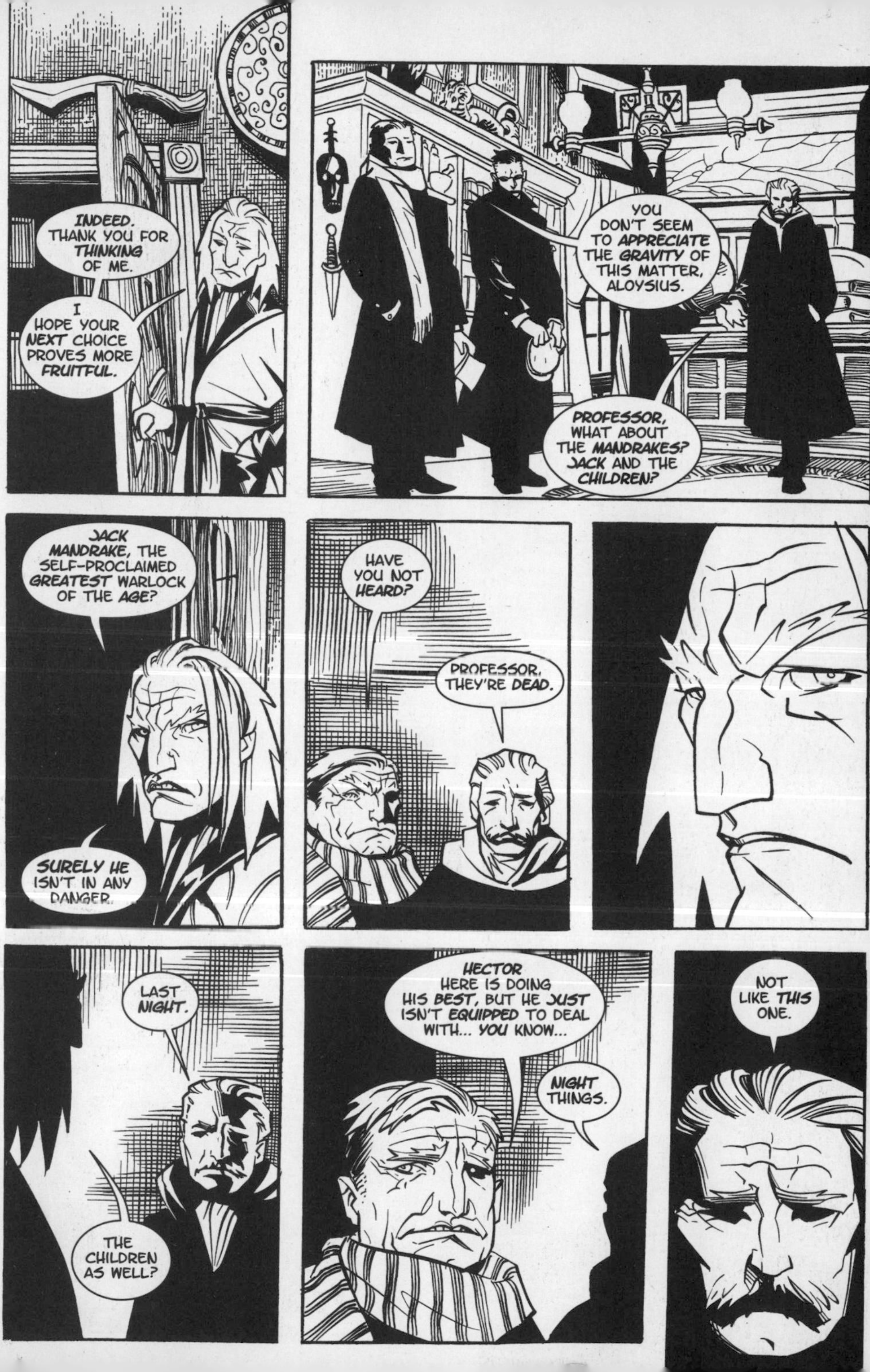
INDEED. THANK YOU FOR THINKING OF ME.
I HOPE YOUR NEXT CHOICE PROVES MORE FRUITFUL.
YOU DON'T SEEM TO APPRECIATE THE GRAVITY OF THIS MATTER, ALOYSIUS.
PROFESSOR, WHAT ABOUT THE MANDRAKES? JACK AND THE CHILDREN?
JACK MANDRAKE, THE SELF-PROCLAIMED GREATEST WARLOCK OF THE AGE?
SURELY HE ISN'T IN ANY DANGER.
HAVE YOU NOT HEARD?
PROFESSOR, THEY'RE DEAD.
LAST NIGHT.
THE CHILDREN AS WELL?
HECTOR HERE IS DOING HIS BEST, BUT HE JUST ISN'T EQUIPPED TO DEAL WITH... YOU KNOW...
NIGHT THINGS.
NOT LIKE THIS ONE.

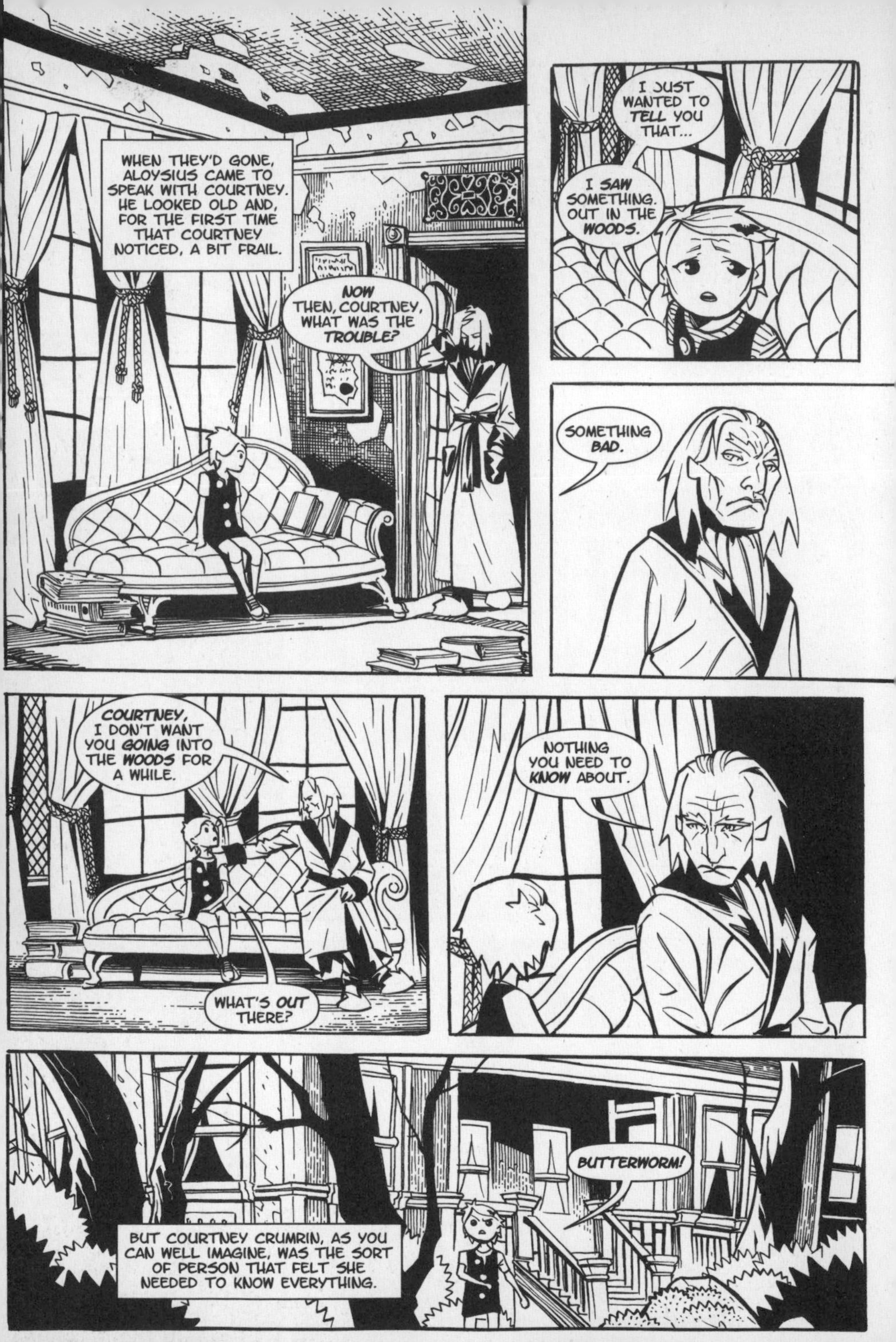
WHEN THEY'D GONE, ALOYSIUS CAME TO SPEAK WITH COURTNEY. HE LOOKED OLD AND, FOR THE FIRST TIME THAT COURTNEY NOTICED, A BIT FRAIL.
NOW THEN, COURTNEY, WHAT WAS THE TROUBLE?
I JUST WANTED TO TELL YOU THAT...
I SAW SOMETHING. OUT IN THE WOODS.
SOMETHING BAD.
COURTNEY, I DON'T WANT YOU GOING INTO THE WOODS FOR A WHILE.
WHAT'S OUT THERE?
NOTHING YOU NEED TO KNOW ABOUT.
BUTTERWORM!
BUT COURTNEY CRUMRIN, AS YOU CAN WELL IMAGINE, WAS THE SORT OF PERSON THAT FELT SHE NEEDED TO KNOW EVERYTHING.

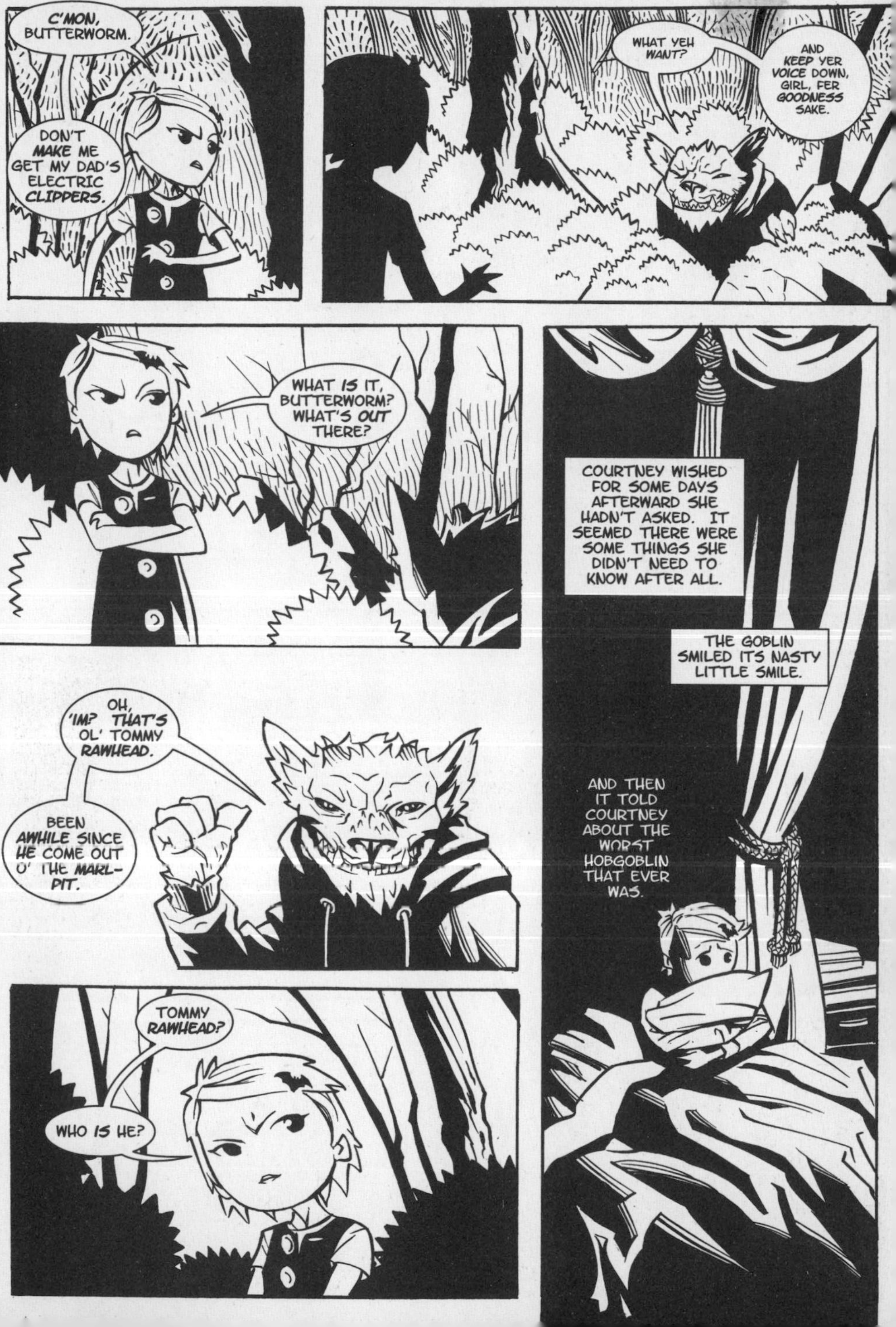
C'MON, BUTTERWORM.
DON'T MAKE ME GET MY DAD'S ELECTRIC CLIPPERS.
WHAT YEH WANT?
AND KEEP YER VOICE DOWN, GIRL, FER GOODNESS SAKE.
WHAT IS IT, BUTTERWORM? WHAT'S OUT THERE?
OH, 'IM? THAT'S OL' TOMMY RAWHEAD.
BEEN AWHILE SINCE HE COME OUT O' THE MARL-PIT.
TOMMY RAWHEAD?
WHO IS HE?
COURTNEY WISHED FOR SOME DAYS AFTERWARD SHE HADN'T ASKED. IT SEEMED THERE WERE SOME THINGS SHE DIDN'T NEED TO KNOW AFTER ALL.
THE GOBLIN SMILED ITS NASTY LITTLE SMILE.
AND THEN IT TOLD COURTNEY ABOUT THE WORST HOBGOBLIN THAT EVER WAS.

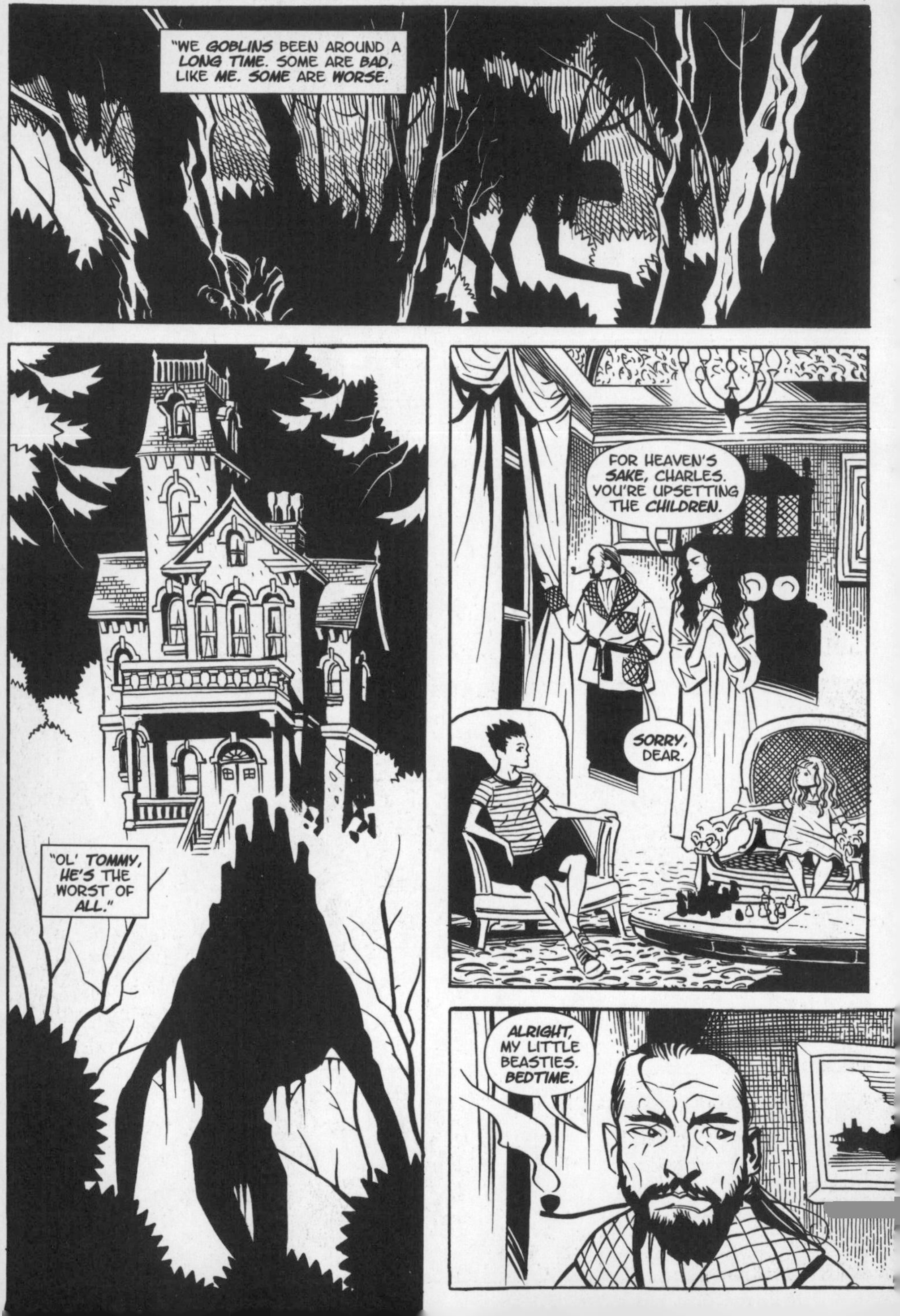
"WE GOBLINS BEEN AROUND A LONG TIME. SOME ARE BAD, LIKE ME. SOME ARE WORSE.
"OL' TOMMY, HE'S THE WORST OF ALL."
FOR HEAVEN'S SAKE, CHARLES. YOU'RE UPSETTING THE CHILDREN.
SORRY, DEAR.
ALRIGHT, MY LITTLE BEASTIES. BEDTIME.

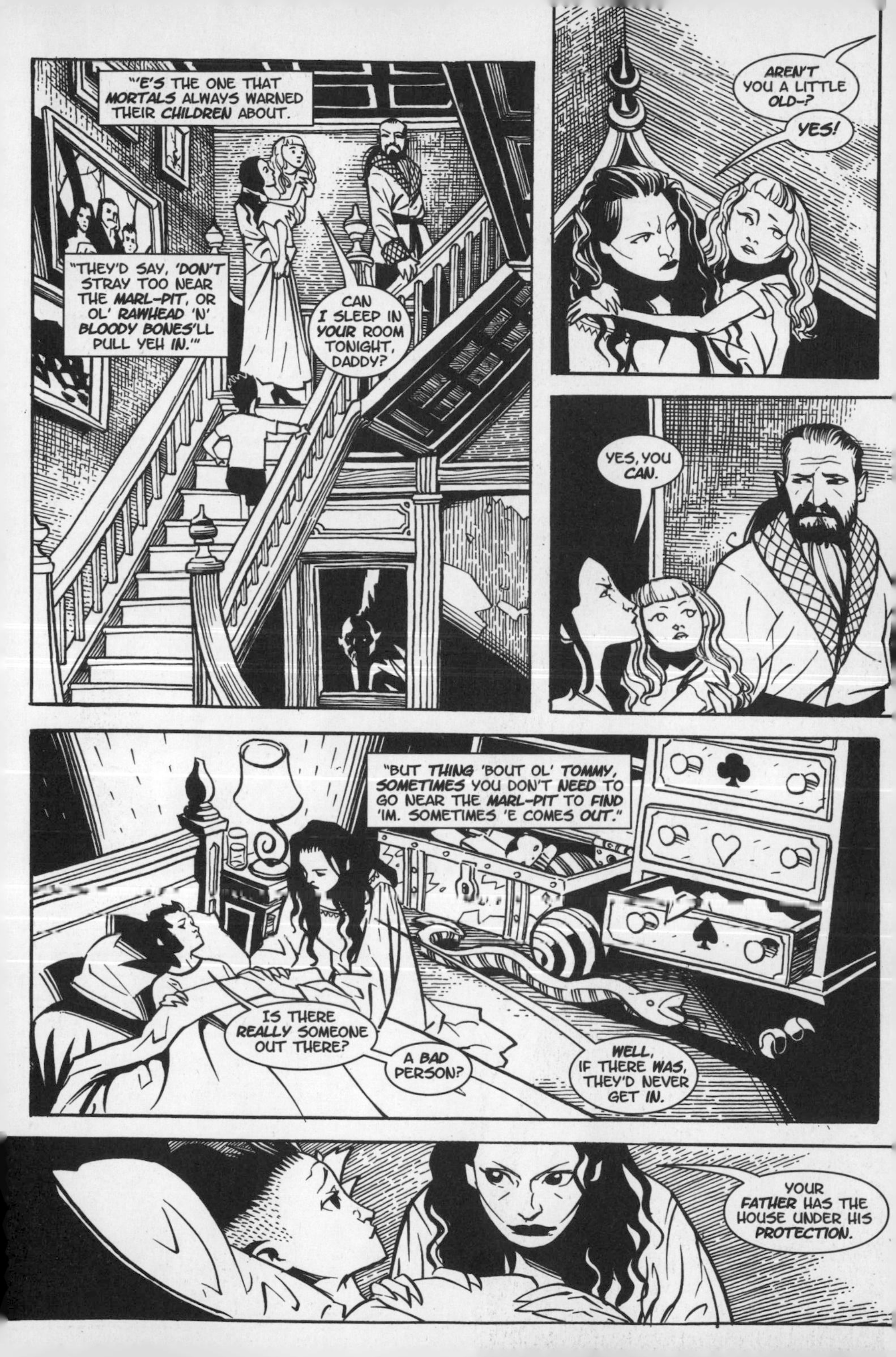
"'E'S THE ONE THAT MORTALS ALWAYS WARNED THEIR CHILDREN ABOUT.
"THEY'D SAY, 'DON'T STRAY TOO NEAR THE MARL-PIT, OR OL' RAWHEAD 'N' BLOODY BONES'LL PULL YEH IN.'"
CAN I SLEEP IN YOUR ROOM TONIGHT, DADDY?
AREN'T YOU A LITTLE OLD-?
YES!
YES, YOU CAN.
"BUT THING 'BOUT OL' TOMMY, SOMETIMES YOU DON'T NEED TO GO NEAR THE MARL-PIT TO FIND 'IM. SOMETIMES 'E COMES OUT."
IS THERE REALLY SOMEONE OUT THERE?
A BAD PERSON?
WELL, IF THERE WAS, THEY'D NEVER GET IN.
YOUR FATHER HAS THE HOUSE UNDER HIS PROTECTION.

"AN' WHEN 'E WANTS BLOOD, THERE'S NOTHIN' CAN STOP 'IM.

"NO SPELL, NO CURSE...

"NO MAGIC, HOWEVER POWERFUL CAN PROTECT YEH FROM 'IM.

"AN' IF 'E WANTS YEH, 'E'LL 'AVE YEH. O' THAT YEH CAN BE SURE.

" 'IS ARMS IS SO LONG, 'E CAN REACH INTO THE FURTHEST HIDIN' PLACES.

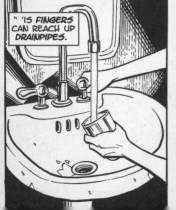

" 'IS FINGERS CAN REACH UP DRAINPIPES.

"BUT THE FUNNIEST THING 'BOUT 'IM, EVEN THOUGH 'E'S A GREAT HUGE BUGGER...

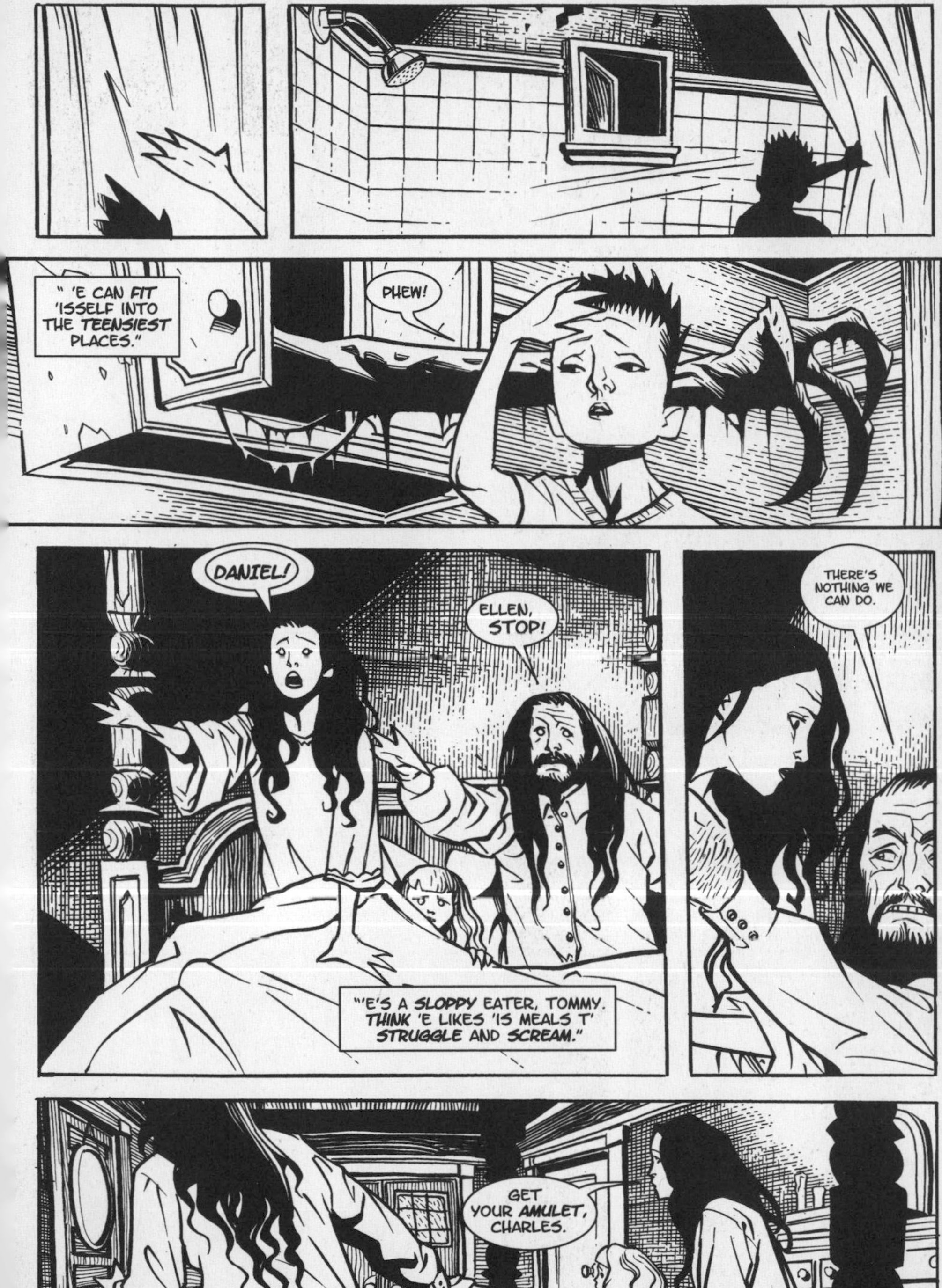
" 'E CAN FIT 'ISSELF INTO THE TEENSIEST PLACES."
PHEW!
DANIEL!
ELLEN, STOP!
"'E'S A SLOPPY EATER, TOMMY. THINK 'E LIKES 'IS MEALS T' STRUGGLE AND SCREAM."
THERE'S NOTHING WE CAN DO.
GET YOUR AMULET, CHARLES.

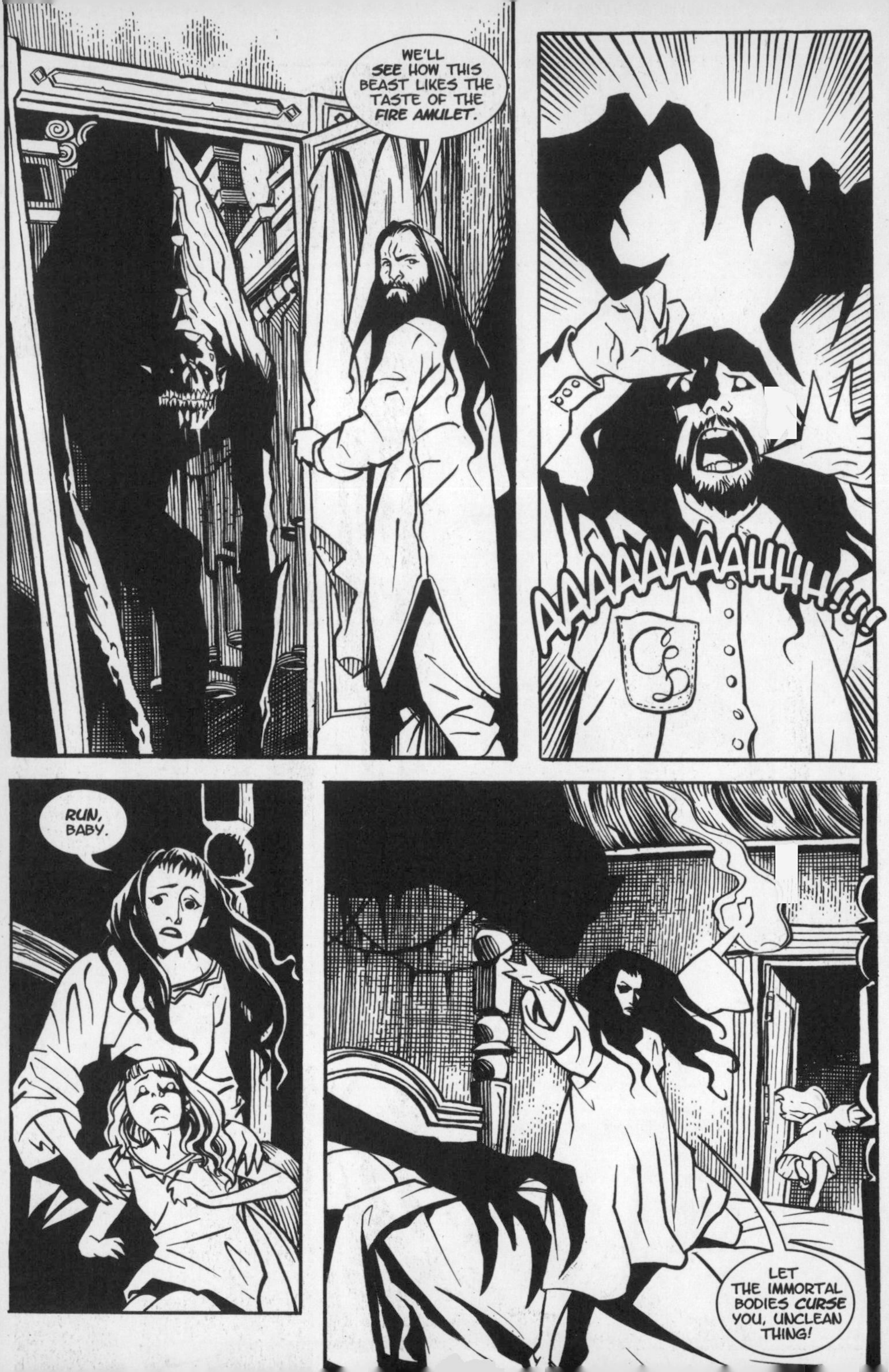
WE'LL SEE HOW THIS BEAST LIKES THE TASTE OF THE FIRE AMULET.
AAAAAAAAAHHH!!!!
RUN, BABY.
LET THE IMMORTAL BODIES CURSE YOU, UNCLEAN THING!

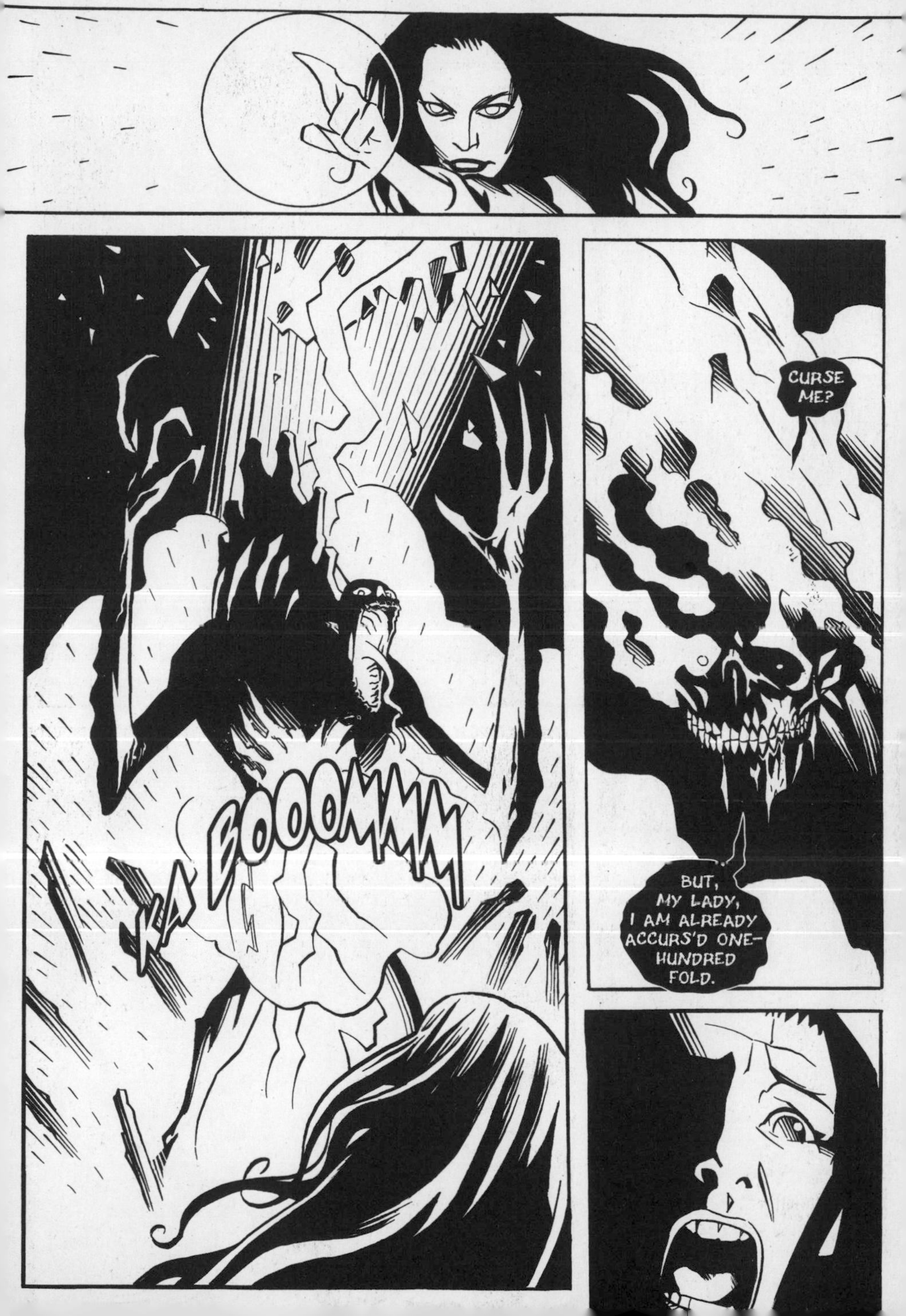
KA BOOOMMM
CURSE ME?
BUT, MY LADY, I AM ALREADY ACCURS'D ONE-HUNDRED FOLD.

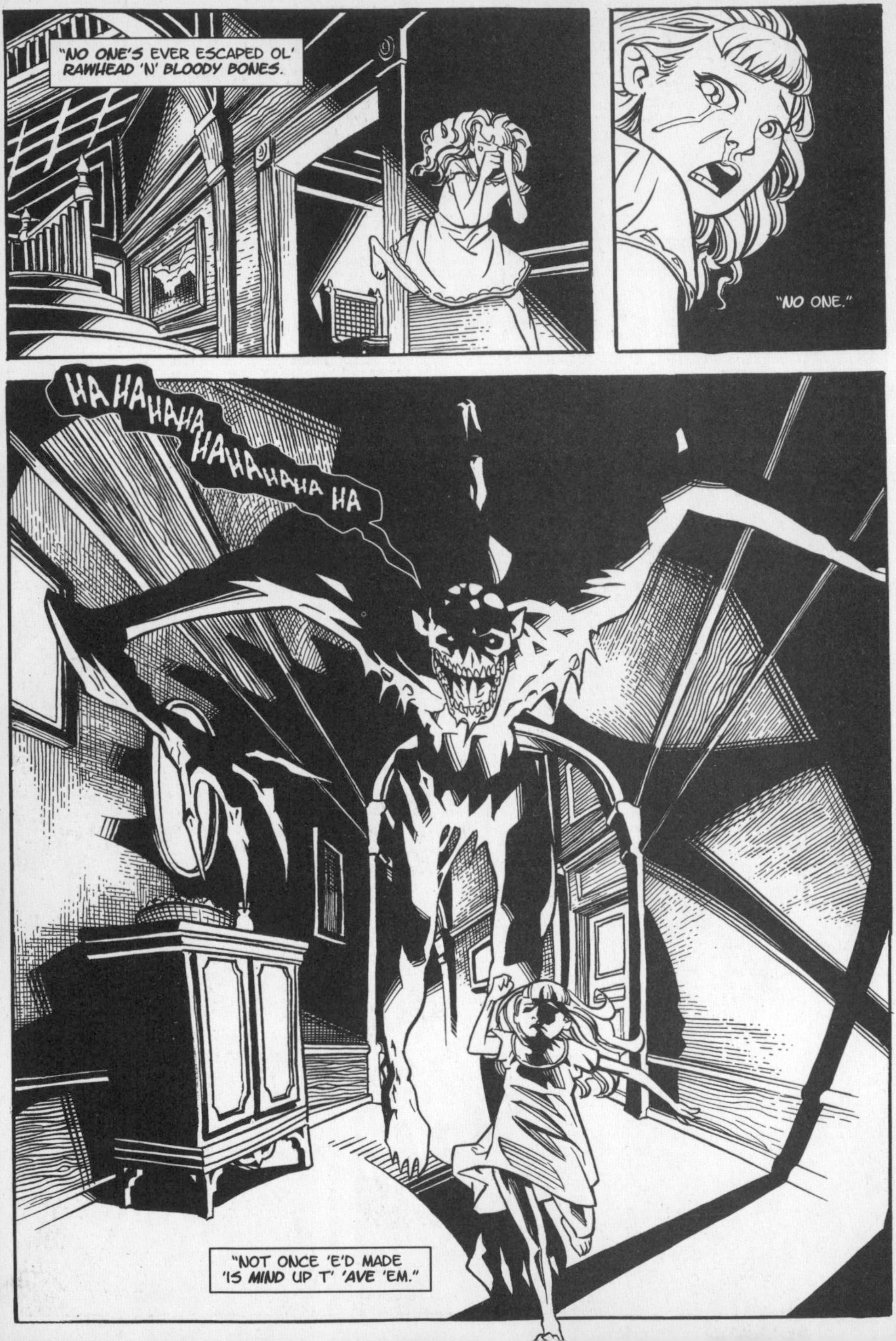
"NO ONE'S EVER ESCAPED OL' RAWHEAD 'N' BLOODY BONES.
"NO ONE."
HA HA HAHAHA HAHAHAHA HA
"NOT ONCE 'E'D MADE 'IS MIND UP T' 'AVE 'EM."

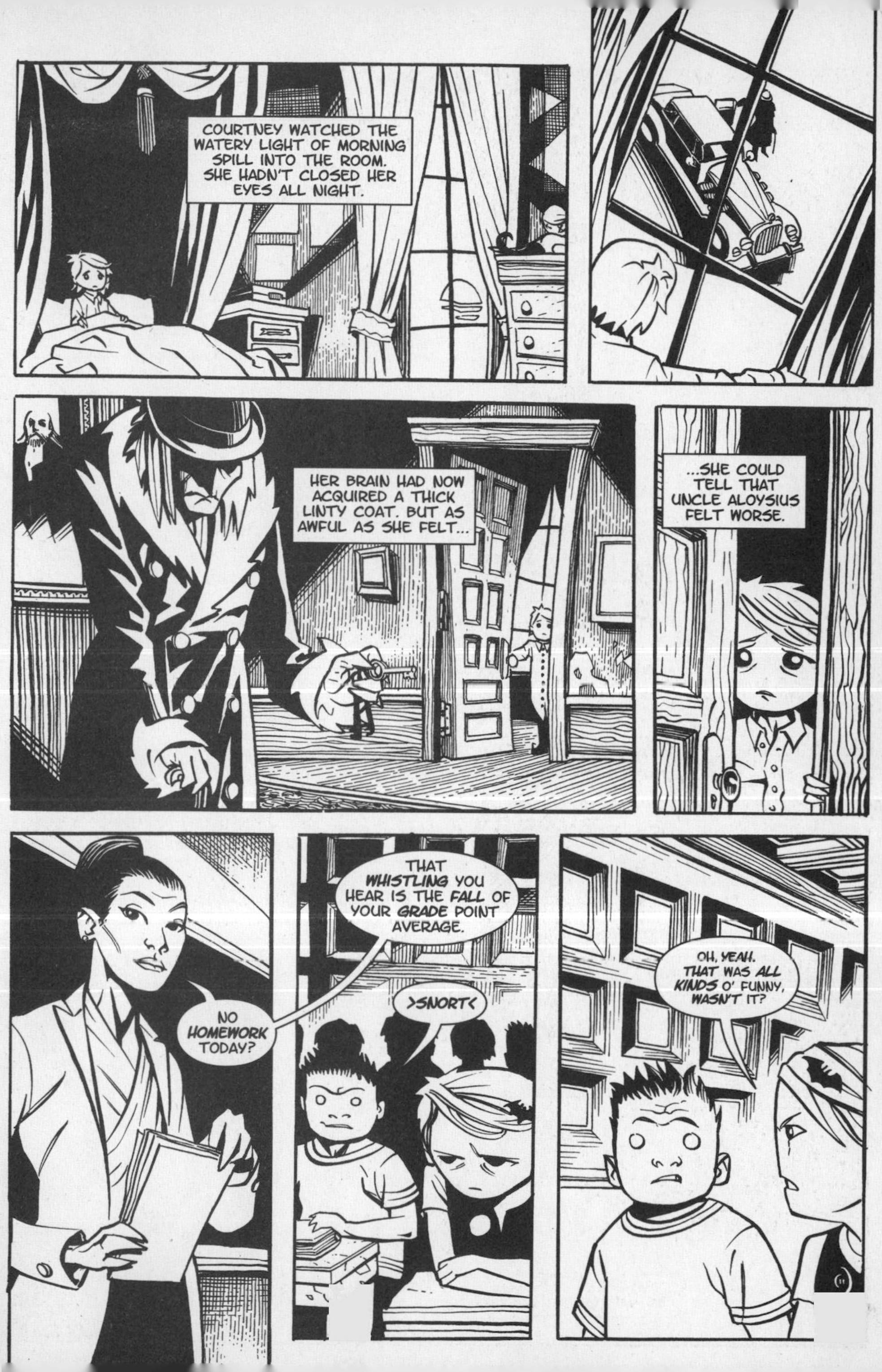
COURTNEY WATCHED THE WATERY LIGHT OF MORNING SPILL INTO THE ROOM. SHE HADN'T CLOSED HER EYES ALL NIGHT.
HER BRAIN HAD NOW ACQUIRED A THICK LINTY COAT. BUT AS AWFUL AS SHE FELT...
...SHE COULD TELL THAT UNCLE ALOYSIUS FELT WORSE.
NO HOMEWORK TODAY?
THAT WHISTLING YOU HEAR IS THE FALL OF YOUR GRADE POINT AVERAGE.
>SNORT<
OH, YEAH. THAT WAS ALL KINDS O' FUNNY, WASN'T IT?

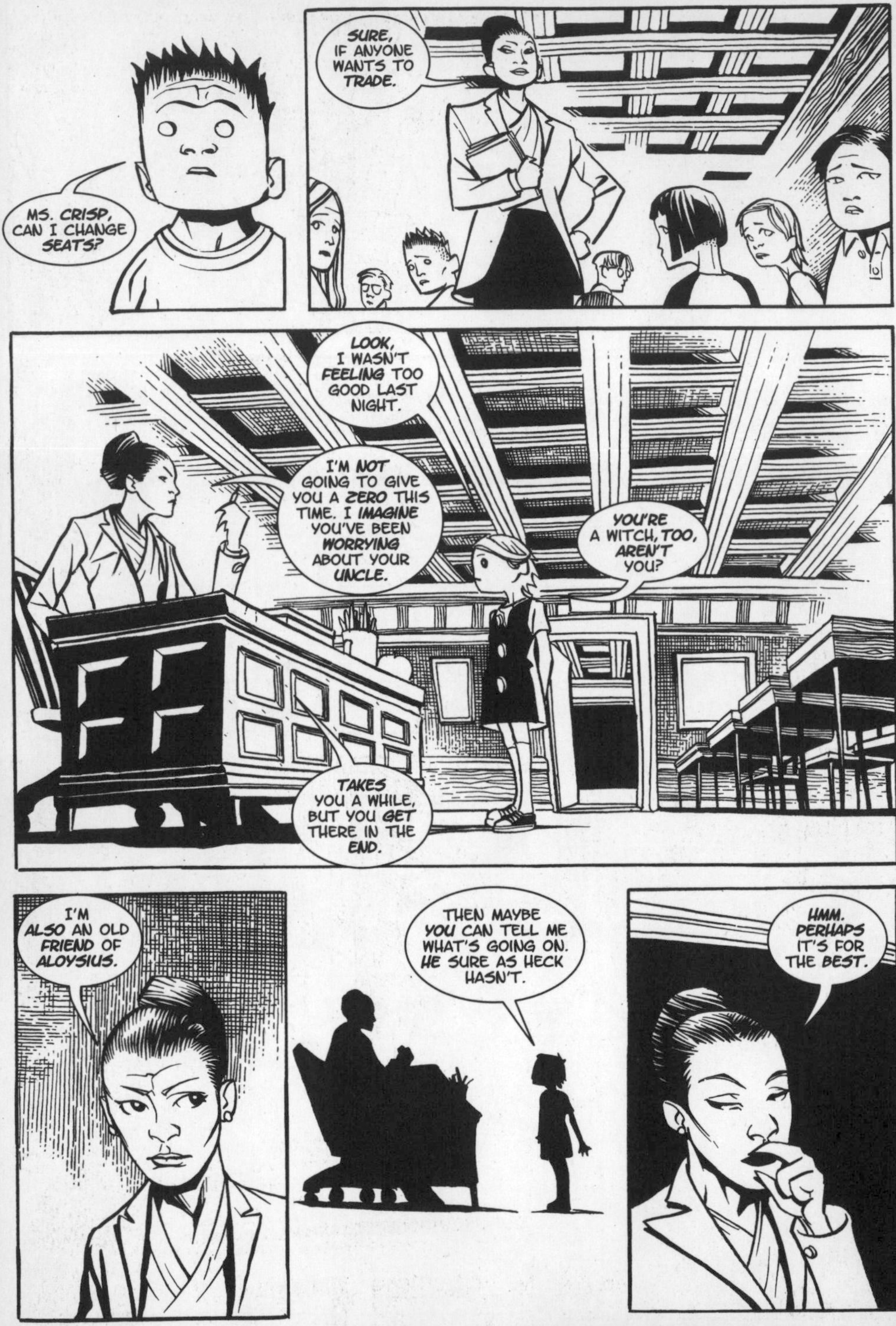
MS. CRISP, CAN I CHANGE SEATS?
SURE, IF ANYONE WANTS TO TRADE.
LOOK, I WASN'T FEELING TOO GOOD LAST NIGHT.
I'M NOT GOING TO GIVE YOU A ZERO THIS TIME. I IMAGINE YOU'VE BEEN WORRYING ABOUT YOUR UNCLE.
YOU'RE A WITCH, TOO, AREN'T YOU?
TAKES YOU A WHILE, BUT YOU GET THERE IN THE END.
I'M ALSO AN OLD FRIEND OF ALOYSIUS.
THEN MAYBE YOU CAN TELL ME WHAT'S GOING ON. HE SURE AS HECK HASN'T.
HMM. PERHAPS IT'S FOR THE BEST.

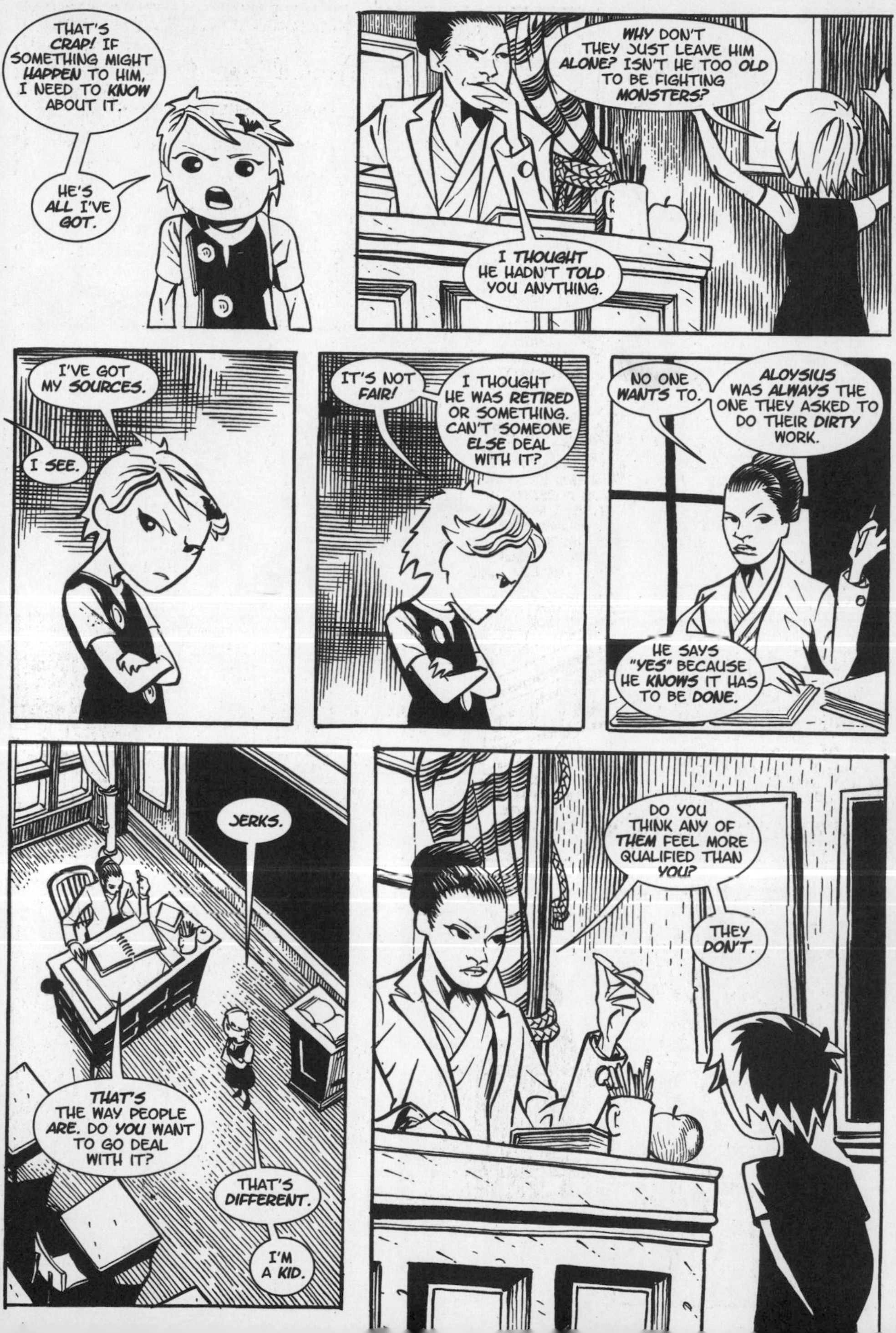

THAT'S CRAP! IF SOMETHING MIGHT HAPPEN TO HIM, I NEED TO KNOW ABOUT IT.
HE'S ALL I'VE GOT.
WHY DON'T THEY JUST LEAVE HIM ALONE? ISN'T HE TOO OLD TO BE FIGHTING MONSTERS?
I THOUGHT HE HADN'T TOLD YOU ANYTHING.
I'VE GOT MY SOURCES.
I SEE.
IT'S NOT FAIR!
I THOUGHT HE WAS RETIRED OR SOMETHING. CAN'T SOMEONE ELSE DEAL WITH IT?
NO ONE WANTS TO.
ALOYSIUS WAS ALWAYS THE ONE THEY ASKED TO DO THEIR DIRTY WORK.
HE SAYS "YES" BECAUSE HE KNOWS IT HAS TO BE DONE.
JERKS.
THAT'S THE WAY PEOPLE ARE. DO YOU WANT TO GO DEAL WITH IT?
THAT'S DIFFERENT.
I'M A KID.
DO YOU THINK ANY OF THEM FEEL MORE QUALIFIED THAN YOU?
THEY DON'T.

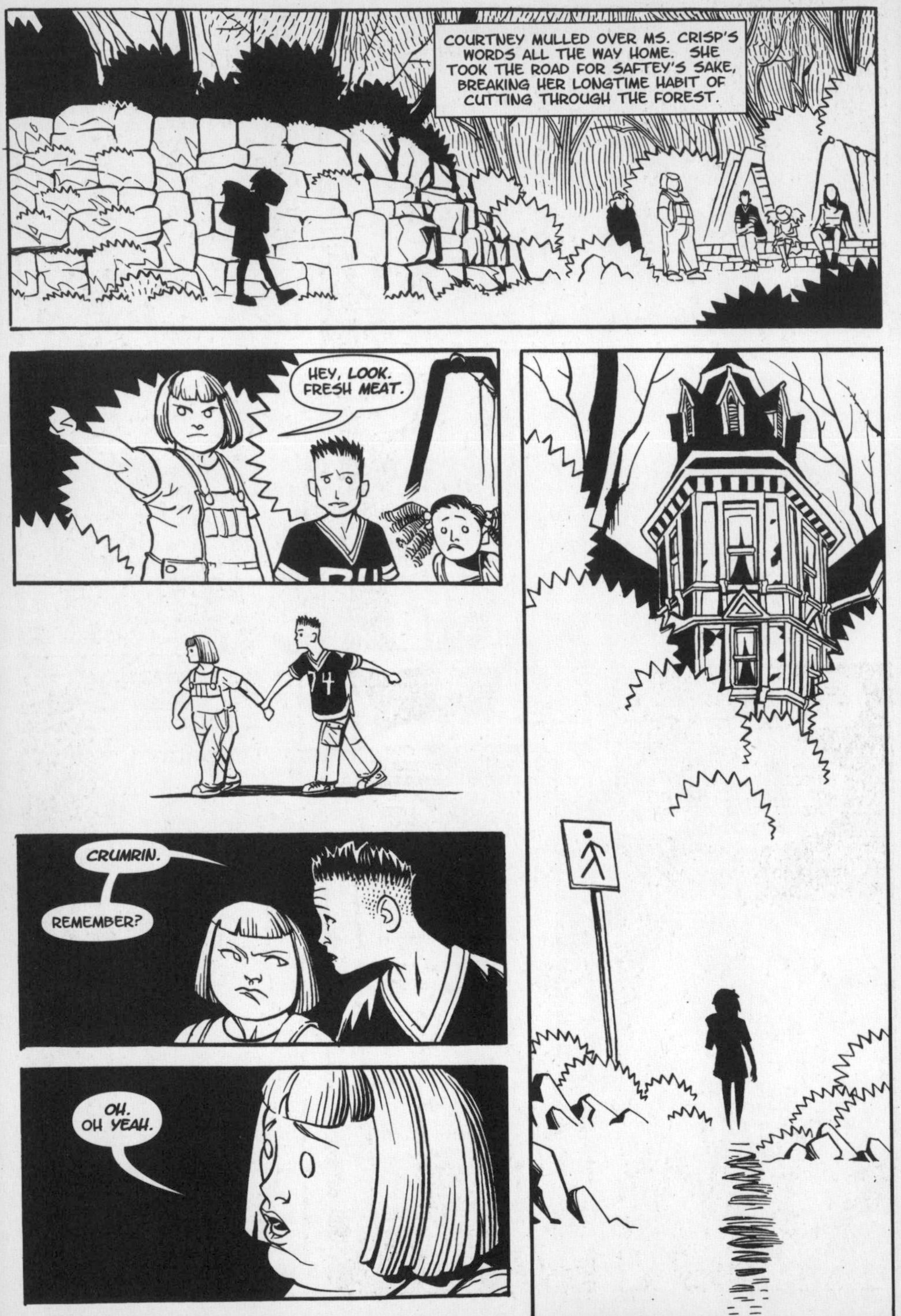
COURTNEY MULLED OVER MS. CRISP'S WORDS ALL THE WAY HOME. SHE TOOK THE ROAD FOR SAFTEY'S SAKE, BREAKING HER LONGTIME HABIT OF CUTTING THROUGH THE FOREST.
HEY, LOOK. FRESH MEAT.
CRUMRIN.
REMEMBER?
OH. OH YEAH.

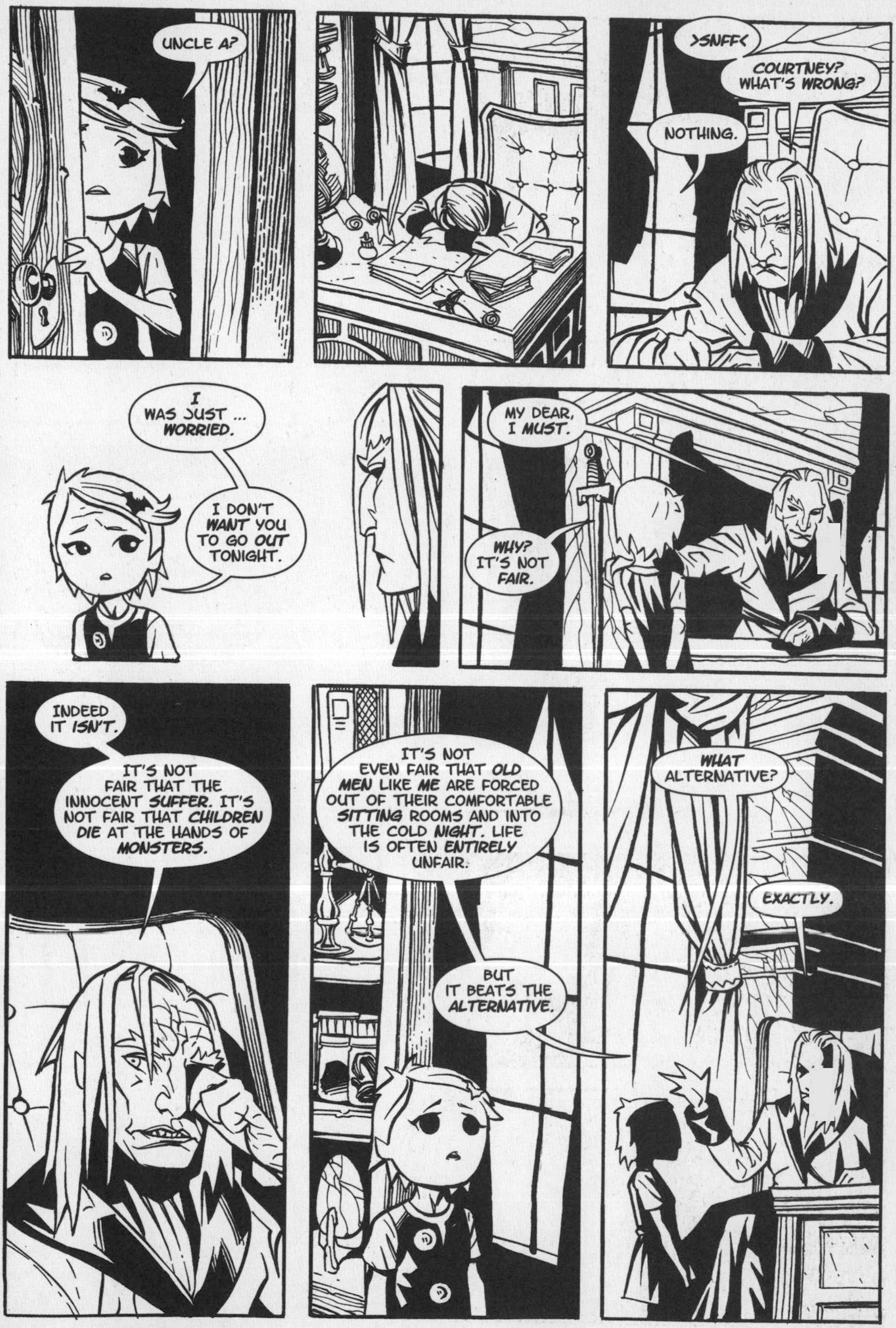
UNCLE A?
>SNFF<
COURTNEY? WHAT'S WRONG?
NOTHING.
I WAS JUST ... WORRIED.
I DON'T WANT YOU TO GO OUT TONIGHT.
MY DEAR, I MUST.
WHY? IT'S NOT FAIR.
INDEED IT ISN'T.
IT'S NOT FAIR THAT THE INNOCENT SUFFER. IT'S NOT FAIR THAT CHILDREN DIE AT THE HANDS OF MONSTERS.
IT'S NOT EVEN FAIR THAT OLD MEN LIKE ME ARE FORCED OUT OF THEIR COMFORTABLE SITTING ROOMS AND INTO THE COLD NIGHT. LIFE IS OFTEN ENTIRELY UNFAIR.
BUT IT BEATS THE ALTERNATIVE.
WHAT ALTERNATIVE?
EXACTLY.

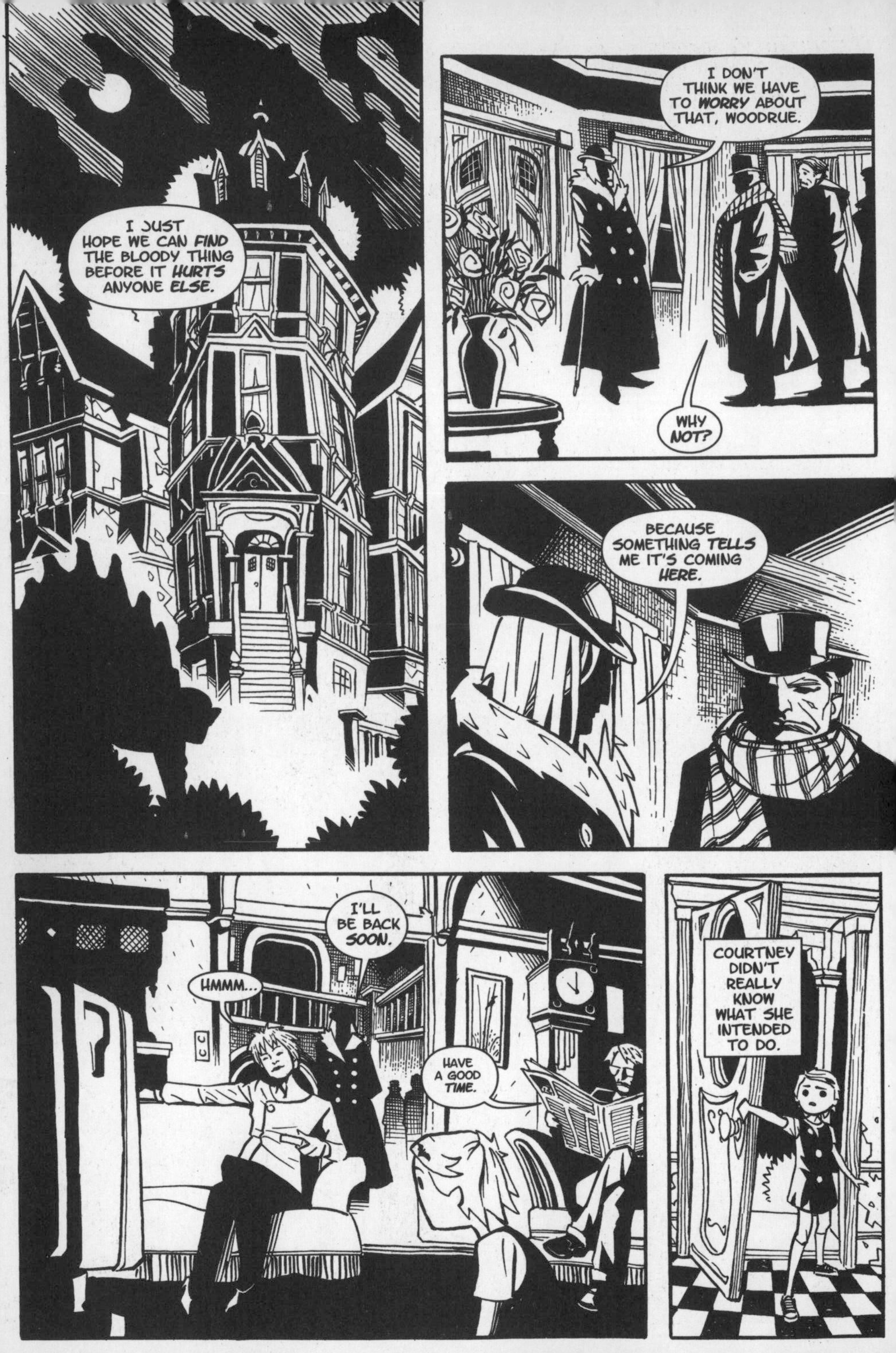
I JUST HOPE WE CAN FIND THE BLOODY THING BEFORE IT HURTS ANYONE ELSE.
I DON'T THINK WE HAVE TO WORRY ABOUT THAT, WOODRUE.
WHY NOT?
BECAUSE SOMETHING TELLS ME IT'S COMING HERE.
I'LL BE BACK SOON.
HMMM...
HAVE A GOOD TIME.
COURTNEY DIDN'T REALLY KNOW WHAT SHE INTENDED TO DO.

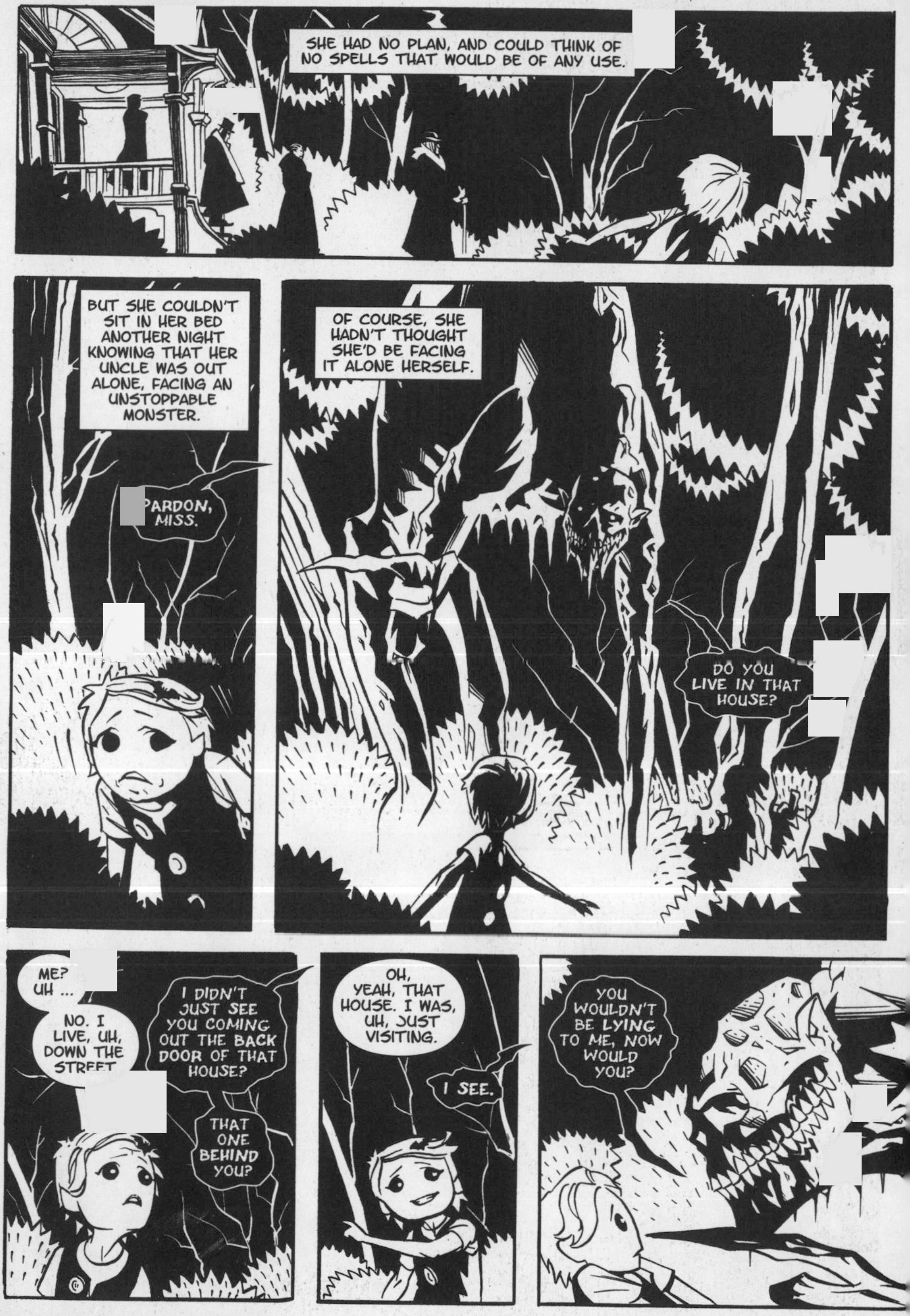
SHE HAD NO PLAN, AND COULD THINK OF NO SPELLS THAT WOULD BE OF ANY USE.
BUT SHE COULDN'T SIT IN HER BED ANOTHER NIGHT KNOWING THAT HER UNCLE WAS OUT ALONE, FACING AN UNSTOPPABLE MONSTER.
PARDON, MISS.
OF COURSE, SHE HADN'T THOUGHT SHE'D BE FACING IT ALONE HERSELF.
DO YOU LIVE IN THAT HOUSE?
ME? UH ...
NO. I LIVE, UH, DOWN THE STREET
I DIDN'T JUST SEE YOU COMING OUT THE BACK DOOR OF THAT HOUSE?
THAT ONE BEHIND YOU?
OH, YEAH, THAT HOUSE. I WAS, UH, JUST VISITING.
I SEE.
YOU WOULDN'T BE LYING TO ME, NOW WOULD YOU?

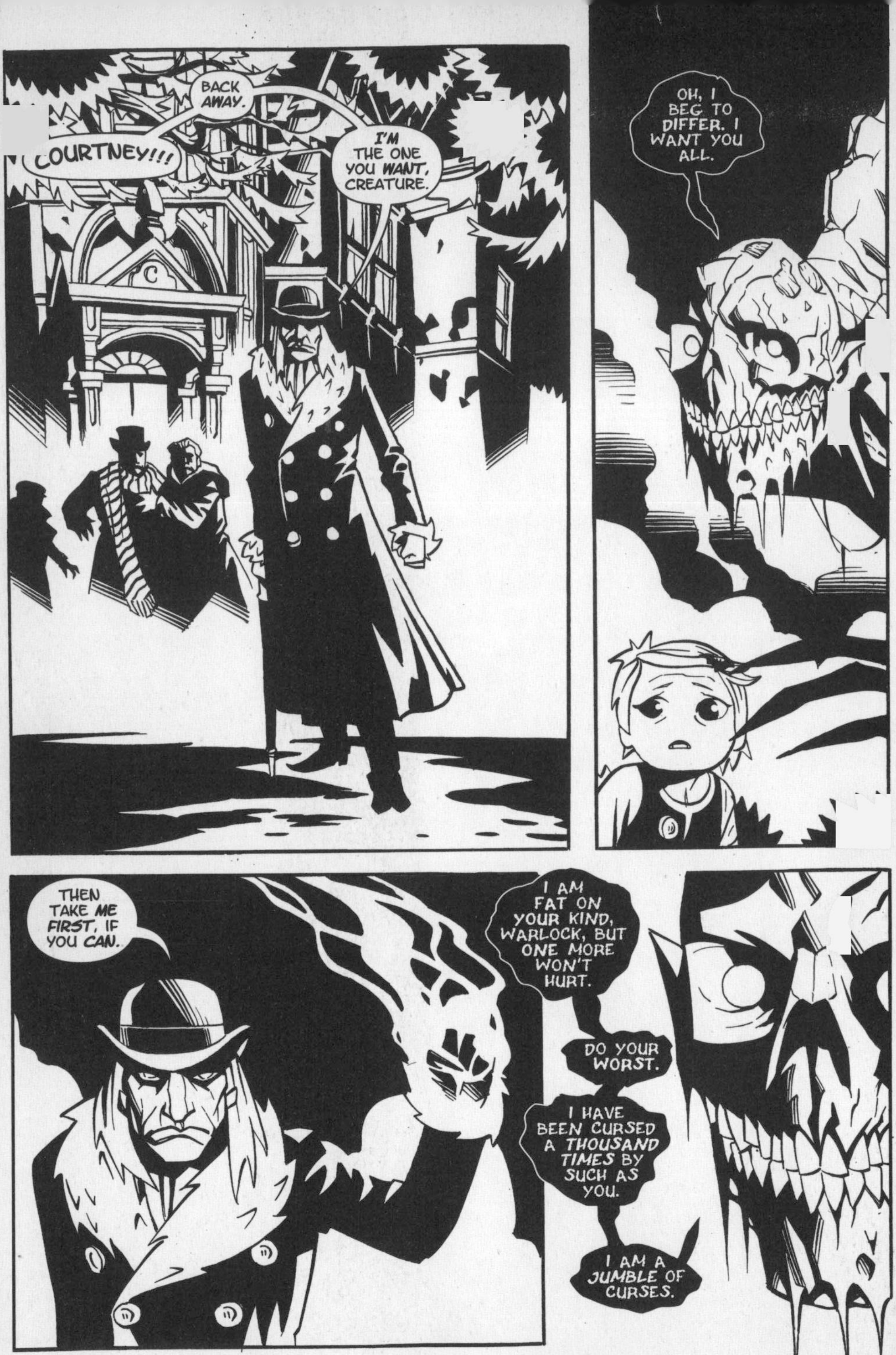
COURTNEY!!!!
BACK AWAY.
I'M THE ONE YOU WANT, CREATURE.
OH, I BEG TO DIFFER. I WANT YOU ALL.
THEN TAKE ME FIRST, IF YOU CAN.
I AM FAT ON YOUR KIND, WARLOCK, BUT ONE MORE WON'T HURT.
DO YOUR WORST.
I HAVE BEEN CURSED A THOUSAND TIMES BY SUCH AS YOU.
I AM A JUMBLE OF CURSES.

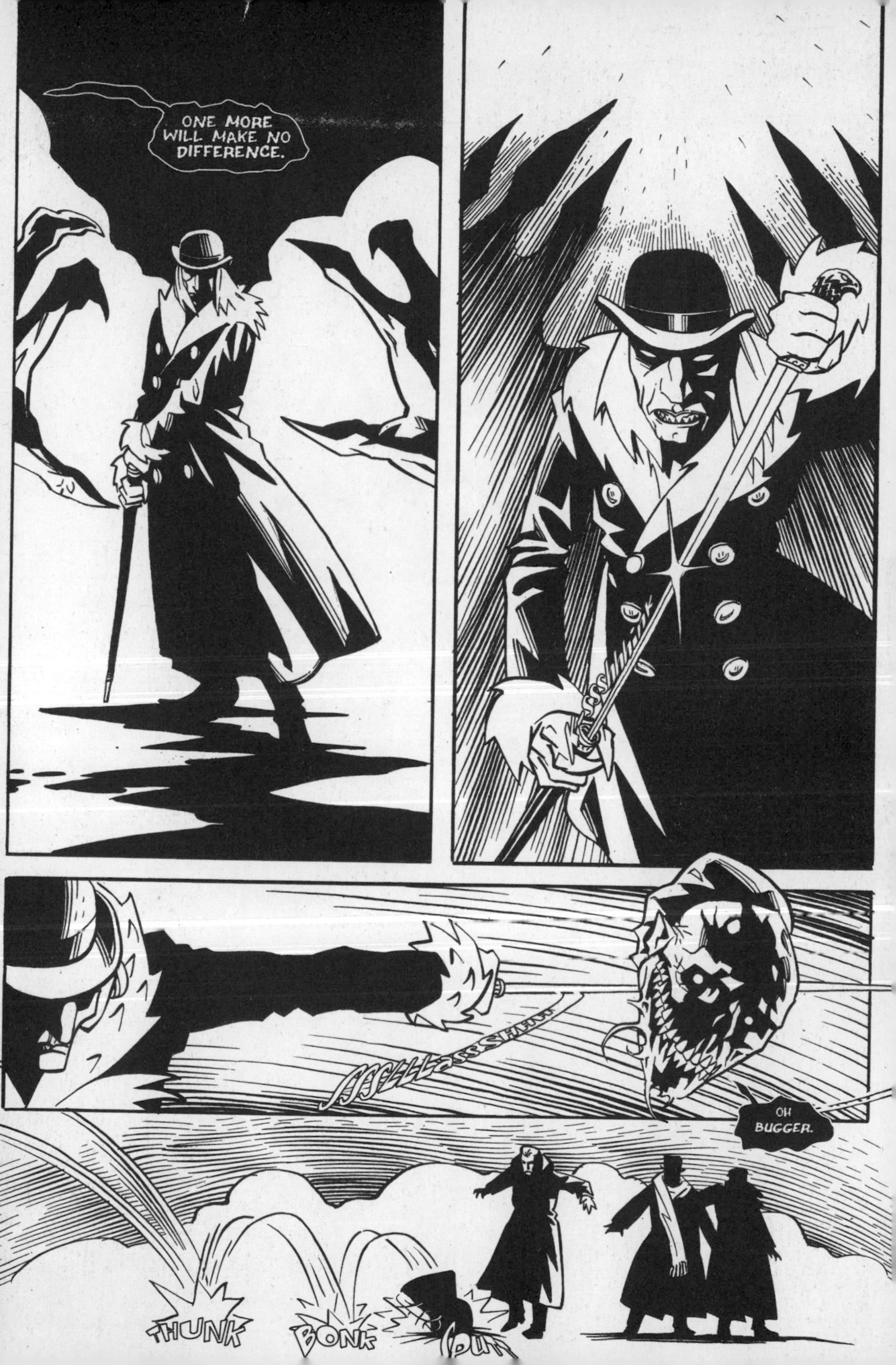
ONE MORE WILL MAKE NO DIFFERENCE.
OH BUGGER.
THUNK
BONK

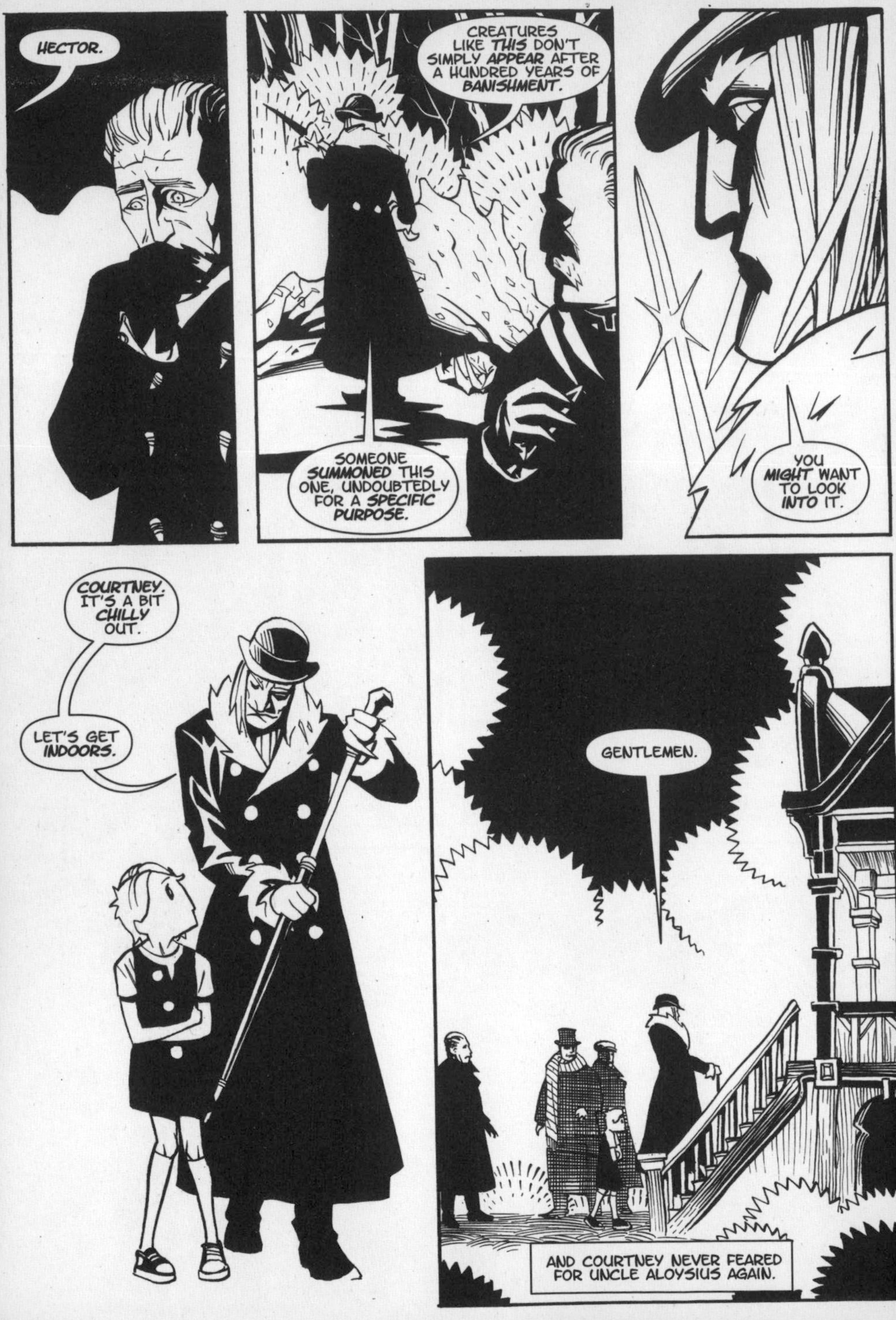
HECTOR.
CREATURES LIKE THIS DON'T SIMPLY APPEAR AFTER A HUNDRED YEARS OF BANISHMENT.
SOMEONE SUMMONED THIS ONE, UNDOUBTEDLY FOR A SPECIFIC PURPOSE.
YOU MIGHT WANT TO LOOK INTO IT.
COURTNEY. IT'S A BIT CHILLY OUT.
LET'S GET INDOORS.
GENTLEMEN.
AND COURTNEY NEVER FEARED FOR UNCLE ALOYSIUS AGAIN.

CHAPTER TWO

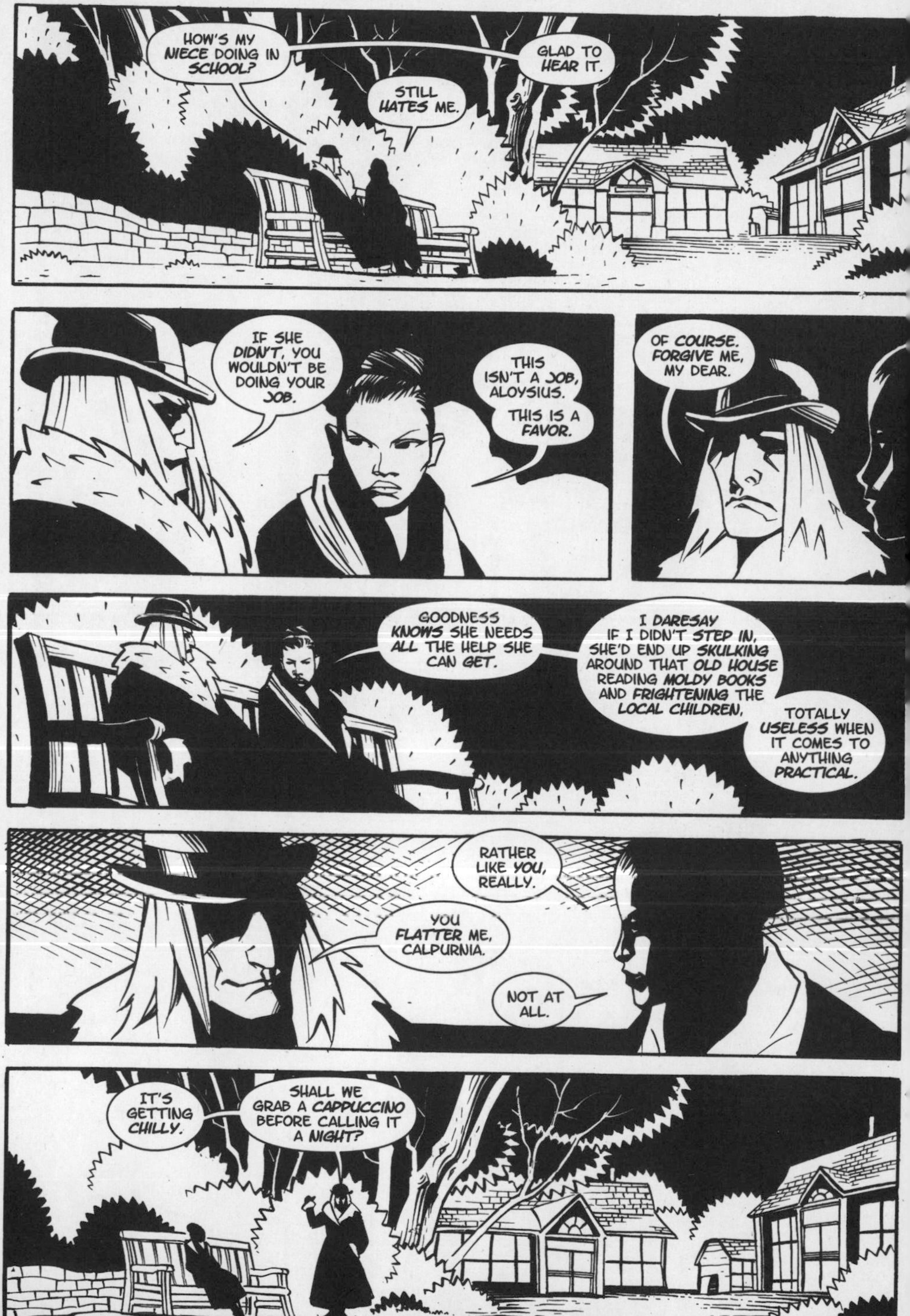
HOW'S MY NIECE DOING IN SCHOOL?
STILL HATES ME.
GLAD TO HEAR IT.
IF SHE DIDN'T, YOU WOULDN'T BE DOING YOUR JOB.
THIS ISN'T A JOB, ALOYSIUS.
THIS IS A FAVOR.
OF COURSE. FORGIVE ME, MY DEAR.
GOODNESS KNOWS SHE NEEDS ALL THE HELP SHE CAN GET.
I DARESAY IF I DIDN'T STEP IN, SHE'D END UP SKULKING AROUND THAT OLD HOUSE READING MOLDY BOOKS AND FRIGHTENING THE LOCAL CHILDREN.
TOTALLY USELESS WHEN IT COMES TO ANYTHING PRACTICAL.
RATHER LIKE YOU, REALLY.
YOU FLATTER ME, CALPURNIA.
NOT AT ALL.
IT'S GETTING CHILLY.
SHALL WE GRAB A CAPPUCCINO BEFORE CALLING IT A NIGHT?

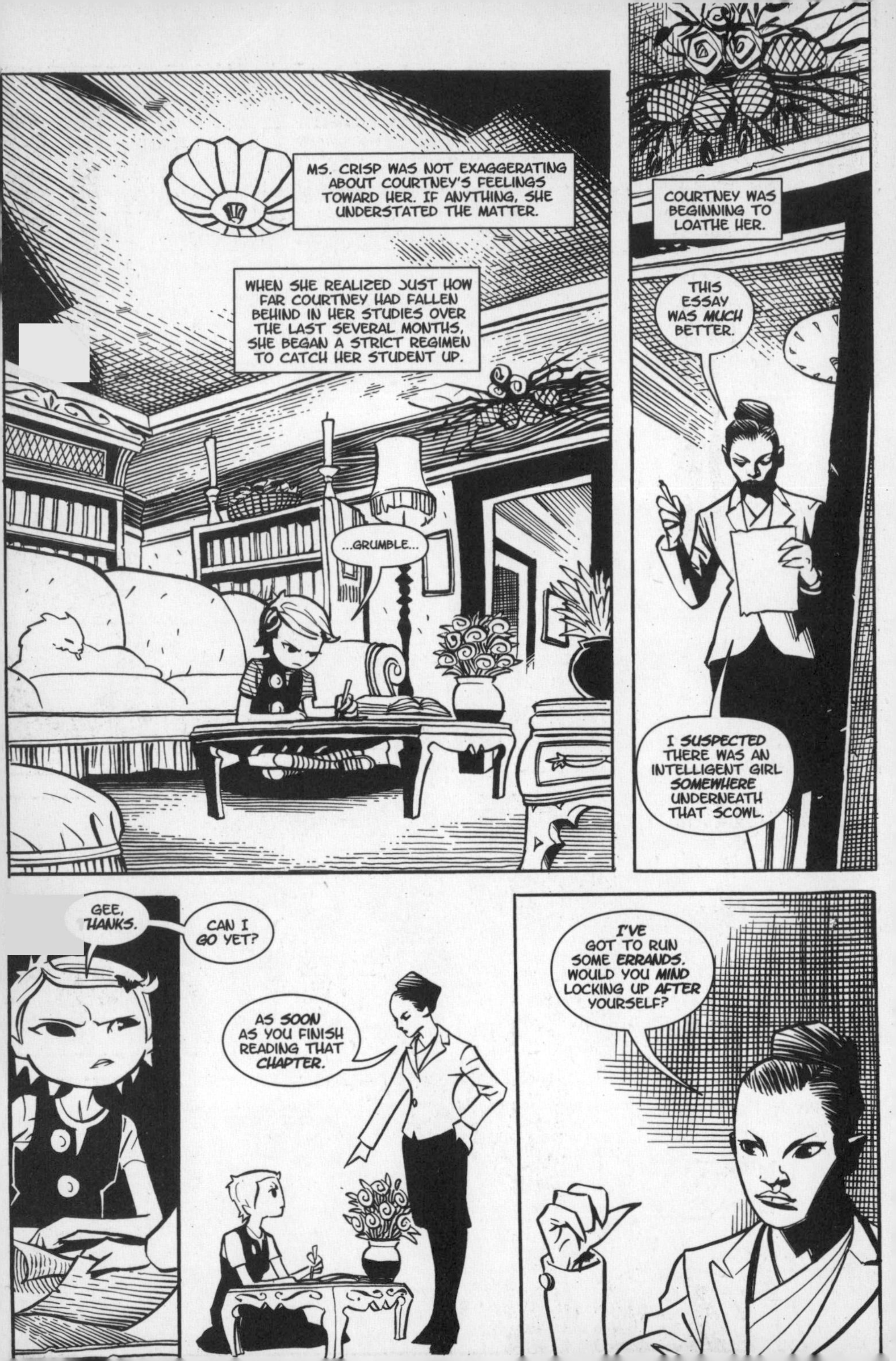

MS. CRISP WAS NOT EXAGGERATING ABOUT COURTNEY'S FEELINGS TOWARD HER. IF ANYTHING, SHE UNDERSTATED THE MATTER.
WHEN SHE REALIZED JUST HOW FAR COURTNEY HAD FALLEN BEHIND IN HER STUDIES OVER THE LAST SEVERAL MONTHS, SHE BEGAN A STRICT REGIMEN TO CATCH HER STUDENT UP.
...GRUMBLE...
COURTNEY WAS BEGINNING TO LOATHE HER.
THIS ESSAY WAS MUCH BETTER.
I SUSPECTED THERE WAS AN INTELLIGENT GIRL SOMEWHERE UNDERNEATH THAT SCOWL.
GEE, THANKS.
CAN I GO YET?
AS SOON AS YOU FINISH READING THAT CHAPTER.
I'VE GOT TO RUN SOME ERRANDS. WOULD YOU MIND LOCKING UP AFTER YOURSELF?

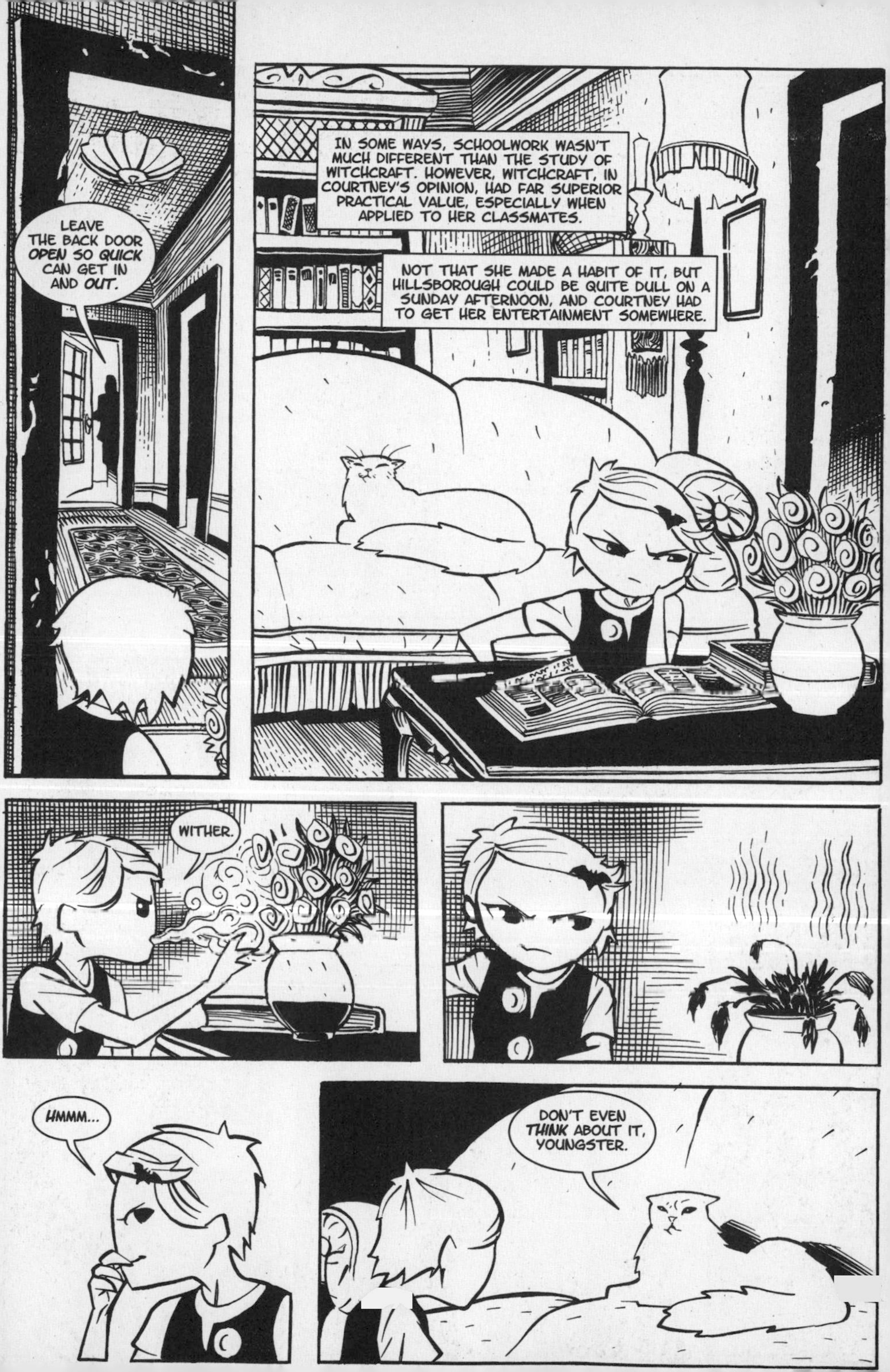
LEAVE THE BACK DOOR OPEN SO QUICK CAN GET IN AND OUT.
IN SOME WAYS, SCHOOLWORK WASN'T MUCH DIFFERENT THAN THE STUDY OF WITCHCRAFT. HOWEVER, WITCHCRAFT, IN COURTNEY'S OPINION, HAD FAR SUPERIOR PRACTICAL VALUE, ESPECIALLY WHEN APPLIED TO HER CLASSMATES.
NOT THAT SHE MADE A HABIT OF IT, BUT HILLSBOROUGH COULD BE QUITE DULL ON A SUNDAY AFTERNOON, AND COURTNEY HAD TO GET HER ENTERTAINMENT SOMEWHERE.
WITHER.
HMMM...
DON'T EVEN THINK ABOUT IT, YOUNGSTER.

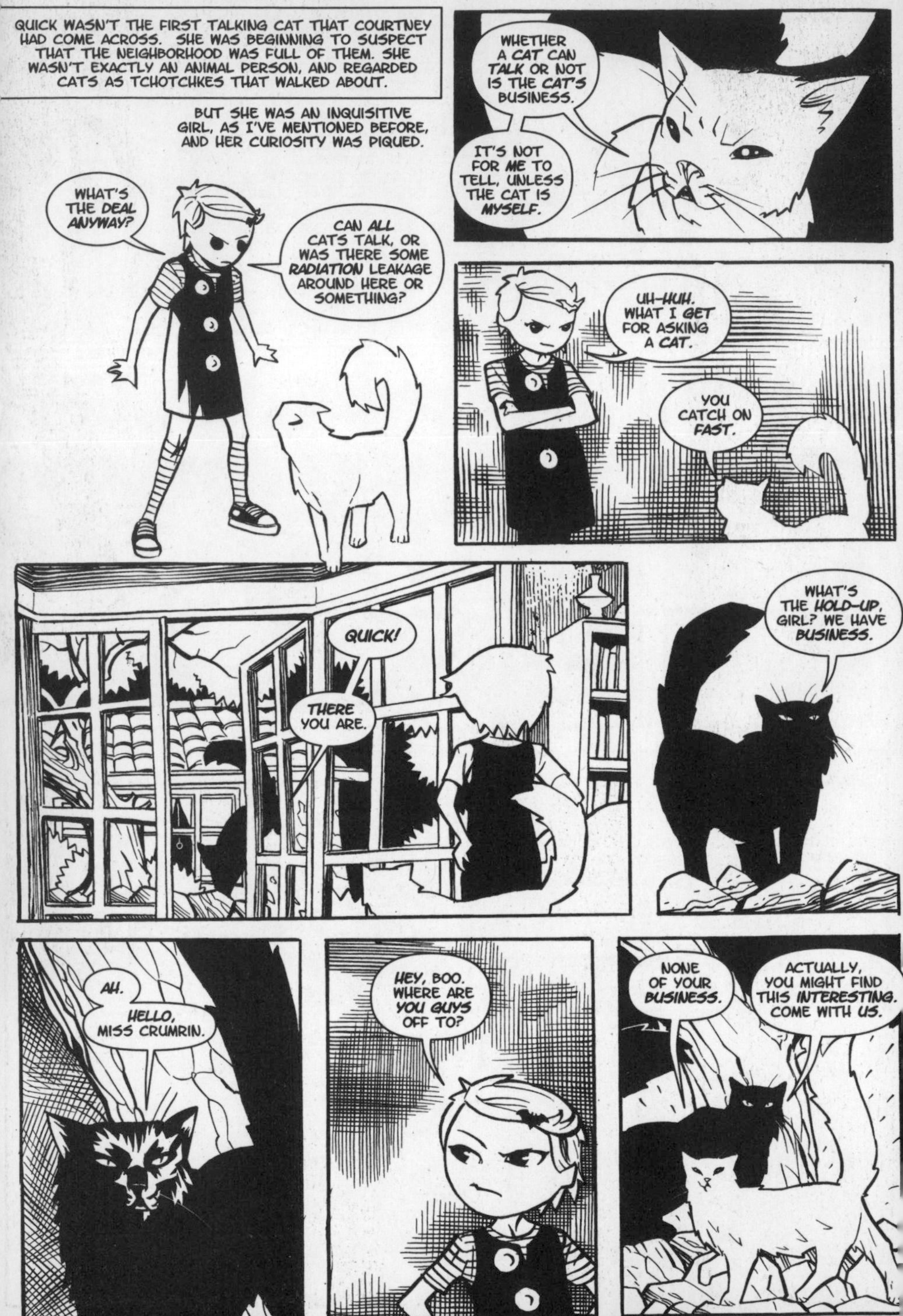
QUICK WASN'T THE FIRST TALKING CAT THAT COURTNEY HAD COME ACROSS. SHE WAS BEGINNING TO SUSPECT THAT THE NEIGHBORHOOD WAS FULL OF THEM. SHE WASN'T EXACTLY AN ANIMAL PERSON, AND REGARDED CATS AS TCHOTCHKES THAT WALKED ABOUT.
BUT SHE WAS AN INQUISITIVE GIRL, AS I'VE MENTIONED BEFORE, AND HER CURIOSITY WAS PIQUED.
WHAT'S THE DEAL ANYWAY?
CAN ALL CATS TALK, OR WAS THERE SOME RADIATION LEAKAGE AROUND HERE OR SOMETHING?
WHETHER A CAT CAN TALK OR NOT IS THE CAT'S BUSINESS.
IT'S NOT FOR ME TO TELL, UNLESS THE CAT IS MYSELF.
UH-HUH. WHAT I GET FOR ASKING A CAT.
YOU CATCH ON FAST.
QUICK!
THERE YOU ARE.
WHAT'S THE HOLD-UP, GIRL? WE HAVE BUSINESS.
AH.
HELLO, MISS CRUMRIN.
HEY, BOO. WHERE ARE YOU GUYS OFF TO?
NONE OF YOUR BUSINESS.
ACTUALLY, YOU MIGHT FIND THIS INTERESTING. COME WITH US.

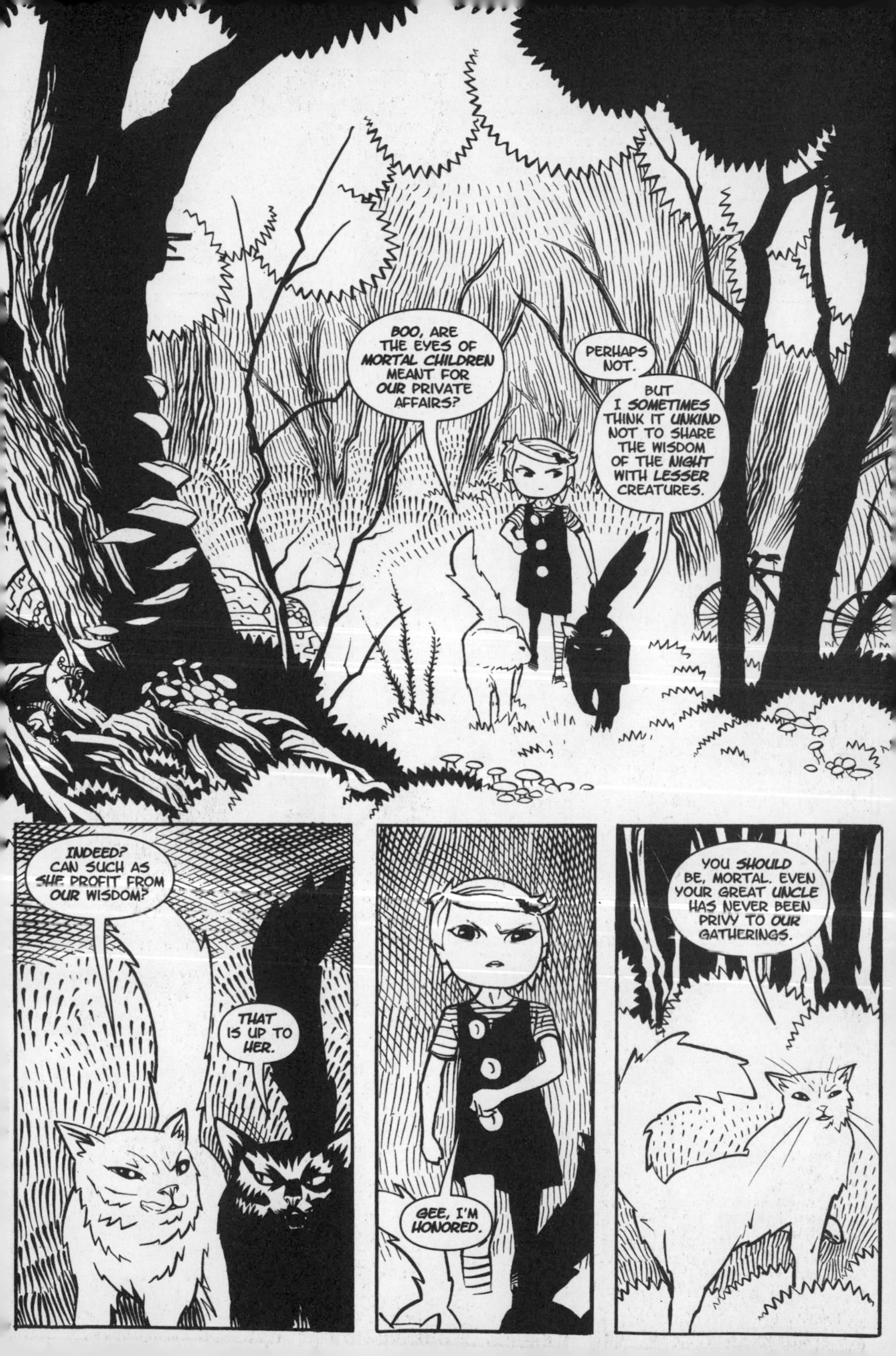

BOO, ARE THE EYES OF MORTAL CHILDREN MEANT FOR OUR PRIVATE AFFAIRS?
PERHAPS NOT.
BUT I SOMETIMES THINK IT UNKIND NOT TO SHARE THE WISDOM OF THE NIGHT WITH LESSER CREATURES.
INDEED? CAN SUCH AS SHE PROFIT FROM OUR WISDOM?
THAT IS UP TO HER.
GEE, I'M HONORED.
YOU SHOULD BE, MORTAL. EVEN YOUR GREAT UNCLE HAS NEVER BEEN PRIVY TO OUR GATHERINGS.

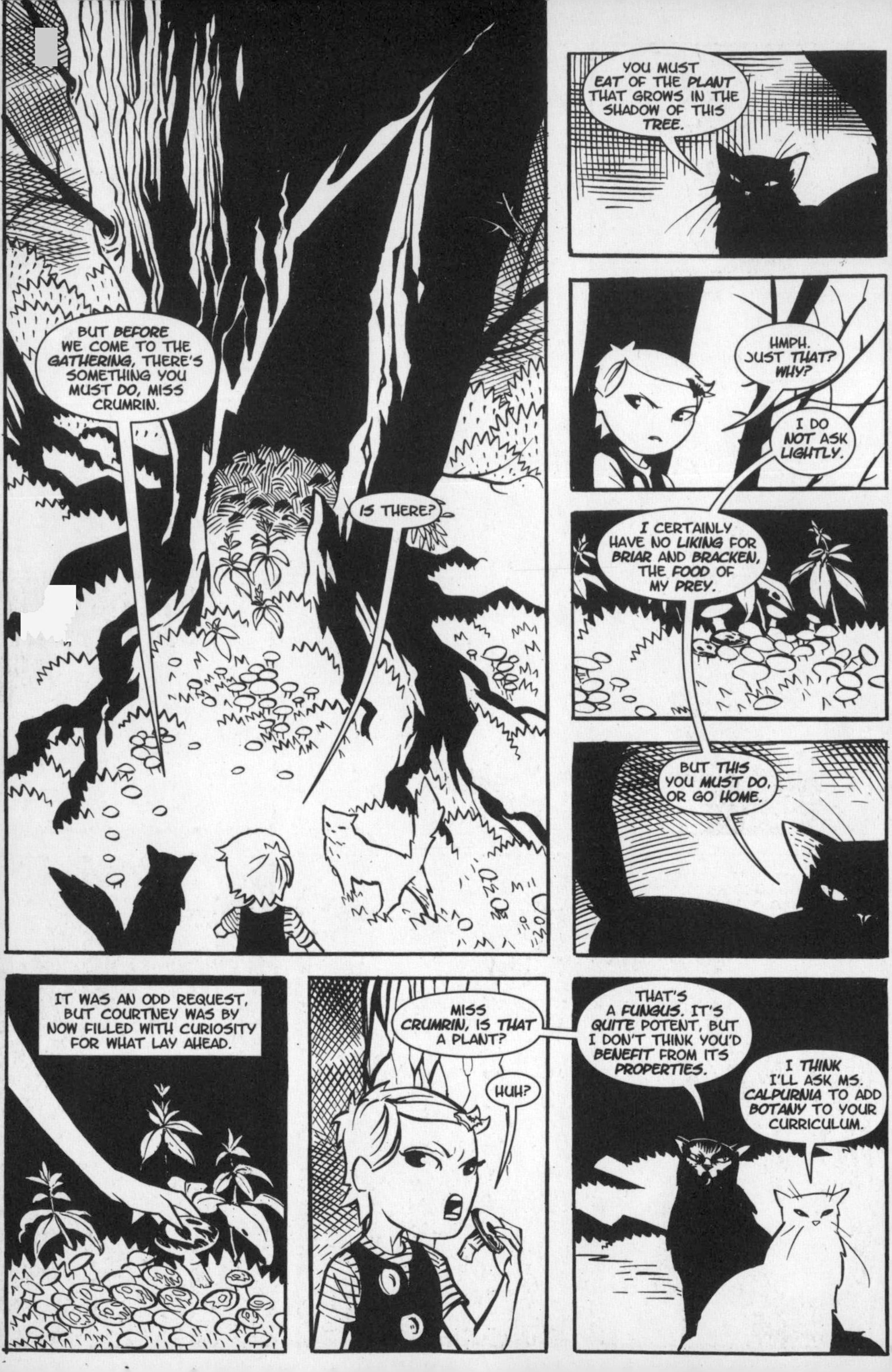
BUT BEFORE WE COME TO THE GATHERING, THERE'S SOMETHING YOU MUST DO, MISS CRUMRIN.
IS THERE?
YOU MUST EAT OF THE PLANT THAT GROWS IN THE SHADOW OF THIS TREE.
HMPH. JUST THAT? WHY?
I DO NOT ASK LIGHTLY.
I CERTAINLY HAVE NO LIKING FOR BRIAR AND BRACKEN, THE FOOD OF MY PREY.
BUT THIS YOU MUST DO, OR GO HOME.
IT WAS AN ODD REQUEST, BUT COURTNEY WAS BY NOW FILLED WITH CURIOSITY FOR WHAT LAY AHEAD.
MISS CRUMRIN, IS THAT A PLANT?
HUH?
THAT'S A FUNGUS. IT'S QUITE POTENT, BUT I DON'T THINK YOU'D BENEFIT FROM ITS PROPERTIES.
I THINK I'LL ASK MS. CALPURNIA TO ADD BOTANY TO YOUR CURRICULUM.

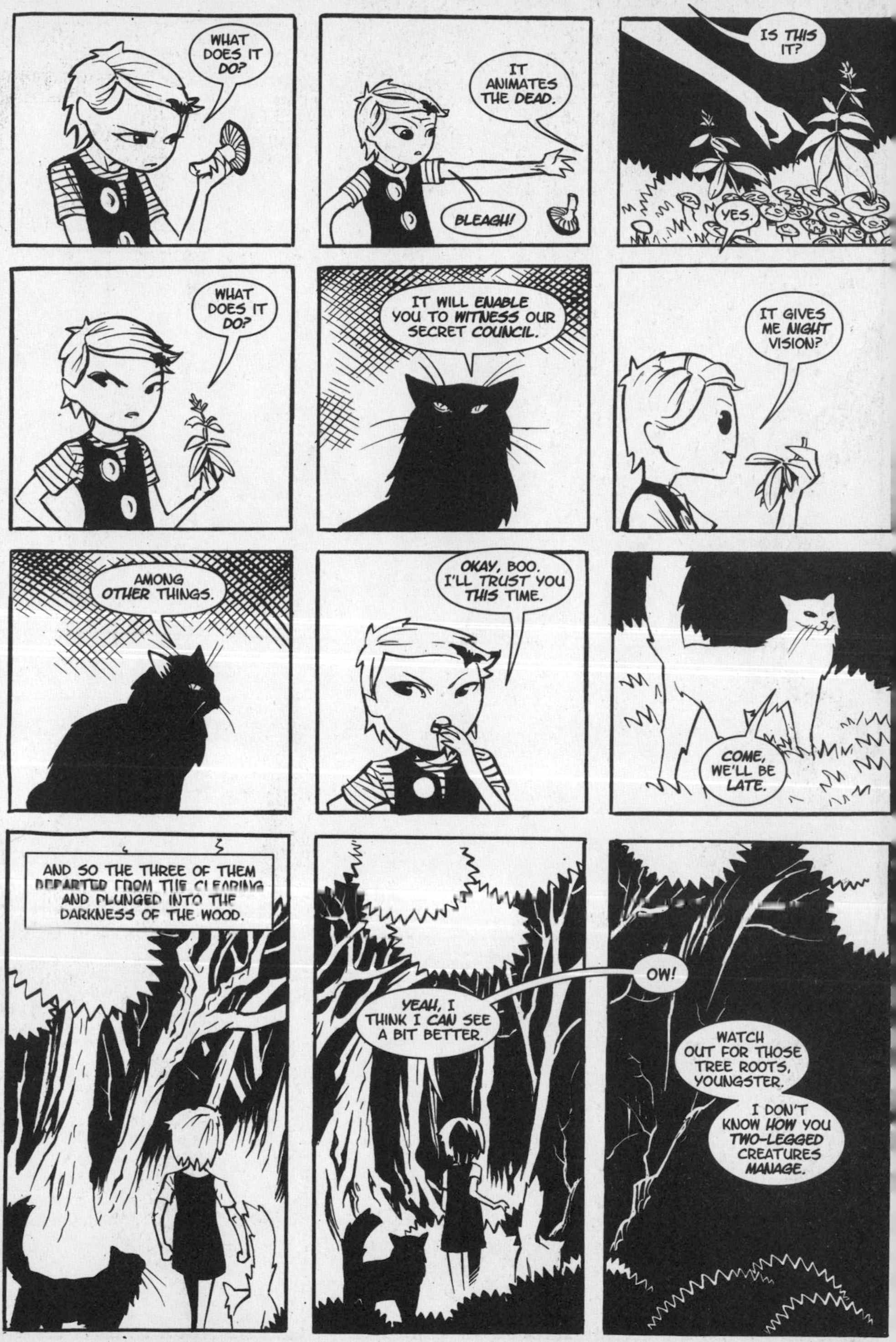
WHAT DOES IT DO?
IT ANIMATES THE DEAD.
BLEAGH!
IS THIS IT?
YES.
WHAT DOES IT DO?
IT WILL ENABLE YOU TO WITNESS OUR SECRET COUNCIL.
IT GIVES ME NIGHT VISION?
AMONG OTHER THINGS.
OKAY, BOO. I'LL TRUST YOU THIS TIME.
COME, WE'LL BE LATE.
AND SO THE THREE OF THEM DEPARTED FROM THE CLEARING AND PLUNGED INTO THE DARKNESS OF THE WOOD.
YEAH, I THINK I CAN SEE A BIT BETTER.
OW!
WATCH OUT FOR THOSE TREE ROOTS, YOUNGSTER.
I DON'T KNOW HOW YOU TWO-LEGGED CREATURES MANAGE.

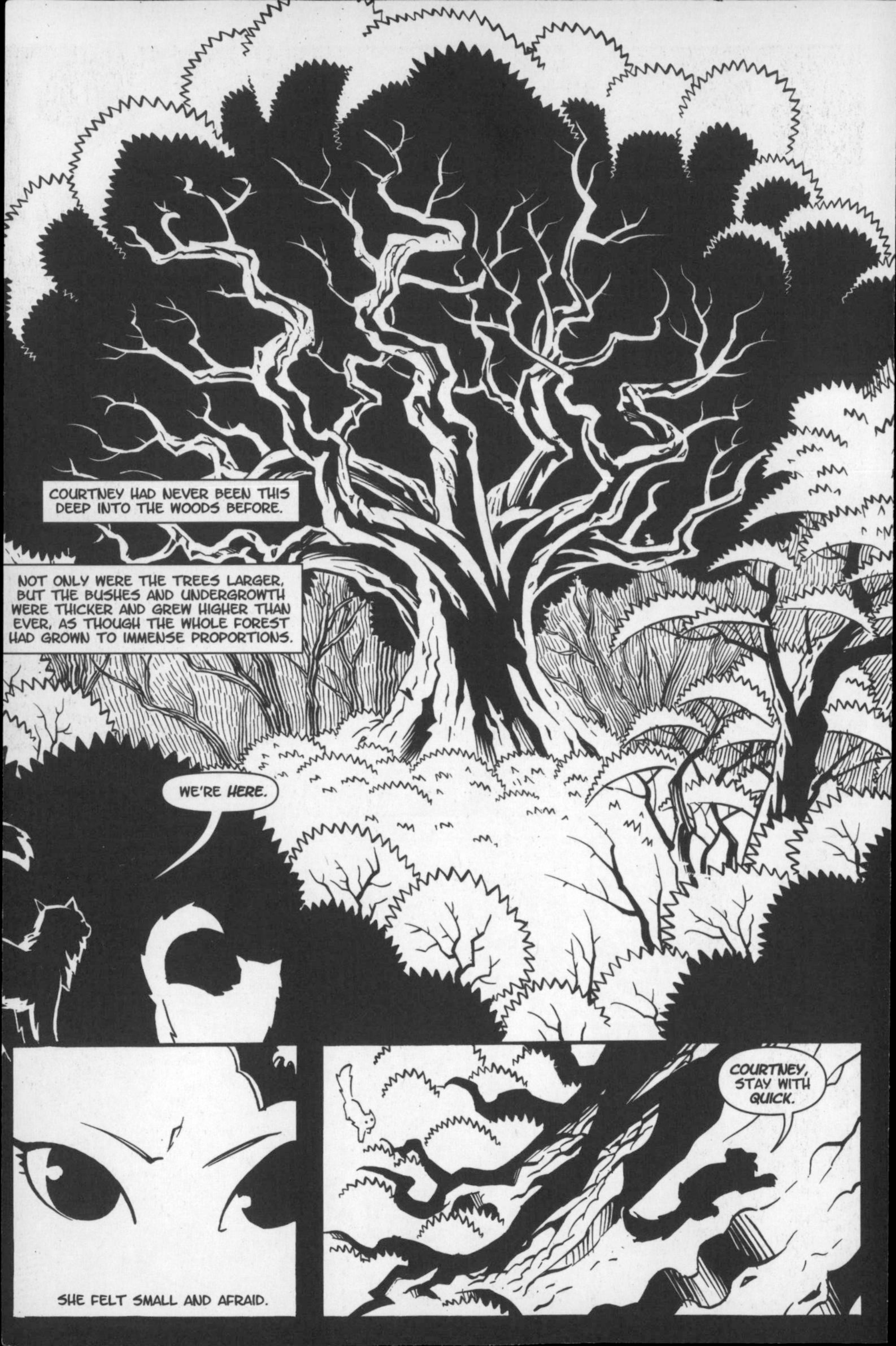
COURTNEY HAD NEVER BEEN THIS DEEP INTO THE WOODS BEFORE.
NOT ONLY WERE THE TREES LARGER, BUT THE BUSHES AND UNDERGROWTH WERE THICKER AND GREW HIGHER THAN EVER, AS THOUGH THE WHOLE FOREST HAD GROWN TO IMMENSE PROPORTIONS.
WE'RE *HERE*.
SHE FELT SMALL AND AFRAID.
COURTNEY, STAY WITH QUICK.

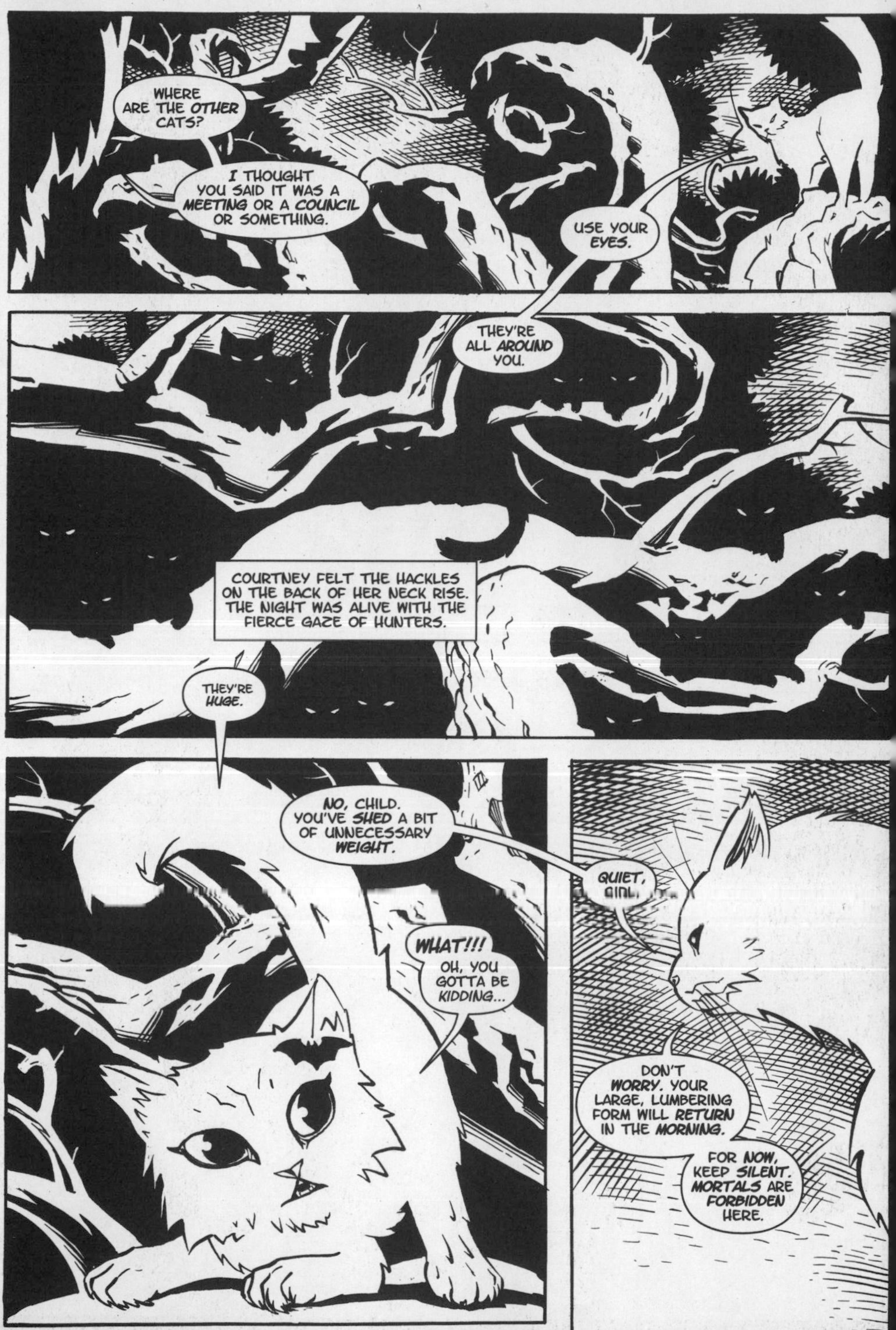
WHERE ARE THE OTHER CATS?
I THOUGHT YOU SAID IT WAS A MEETING OR A COUNCIL OR SOMETHING.
USE YOUR EYES.
THEY'RE ALL AROUND YOU.
COURTNEY FELT THE HACKLES ON THE BACK OF HER NECK RISE. THE NIGHT WAS ALIVE WITH THE FIERCE GAZE OF HUNTERS.
THEY'RE HUGE.
NO, CHILD. YOU'VE SHED A BIT OF UNNECESSARY WEIGHT.
QUIET, GIRL.
WHAT!!! OH, YOU GOTTA BE KIDDING...
DON'T WORRY. YOUR LARGE, LUMBERING FORM WILL RETURN IN THE MORNING.
FOR NOW, KEEP SILENT. MORTALS ARE FORBIDDEN HERE.

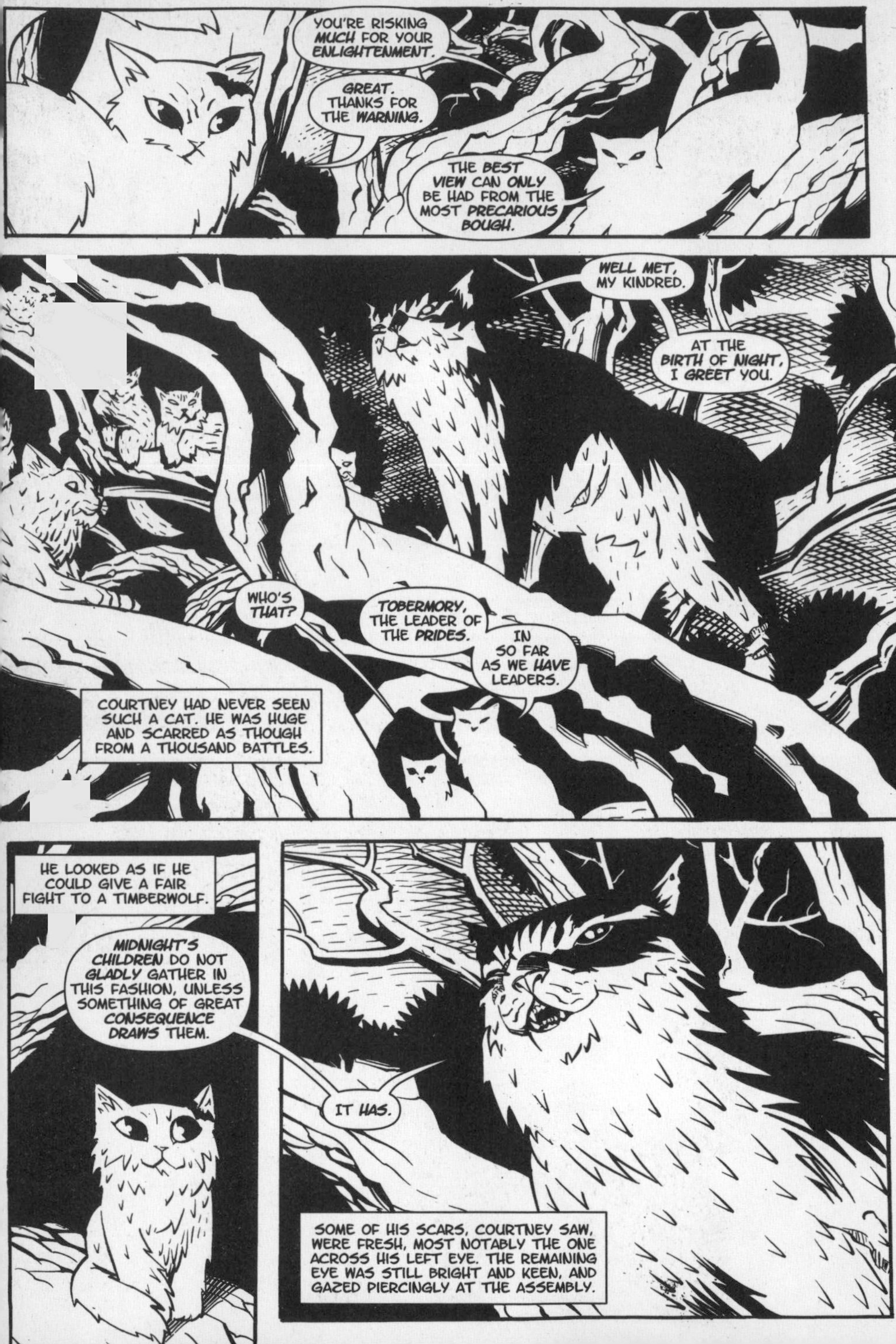

YOU'RE RISKING MUCH FOR YOUR ENLIGHTENMENT.
GREAT. THANKS FOR THE WARNING.
THE BEST VIEW CAN ONLY BE HAD FROM THE MOST PRECARIOUS BOUGH.
WELL MET, MY KINDRED.
AT THE BIRTH OF NIGHT, I GREET YOU.
WHO'S THAT?
TOBERMORY, THE LEADER OF THE PRIDES.
IN SO FAR AS WE HAVE LEADERS.
COURTNEY HAD NEVER SEEN SUCH A CAT. HE WAS HUGE AND SCARRED AS THOUGH FROM A THOUSAND BATTLES.
HE LOOKED AS IF HE COULD GIVE A FAIR FIGHT TO A TIMBERWOLF.
MIDNIGHT'S CHILDREN DO NOT GLADLY GATHER IN THIS FASHION, UNLESS SOMETHING OF GREAT CONSEQUENCE DRAWS THEM.
IT HAS.
SOME OF HIS SCARS, COURTNEY SAW, WERE FRESH, MOST NOTABLY THE ONE ACROSS HIS LEFT EYE. THE REMAINING EYE WAS STILL BRIGHT AND KEEN, AND GAZED PIERCINGLY AT THE ASSEMBLY.

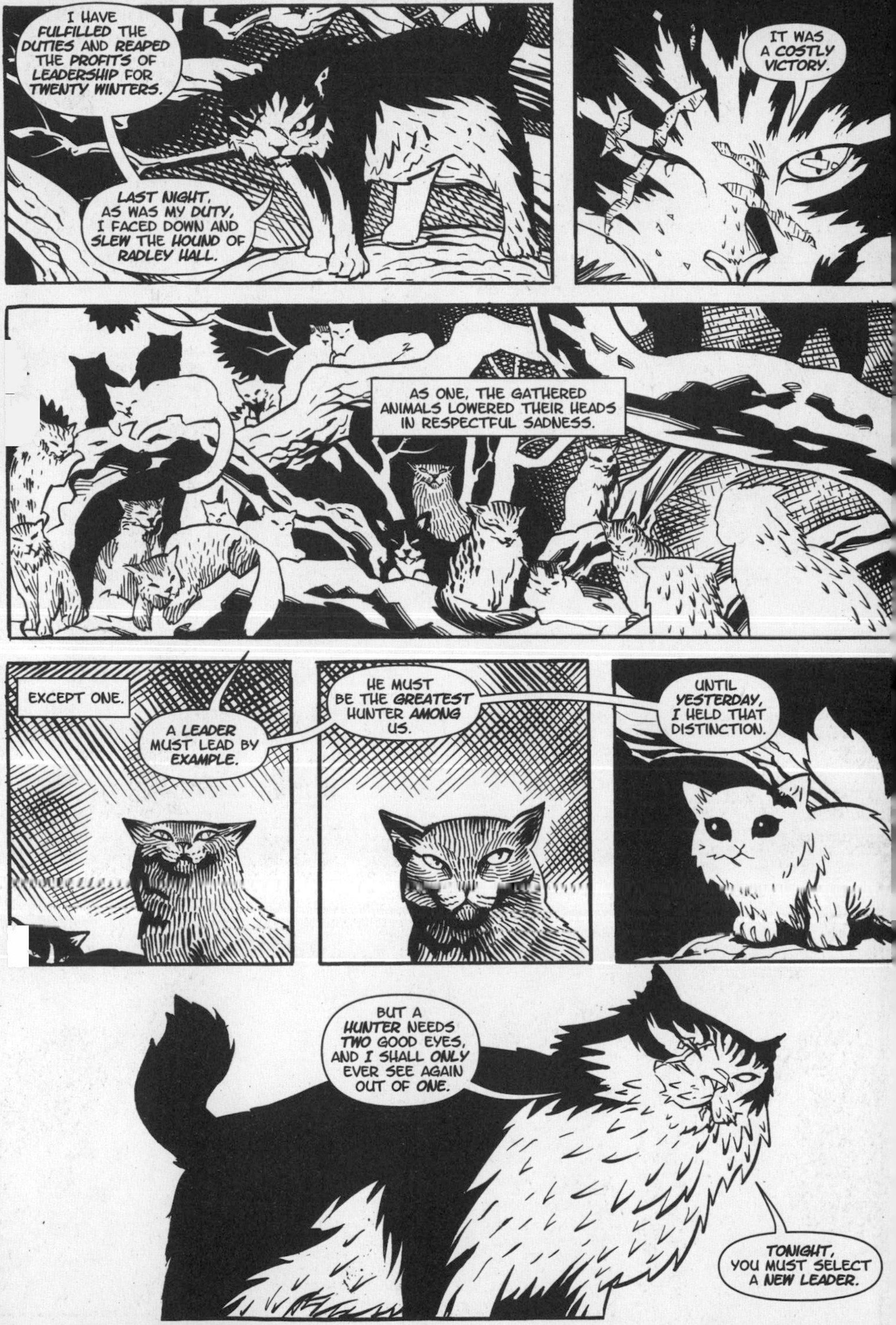
I HAVE FULFILLED THE DUTIES AND REAPED THE PROFITS OF LEADERSHIP FOR TWENTY WINTERS.
LAST NIGHT, AS WAS MY DUTY, I FACED DOWN AND SLEW THE HOUND OF RADLEY HALL.
IT WAS A COSTLY VICTORY.
AS ONE, THE GATHERED ANIMALS LOWERED THEIR HEADS IN RESPECTFUL SADNESS.
EXCEPT ONE.
A LEADER MUST LEAD BY EXAMPLE.
HE MUST BE THE GREATEST HUNTER AMONG US.
UNTIL YESTERDAY, I HELD THAT DISTINCTION.
BUT A HUNTER NEEDS TWO GOOD EYES, AND I SHALL ONLY EVER SEE AGAIN OUT OF ONE.
TONIGHT, YOU MUST SELECT A NEW LEADER.

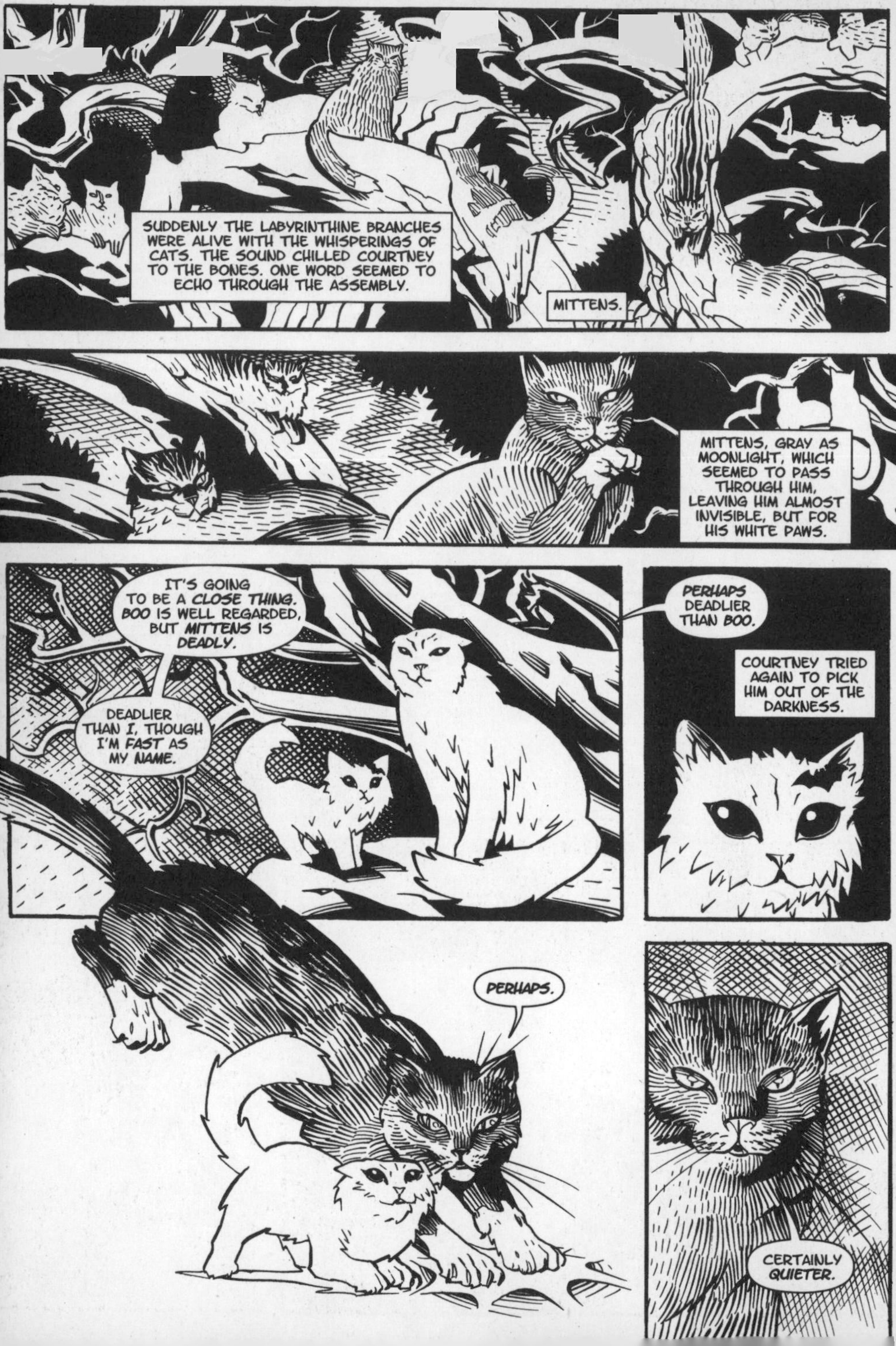
SUDDENLY THE LABYRINTHINE BRANCHES WERE ALIVE WITH THE WHISPERINGS OF CATS. THE SOUND CHILLED COURTNEY TO THE BONES. ONE WORD SEEMED TO ECHO THROUGH THE ASSEMBLY.
MITTENS.
MITTENS, GRAY AS MOONLIGHT, WHICH SEEMED TO PASS THROUGH HIM, LEAVING HIM ALMOST INVISIBLE, BUT FOR HIS WHITE PAWS.
IT'S GOING TO BE A *CLOSE THING.* *BOO* IS WELL REGARDED, BUT *MITTENS* IS *DEADLY.*
DEADLIER THAN *I,* THOUGH I'M *FAST* AS MY *NAME.*
PERHAPS DEADLIER THAN *BOO.*
COURTNEY TRIED AGAIN TO PICK HIM OUT OF THE DARKNESS.
PERHAPS.
CERTAINLY *QUIETER.*

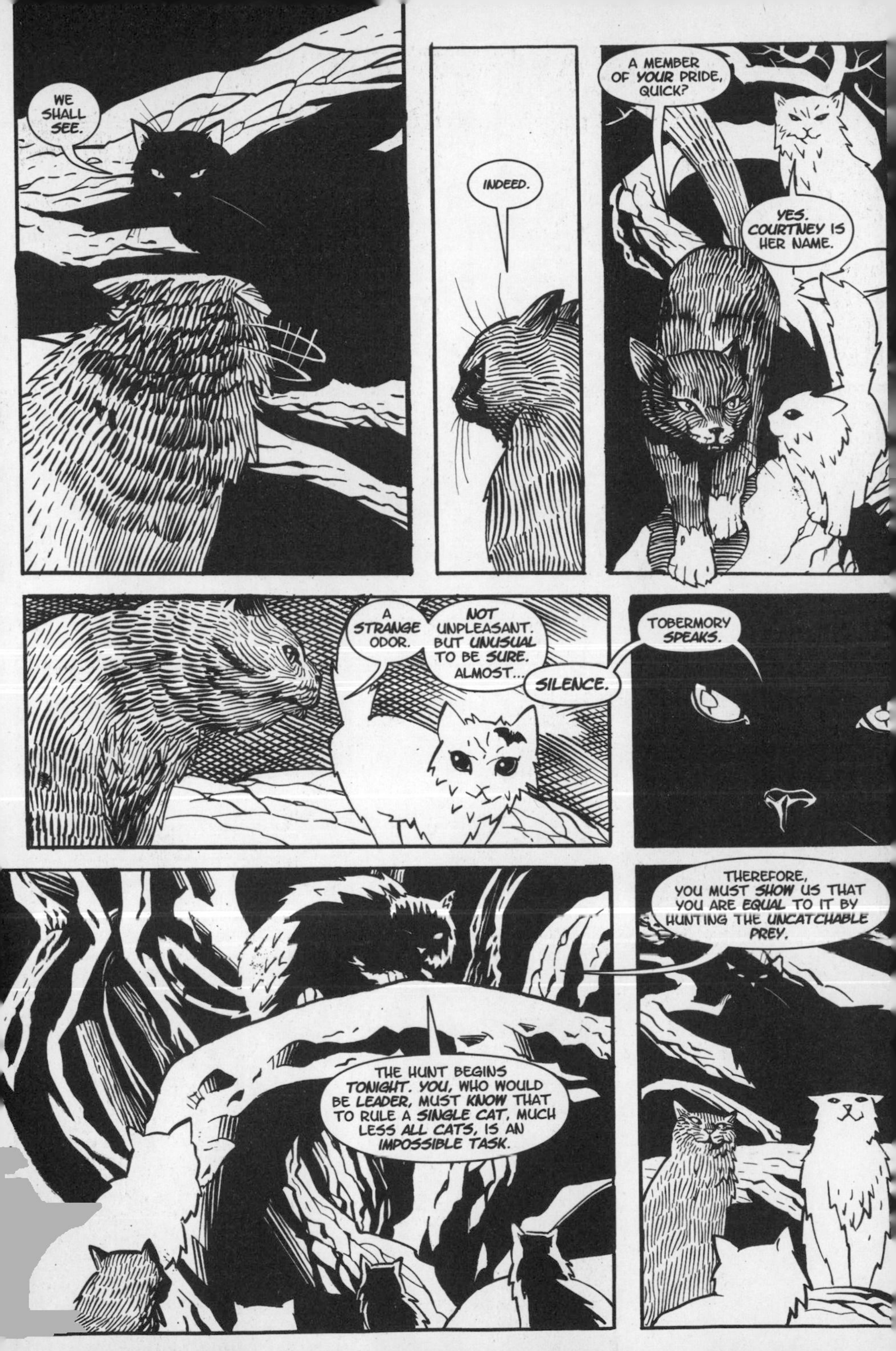
WE SHALL SEE.
INDEED.
A MEMBER OF YOUR PRIDE, QUICK?
YES. COURTNEY IS HER NAME.
A STRANGE ODOR.
NOT UNPLEASANT. BUT UNUSUAL TO BE SURE. ALMOST...
SILENCE.
TOBERMORY SPEAKS.
THE HUNT BEGINS TONIGHT. YOU, WHO WOULD BE LEADER, MUST KNOW THAT TO RULE A SINGLE CAT, MUCH LESS ALL CATS, IS AN IMPOSSIBLE TASK.
THEREFORE, YOU MUST SHOW US THAT YOU ARE EQUAL TO IT BY HUNTING THE UNCATCHABLE PREY.

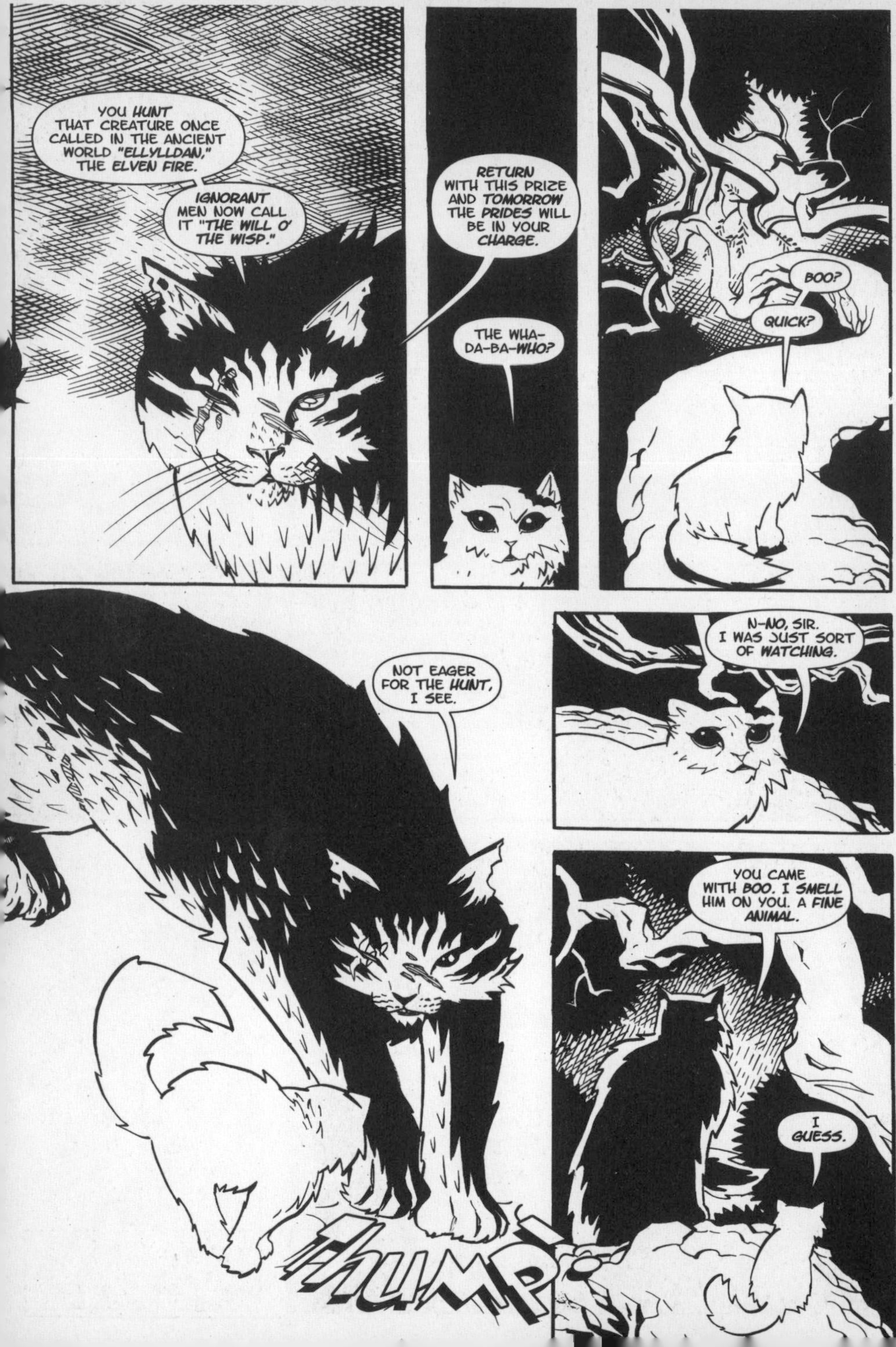
YOU HUNT THAT CREATURE ONCE CALLED IN THE ANCIENT WORLD "ELLYLLDAN," THE ELVEN FIRE.
IGNORANT MEN NOW CALL IT "THE WILL O' THE WISP."
RETURN WITH THIS PRIZE AND TOMORROW THE PRIDES WILL BE IN YOUR CHARGE.
THE WHA-DA-BA-WHO?
BOO?
QUICK?
NOT EAGER FOR THE HUNT, I SEE.
N-NO, SIR. I WAS JUST SORT OF WATCHING.
YOU CAME WITH BOO. I SMELL HIM ON YOU. A FINE ANIMAL.
I GUESS.
THUMP

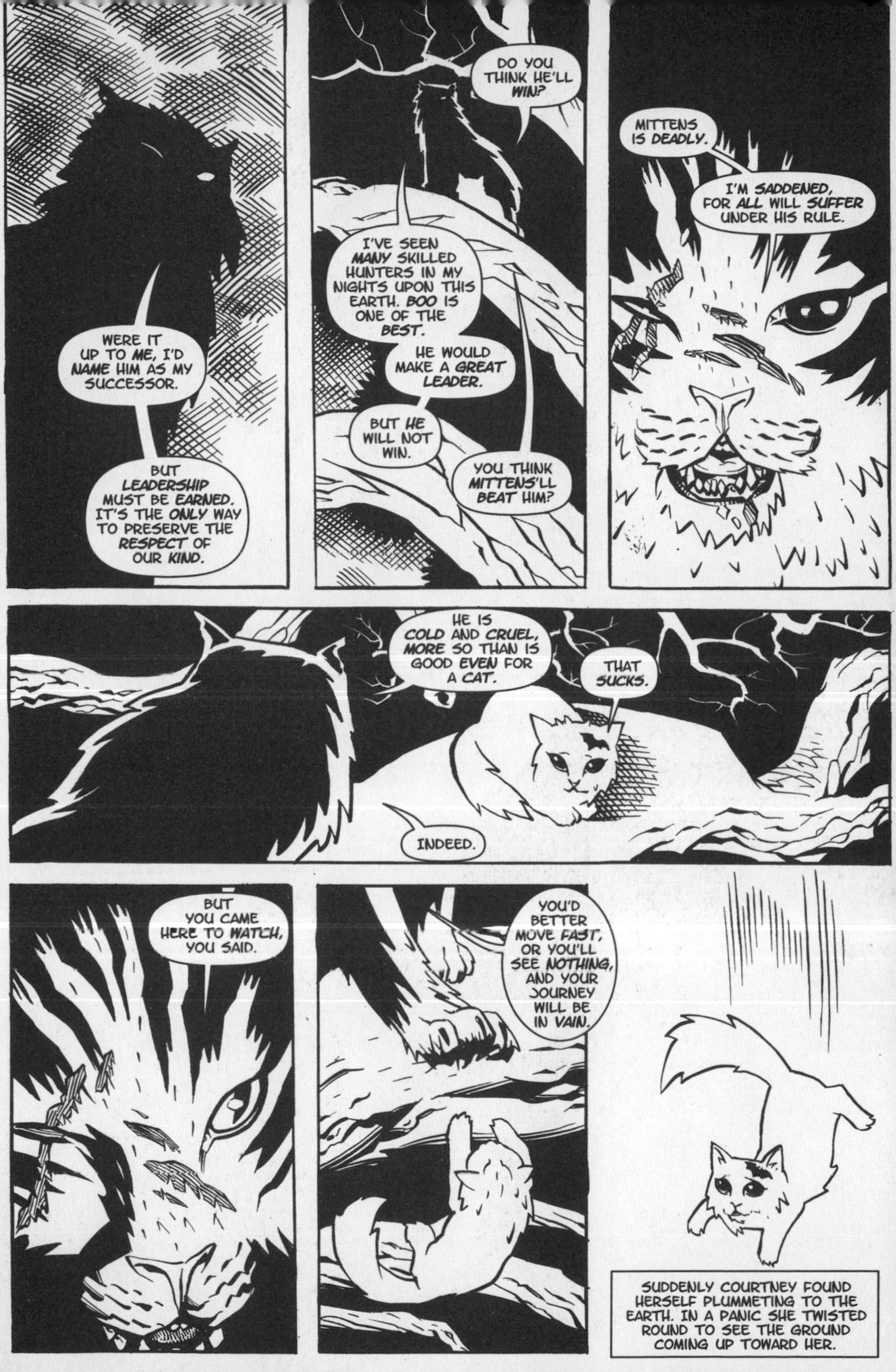
WERE IT UP TO ME, I'D NAME HIM AS MY SUCCESSOR.
BUT LEADERSHIP MUST BE EARNED. IT'S THE ONLY WAY TO PRESERVE THE RESPECT OF OUR KIND.
DO YOU THINK HE'LL WIN?
I'VE SEEN MANY SKILLED HUNTERS IN MY NIGHTS UPON THIS EARTH. BOO IS ONE OF THE BEST.
HE WOULD MAKE A GREAT LEADER.
BUT HE WILL NOT WIN.
YOU THINK MITTENS'LL BEAT HIM?
MITTENS IS DEADLY.
I'M SADDENED, FOR ALL WILL SUFFER UNDER HIS RULE.
HE IS COLD AND CRUEL, MORE SO THAN IS GOOD EVEN FOR A CAT.
THAT SUCKS.
INDEED.
BUT YOU CAME HERE TO WATCH, YOU SAID.
YOU'D BETTER MOVE FAST, OR YOU'LL SEE NOTHING, AND YOUR JOURNEY WILL BE IN VAIN.
SUDDENLY COURTNEY FOUND HERSELF PLUMMETING TO THE EARTH. IN A PANIC SHE TWISTED ROUND TO SEE THE GROUND COMING UP TOWARD HER.

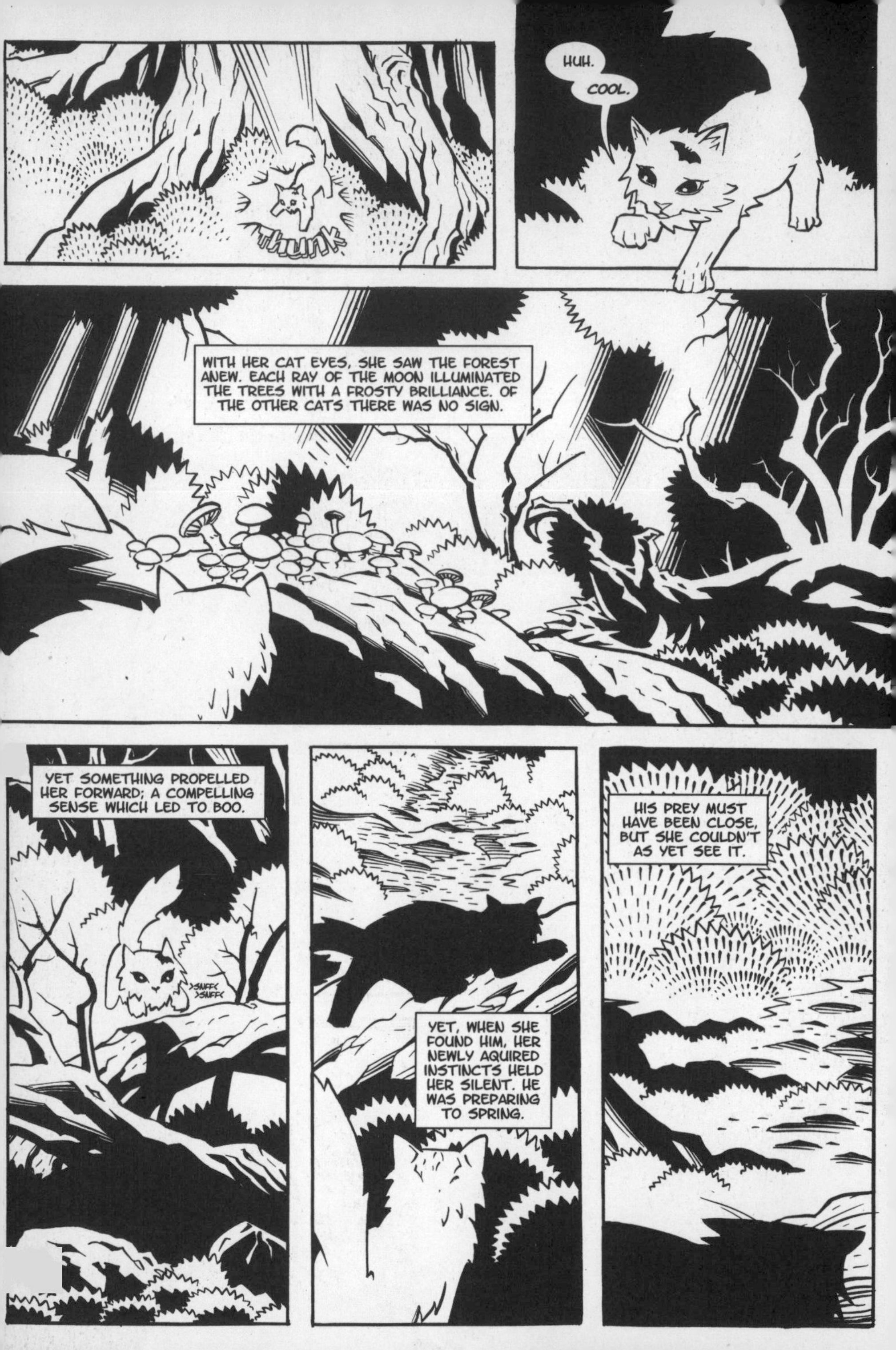
thunk
HUH.
COOL.
WITH HER CAT EYES, SHE SAW THE FOREST ANEW. EACH RAY OF THE MOON ILLUMINATED THE TREES WITH A FROSTY BRILLIANCE. OF THE OTHER CATS THERE WAS NO SIGN.
YET SOMETHING PROPELLED HER FORWARD; A COMPELLING SENSE WHICH LED TO BOO.
>SNIFF< >SNIFF<
YET, WHEN SHE FOUND HIM, HER NEWLY AQUIRED INSTINCTS HELD HER SILENT. HE WAS PREPARING TO SPRING.
HIS PREY MUST HAVE BEEN CLOSE, BUT SHE COULDN'T AS YET SEE IT.

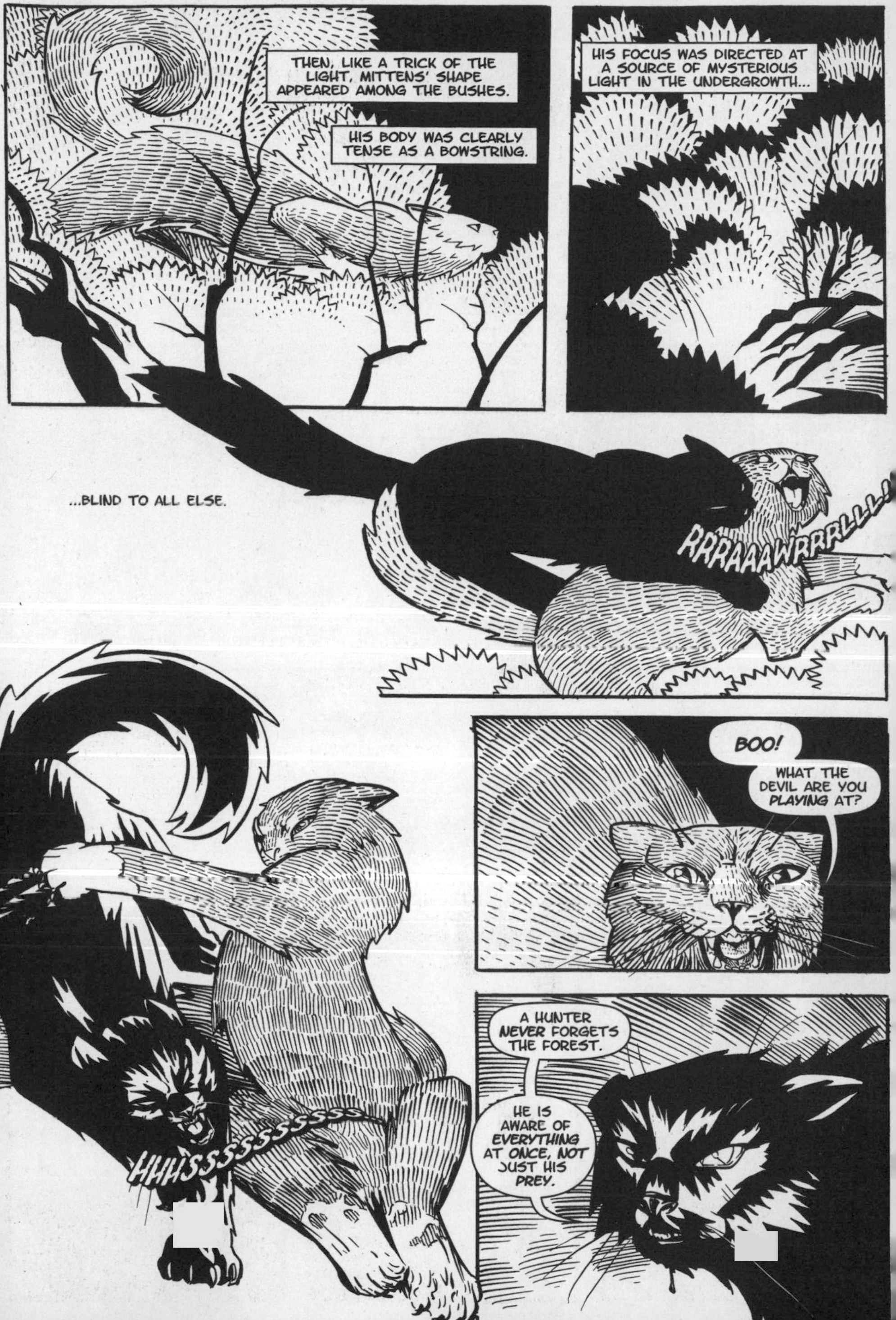
THEN, LIKE A TRICK OF THE LIGHT, MITTENS' SHAPE APPEARED AMONG THE BUSHES.
HIS BODY WAS CLEARLY TENSE AS A BOWSTRING.
HIS FOCUS WAS DIRECTED AT A SOURCE OF MYSTERIOUS LIGHT IN THE UNDERGROWTH...
...BLIND TO ALL ELSE.
RRRAAAWRRRLLL!
HHHSSSSSSSSSSS
BOO!
WHAT THE DEVIL ARE YOU *PLAYING* AT?
A HUNTER *NEVER* FORGETS THE FOREST.
HE IS AWARE OF *EVERYTHING* AT *ONCE*, NOT JUST HIS *PREY*.

TRUE. I SHALL NOT FORGET AGAIN.

THEN HE MELTED INTO THE NIGHT.

YOU OKAY?

YES, BUT NOW HE'LL MORE EASILY SMELL MY COMING.

SHOULDN'T YOU BE TRYING TO CATCH THE THING YOURSELF?

PERHAPS. I CERTAINLY SHOULDN'T BE SITTING HERE LICKING MY WOUNDS. FAREWELL.

BOO SLIPPED LIKE A SHADOW INTO THE DARKNESS, LEAVING COURTNEY ALONE ONCE AGAIN.

JUST AS SHE RESOLVED TO FOLLOW, SHE HEARD STRANGE NOISES.

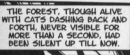

THE FOREST, THOUGH ALIVE WITH CATS DASHING BACK AND FORTH, NEVER VISIBLE FOR MORE THAN A SECOND, HAD BEEN SILENT UP TILL NOW.

SUCH A TERRIFIC CLAMOR SHATTERED THE SILENCE THAT SHE WAS CONVINCED A BULLDOZER WAS MOVING THROUGH THE TREES.

THEN SHE HEARD VOICES.

HUMAN VOICES.

THERE. DO YOU SEE THE TRACK?

THE BEAST CAN'T BE FAR. THE UNDERBRUSH IS STILL MOVING.

COURTNEY TRIED TO SUPPRESS HERSELF, BUT BY THEN HER NERVES WERE ON EDGE.

RAERRRR!

WAS THAT IT?

NO, BUT I'LL WAGER IT'S NEAR.

THERE.

THE FOREST IS *FULL* OF CATS TONIGHT, BUT *THAT'S* THE FIRST ONE I'VE *HEARD.*

SOMETHING STARTLED IT.

THE HUGE MEN CRASH OFF THROUGH THE BUSHES LIKE ELEPHANTS. COURTNEY KNEW THAT SHE'D LEAD THEM RIGHT TO THEIR QUARRY, AND DIDN'T FEEL GOOD ABOUT IT. HER INQUISITIVENESS UNQUENCHED, SHE RESOLVED TO FOLLOW.

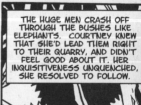

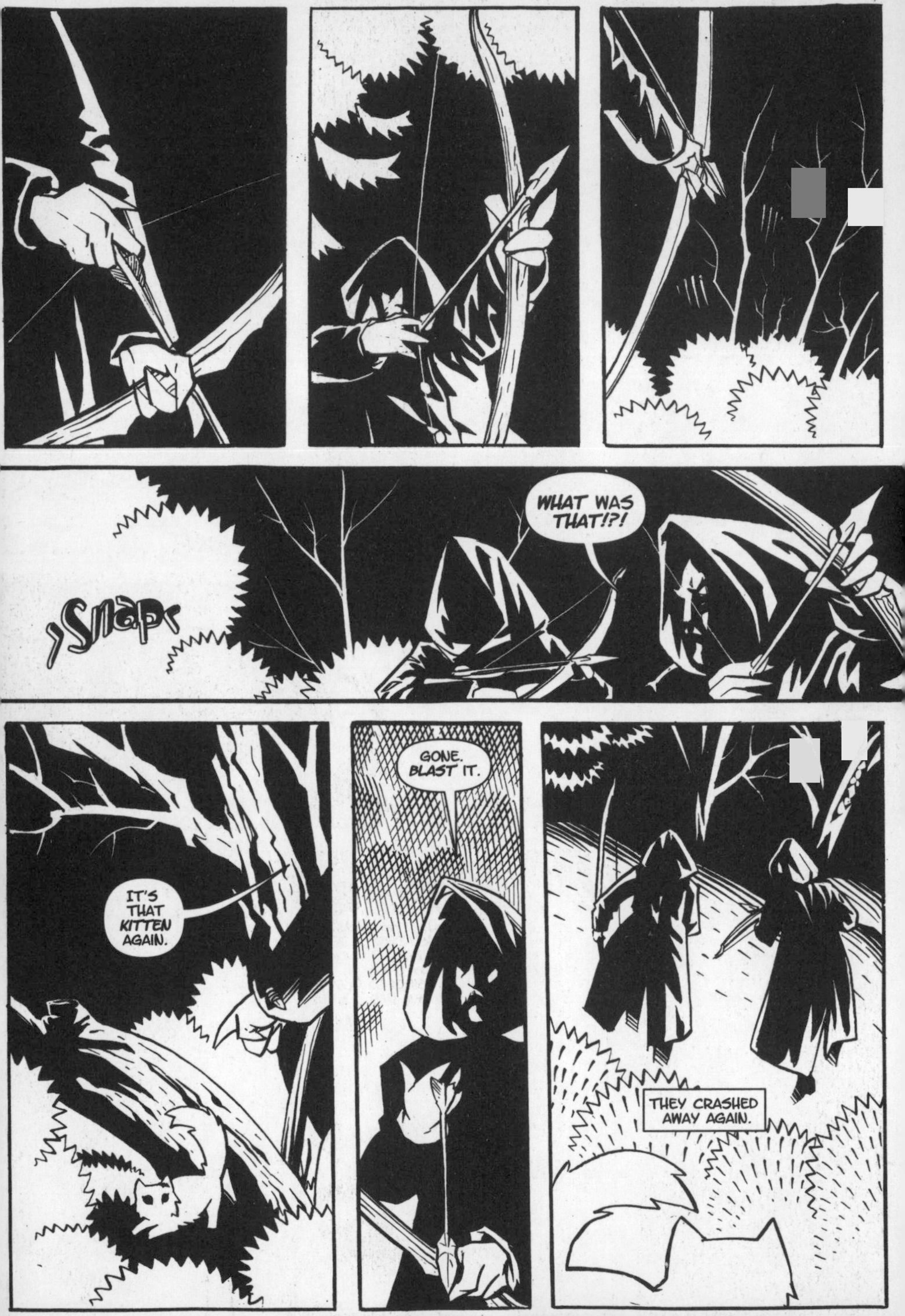
SNAP
WHAT WAS THAT!?!
IT'S THAT KITTEN AGAIN.
GONE. BLAST IT.
THEY CRASHED AWAY AGAIN.

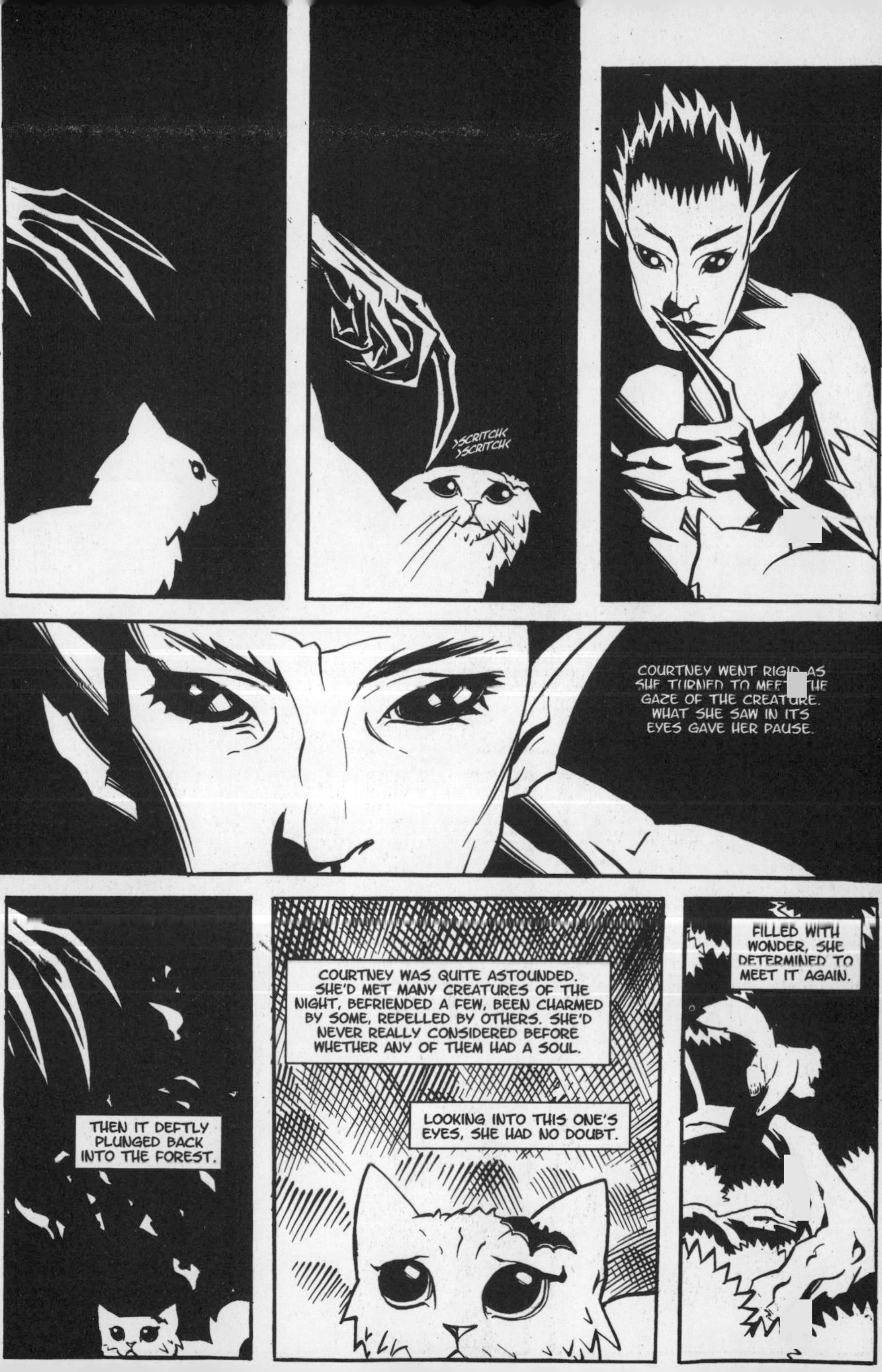

>SCRITCH<
>SCRITCH<
COURTNEY WENT RIGID AS SHE TURNED TO MEET THE GAZE OF THE CREATURE. WHAT SHE SAW IN ITS EYES GAVE HER PAUSE.
THEN IT DEFTLY PLUNGED BACK INTO THE FOREST.
COURTNEY WAS QUITE ASTOUNDED. SHE'D MET MANY CREATURES OF THE NIGHT, BEFRIENDED A FEW, BEEN CHARMED BY SOME, REPELLED BY OTHERS. SHE'D NEVER REALLY CONSIDERED BEFORE WHETHER ANY OF THEM HAD A SOUL.
LOOKING INTO THIS ONE'S EYES, SHE HAD NO DOUBT.
FILLED WITH WONDER, SHE DETERMINED TO MEET IT AGAIN.

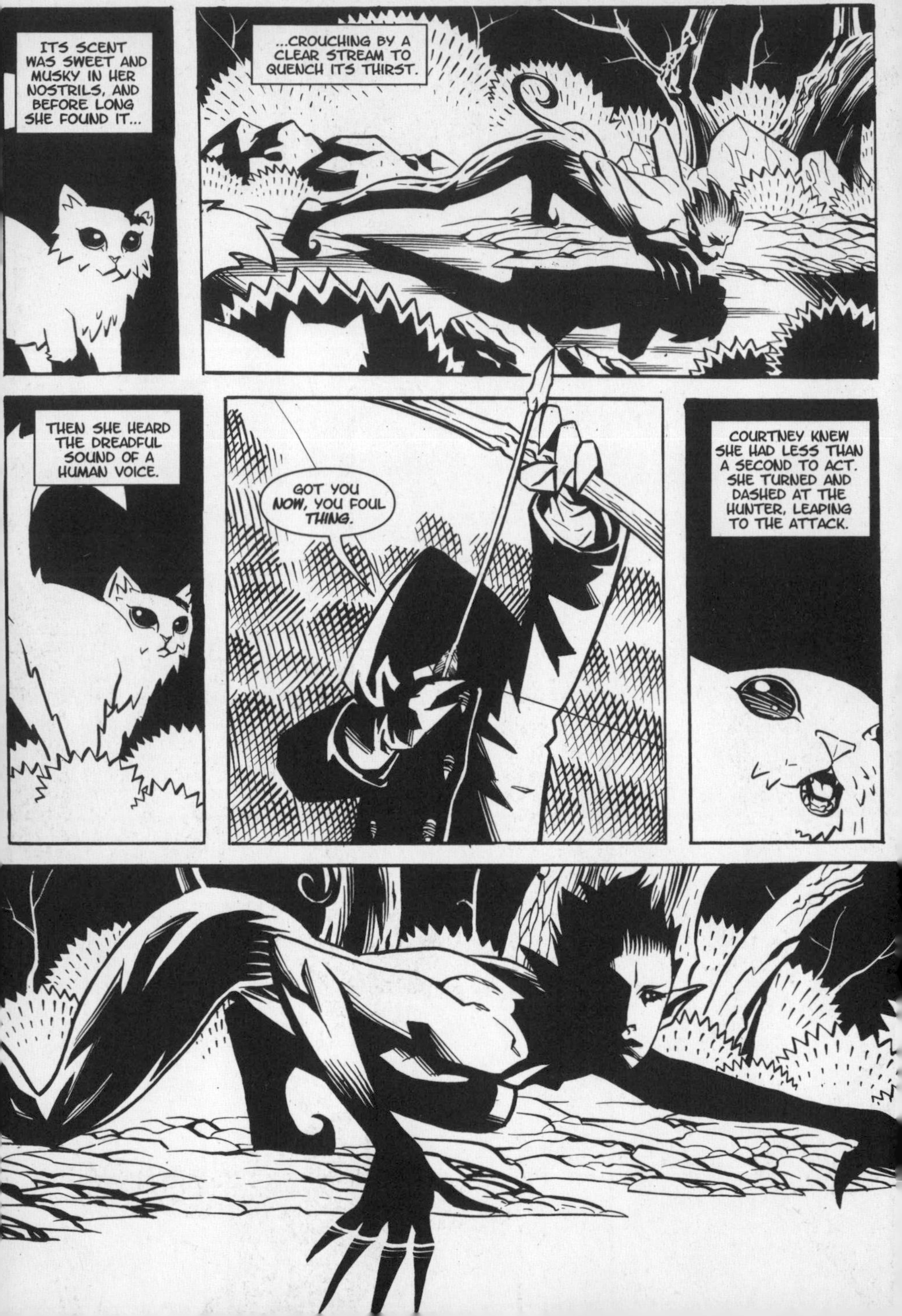
ITS SCENT WAS SWEET AND MUSKY IN HER NOSTRILS, AND BEFORE LONG SHE FOUND IT...
...CROUCHING BY A CLEAR STREAM TO QUENCH ITS THIRST.
THEN SHE HEARD THE DREADFUL SOUND OF A HUMAN VOICE.
GOT YOU NOW, YOU FOUL THING.
COURTNEY KNEW SHE HAD LESS THAN A SECOND TO ACT. SHE TURNED AND DASHED AT THE HUNTER, LEAPING TO THE ATTACK.

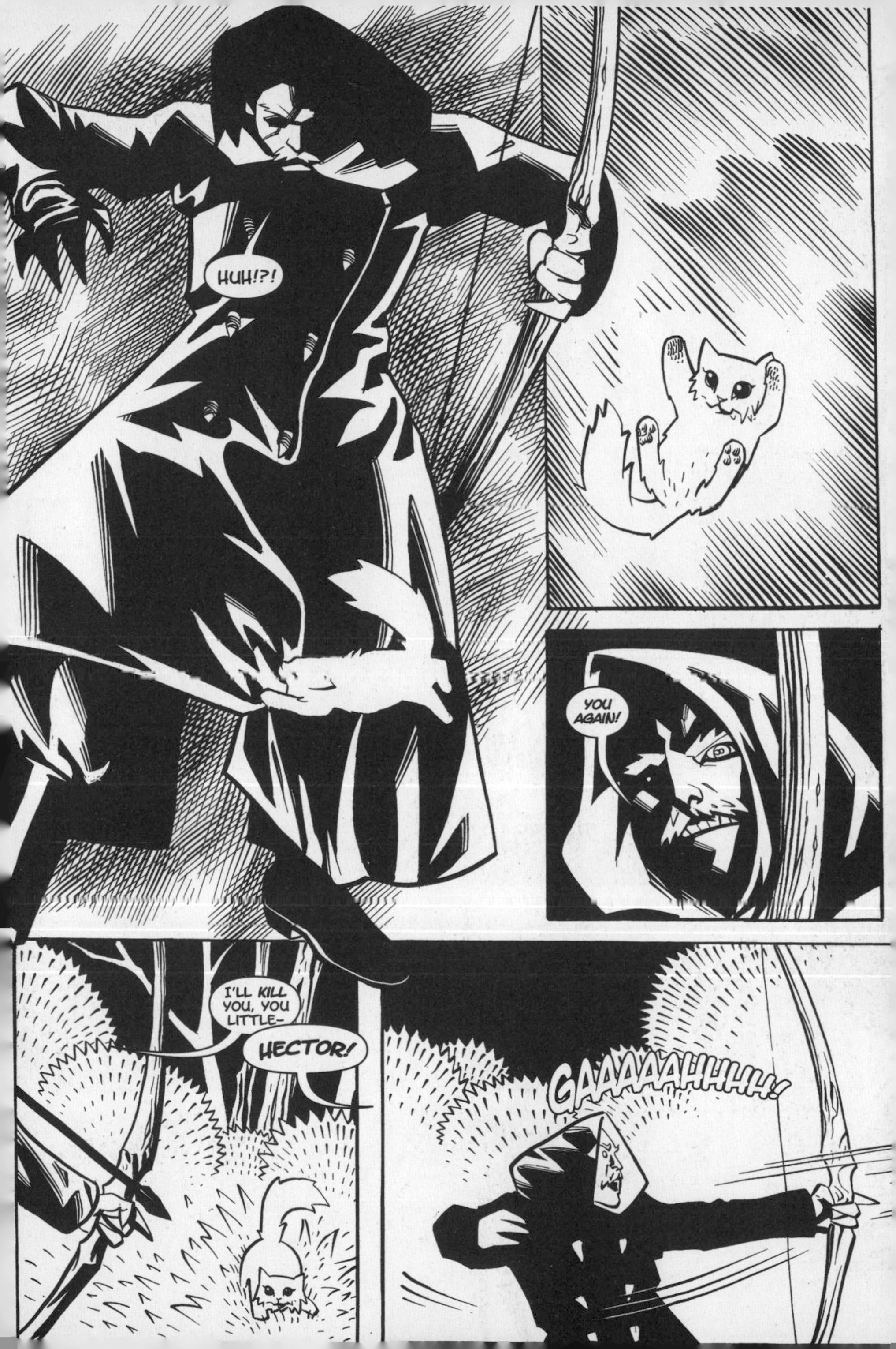
HUH!?!
YOU AGAIN!
I'LL KILL YOU, YOU LITTLE-
HECTOR!
GAAAAAHHHH!

EHEM.

PROFESSOR!?! WHAT ARE YOU DOING HERE?

I MIGHT ASK YOU THE SAME QUESTION.

RATHER UNSPORTSMANLIKE CHOICE OF QUARRY, DON'T YOU THINK?

I'M SO SORRY, PROFESSOR. I WAS HUNTING—

I KNOW WHAT YOU WERE HUNTING.

I THINK YOU SHOULD GO HOME NOW.

BUT PROFESSOR...

YES, SIR.

AND YOU TOO, YOUNG LADY.

IT'S PAST YOUR BEDTIME.

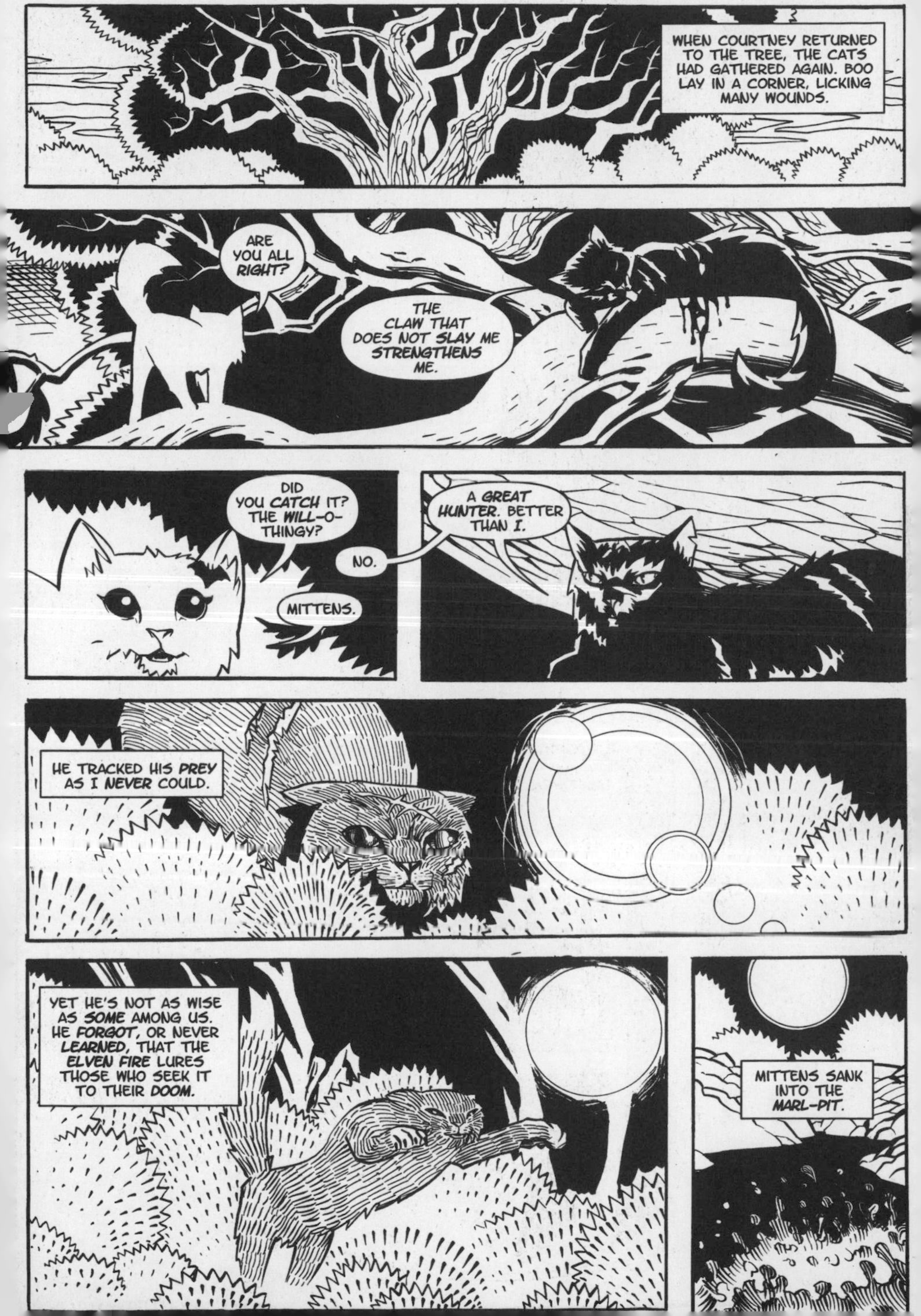
WHEN COURTNEY RETURNED TO THE TREE, THE CATS HAD GATHERED AGAIN. BOO LAY IN A CORNER, LICKING MANY WOUNDS.
ARE YOU ALL RIGHT?
THE CLAW THAT DOES NOT SLAY ME STRENGTHENS ME.
DID YOU CATCH IT? THE WILL-O-THINGY?
NO.
MITTENS.
A GREAT HUNTER. BETTER THAN I.
HE TRACKED HIS PREY AS I NEVER COULD.
YET HE'S NOT AS WISE AS SOME AMONG US. HE FORGOT, OR NEVER LEARNED, THAT THE ELVEN FIRE LURES THOSE WHO SEEK IT TO THEIR DOOM.
MITTENS SANK INTO THE MARL-PIT.

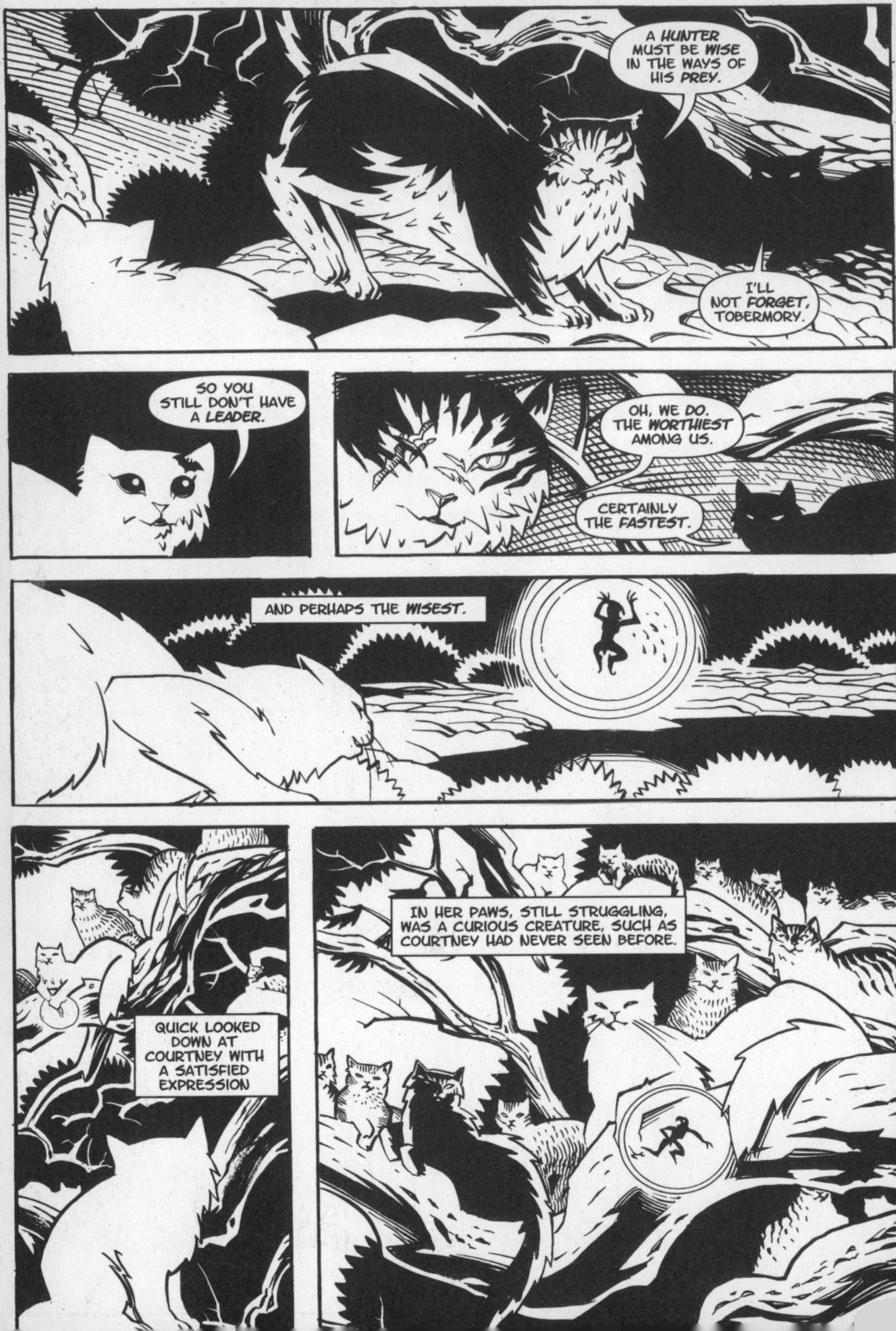
A HUNTER MUST BE WISE IN THE WAYS OF HIS PREY.
I'LL NOT FORGET, TOBERMORY.
SO YOU STILL DON'T HAVE A LEADER.
OH, WE DO. THE WORTHIEST AMONG US.
CERTAINLY THE FASTEST.
AND PERHAPS THE WISEST.
QUICK LOOKED DOWN AT COURTNEY WITH A SATISFIED EXPRESSION
IN HER PAWS, STILL STRUGGLING, WAS A CURIOUS CREATURE, SUCH AS COURTNEY HAD NEVER SEEN BEFORE.

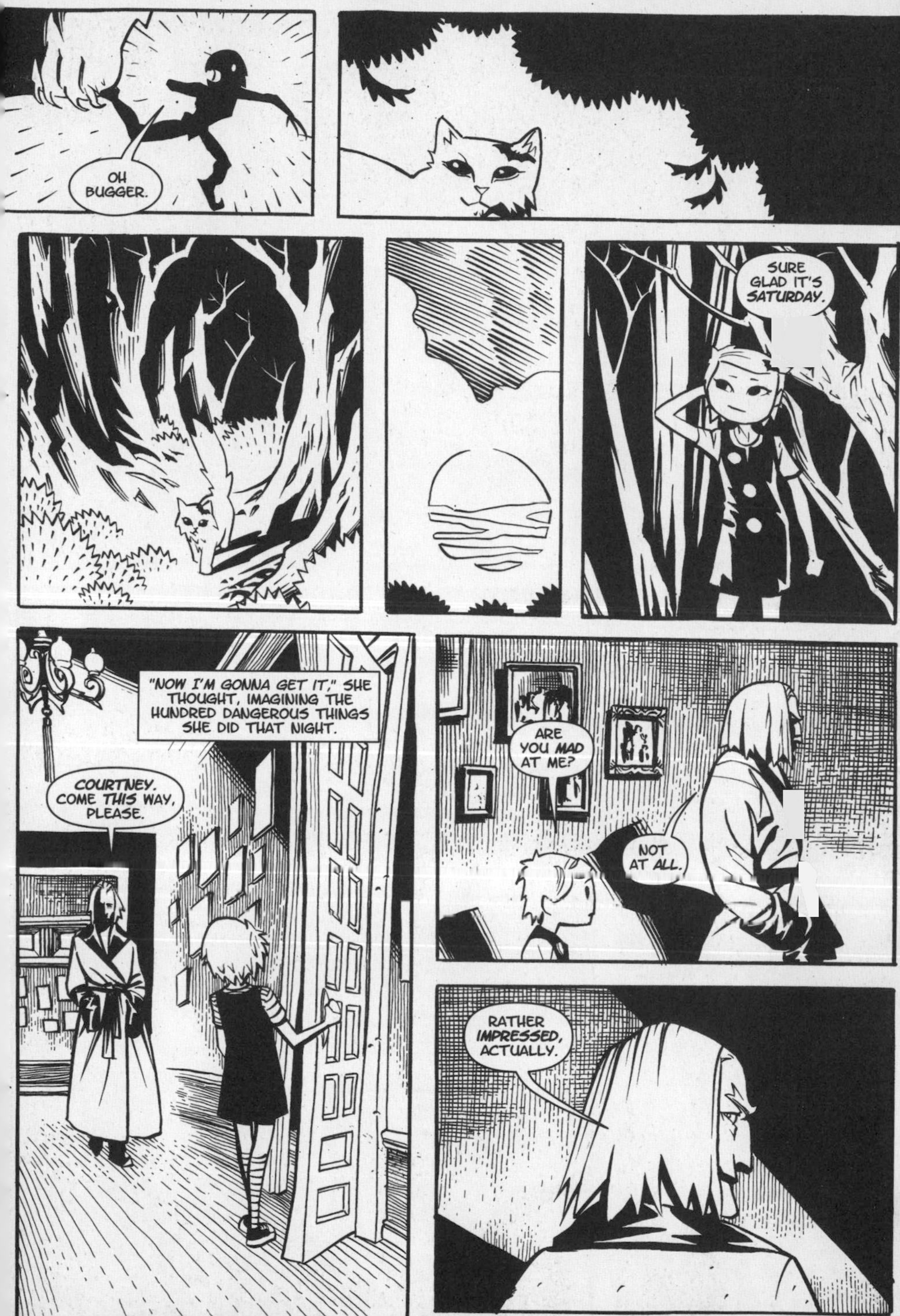
OH BUGGER.
SURE GLAD IT'S SATURDAY.
"NOW I'M GONNA GET IT," SHE THOUGHT, IMAGINING THE HUNDRED DANGEROUS THINGS SHE DID THAT NIGHT.
COURTNEY. COME THIS WAY, PLEASE.
ARE YOU MAD AT ME?
NOT AT ALL.
RATHER IMPRESSED, ACTUALLY.

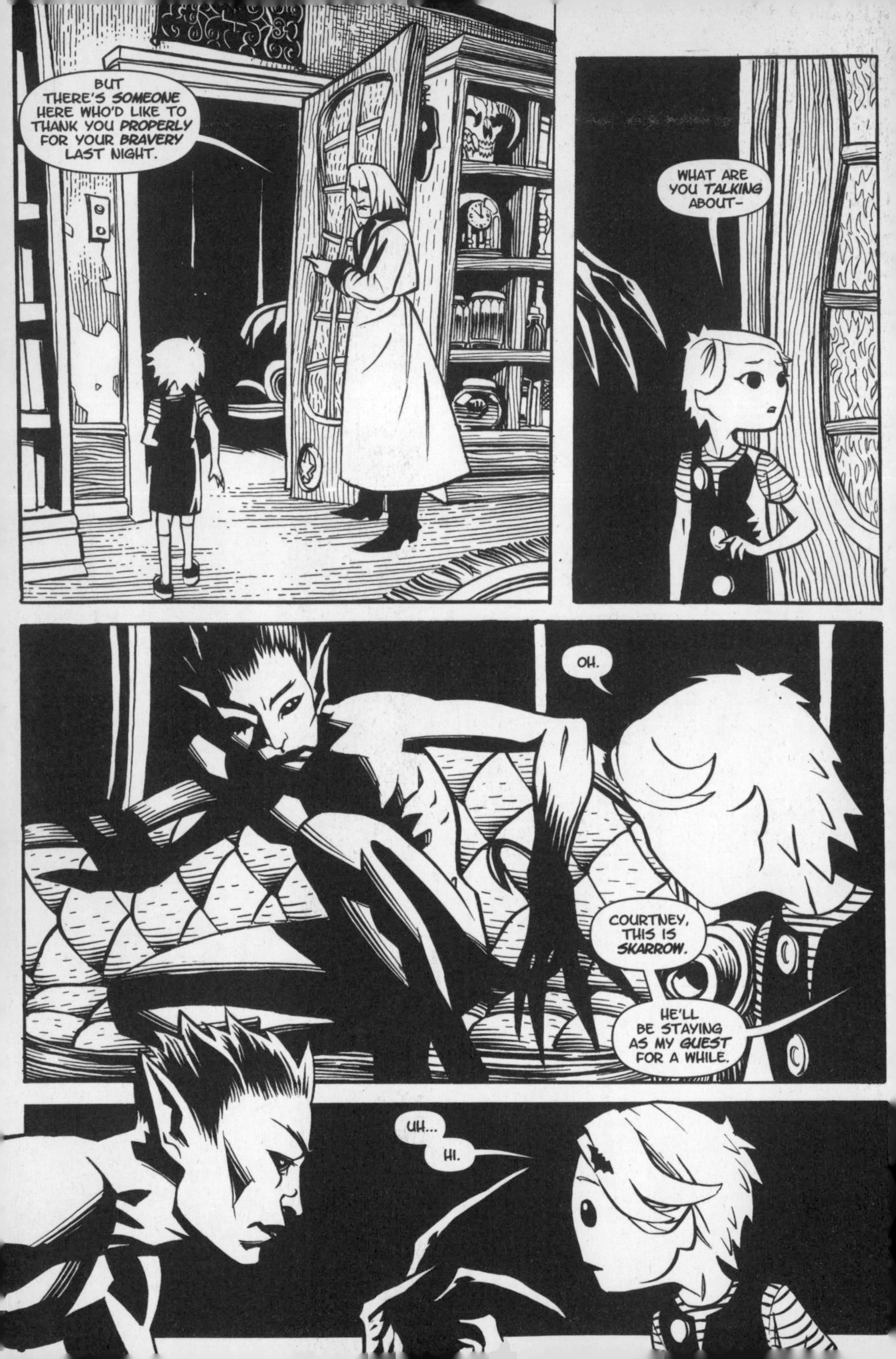
BUT THERE'S SOMEONE HERE WHO'D LIKE TO THANK YOU PROPERLY FOR YOUR BRAVERY LAST NIGHT.
WHAT ARE YOU TALKING ABOUT-
OH.
COURTNEY, THIS IS SKARROW.
HE'LL BE STAYING AS MY GUEST FOR A WHILE.
UH...
HI.

CHAPTER THREE

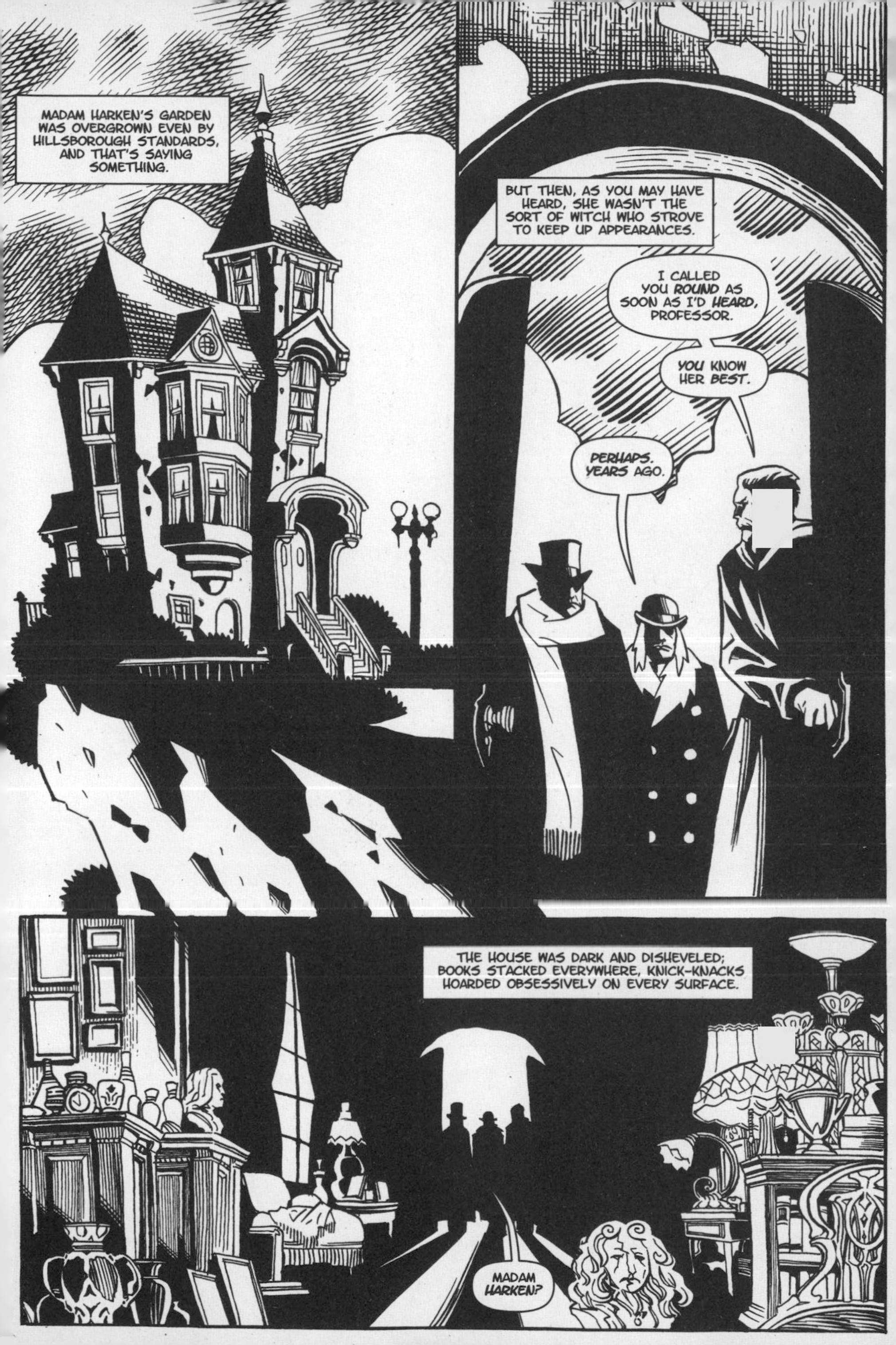
MADAM HARKEN'S GARDEN WAS OVERGROWN EVEN BY HILLSBOROUGH STANDARDS, AND THAT'S SAYING SOMETHING.
BUT THEN, AS YOU MAY HAVE HEARD, SHE WASN'T THE SORT OF WITCH WHO STROVE TO KEEP UP APPEARANCES.
I CALLED YOU ROUND AS SOON AS I'D HEARD, PROFESSOR.
YOU KNOW HER BEST.
PERHAPS. YEARS AGO.
THE HOUSE WAS DARK AND DISHEVELED; BOOKS STACKED EVERYWHERE, KNICK-KNACKS HOARDED OBSESSIVELY ON EVERY SURFACE.
MADAM HARKEN?

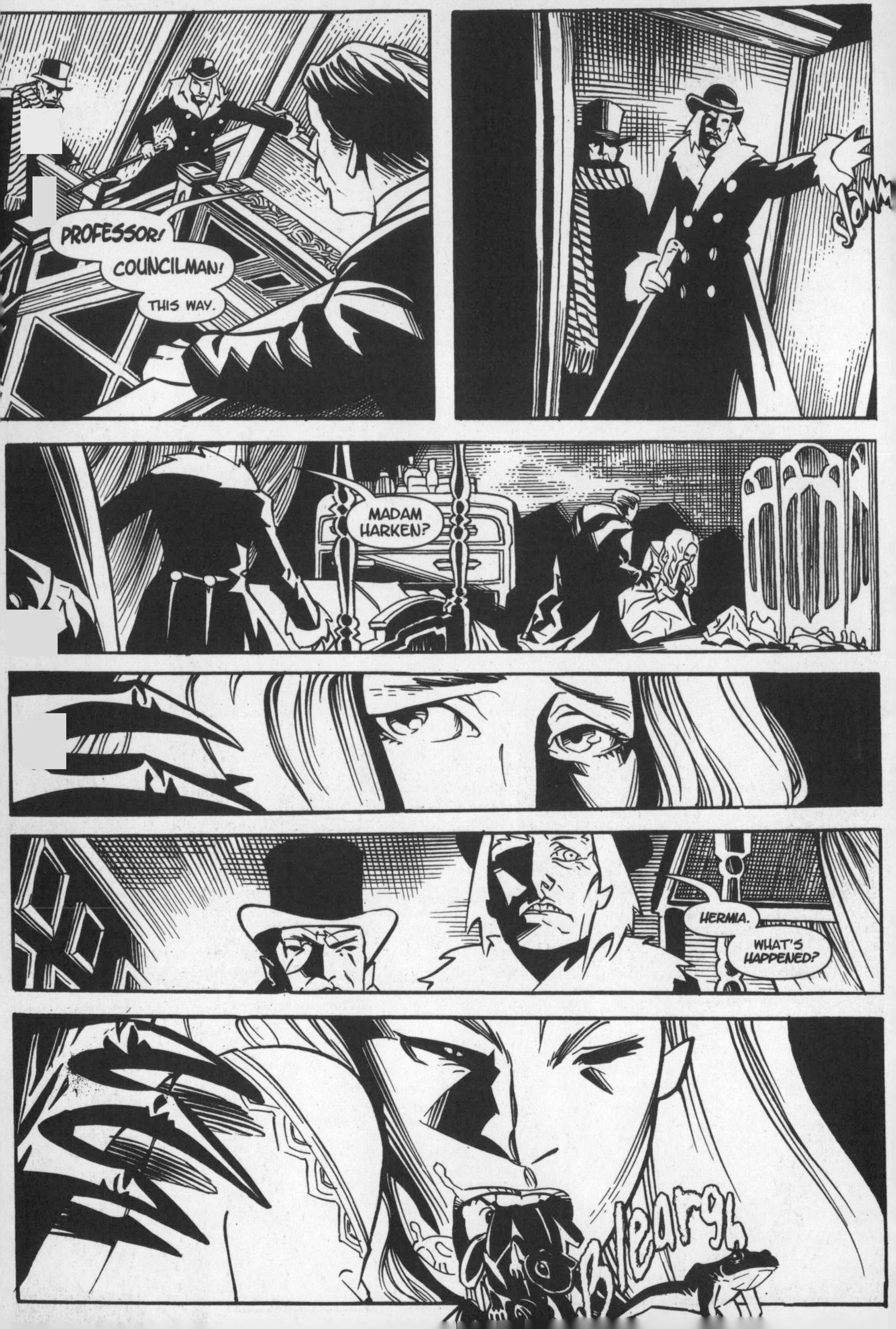
PROFESSOR!
COUNCILMAN!
THIS WAY.
SLAMM
MADAM HARKEN?
HERMIA.
WHAT'S HAPPENED?
BLEARGH

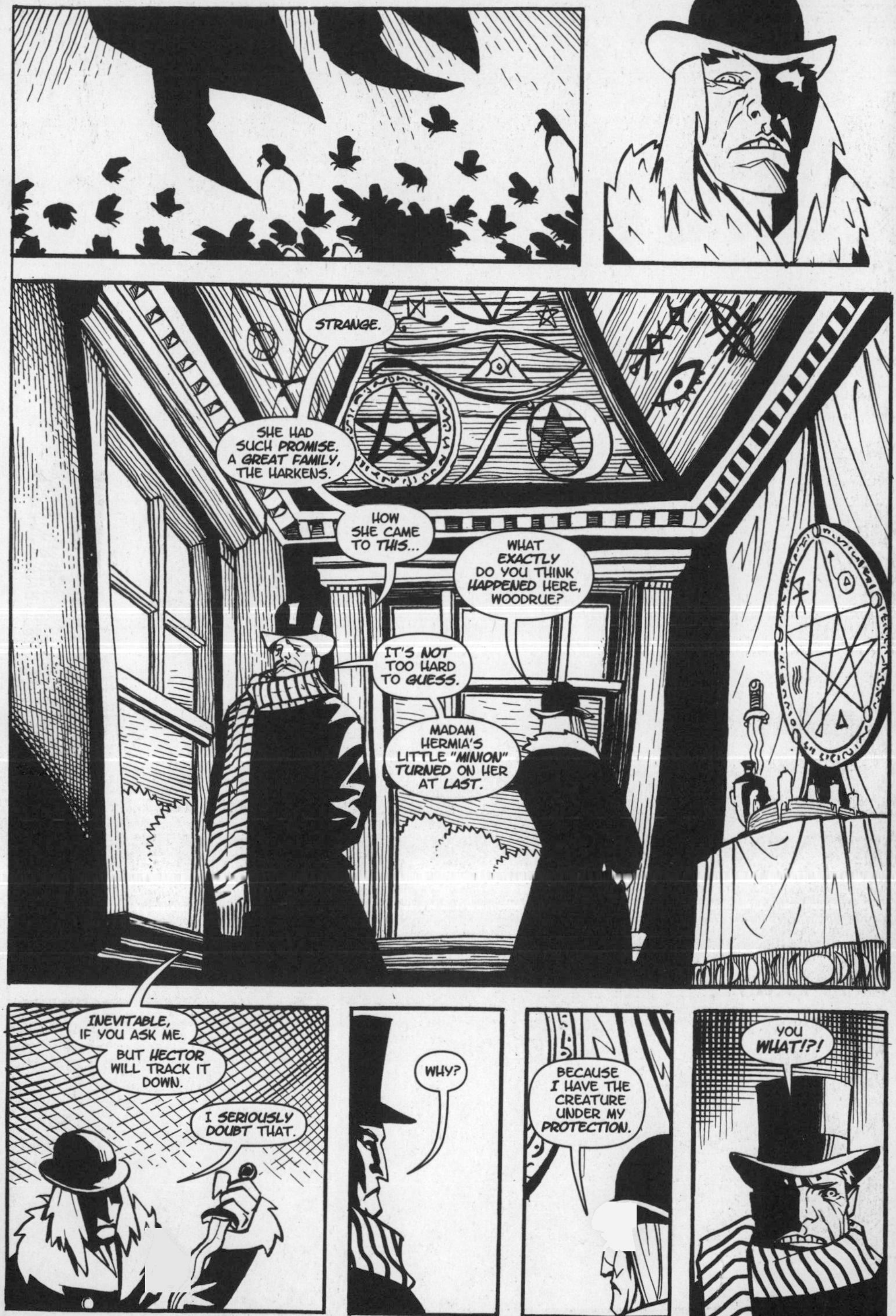
STRANGE.
SHE HAD SUCH PROMISE. A GREAT FAMILY, THE HARKENS.
HOW SHE CAME TO THIS...
WHAT EXACTLY DO YOU THINK HAPPENED HERE, WOODRUE?
IT'S NOT TOO HARD TO GUESS.
MADAM HERMIA'S LITTLE "MINION" TURNED ON HER AT LAST.
INEVITABLE, IF YOU ASK ME.
BUT HECTOR WILL TRACK IT DOWN.
I SERIOUSLY DOUBT THAT.
WHY?
BECAUSE I HAVE THE CREATURE UNDER MY PROTECTION.
YOU WHAT!?!

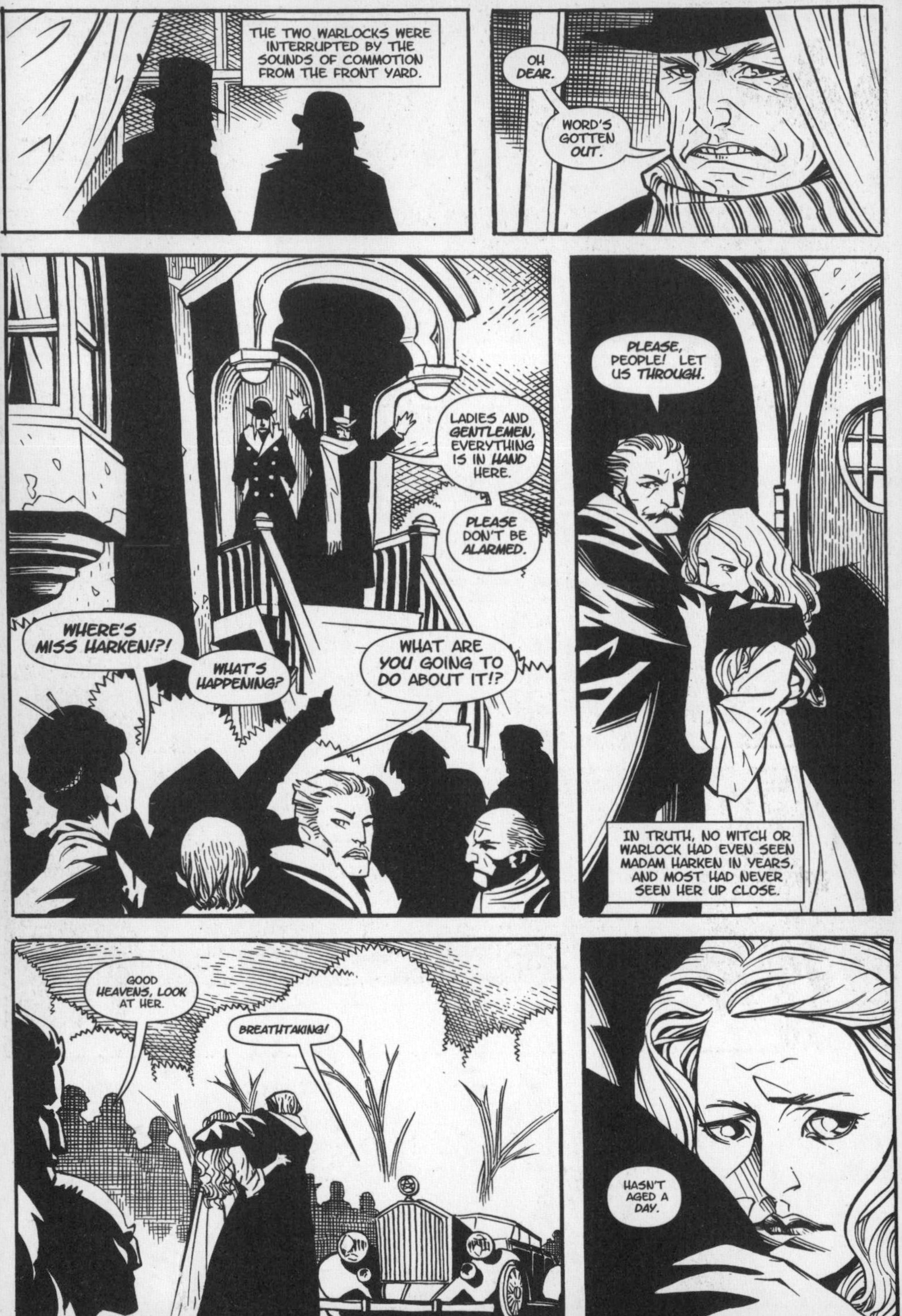
THE TWO WARLOCKS WERE INTERRUPTED BY THE SOUNDS OF COMMOTION FROM THE FRONT YARD.
OH DEAR.
WORD'S GOTTEN OUT.
LADIES AND GENTLEMEN, EVERYTHING IS IN HAND HERE.
PLEASE DON'T BE ALARMED.
WHERE'S MISS HARKEN!?!
WHAT'S HAPPENING?
WHAT ARE YOU GOING TO DO ABOUT IT!?
PLEASE, PEOPLE! LET US THROUGH.
IN TRUTH, NO WITCH OR WARLOCK HAD EVEN SEEN MADAM HARKEN IN YEARS, AND MOST HAD NEVER SEEN HER UP CLOSE.
GOOD HEAVENS, LOOK AT HER.
BREATHTAKING!
HASN'T AGED A DAY.

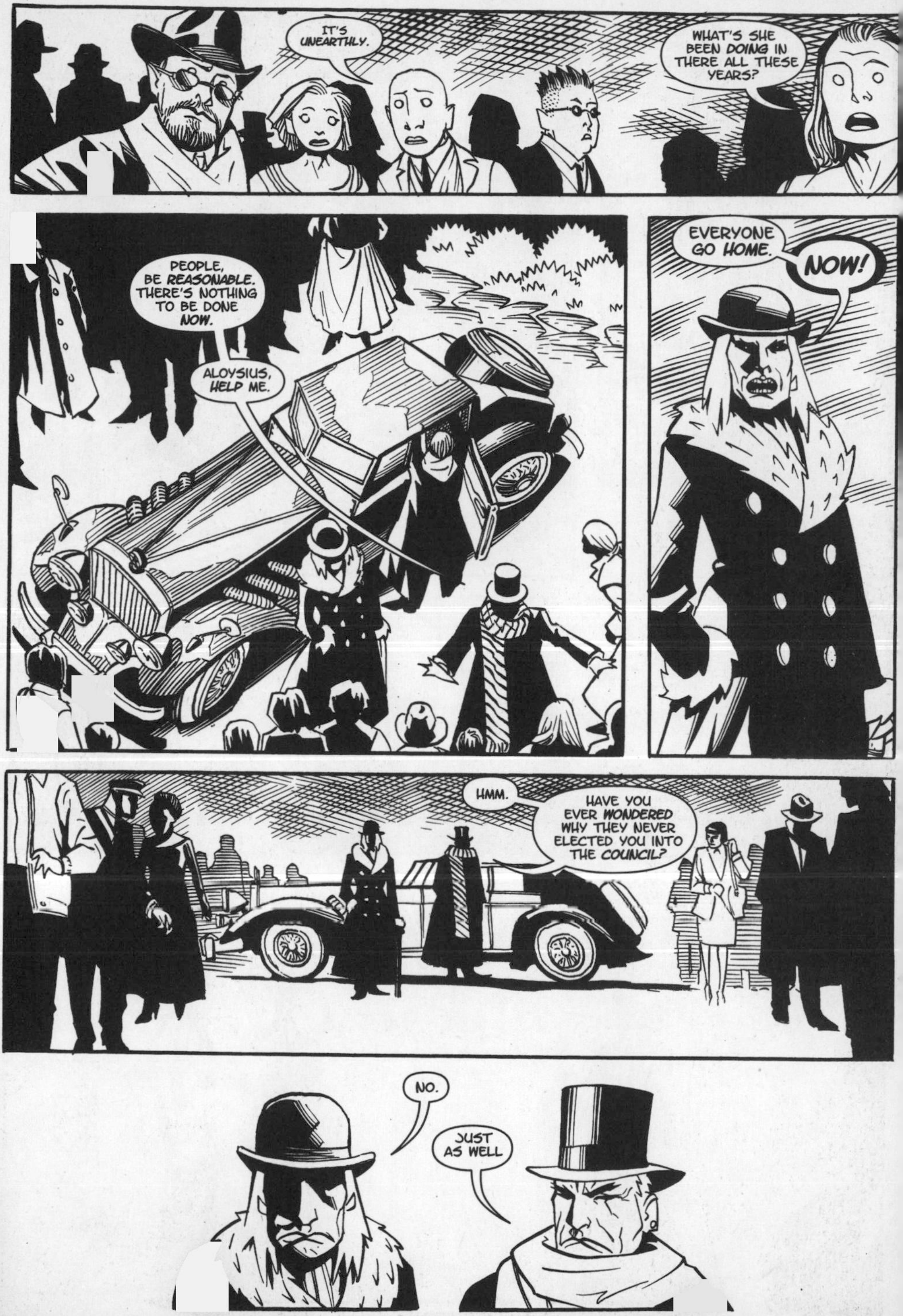
IT'S UNEARTHLY.
WHAT'S SHE BEEN DOING IN THERE ALL THESE YEARS?
PEOPLE, BE REASONABLE. THERE'S NOTHING TO BE DONE NOW.
ALOYSIUS, HELP ME.
EVERYONE GO HOME.
NOW!
HMM.
HAVE YOU EVER WONDERED WHY THEY NEVER ELECTED YOU INTO THE COUNCIL?
NO.
JUST AS WELL

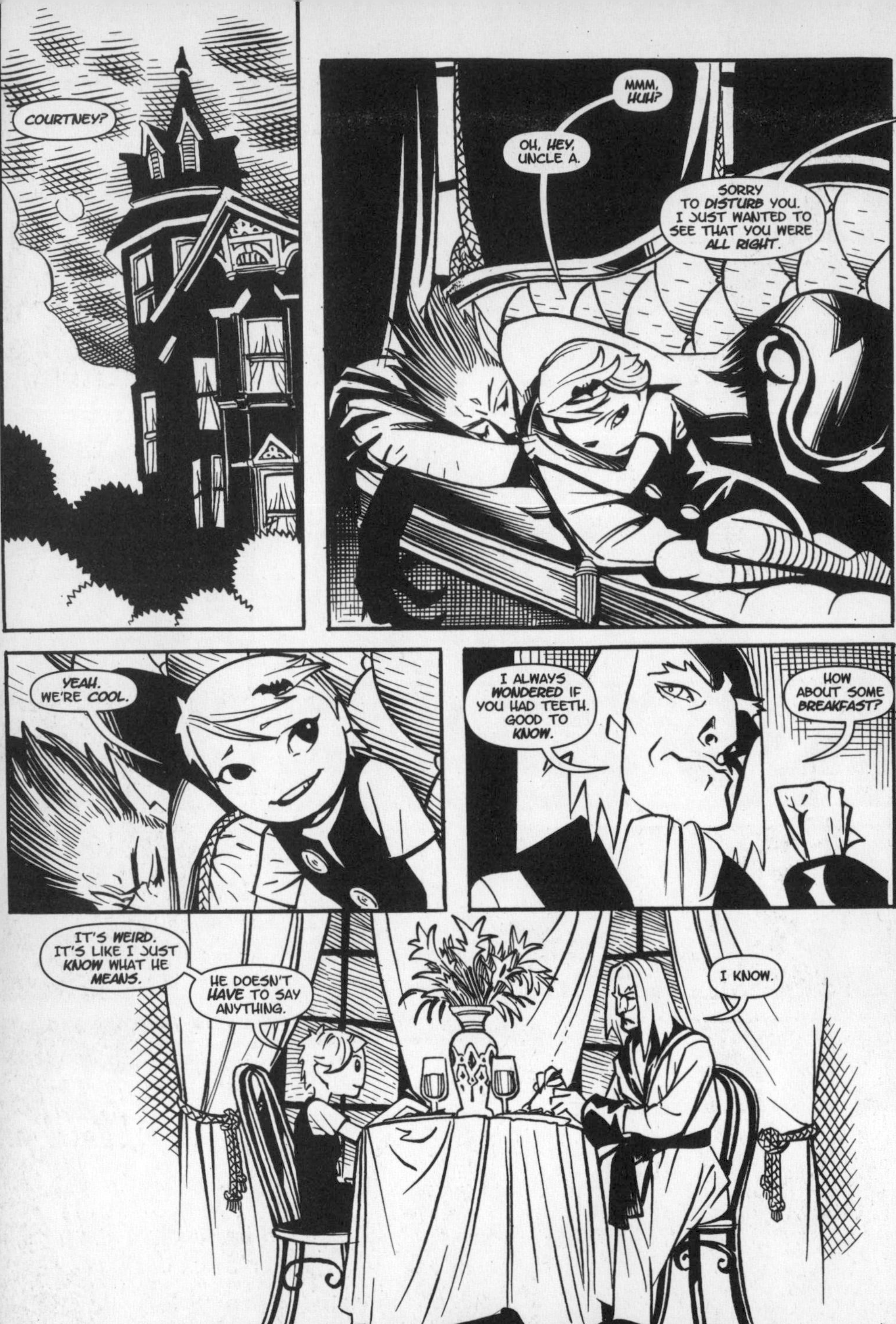
COURTNEY?
MMM, HUH?
OH, HEY, UNCLE A.
SORRY TO DISTURB YOU. I JUST WANTED TO SEE THAT YOU WERE ALL RIGHT.
YEAH. WE'RE COOL.
I ALWAYS WONDERED IF YOU HAD TEETH. GOOD TO KNOW.
HOW ABOUT SOME BREAKFAST?
IT'S WEIRD. IT'S LIKE I JUST KNOW WHAT HE MEANS.
HE DOESN'T HAVE TO SAY ANYTHING.
I KNOW.

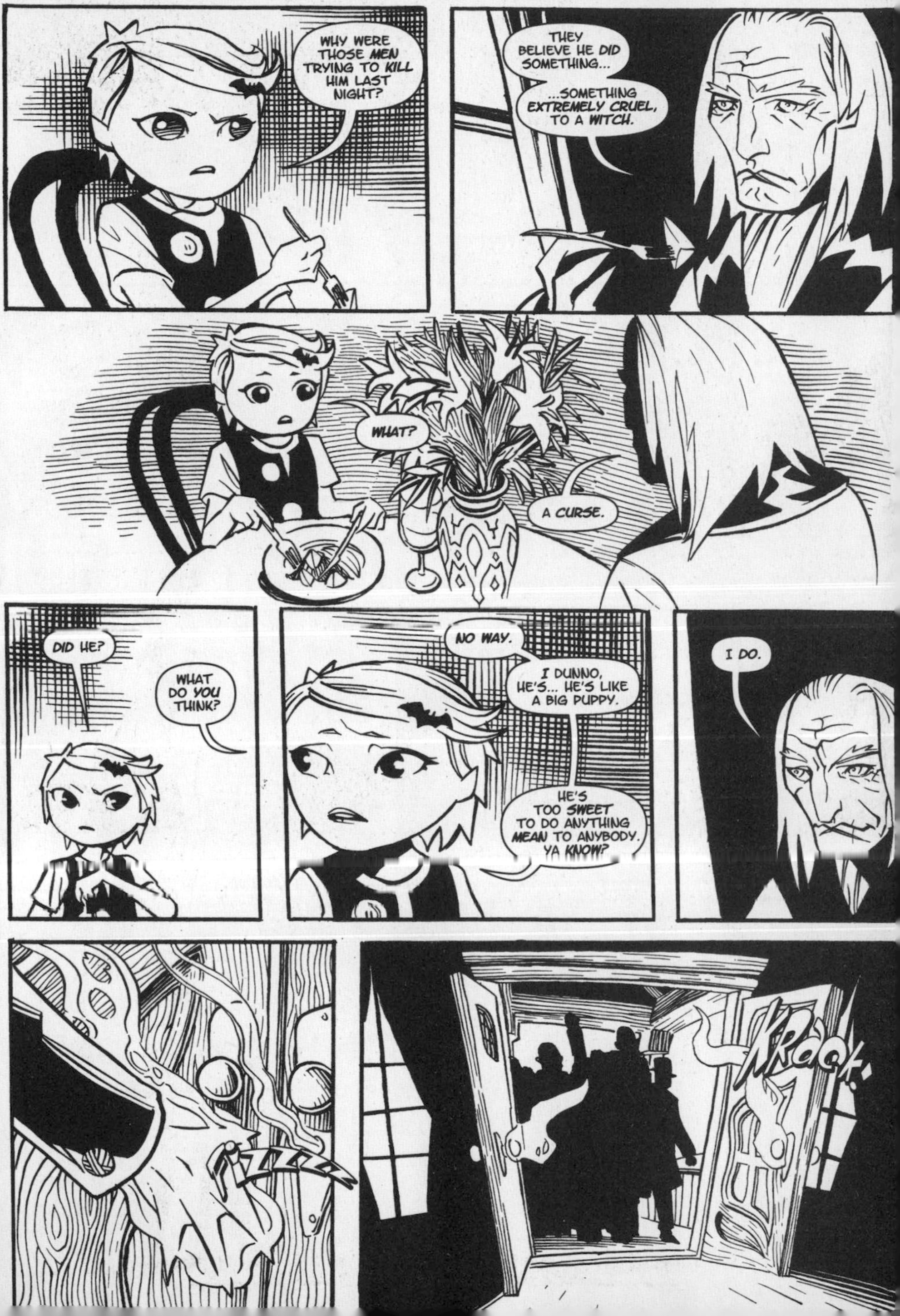
WHY WERE THOSE MEN TRYING TO KILL HIM LAST NIGHT?
THEY BELIEVE HE DID SOMETHING...
...SOMETHING EXTREMELY CRUEL, TO A WITCH.
WHAT?
A CURSE.
DID HE?
WHAT DO YOU THINK?
NO WAY.
I DUNNO, HE'S... HE'S LIKE A BIG PUPPY.
HE'S TOO SWEET TO DO ANYTHING MEAN TO ANYBODY. YA KNOW?
I DO.
KRAAK!

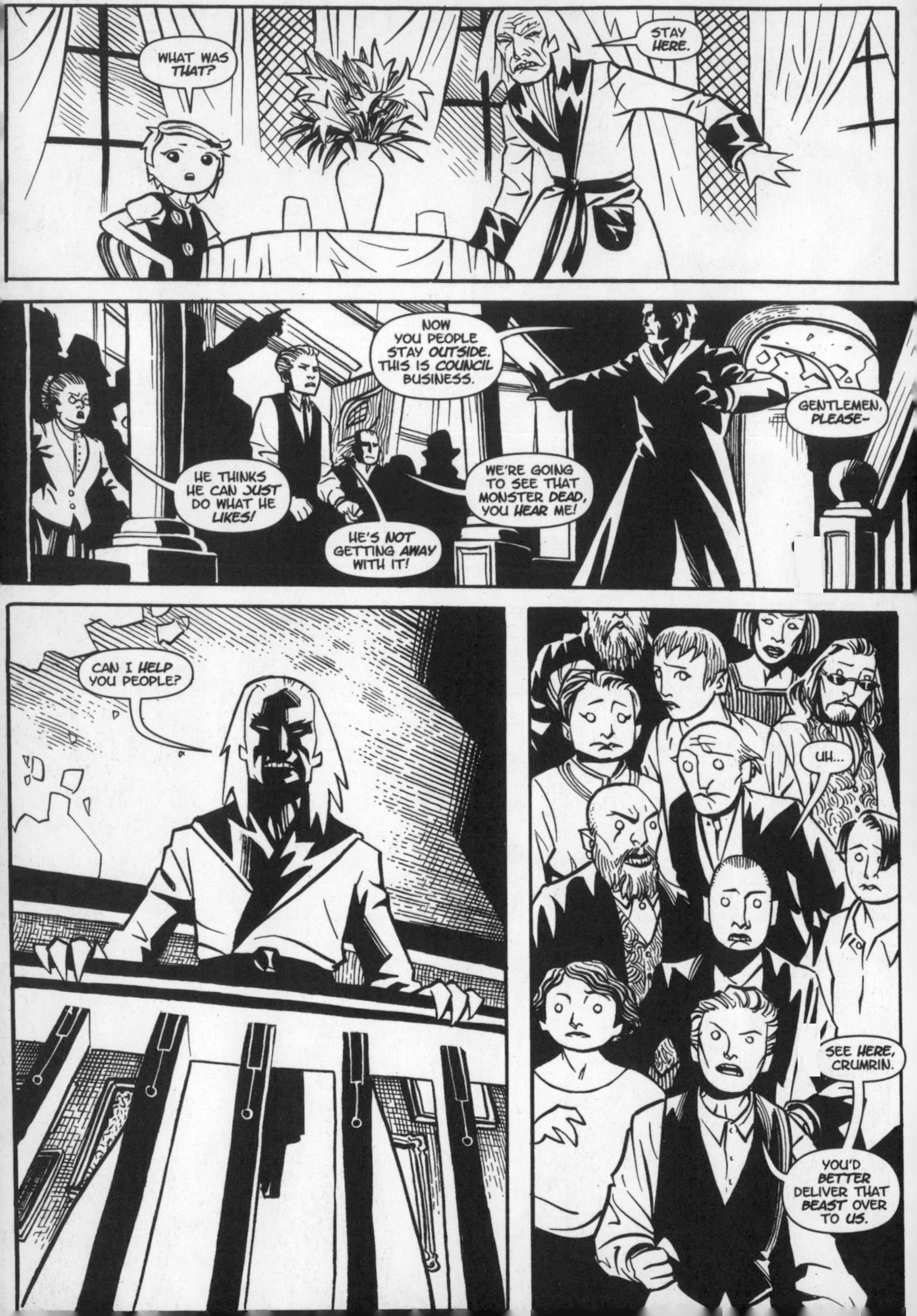
WHAT WAS THAT?
STAY HERE.
NOW YOU PEOPLE STAY OUTSIDE. THIS IS COUNCIL BUSINESS.
GENTLEMEN, PLEASE-
HE THINKS HE CAN JUST DO WHAT HE LIKES!
WE'RE GOING TO SEE THAT MONSTER DEAD, YOU HEAR ME!
HE'S NOT GETTING AWAY WITH IT!
CAN I HELP YOU PEOPLE?
UH...
SEE HERE, CRUMRIN.
YOU'D BETTER DELIVER THAT BEAST OVER TO US.

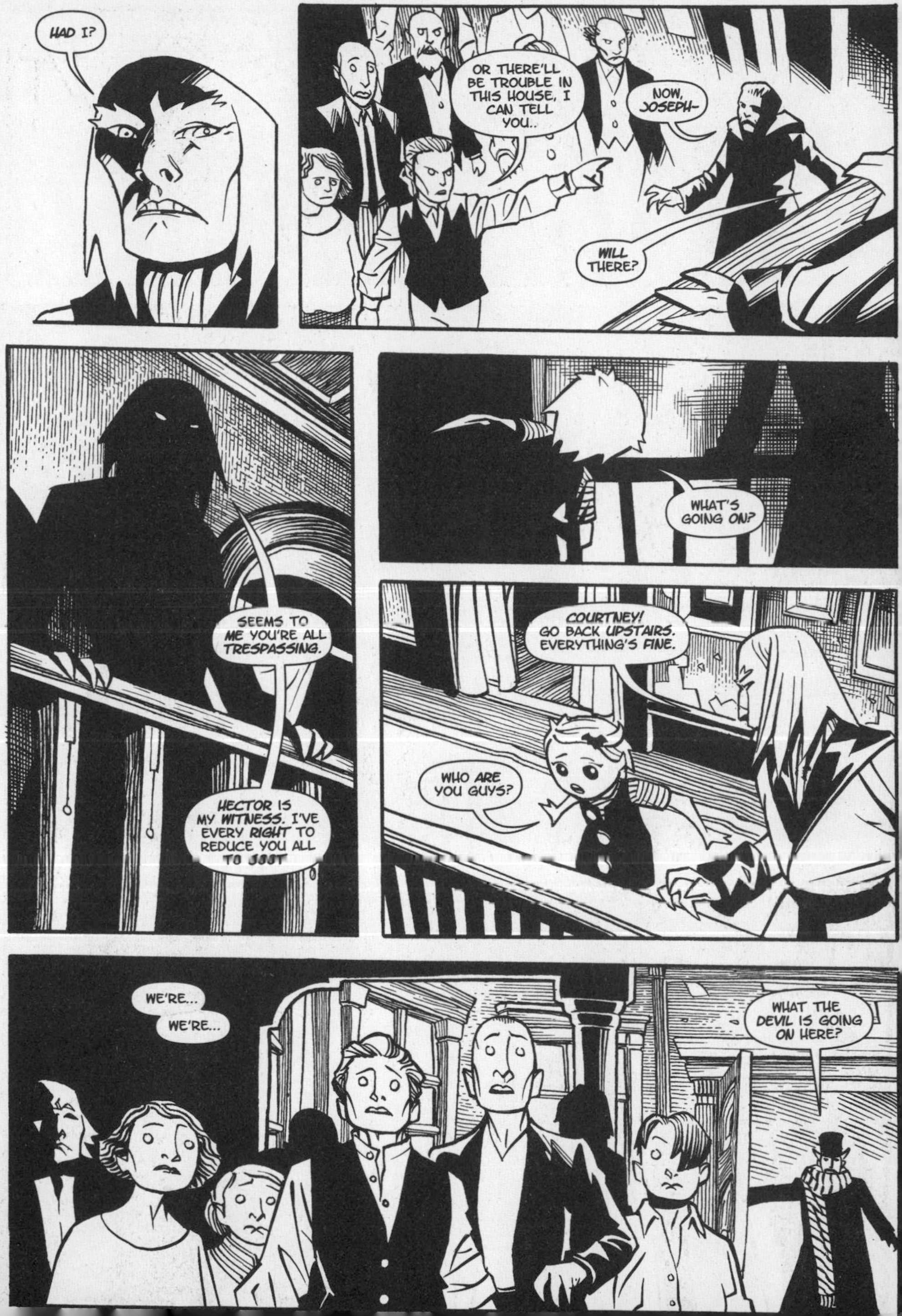

HAD I?
OR THERE'LL BE TROUBLE IN THIS HOUSE, I CAN TELL YOU..
NOW, JOSEPH-
WILL THERE?
SEEMS TO ME YOU'RE ALL TRESPASSING.
HECTOR IS MY WITNESS. I'VE EVERY RIGHT TO REDUCE YOU ALL TO
WHAT'S GOING ON?
COURTNEY! GO BACK UPSTAIRS. EVERYTHING'S FINE.
WHO ARE YOU GUYS?
WE'RE...
WE'RE...
WHAT THE DEVIL IS GOING ON HERE?

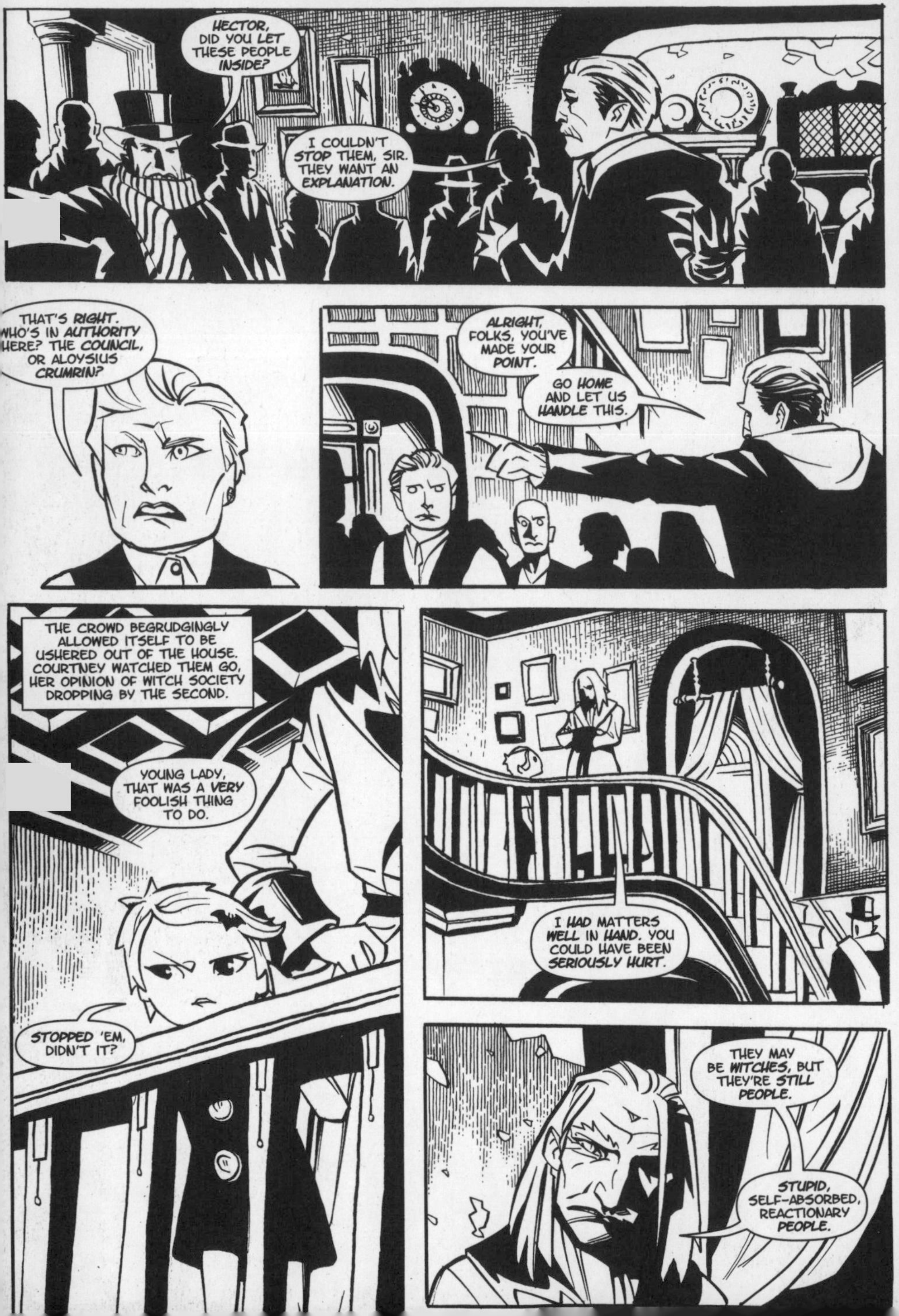
HECTOR, DID YOU LET THESE PEOPLE INSIDE?
I COULDN'T STOP THEM, SIR. THEY WANT AN EXPLANATION.
THAT'S RIGHT. WHO'S IN AUTHORITY HERE? THE COUNCIL, OR ALOYSIUS CRUMRIN?
ALRIGHT, FOLKS, YOU'VE MADE YOUR POINT.
GO HOME AND LET US HANDLE THIS.
THE CROWD BEGRUDGINGLY ALLOWED ITSELF TO BE USHERED OUT OF THE HOUSE. COURTNEY WATCHED THEM GO, HER OPINION OF WITCH SOCIETY DROPPING BY THE SECOND.
YOUNG LADY, THAT WAS A VERY FOOLISH THING TO DO.
I HAD MATTERS WELL IN HAND. YOU COULD HAVE BEEN SERIOUSLY HURT.
STOPPED 'EM, DIDN'T IT?
THEY MAY BE WITCHES, BUT THEY'RE STILL PEOPLE.
STUPID, SELF-ABSORBED, REACTIONARY PEOPLE.

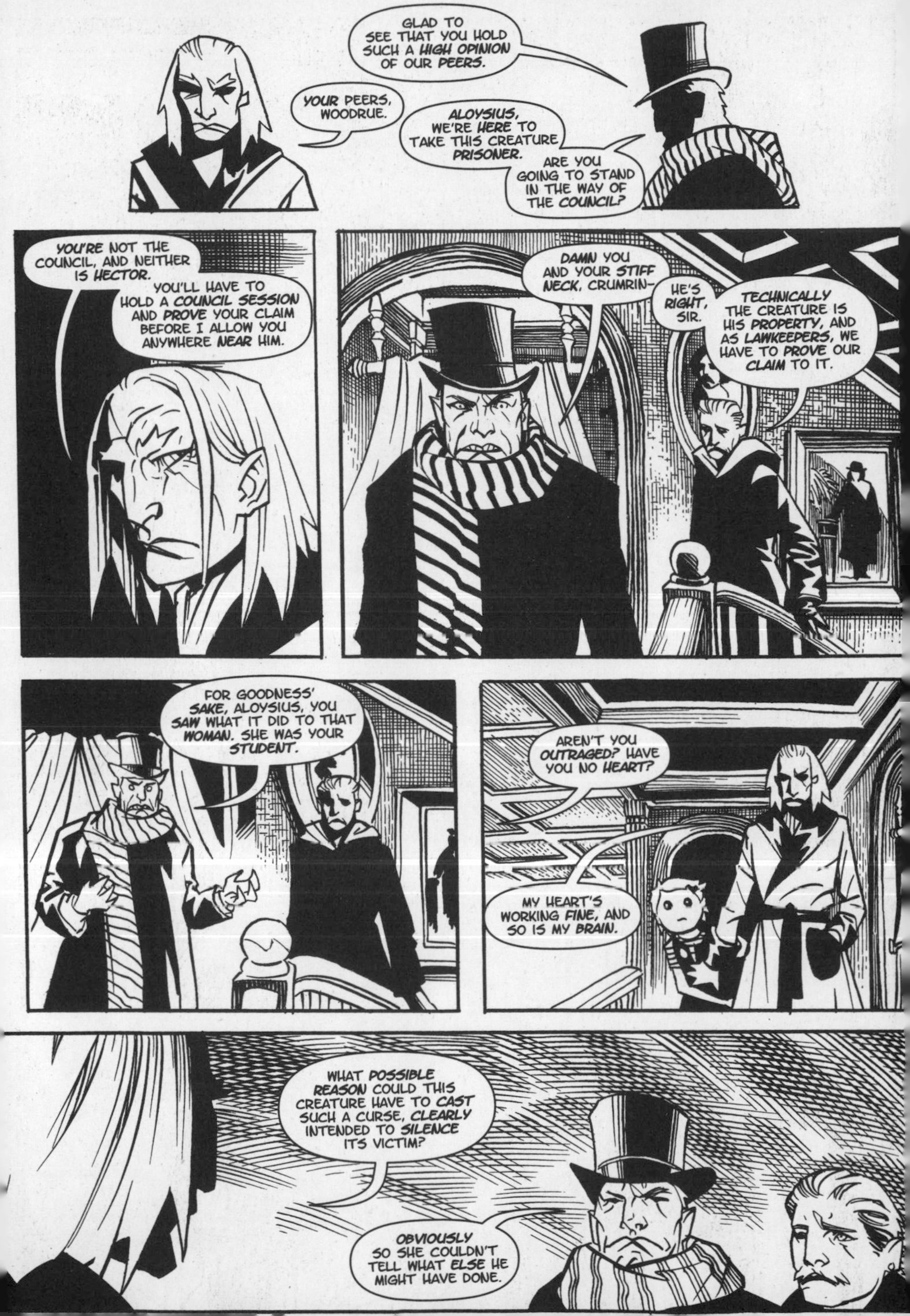
GLAD TO SEE THAT YOU HOLD SUCH A HIGH OPINION OF OUR PEERS.
YOUR PEERS, WOODRUE.
ALOYSIUS, WE'RE HERE TO TAKE THIS CREATURE PRISONER.
ARE YOU GOING TO STAND IN THE WAY OF THE COUNCIL?
YOU'RE NOT THE COUNCIL, AND NEITHER IS HECTOR.
YOU'LL HAVE TO HOLD A COUNCIL SESSION AND PROVE YOUR CLAIM BEFORE I ALLOW YOU ANYWHERE NEAR HIM.
DAMN YOU AND YOUR STIFF NECK, CRUMRIN-
HE'S RIGHT, SIR.
TECHNICALLY THE CREATURE IS HIS PROPERTY, AND AS LAWKEEPERS, WE HAVE TO PROVE OUR CLAIM TO IT.
FOR GOODNESS' SAKE, ALOYSIUS, YOU SAW WHAT IT DID TO THAT WOMAN. SHE WAS YOUR STUDENT.
AREN'T YOU OUTRAGED? HAVE YOU NO HEART?
MY HEART'S WORKING FINE, AND SO IS MY BRAIN.
WHAT POSSIBLE REASON COULD THIS CREATURE HAVE TO CAST SUCH A CURSE, CLEARLY INTENDED TO SILENCE ITS VICTIM?
OBVIOUSLY SO SHE COULDN'T TELL WHAT ELSE HE MIGHT HAVE DONE.

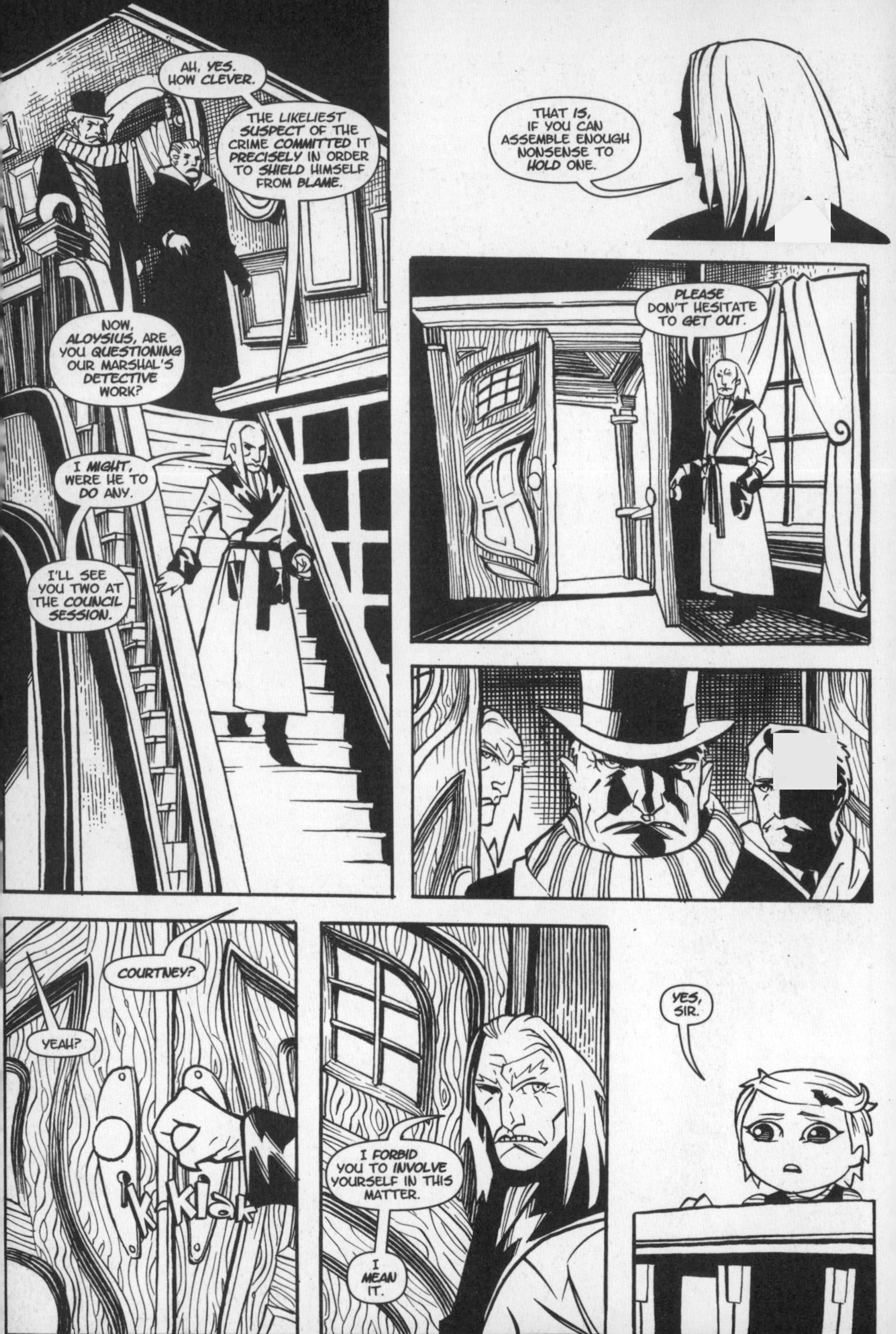
AH, YES. HOW CLEVER.
THE LIKELIEST SUSPECT OF THE CRIME COMMITTED IT PRECISELY IN ORDER TO SHIELD HIMSELF FROM BLAME.
NOW, ALOYSIUS, ARE YOU QUESTIONING OUR MARSHAL'S DETECTIVE WORK?
I MIGHT, WERE HE TO DO ANY.
I'LL SEE YOU TWO AT THE COUNCIL SESSION.
THAT IS, IF YOU CAN ASSEMBLE ENOUGH NONSENSE TO HOLD ONE.
PLEASE DON'T HESITATE TO GET OUT.
COURTNEY?
YEAH?
K-KLAK
I FORBID YOU TO INVOLVE YOURSELF IN THIS MATTER.
I MEAN IT.
YES, SIR.

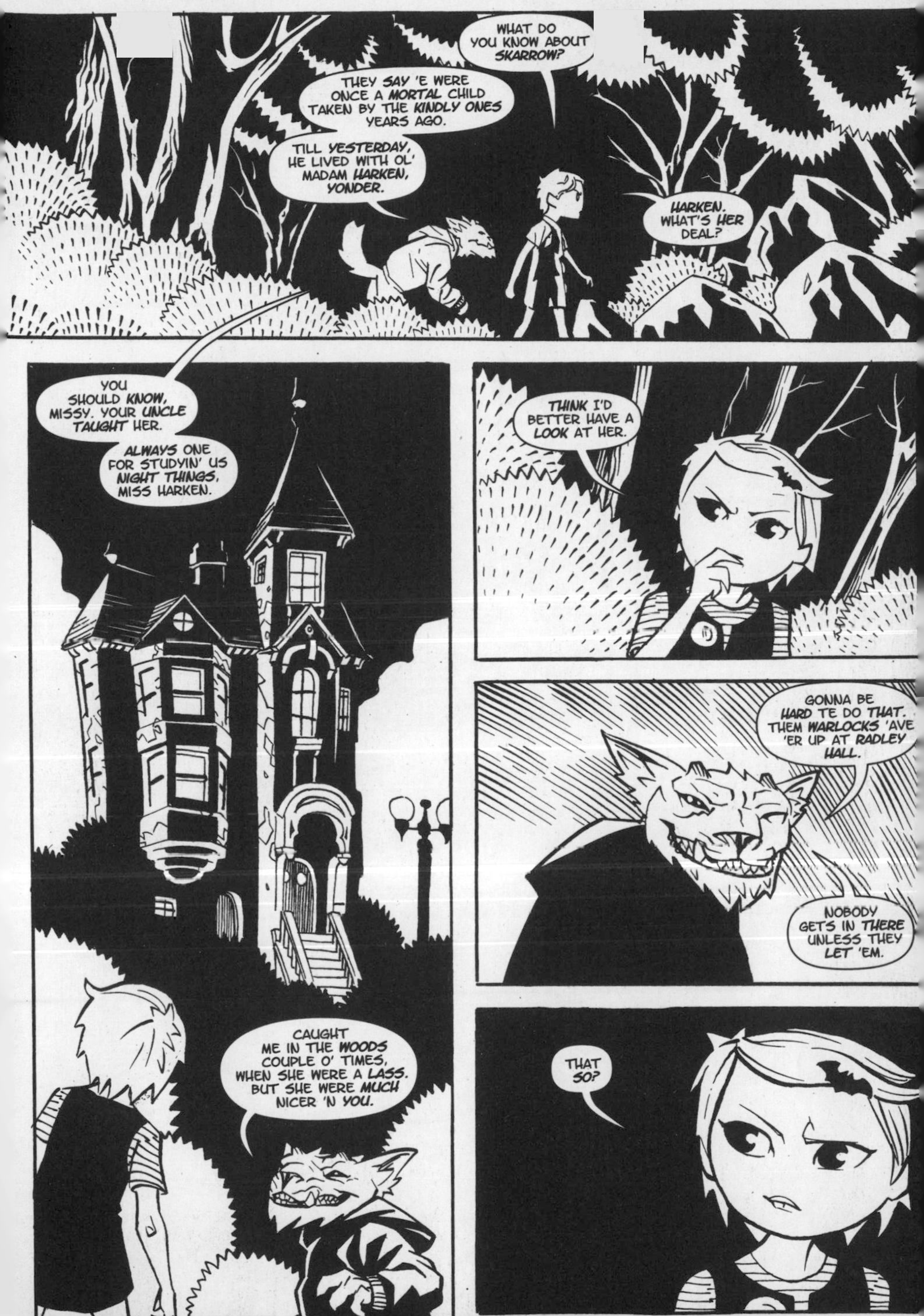
WHAT DO YOU KNOW ABOUT SKARROW?
THEY SAY 'E WERE ONCE A MORTAL CHILD TAKEN BY THE KINDLY ONES YEARS AGO.
TILL YESTERDAY, HE LIVED WITH OL' MADAM HARKEN, YONDER.
HARKEN. WHAT'S HER DEAL?
YOU SHOULD KNOW, MISSY. YOUR UNCLE TAUGHT HER.
ALWAYS ONE FOR STUDYIN' US NIGHT THINGS, MISS HARKEN.
THINK I'D BETTER HAVE A LOOK AT HER.
GONNA BE HARD TE DO THAT. THEM WARLOCKS 'AVE 'ER UP AT RADLEY HALL.
NOBODY GETS IN THERE UNLESS THEY LET 'EM.
CAUGHT ME IN THE WOODS COUPLE O' TIMES, WHEN SHE WERE A LASS. BUT SHE WERE MUCH NICER 'N YOU.
THAT SO?

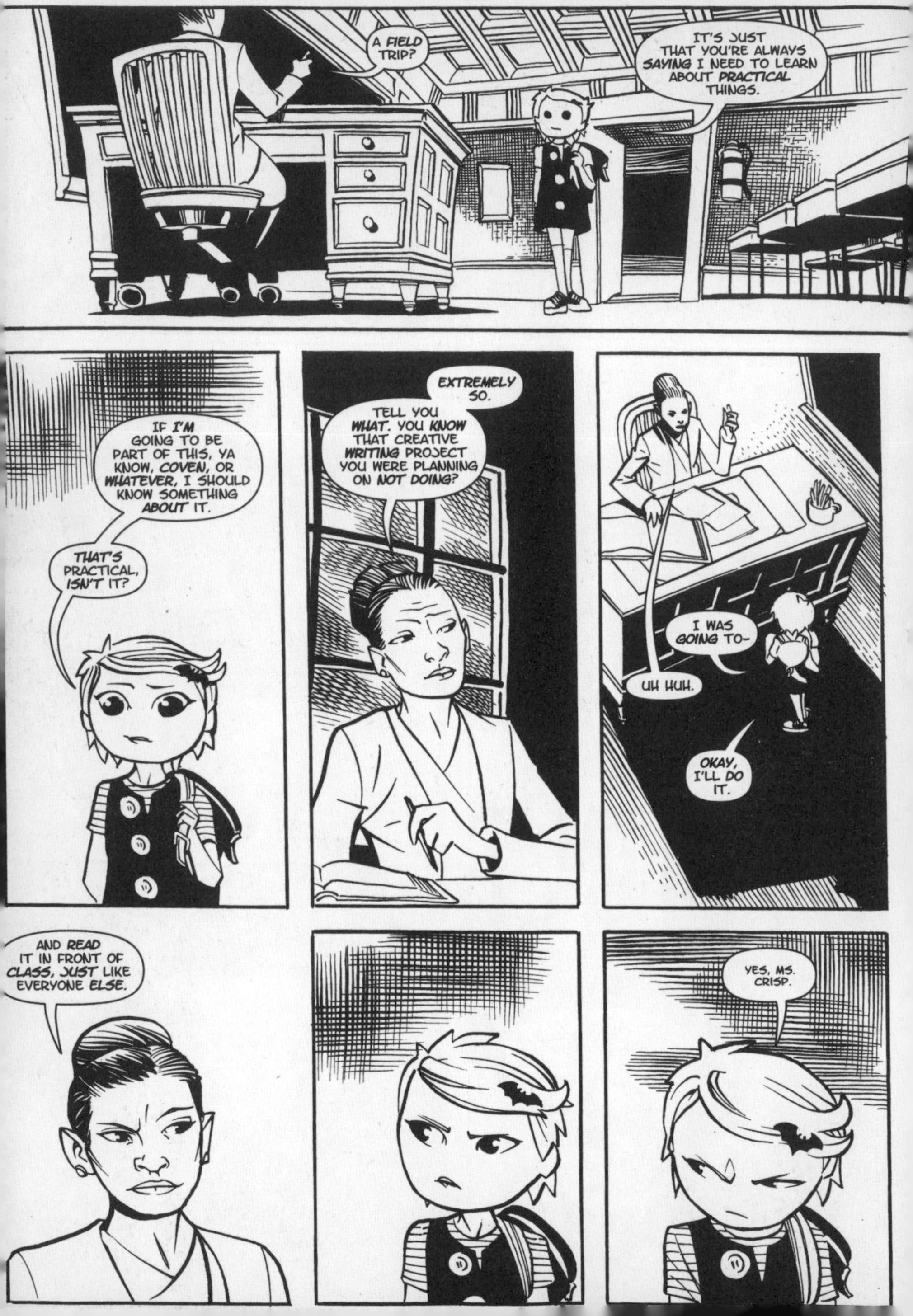
A FIELD TRIP?
IT'S JUST THAT YOU'RE ALWAYS SAYING I NEED TO LEARN ABOUT PRACTICAL THINGS.
IF I'M GOING TO BE PART OF THIS, YA KNOW, COVEN, OR WHATEVER, I SHOULD KNOW SOMETHING ABOUT IT.
THAT'S PRACTICAL, ISN'T IT?
EXTREMELY SO.
TELL YOU WHAT. YOU KNOW THAT CREATIVE WRITING PROJECT YOU WERE PLANNING ON NOT DOING?
I WAS GOING TO-
UH HUH.
OKAY, I'LL DO IT.
AND READ IT IN FRONT OF CLASS, JUST LIKE EVERYONE ELSE.
YES, MS. CRISP.

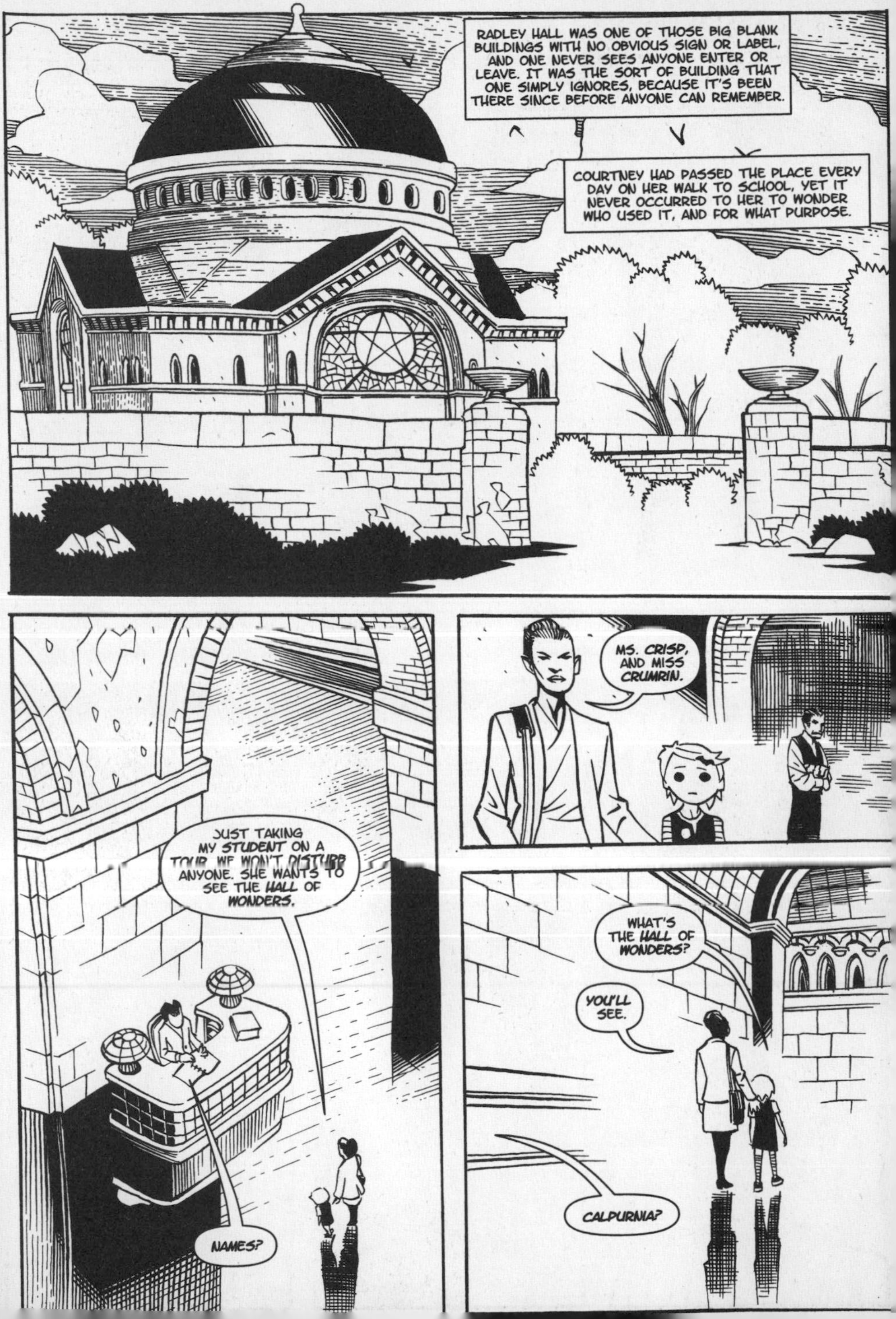
RADLEY HALL WAS ONE OF THOSE BIG BLANK BUILDINGS WITH NO OBVIOUS SIGN OR LABEL, AND ONE NEVER SEES ANYONE ENTER OR LEAVE. IT WAS THE SORT OF BUILDING THAT ONE SIMPLY IGNORES, BECAUSE IT'S BEEN THERE SINCE BEFORE ANYONE CAN REMEMBER.
COURTNEY HAD PASSED THE PLACE EVERY DAY ON HER WALK TO SCHOOL, YET IT NEVER OCCURRED TO HER TO WONDER WHO USED IT, AND FOR WHAT PURPOSE.
NAMES?
MS. CRISP, AND MISS CRUMRIN.
CALPURNIA?
JUST TAKING MY STUDENT ON A TOUR. WE WON'T DISTURB ANYONE. SHE WANTS TO SEE THE HALL OF WONDERS.
WHAT'S THE HALL OF WONDERS?
YOU'LL SEE.

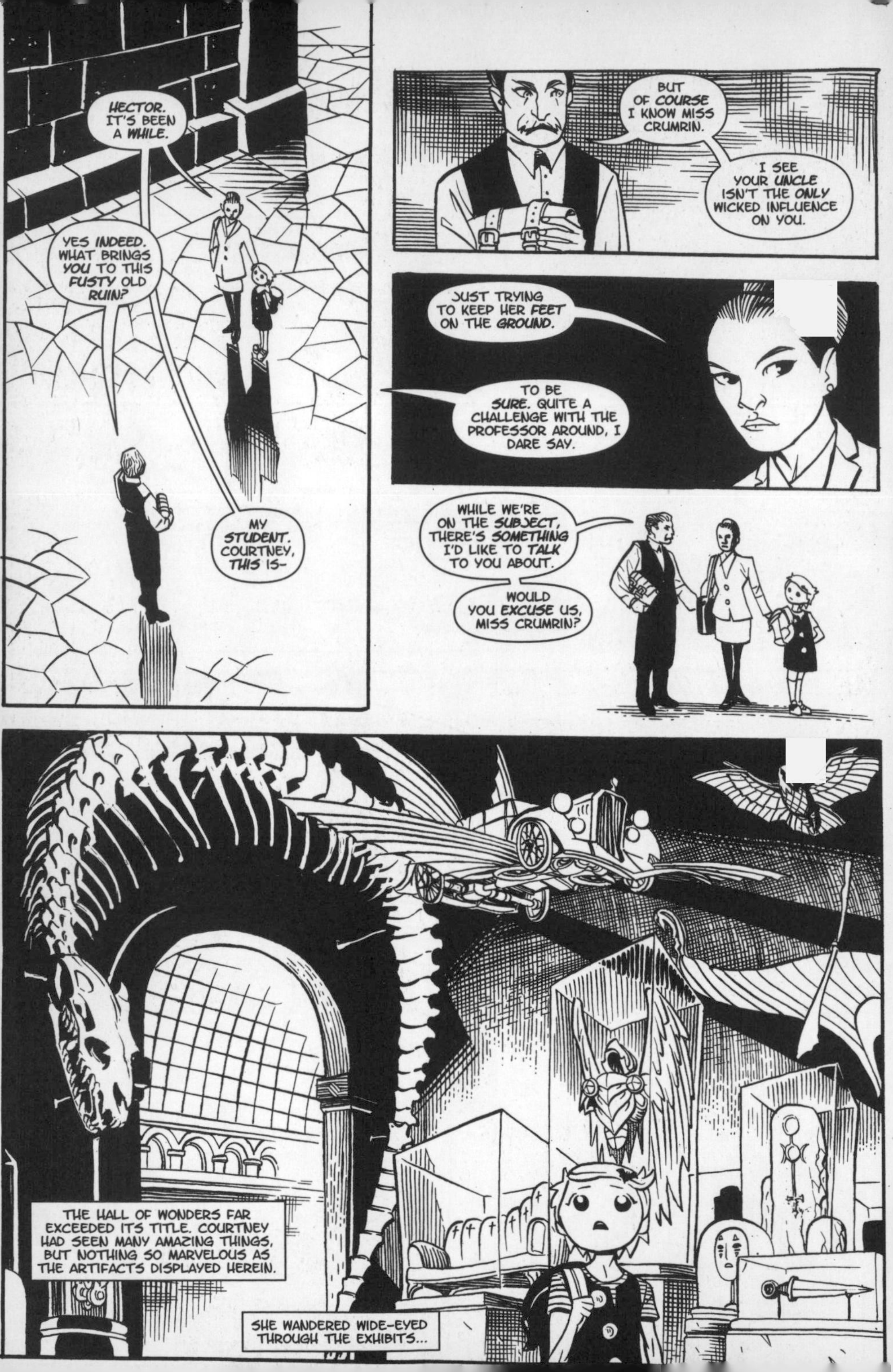
HECTOR. IT'S BEEN A WHILE.
YES INDEED. WHAT BRINGS YOU TO THIS FUSTY OLD RUIN?
MY STUDENT. COURTNEY, THIS IS-
BUT OF COURSE I KNOW MISS CRUMRIN.
I SEE YOUR UNCLE ISN'T THE ONLY WICKED INFLUENCE ON YOU.
JUST TRYING TO KEEP HER FEET ON THE GROUND.
TO BE SURE. QUITE A CHALLENGE WITH THE PROFESSOR AROUND, I DARE SAY.
WHILE WE'RE ON THE SUBJECT, THERE'S SOMETHING I'D LIKE TO TALK TO YOU ABOUT.
WOULD YOU EXCUSE US, MISS CRUMRIN?
THE HALL OF WONDERS FAR EXCEEDED ITS TITLE. COURTNEY HAD SEEN MANY AMAZING THINGS, BUT NOTHING SO MARVELOUS AS THE ARTIFACTS DISPLAYED HEREIN.
SHE WANDERED WIDE-EYED THROUGH THE EXHIBITS...

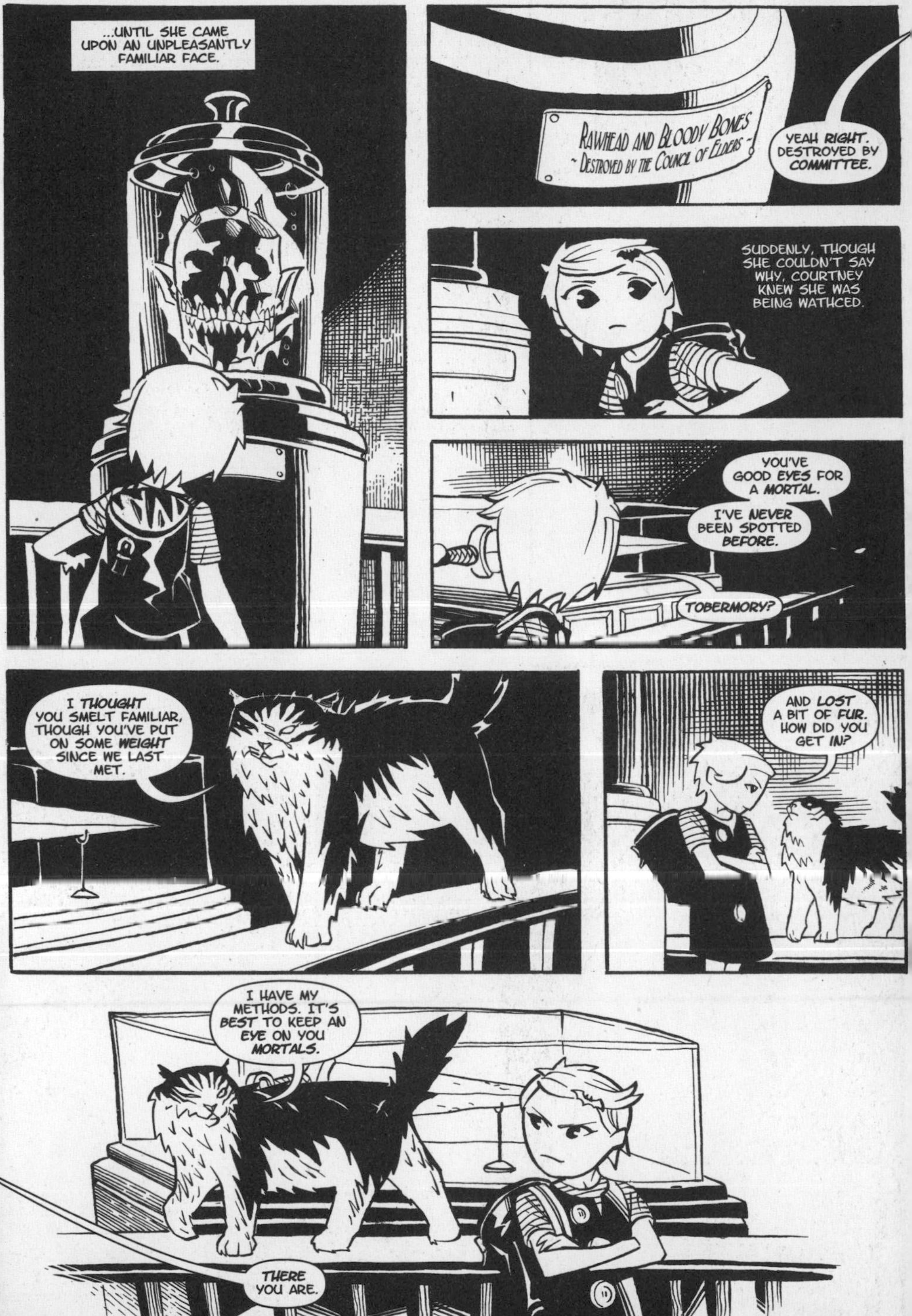

...UNTIL SHE CAME UPON AN UNPLEASANTLY FAMILIAR FACE.
RAWHEAD AND BLOODY BONES ~ DESTROYED BY THE COUNCIL OF ELDERS ~
YEAH RIGHT. DESTROYED BY COMMITTEE.
SUDDENLY, THOUGH SHE COULDN'T SAY WHY, COURTNEY KNEW SHE WAS BEING WATHCED.
YOU'VE GOOD EYES FOR A MORTAL.
I'VE NEVER BEEN SPOTTED BEFORE.
TOBERMORY?
I THOUGHT YOU SMELT FAMILIAR, THOUGH YOU'VE PUT ON SOME WEIGHT SINCE WE LAST MET.
AND LOST A BIT OF FUR. HOW DID YOU GET IN?
I HAVE MY METHODS. IT'S BEST TO KEEP AN EYE ON YOU MORTALS.
THERE YOU ARE.

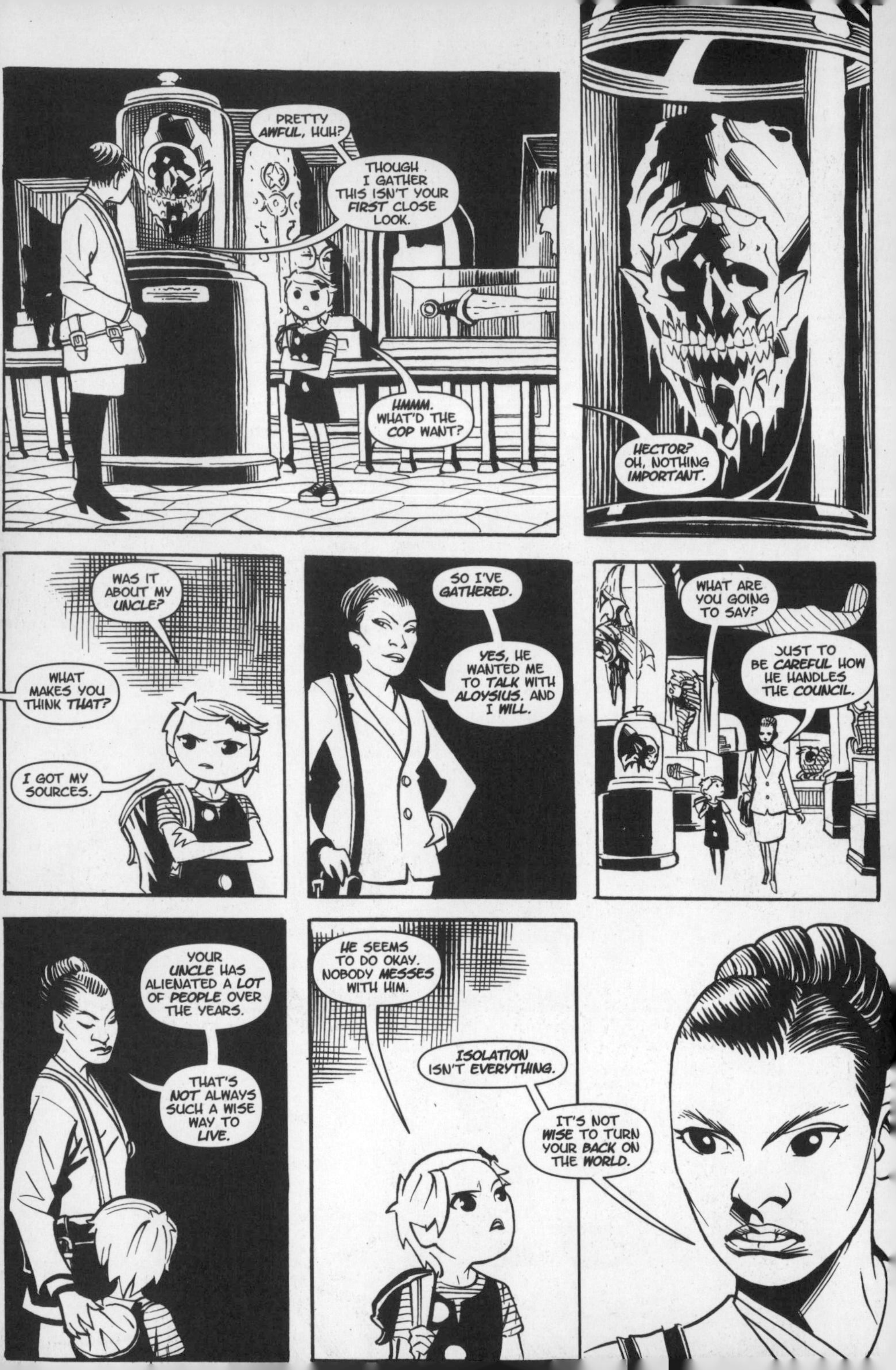
PRETTY AWFUL, HUH?
THOUGH I GATHER THIS ISN'T YOUR FIRST CLOSE LOOK.
HMMM. WHAT'D THE COP WANT?
HECTOR? OH, NOTHING IMPORTANT.
WAS IT ABOUT MY UNCLE?
WHAT MAKES YOU THINK THAT?
I GOT MY SOURCES.
SO I'VE GATHERED.
YES, HE WANTED ME TO TALK WITH ALOYSIUS. AND I WILL.
WHAT ARE YOU GOING TO SAY?
JUST TO BE CAREFUL HOW HE HANDLES THE COUNCIL.
YOUR UNCLE HAS ALIENATED A LOT OF PEOPLE OVER THE YEARS.
THAT'S NOT ALWAYS SUCH A WISE WAY TO LIVE.
HE SEEMS TO DO OKAY. NOBODY MESSES WITH HIM.
ISOLATION ISN'T EVERYTHING.
IT'S NOT WISE TO TURN YOUR BACK ON THE WORLD.

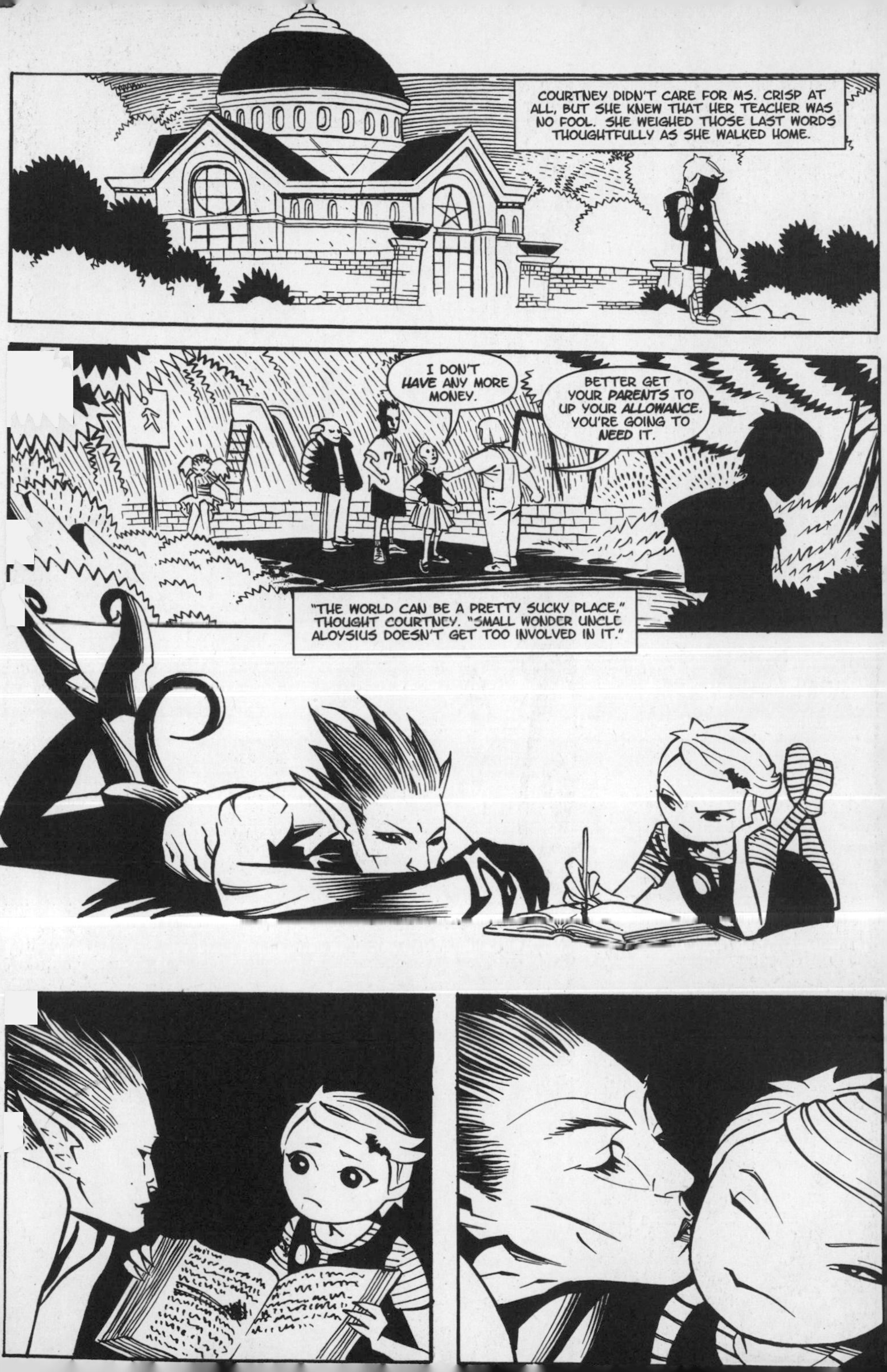
COURTNEY DIDN'T CARE FOR MS. CRISP AT ALL, BUT SHE KNEW THAT HER TEACHER WAS NO FOOL. SHE WEIGHED THOSE LAST WORDS THOUGHTFULLY AS SHE WALKED HOME.
I DON'T HAVE ANY MORE MONEY.
BETTER GET YOUR PARENTS TO UP YOUR ALLOWANCE. YOU'RE GOING TO NEED IT.
"THE WORLD CAN BE A PRETTY SUCKY PLACE," THOUGHT COURTNEY. "SMALL WONDER UNCLE ALOYSIUS DOESN'T GET TOO INVOLVED IN IT."

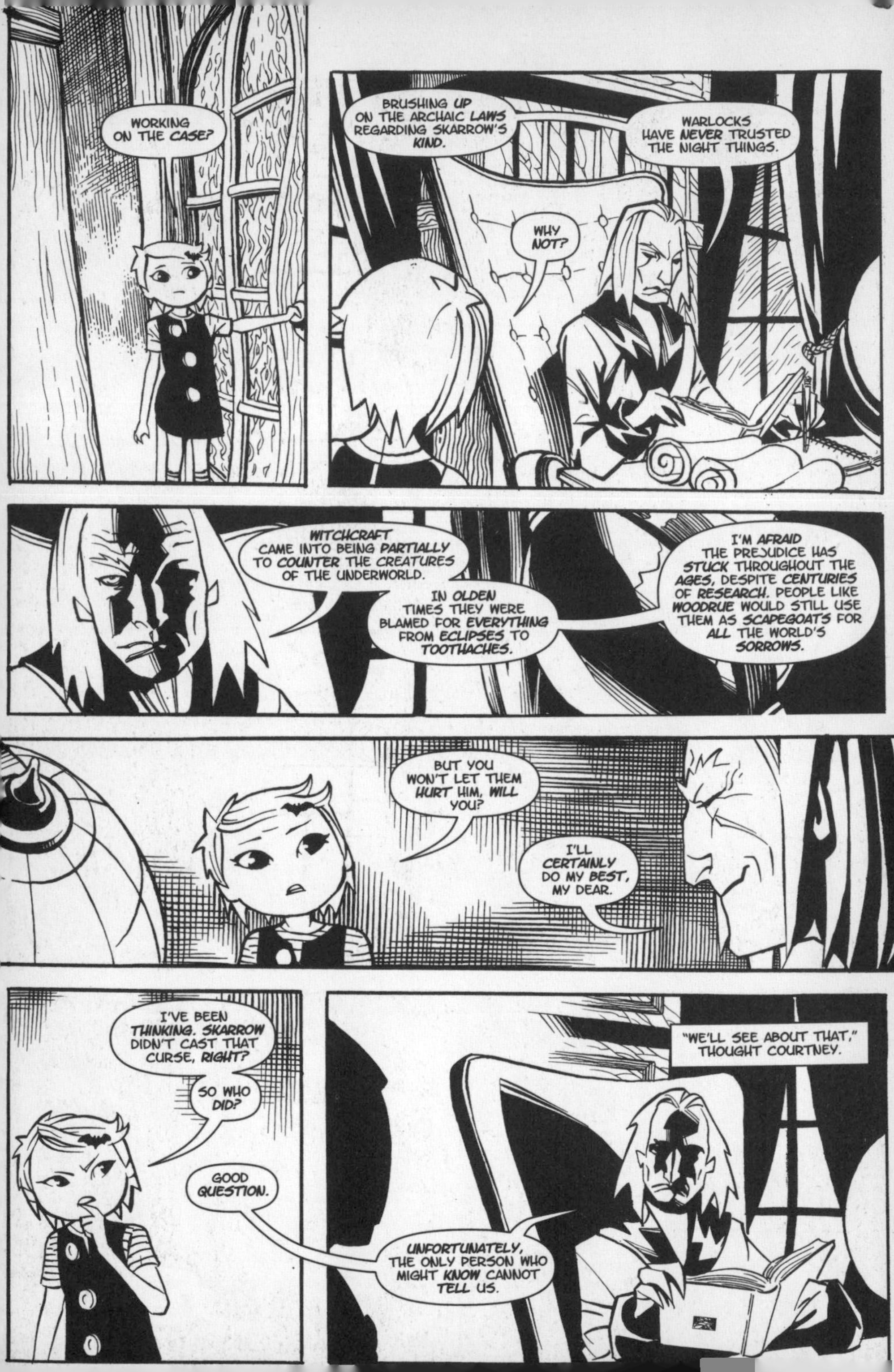
WORKING ON THE CASE?
BRUSHING UP ON THE ARCHAIC LAWS REGARDING SKARROW'S KIND.
WARLOCKS HAVE NEVER TRUSTED THE NIGHT THINGS.
WHY NOT?
WITCHCRAFT CAME INTO BEING PARTIALLY TO COUNTER THE CREATURES OF THE UNDERWORLD.
IN OLDEN TIMES THEY WERE BLAMED FOR EVERYTHING FROM ECLIPSES TO TOOTHACHES.
I'M AFRAID THE PREJUDICE HAS STUCK THROUGHOUT THE AGES, DESPITE CENTURIES OF RESEARCH. PEOPLE LIKE WOODRUE WOULD STILL USE THEM AS SCAPEGOATS FOR ALL THE WORLD'S SORROWS.
BUT YOU WON'T LET THEM HURT HIM, WILL YOU?
I'LL CERTAINLY DO MY BEST, MY DEAR.
I'VE BEEN THINKING. SKARROW DIDN'T CAST THAT CURSE, RIGHT?
SO WHO DID?
GOOD QUESTION.
UNFORTUNATELY, THE ONLY PERSON WHO MIGHT KNOW CANNOT TELL US.
"WE'LL SEE ABOUT THAT," THOUGHT COURTNEY.

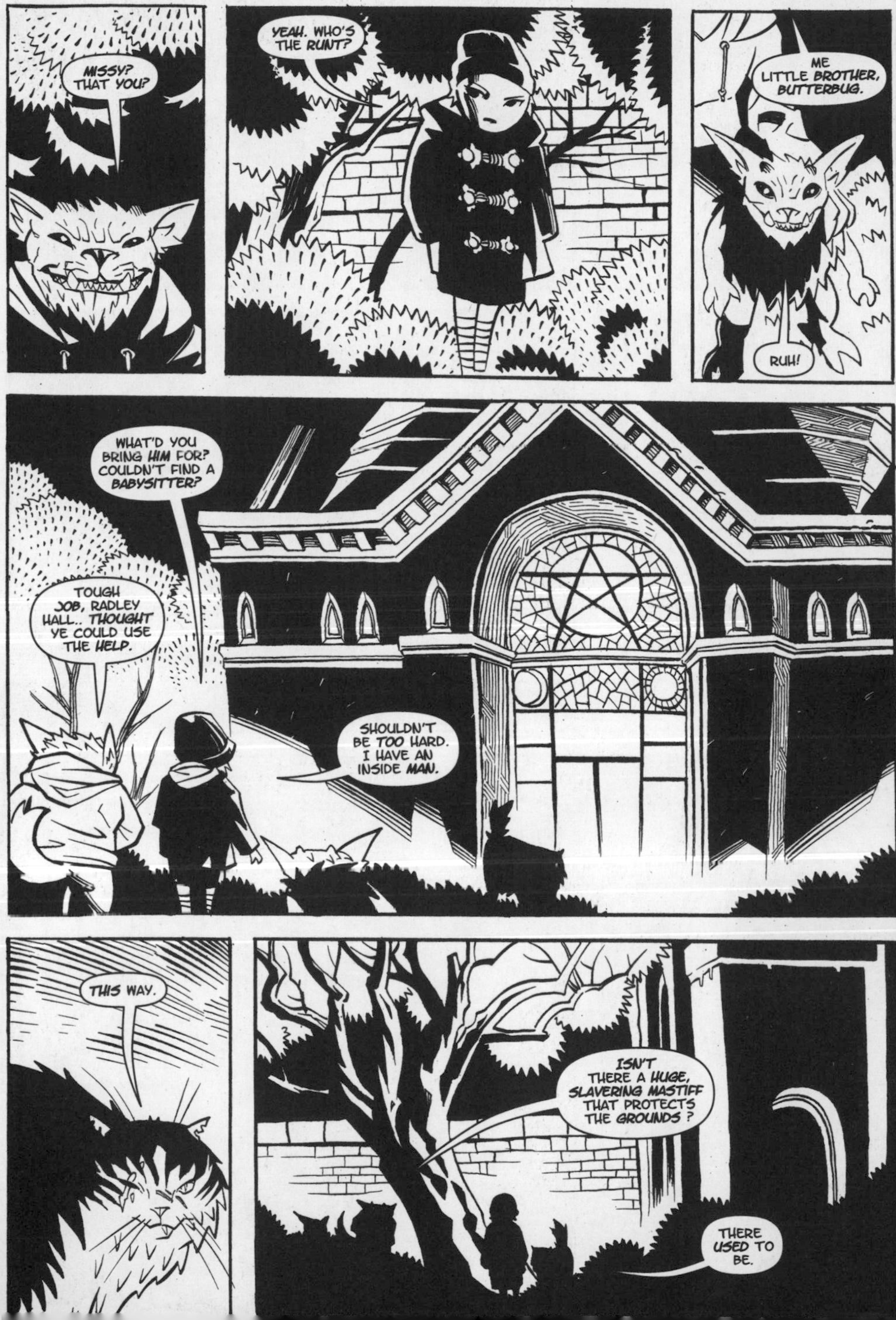
MISSY? THAT YOU?
YEAH. WHO'S THE RUNT?
ME LITTLE BROTHER, BUTTERBUG.
RUH!
WHAT'D YOU BRING HIM FOR? COULDN'T FIND A BABYSITTER?
TOUGH JOB, RADLEY HALL.. THOUGHT YE COULD USE THE HELP.
SHOULDN'T BE TOO HARD. I HAVE AN INSIDE MAN.
THIS WAY.
ISN'T THERE A HUGE, SLAVERING MASTIFF THAT PROTECTS THE GROUNDS ?
THERE USED TO BE.

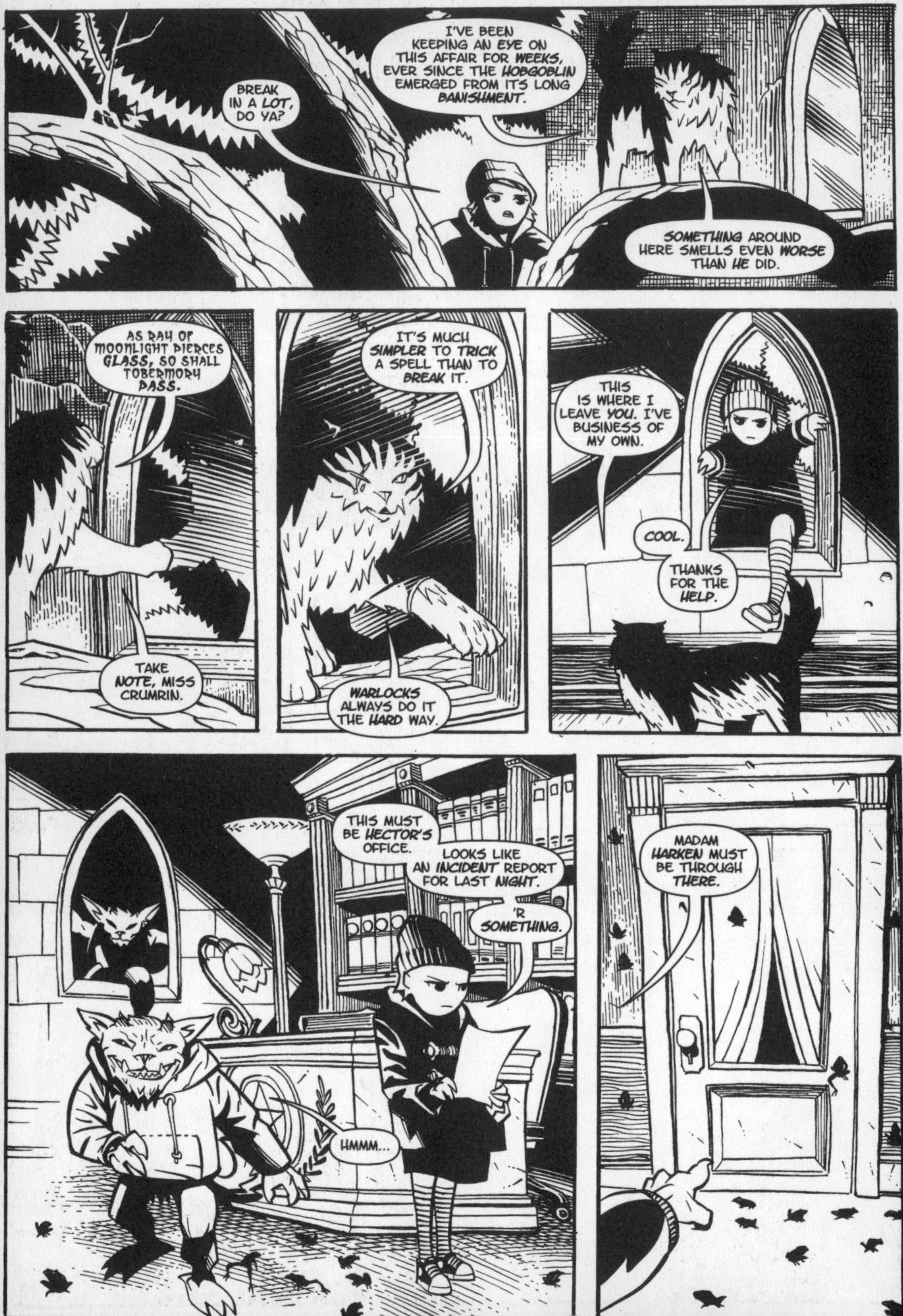
BREAK IN A LOT, DO YA?
I'VE BEEN KEEPING AN EYE ON THIS AFFAIR FOR WEEKS, EVER SINCE THE HOBGOBLIN EMERGED FROM ITS LONG BANISHMENT.
SOMETHING AROUND HERE SMELLS EVEN WORSE THAN HE DID.
AS RAY OF MOONLIGHT PIERCES GLASS, SO SHALL TOBERMORY PASS.
TAKE NOTE, MISS CRUMRIN.
IT'S MUCH SIMPLER TO TRICK A SPELL THAN TO BREAK IT.
WARLOCKS ALWAYS DO IT THE HARD WAY.
THIS IS WHERE I LEAVE YOU. I'VE BUSINESS OF MY OWN.
COOL.
THANKS FOR THE HELP.
THIS MUST BE HECTOR'S OFFICE.
LOOKS LIKE AN INCIDENT REPORT FOR LAST NIGHT.
'R SOMETHING.
HMMM...
MADAM HARKEN MUST BE THROUGH THERE.

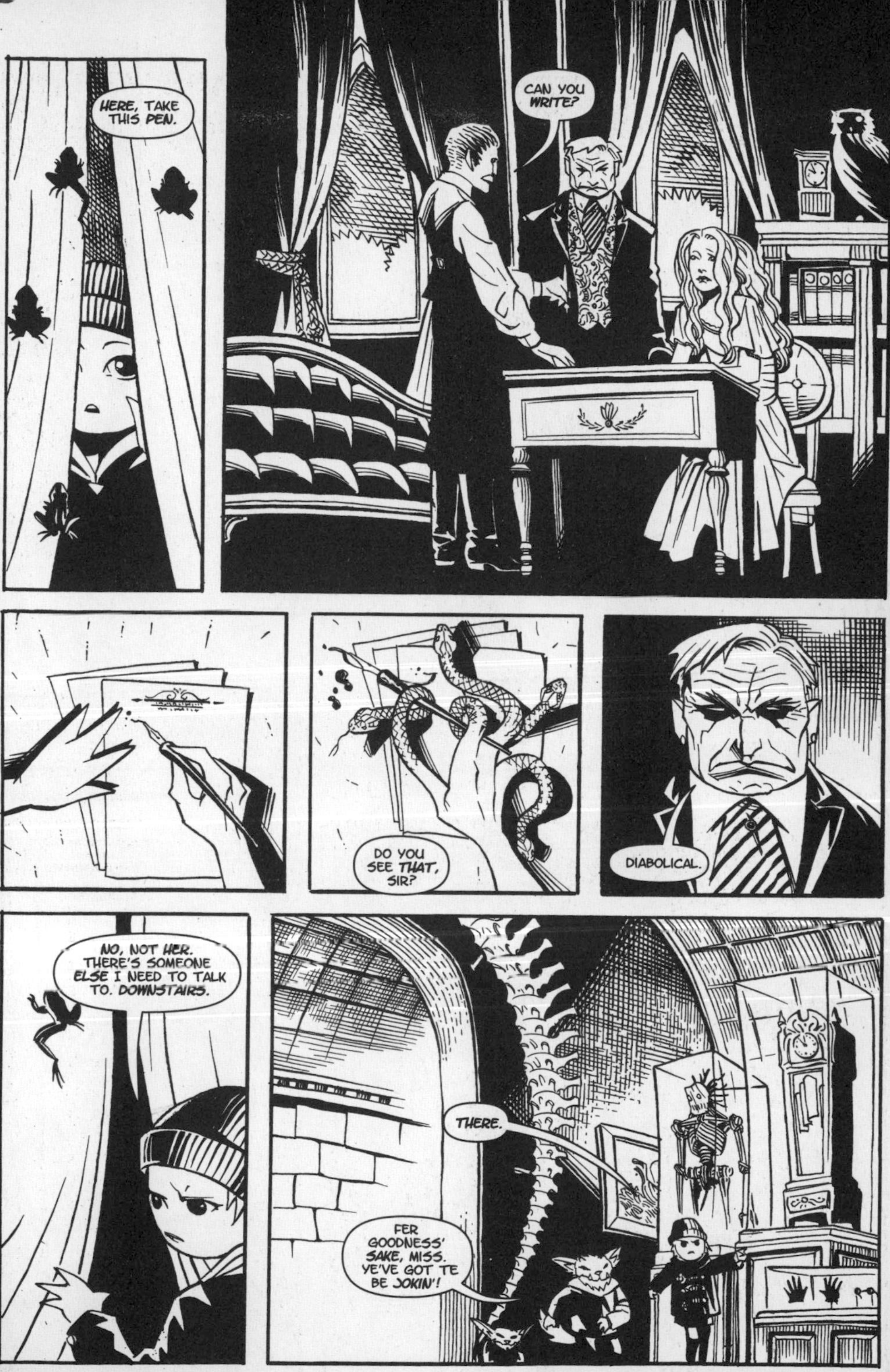
HERE, TAKE THIS PEN.
CAN YOU WRITE?
DO YOU SEE THAT, SIR?
DIABOLICAL.
NO, NOT HER. THERE'S SOMEONE ELSE I NEED TO TALK TO. DOWNSTAIRS.
THERE.
FER GOODNESS' SAKE, MISS. YE'VE GOT TE BE JOKIN'!

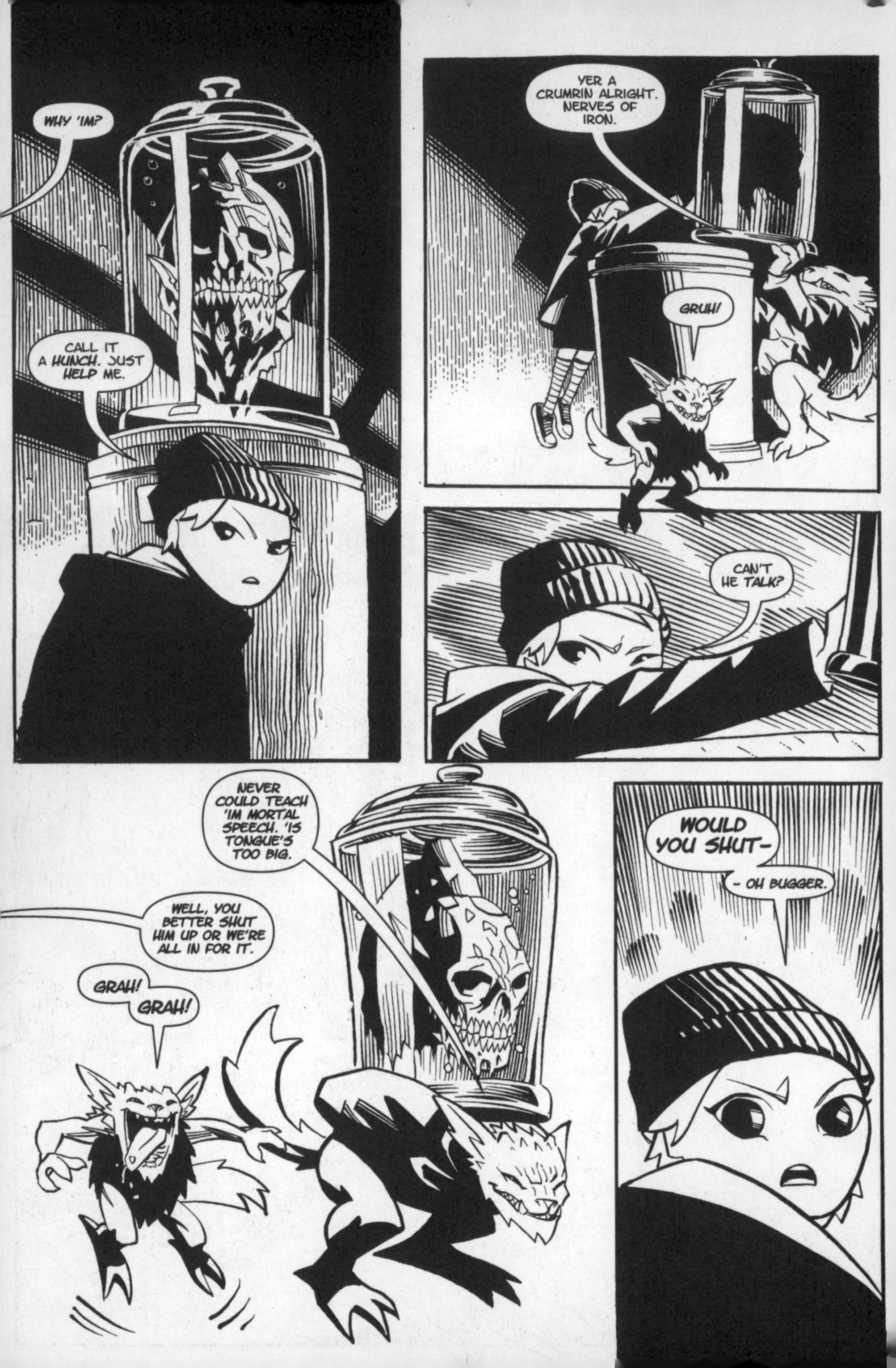
WHY 'IM?
CALL IT A HUNCH. JUST HELP ME.
YER A CRUMRIN ALRIGHT. NERVES OF IRON.
GRUH!
CAN'T HE TALK?
NEVER COULD TEACH 'IM MORTAL SPEECH. 'IS TONGUE'S TOO BIG.
WELL, YOU BETTER SHUT HIM UP OR WE'RE ALL IN FOR IT.
GRAH!
GRAH!
WOULD YOU SHUT-
- OH BUGGER.

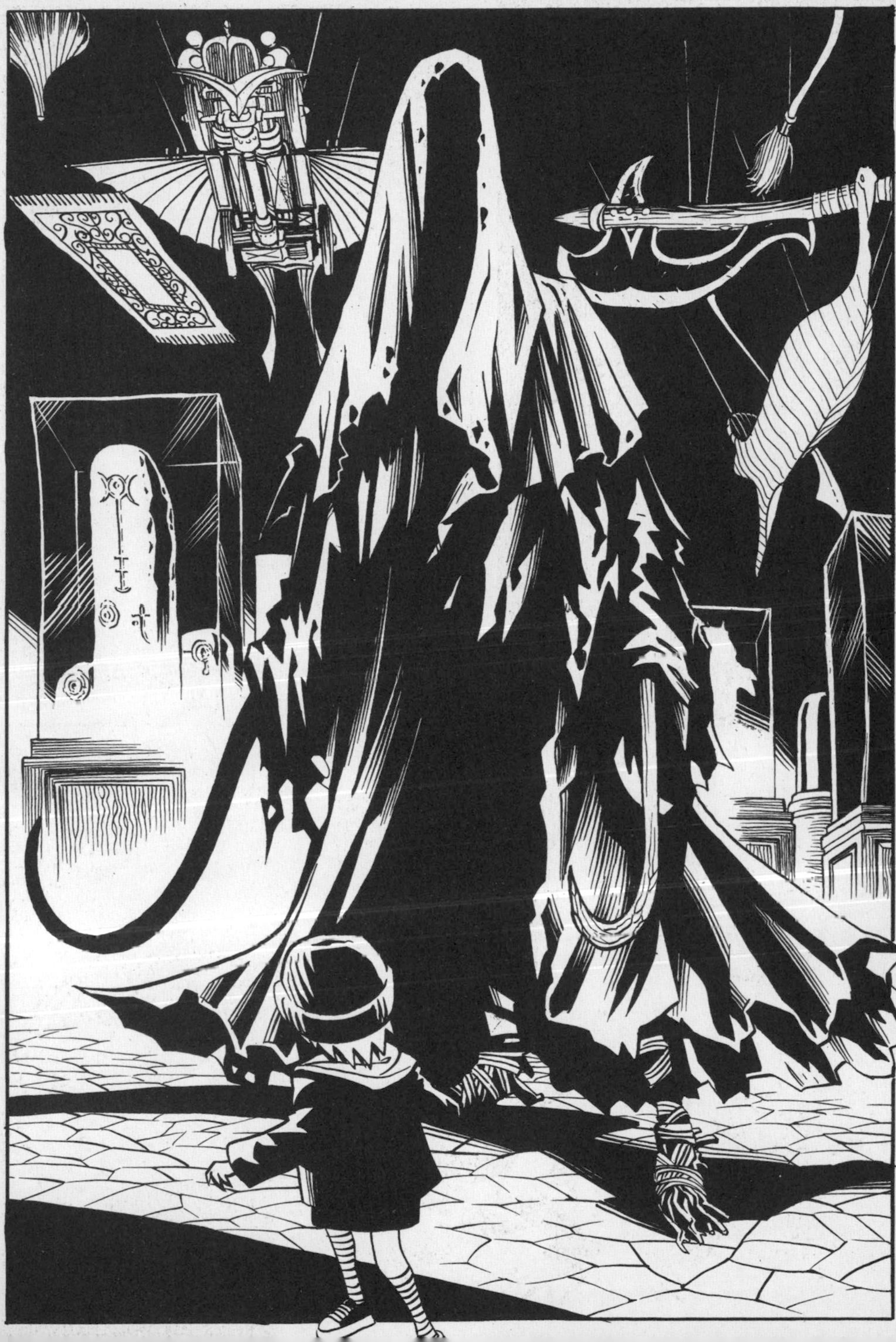

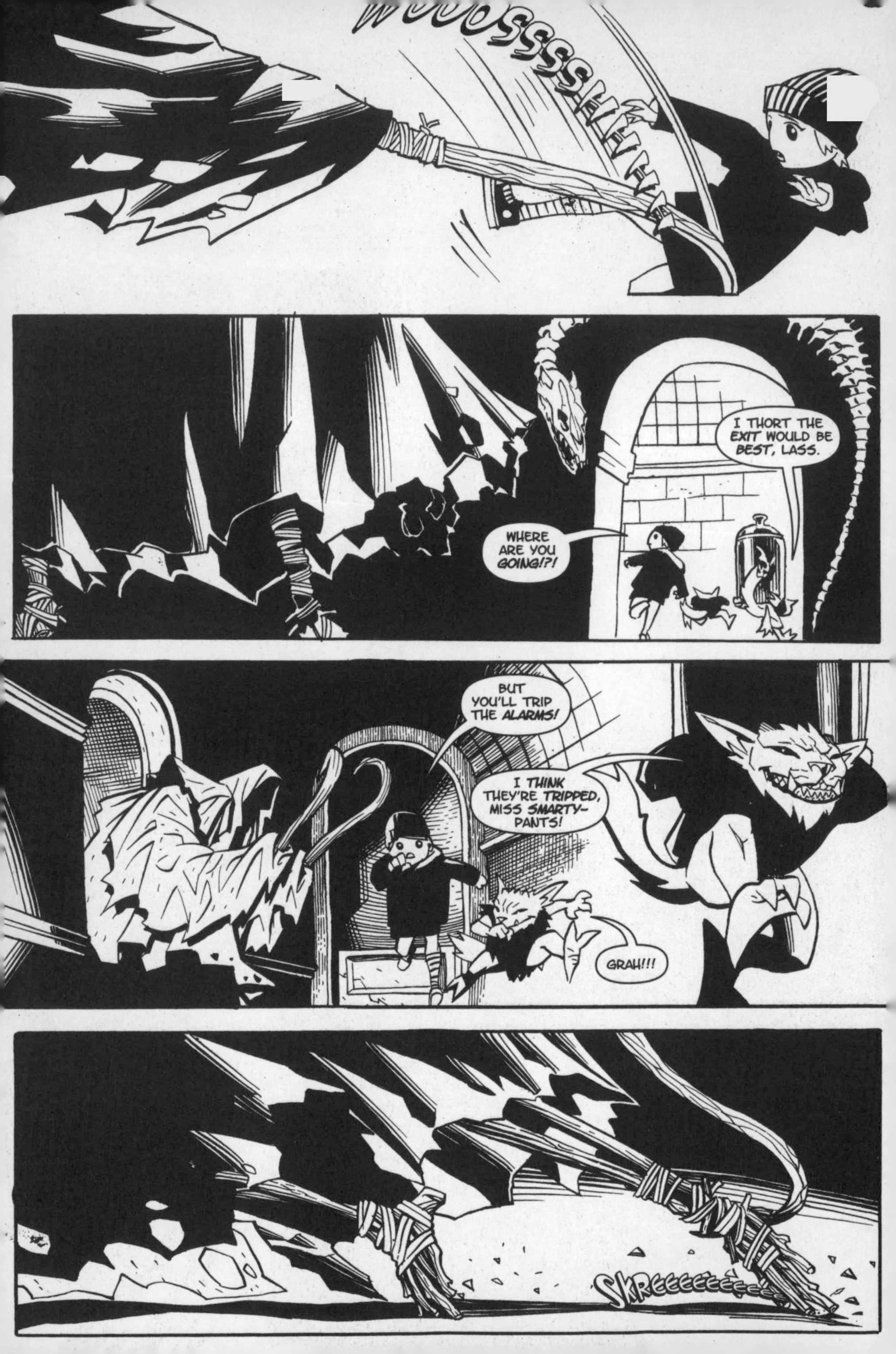
WOOOSSSSSHHHHH
I THORT THE EXIT WOULD BE BEST, LASS.
WHERE ARE YOU GOING!?!
BUT YOU'LL TRIP THE ALARMS!
I THINK THEY'RE TRIPPED, MISS SMARTY-PANTS!
GRAH!!!
SKREEEEEEEEEEE

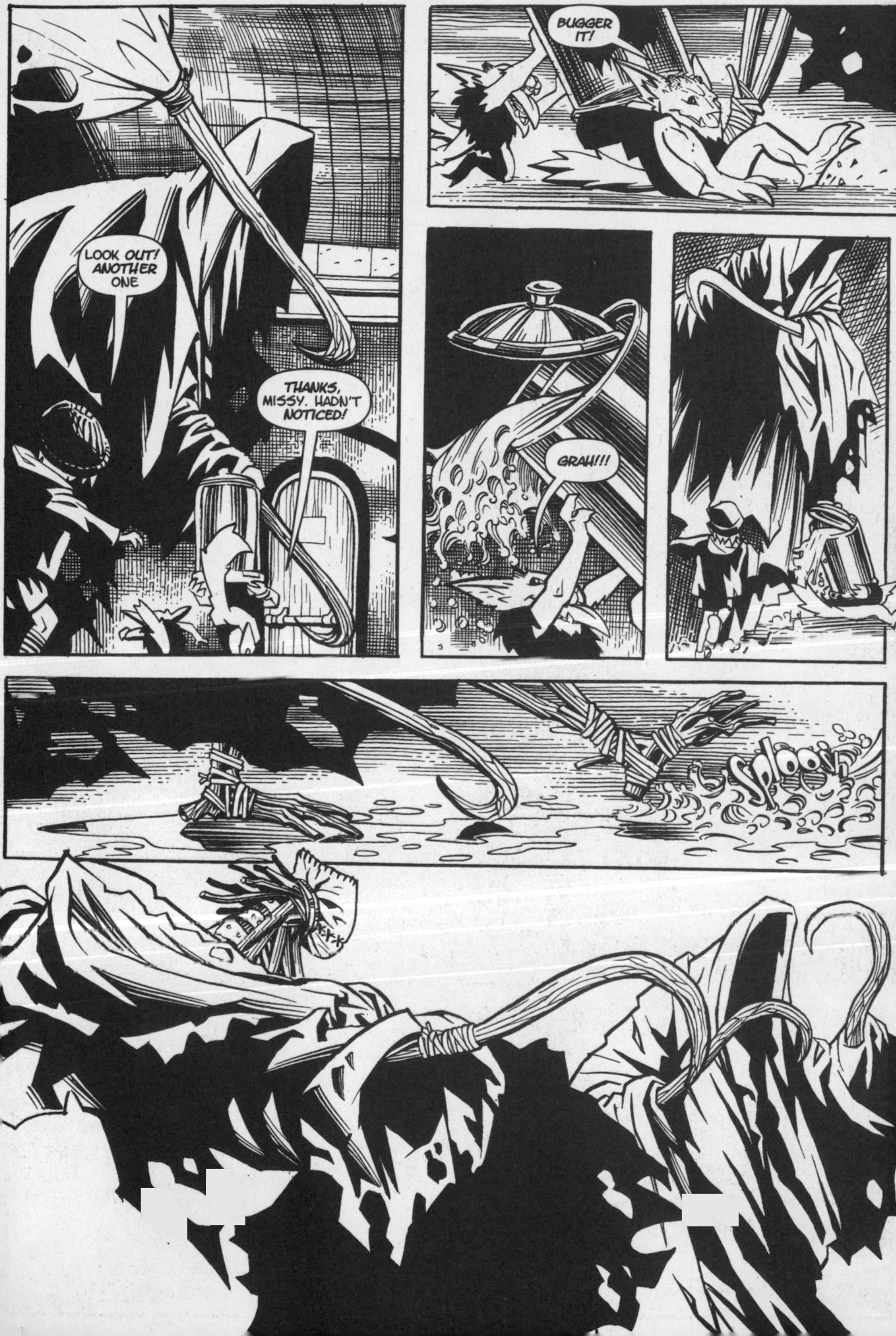
LOOK OUT! ANOTHER ONE
THANKS, MISSY. HADN'T NOTICED!
BUGGER IT!
GRAH!!!
sploosh

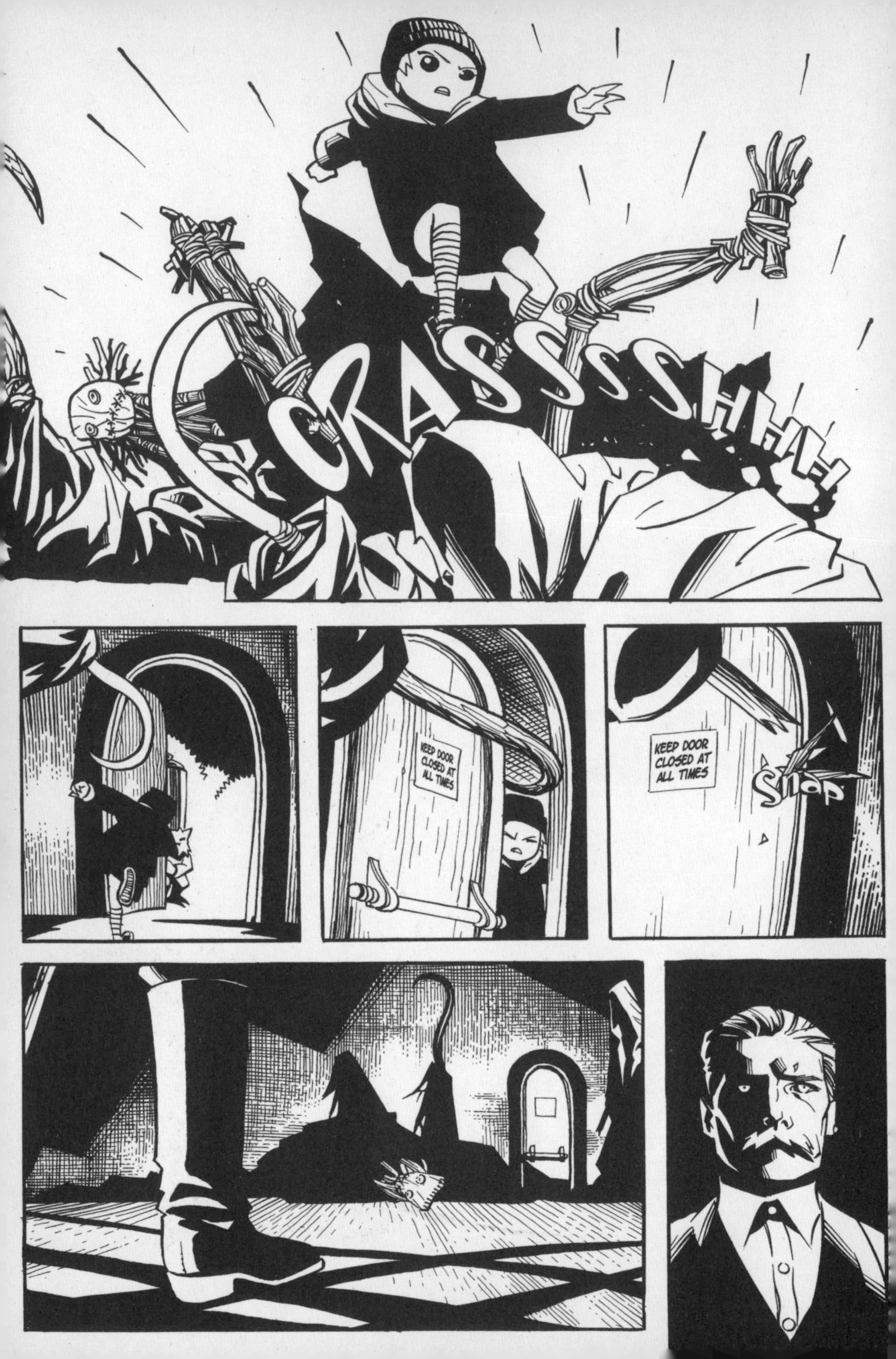
CRASSSSHHH!!
KEEP DOOR CLOSED AT ALL TIMES
KEEP DOOR CLOSED AT ALL TIMES
Snap

CHAPTER FOUR

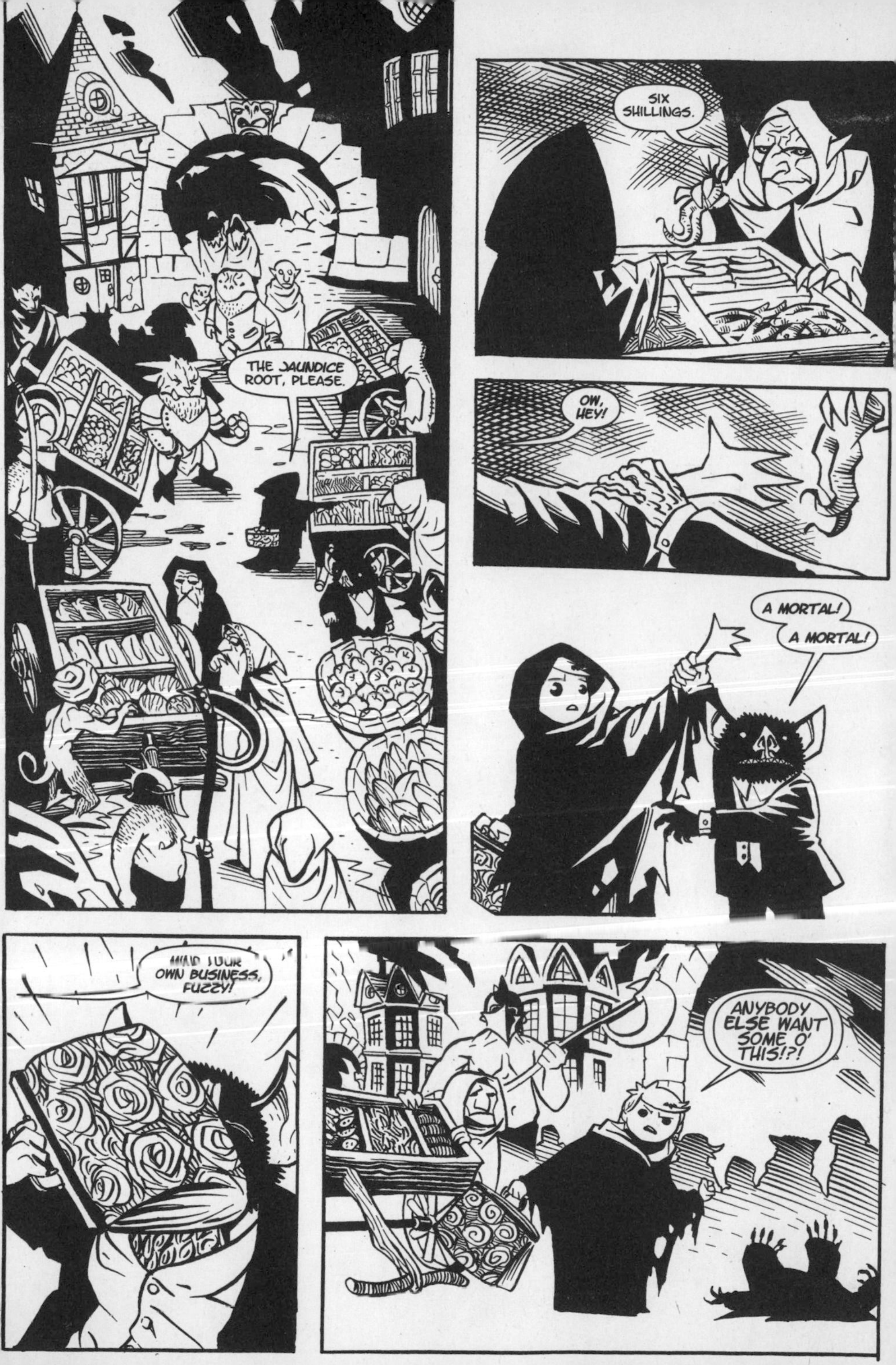
THE JAUNDICE ROOT, PLEASE.
SIX SHILLINGS.
OW, HEY!
A MORTAL!
A MORTAL!
OWN BUSINESS, FUZZY!
ANYBODY ELSE WANT SOME O' THIS!?!

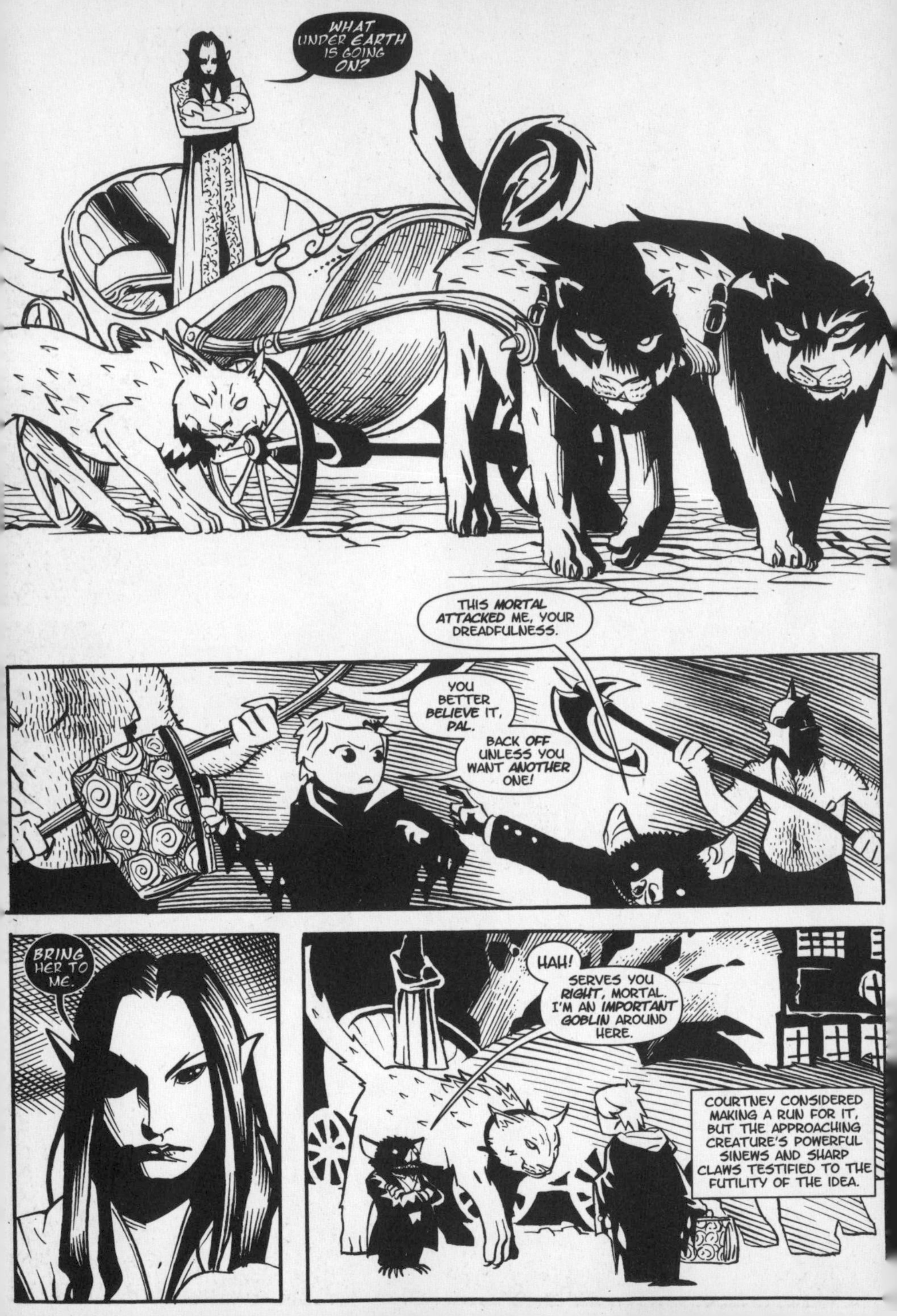
WHAT UNDER EARTH IS GOING ON?
THIS MORTAL ATTACKED ME, YOUR DREADFULNESS.
YOU BETTER BELIEVE IT, PAL.
BACK OFF UNLESS YOU WANT ANOTHER ONE!
BRING HER TO ME.
HAH!
SERVES YOU RIGHT, MORTAL. I'M AN IMPORTANT GOBLIN AROUND HERE.
COURTNEY CONSIDERED MAKING A RUN FOR IT, BUT THE APPROACHING CREATURE'S POWERFUL SINEWS AND SHARP CLAWS TESTIFIED TO THE FUTILITY OF THE IDEA.

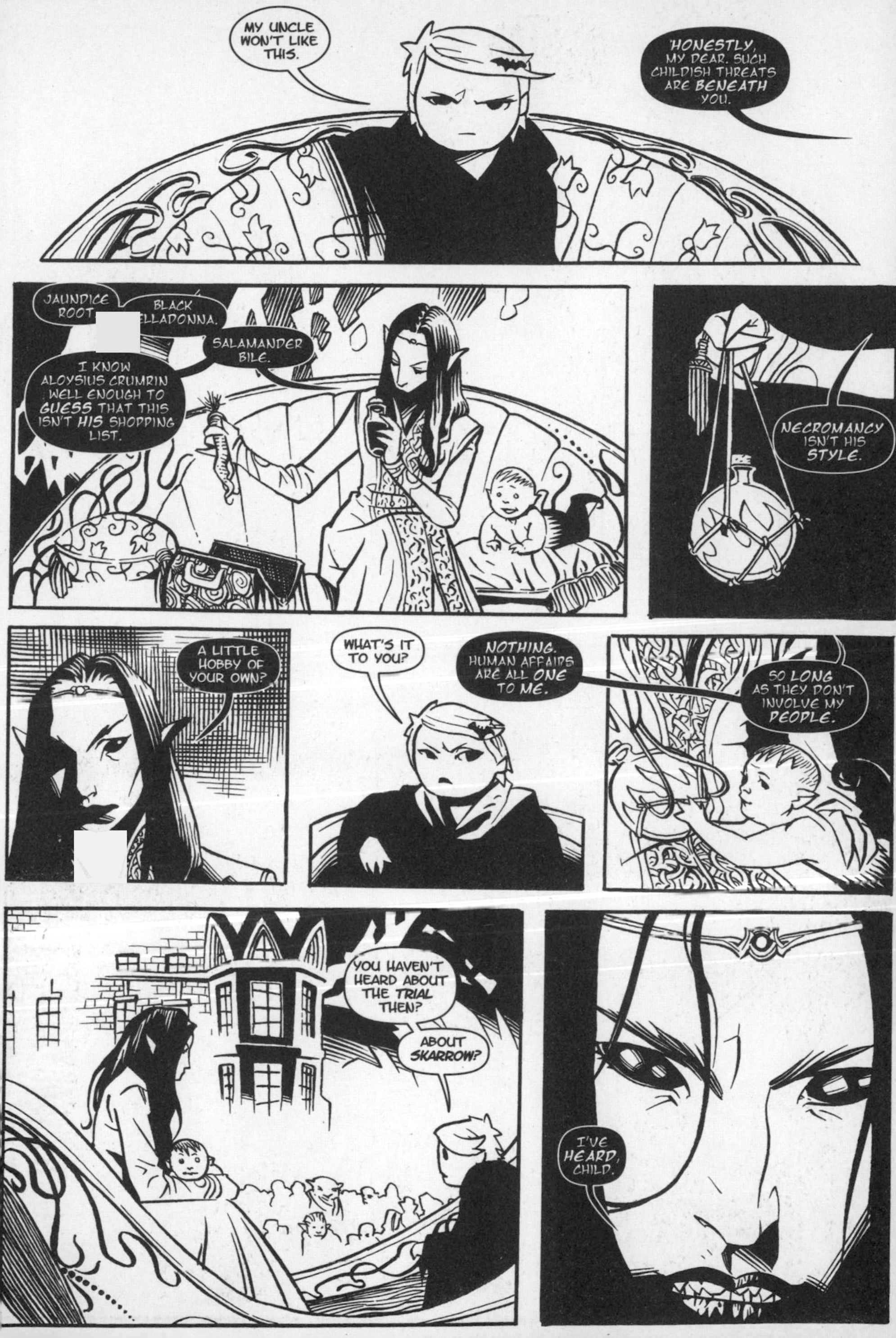
MY UNCLE WON'T LIKE THIS.
HONESTLY, MY DEAR. SUCH CHILDISH THREATS ARE BENEATH YOU.
JAUNDICE ROOT.
BLACK ELLADONNA.
SALAMANDER BILE.
I KNOW ALOYSIUS CRUMRIN WELL ENOUGH TO GUESS THAT THIS ISN'T HIS SHOPPING LIST.
NECROMANCY ISN'T HIS STYLE.
A LITTLE HOBBY OF YOUR OWN?
WHAT'S IT TO YOU?
NOTHING. HUMAN AFFAIRS ARE ALL ONE TO ME.
SO LONG AS THEY DON'T INVOLVE MY PEOPLE.
YOU HAVEN'T HEARD ABOUT THE TRIAL THEN?
ABOUT SKARROW?
I'VE HEARD, CHILD.

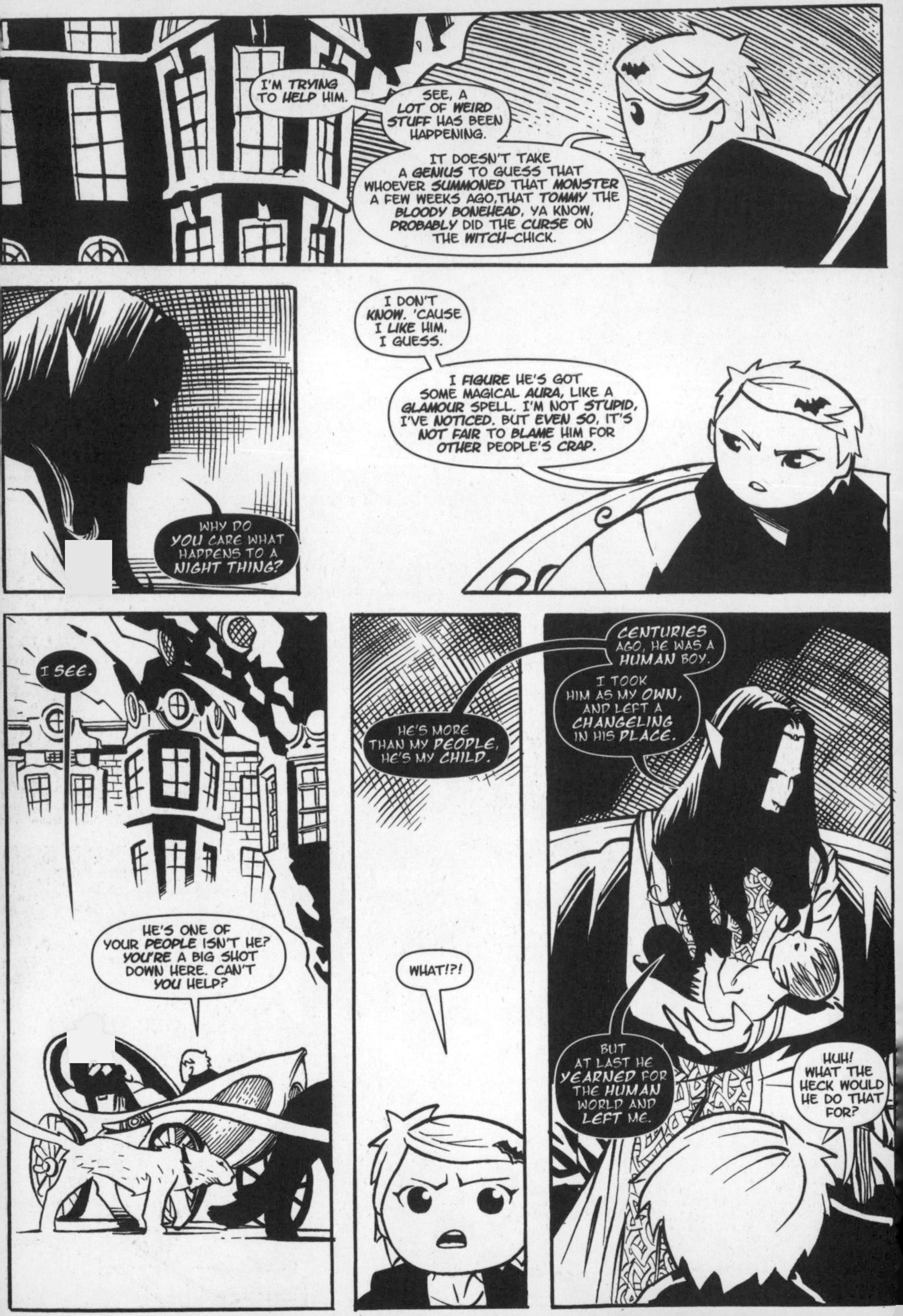
I'M TRYING TO HELP HIM.
SEE, A LOT OF WEIRD STUFF HAS BEEN HAPPENING.
IT DOESN'T TAKE A GENIUS TO GUESS THAT WHOEVER SUMMONED THAT MONSTER A FEW WEEKS AGO,THAT TOMMY THE BLOODY BONEHEAD, YA KNOW, PROBABLY DID THE CURSE ON THE WITCH-CHICK.
WHY DO YOU CARE WHAT HAPPENS TO A NIGHT THING?
I DON'T KNOW. 'CAUSE I LIKE HIM, I GUESS.
I FIGURE HE'S GOT SOME MAGICAL AURA, LIKE A GLAMOUR SPELL. I'M NOT STUPID, I'VE NOTICED. BUT EVEN SO, IT'S NOT FAIR TO BLAME HIM FOR OTHER PEOPLE'S CRAP.
I SEE.
HE'S ONE OF YOUR PEOPLE ISN'T HE? YOU'RE A BIG SHOT DOWN HERE. CAN'T YOU HELP?
HE'S MORE THAN MY PEOPLE, HE'S MY CHILD.
WHAT!?!
CENTURIES AGO, HE WAS A HUMAN BOY.
I TOOK HIM AS MY OWN, AND LEFT A CHANGELING IN HIS PLACE.
BUT AT LAST HE YEARNED FOR THE HUMAN WORLD AND LEFT ME.
HUH! WHAT THE HECK WOULD HE DO THAT FOR?

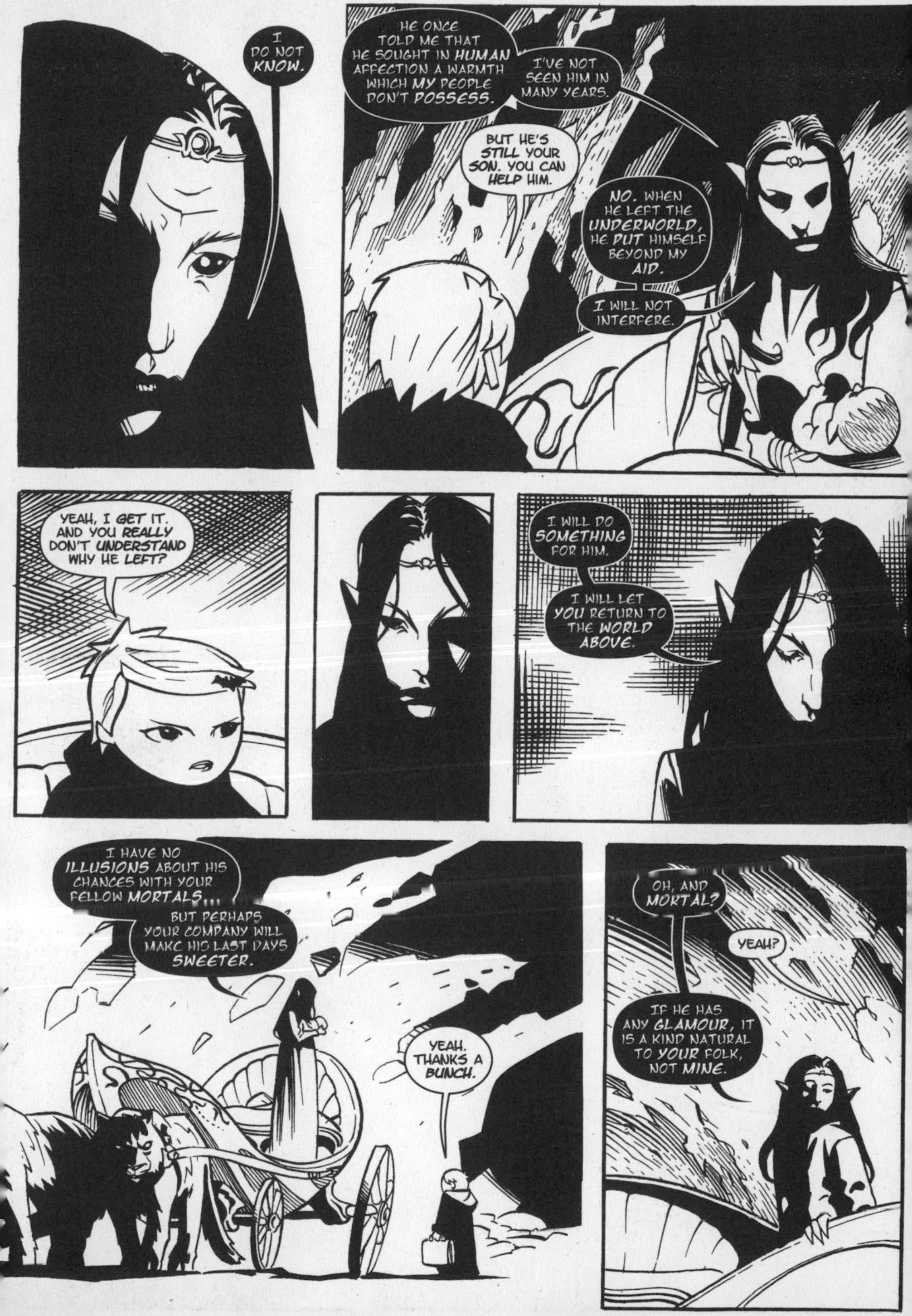
I DO NOT KNOW.
HE ONCE TOLD ME THAT HE SOUGHT IN HUMAN AFFECTION A WARMTH WHICH MY PEOPLE DON'T POSSESS.
I'VE NOT SEEN HIM IN MANY YEARS.
BUT HE'S STILL YOUR SON. YOU CAN HELP HIM.
NO. WHEN HE LEFT THE UNDERWORLD, HE PUT HIMSELF BEYOND MY AID.
I WILL NOT INTERFERE.
YEAH, I GET IT. AND YOU REALLY DON'T UNDERSTAND WHY HE LEFT?
I WILL DO SOMETHING FOR HIM.
I WILL LET YOU RETURN TO THE WORLD ABOVE.
I HAVE NO ILLUSIONS ABOUT HIS CHANCES WITH YOUR FELLOW MORTALS...
BUT PERHAPS YOUR COMPANY WILL MAKE HIS LAST DAYS SWEETER.
YEAH. THANKS A BUNCH.
OH, AND MORTAL?
YEAH?
IF HE HAS ANY GLAMOUR, IT IS A KIND NATURAL TO YOUR FOLK, NOT MINE.

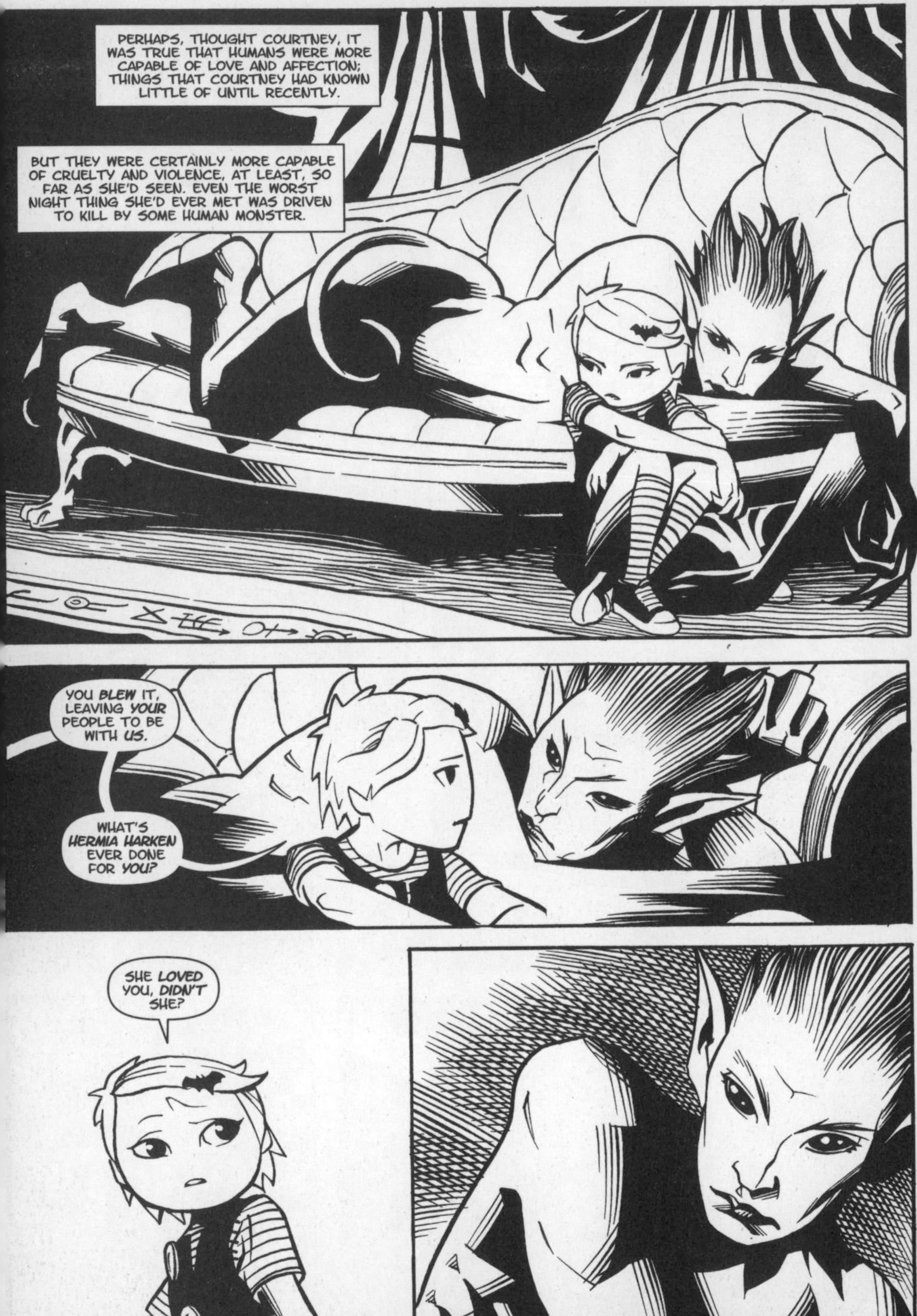
PERHAPS, THOUGHT COURTNEY, IT WAS TRUE THAT HUMANS WERE MORE CAPABLE OF LOVE AND AFFECTION; THINGS THAT COURTNEY HAD KNOWN LITTLE OF UNTIL RECENTLY.
BUT THEY WERE CERTAINLY MORE CAPABLE OF CRUELTY AND VIOLENCE, AT LEAST, SO FAR AS SHE'D SEEN. EVEN THE WORST NIGHT THING SHE'D EVER MET WAS DRIVEN TO KILL BY SOME HUMAN MONSTER.
YOU BLEW IT, LEAVING YOUR PEOPLE TO BE WITH US.
WHAT'S HERMIA HARKEN EVER DONE FOR YOU?
SHE LOVED YOU, DIDN'T SHE?

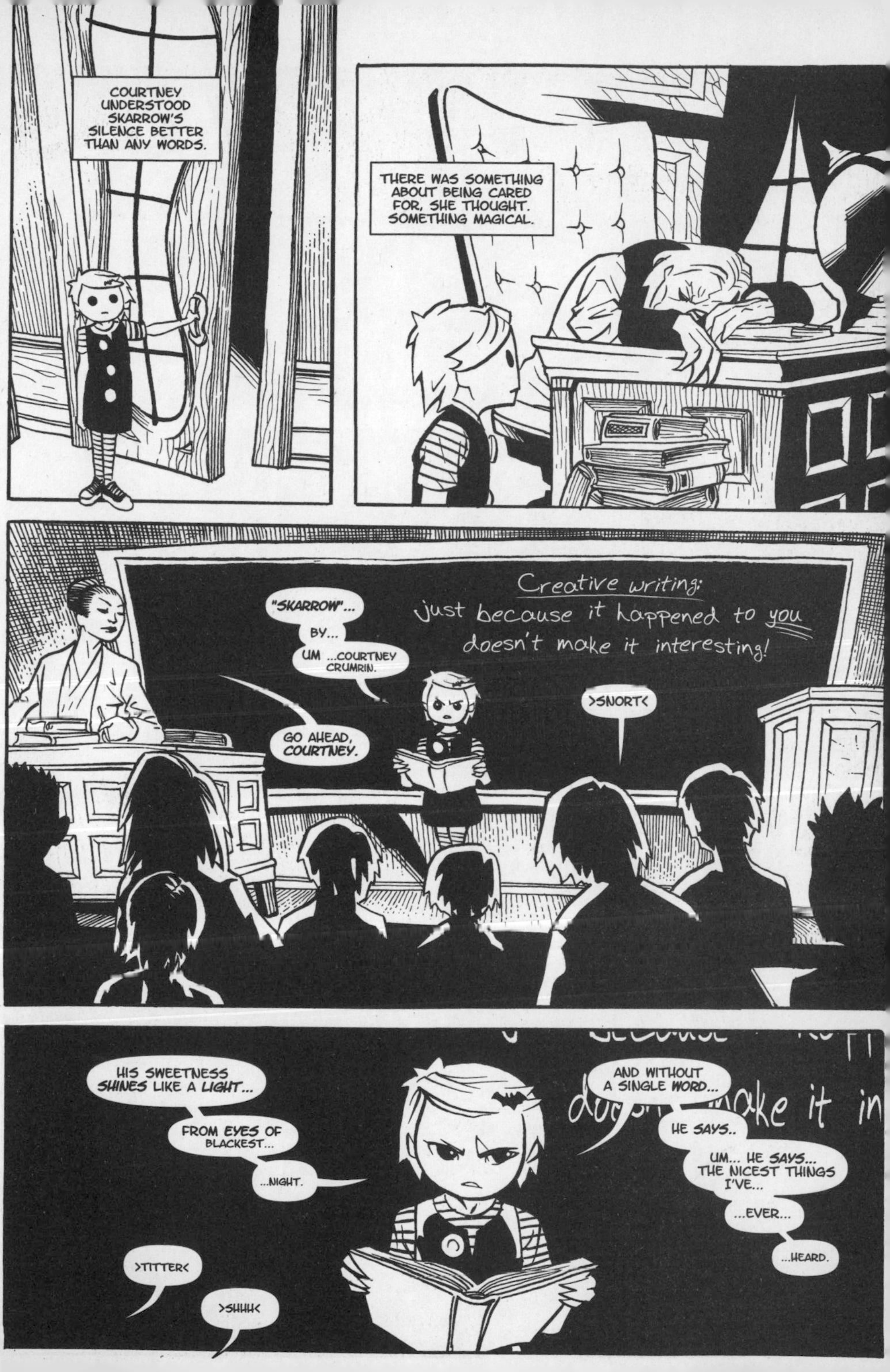
COURTNEY UNDERSTOOD SKARROW'S SILENCE BETTER THAN ANY WORDS.
THERE WAS SOMETHING ABOUT BEING CARED FOR, SHE THOUGHT. SOMETHING MAGICAL.
Creative writing:
just because it happened to you doesn't make it interesting!
"SKARROW"...
BY...
UM ...COURTNEY CRUMRIN.
GO AHEAD, COURTNEY.
>SNORT<
HIS SWEETNESS SHINES LIKE A LIGHT...
FROM EYES OF BLACKEST...
...NIGHT.
AND WITHOUT A SINGLE WORD...
HE SAYS..
UM... HE SAYS... THE NICEST THINGS I'VE...
...EVER...
...HEARD.
>TITTER<
>SHHH<

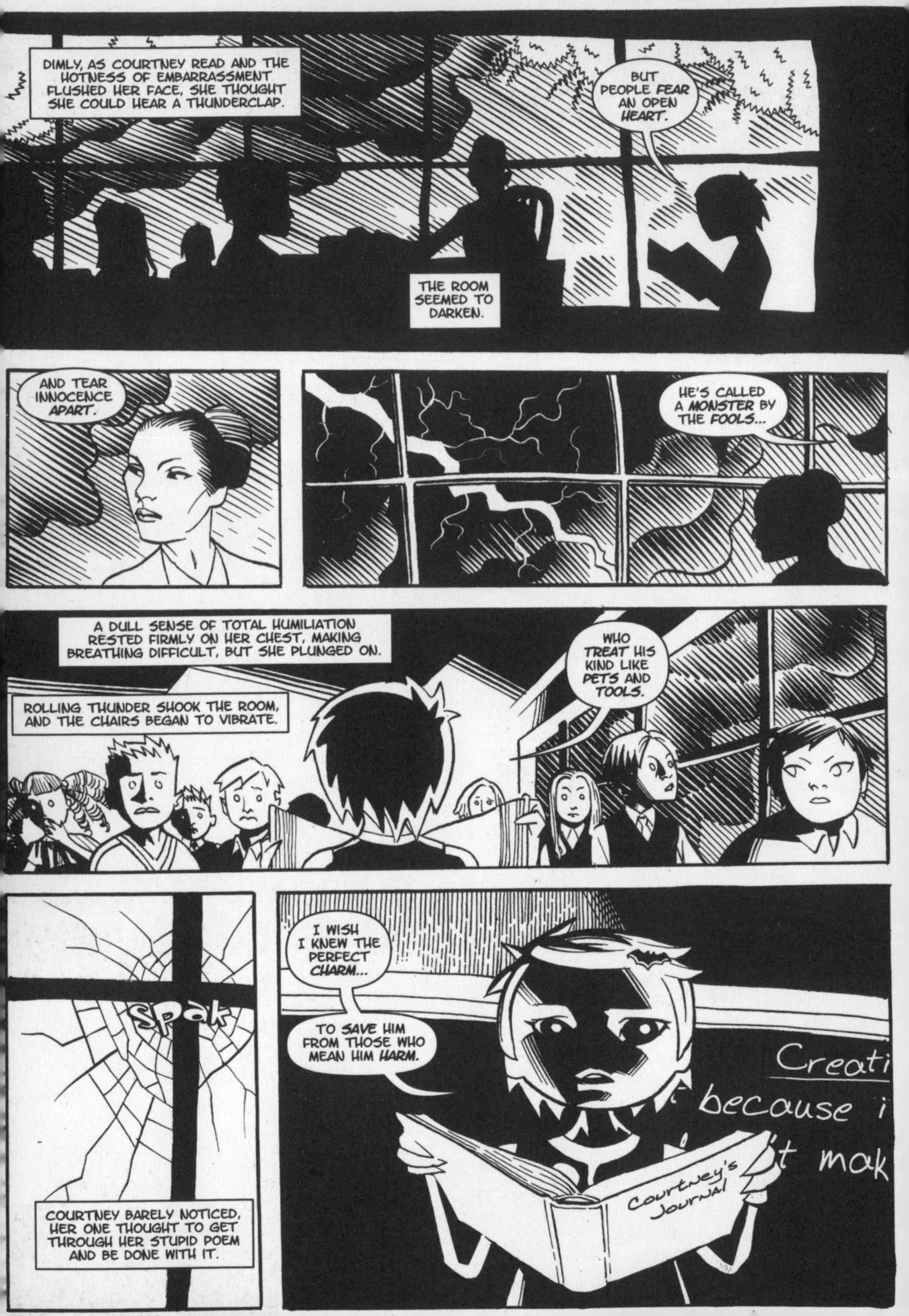
DIMLY, AS COURTNEY READ AND THE HOTNESS OF EMBARRASSMENT FLUSHED HER FACE, SHE THOUGHT SHE COULD HEAR A THUNDERCLAP.
BUT PEOPLE FEAR AN OPEN HEART.
THE ROOM SEEMED TO DARKEN.
AND TEAR INNOCENCE APART.
HE'S CALLED A MONSTER BY THE FOOLS...
A DULL SENSE OF TOTAL HUMILIATION RESTED FIRMLY ON HER CHEST, MAKING BREATHING DIFFICULT, BUT SHE PLUNGED ON.
ROLLING THUNDER SHOOK THE ROOM, AND THE CHAIRS BEGAN TO VIBRATE.
WHO TREAT HIS KIND LIKE PETS AND TOOLS.
SPAK
COURTNEY BARELY NOTICED, HER ONE THOUGHT TO GET THROUGH HER STUPID POEM AND BE DONE WITH IT.
I WISH I KNEW THE PERFECT CHARM...
TO SAVE HIM FROM THOSE WHO MEAN HIM HARM.
Creati
because i
t mak
Courtney's Journal

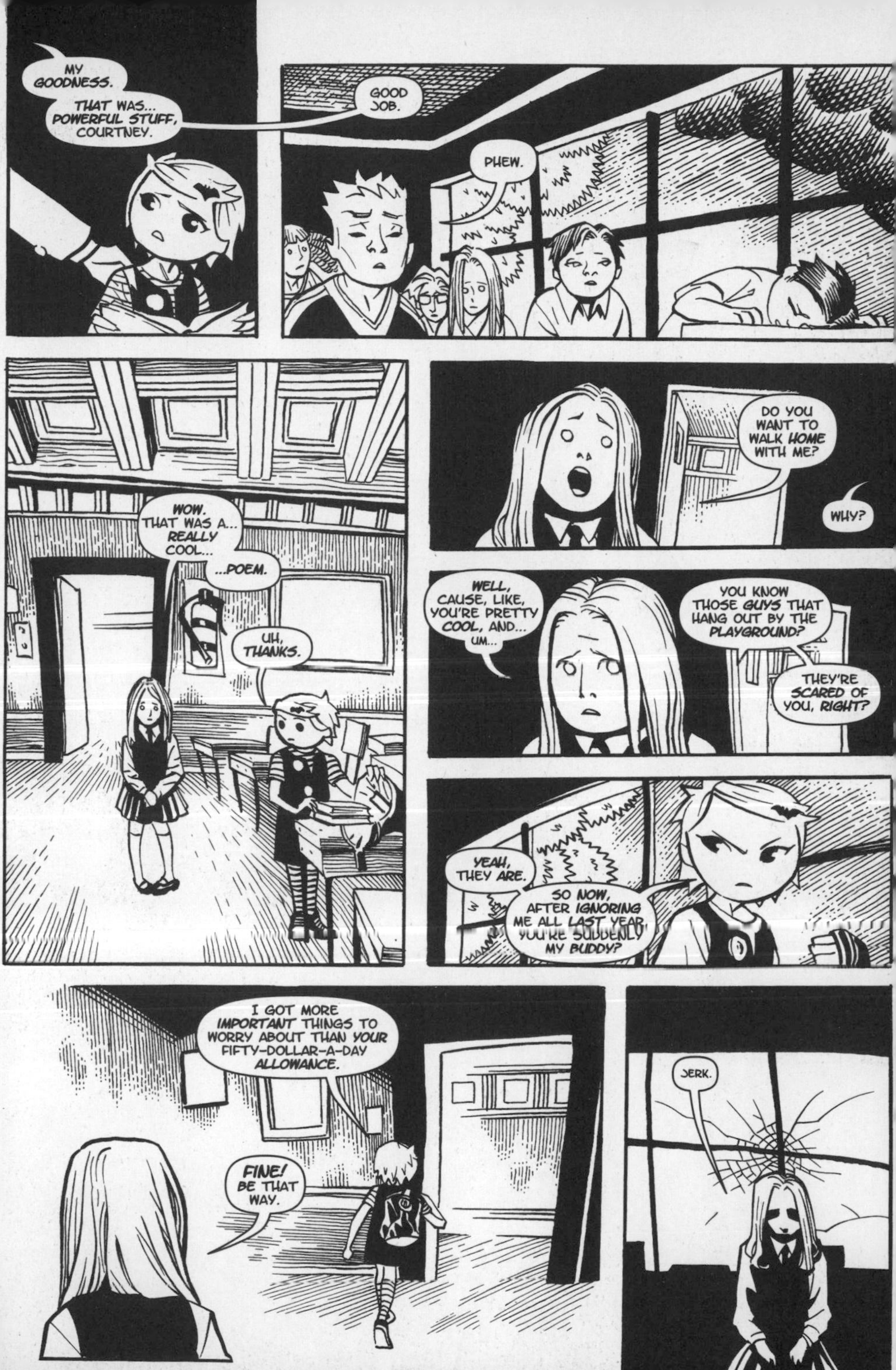
MY GOODNESS.
THAT WAS... POWERFUL STUFF, COURTNEY.
GOOD JOB.
PHEW.
WOW. THAT WAS A... REALLY COOL...
...POEM.
UH, THANKS.
DO YOU WANT TO WALK HOME WITH ME?
WHY?
WELL, CAUSE, LIKE, YOU'RE PRETTY COOL, AND... UM...
YOU KNOW THOSE GUYS THAT HANG OUT BY THE PLAYGROUND?
THEY'RE SCARED OF YOU, RIGHT?
YEAH, THEY ARE.
SO NOW, AFTER IGNORING ME ALL LAST YEAR YOU'RE SUDDENLY MY BUDDY?
I GOT MORE IMPORTANT THINGS TO WORRY ABOUT THAN YOUR FIFTY-DOLLAR-A-DAY ALLOWANCE.
FINE! BE THAT WAY.
JERK.

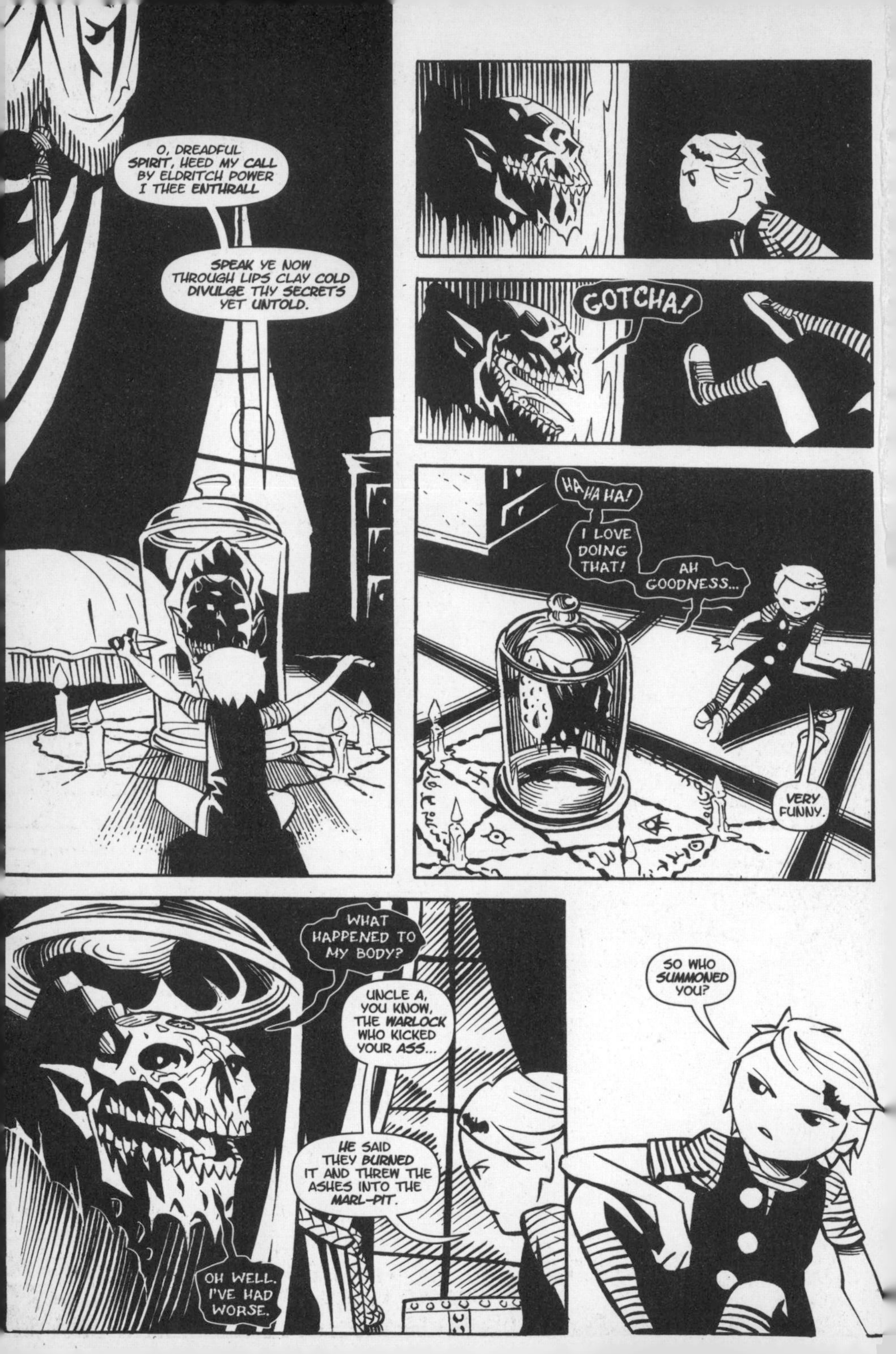
O, DREADFUL SPIRIT, HEED MY CALL BY ELDRITCH POWER I THEE ENTHRALL
SPEAK YE NOW THROUGH LIPS CLAY COLD DIVULGE THY SECRETS YET UNTOLD.
GOTCHA!
HA HA HA!
I LOVE DOING THAT!
AH GOODNESS...
VERY FUNNY.
WHAT HAPPENED TO MY BODY?
UNCLE A, YOU KNOW, THE WARLOCK WHO KICKED YOUR ASS...
HE SAID THEY BURNED IT AND THREW THE ASHES INTO THE MARL-PIT.
OH WELL. I'VE HAD WORSE.
SO WHO SUMMONED YOU?

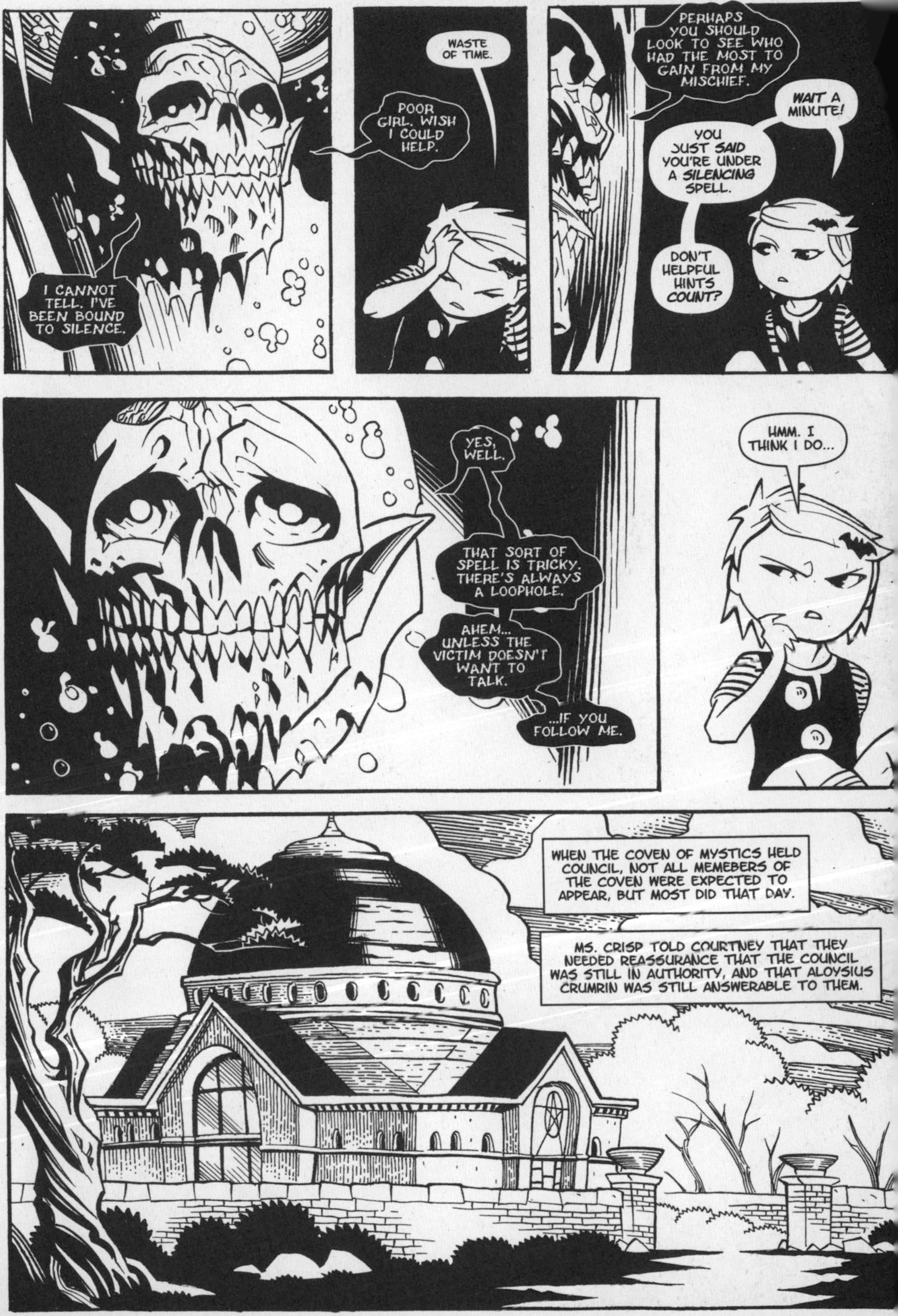
I CANNOT TELL. I'VE BEEN BOUND TO SILENCE.
POOR GIRL. WISH I COULD HELP.
WASTE OF TIME.
PERHAPS YOU SHOULD LOOK TO SEE WHO HAD THE MOST TO GAIN FROM MY MISCHIEF.
WAIT A MINUTE!
YOU JUST SAID YOU'RE UNDER A SILENCING SPELL.
DON'T HELPFUL HINTS COUNT?
YES, WELL.
THAT SORT OF SPELL IS TRICKY. THERE'S ALWAYS A LOOPHOLE.
AHEM... UNLESS THE VICTIM DOESN'T WANT TO TALK.
...IF YOU FOLLOW ME.
HMM. I THINK I DO...
WHEN THE COVEN OF MYSTICS HELD COUNCIL, NOT ALL MEMEBERS OF THE COVEN WERE EXPECTED TO APPEAR, BUT MOST DID THAT DAY.
MS. CRISP TOLD COURTNEY THAT THEY NEEDED REASSURANCE THAT THE COUNCIL WAS STILL IN AUTHORITY, AND THAT ALOYSIUS CRUMRIN WAS STILL ANSWERABLE TO THEM.

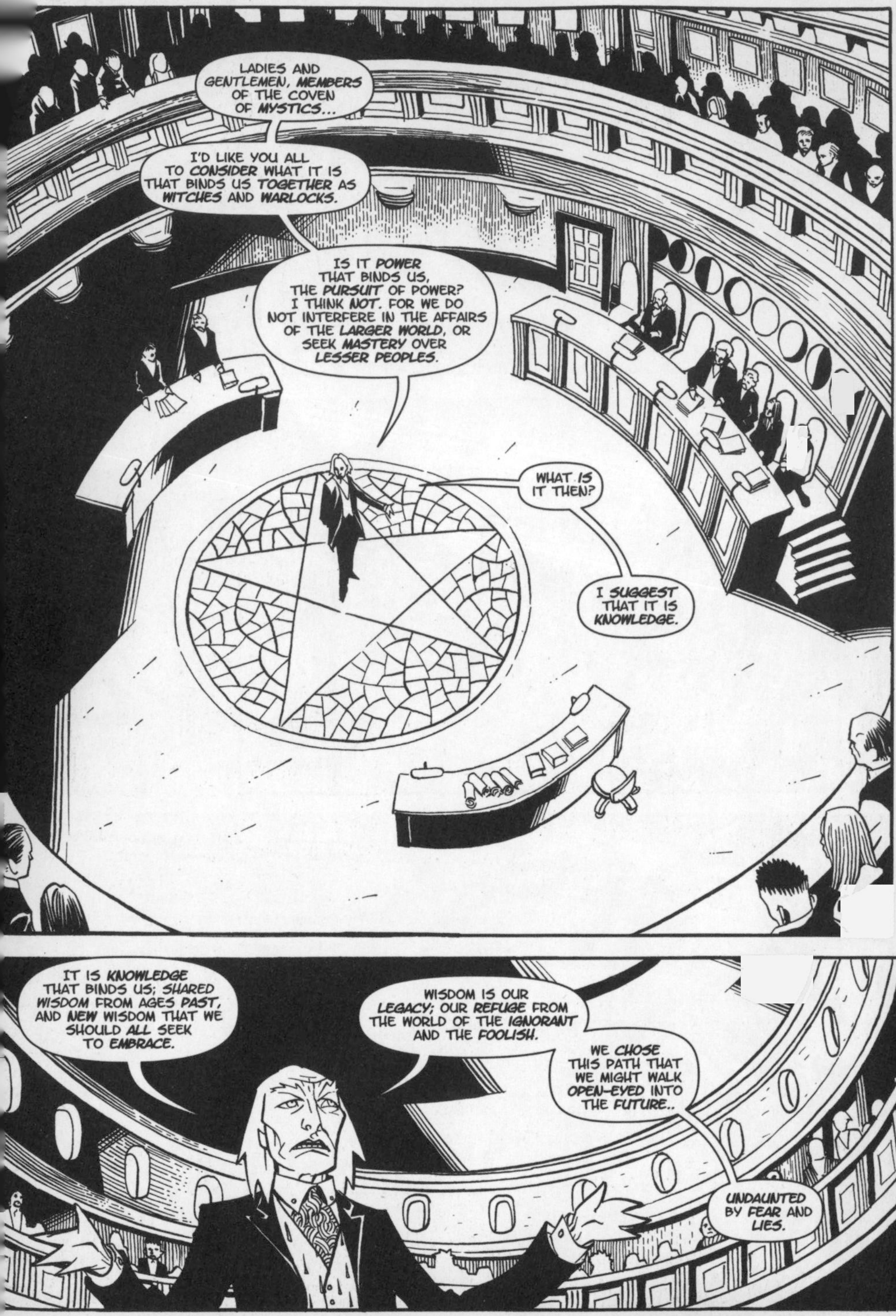
LADIES AND GENTLEMEN, MEMBERS OF THE COVEN OF MYSTICS...
I'D LIKE YOU ALL TO CONSIDER WHAT IT IS THAT BINDS US TOGETHER AS WITCHES AND WARLOCKS.
IS IT POWER THAT BINDS US, THE PURSUIT OF POWER? I THINK NOT. FOR WE DO NOT INTERFERE IN THE AFFAIRS OF THE LARGER WORLD, OR SEEK MASTERY OVER LESSER PEOPLES.
WHAT IS IT THEN?
I SUGGEST THAT IT IS KNOWLEDGE.
IT IS KNOWLEDGE THAT BINDS US; SHARED WISDOM FROM AGES PAST, AND NEW WISDOM THAT WE SHOULD ALL SEEK TO EMBRACE.
WISDOM IS OUR LEGACY; OUR REFUGE FROM THE WORLD OF THE IGNORANT AND THE FOOLISH.
WE CHOSE THIS PATH THAT WE MIGHT WALK OPEN-EYED INTO THE FUTURE..
UNDAUNTED BY FEAR AND LIES.

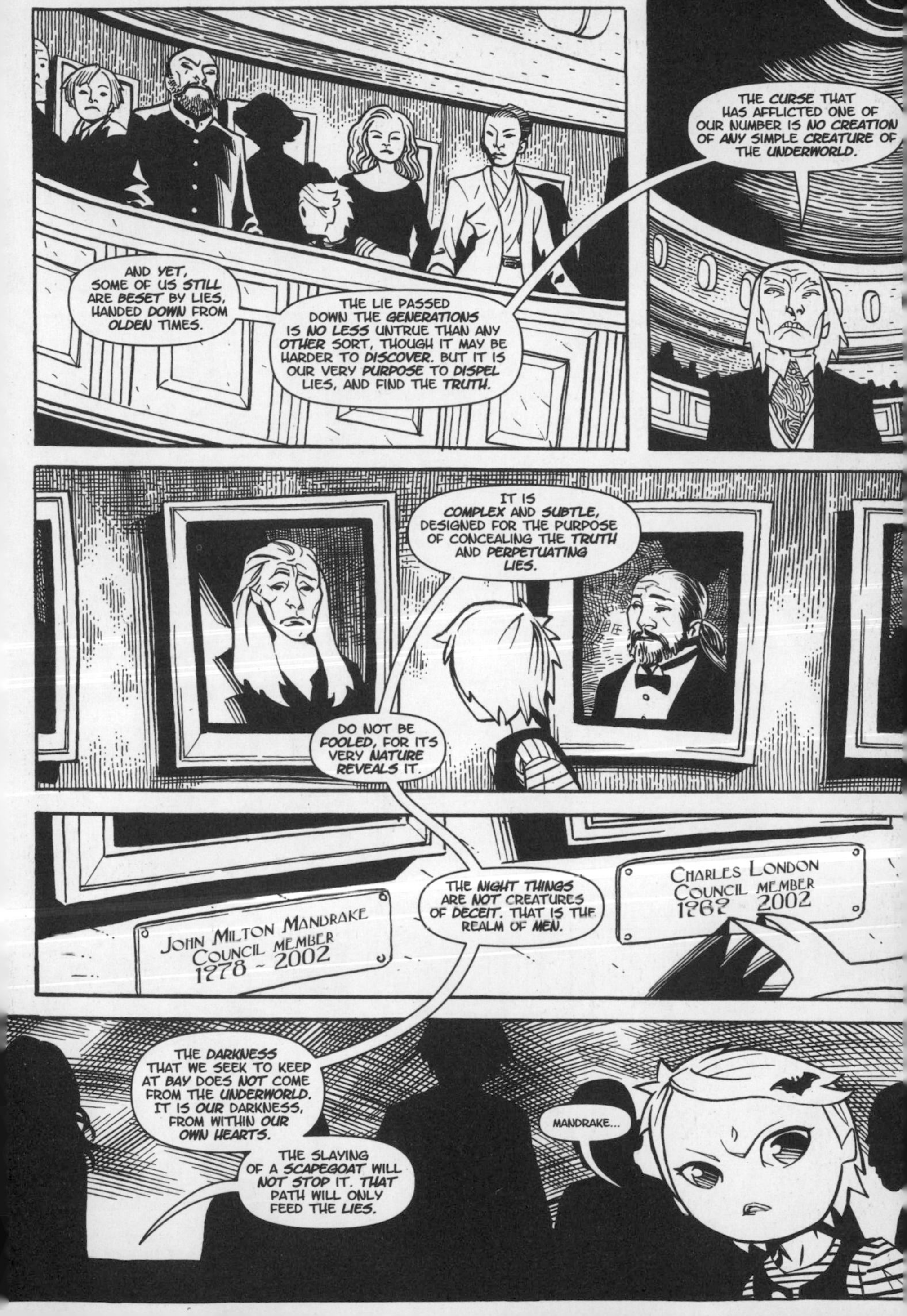

AND YET, SOME OF US STILL ARE BESET BY LIES, HANDED DOWN FROM OLDEN TIMES.
THE LIE PASSED DOWN THE GENERATIONS IS NO LESS UNTRUE THAN ANY OTHER SORT, THOUGH IT MAY BE HARDER TO DISCOVER. BUT IT IS OUR VERY PURPOSE TO DISPEL LIES, AND FIND THE TRUTH.
THE CURSE THAT HAS AFFLICTED ONE OF OUR NUMBER IS NO CREATION OF ANY SIMPLE CREATURE OF THE UNDERWORLD.
IT IS COMPLEX AND SUBTLE, DESIGNED FOR THE PURPOSE OF CONCEALING THE TRUTH AND PERPETUATING LIES.
DO NOT BE FOOLED, FOR ITS VERY NATURE REVEALS IT.
JOHN MILTON MANDRAKE
COUNCIL MEMBER
1978 ~ 2002
THE NIGHT THINGS ARE NOT CREATURES OF DECEIT. THAT IS THE REALM OF MEN.
CHARLES LONDON
COUNCIL MEMBER
1962 2002
THE DARKNESS THAT WE SEEK TO KEEP AT BAY DOES NOT COME FROM THE UNDERWORLD. IT IS OUR DARKNESS, FROM WITHIN OUR OWN HEARTS.
THE SLAYING OF A SCAPEGOAT WILL NOT STOP IT. THAT PATH WILL ONLY FEED THE LIES.
MANDRAKE...

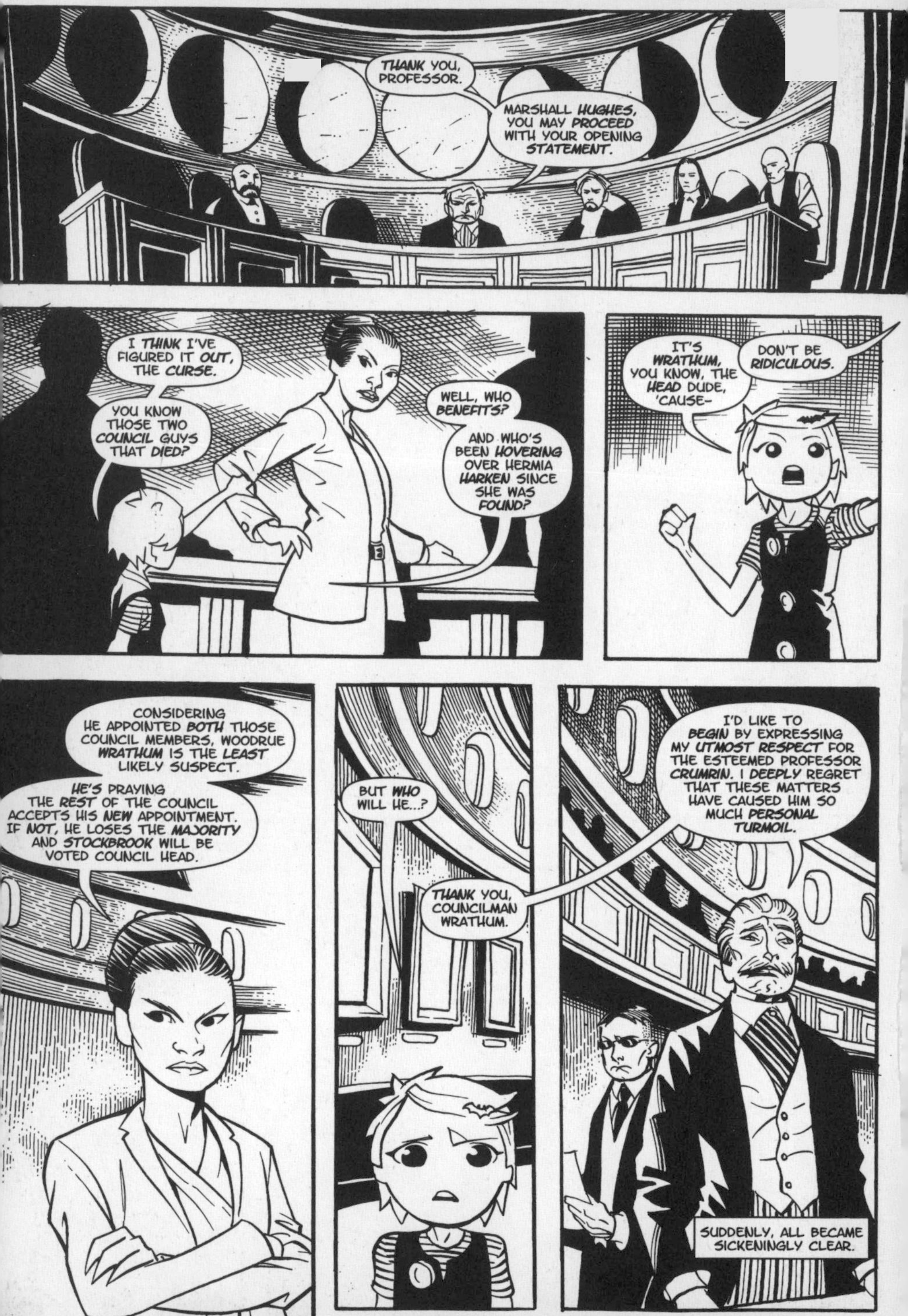
THANK YOU, PROFESSOR.
MARSHALL HUGHES, YOU MAY PROCEED WITH YOUR OPENING STATEMENT.
I THINK I'VE FIGURED IT OUT, THE CURSE.
YOU KNOW THOSE TWO COUNCIL GUYS THAT DIED?
WELL, WHO BENEFITS?
AND WHO'S BEEN HOVERING OVER HERMIA HARKEN SINCE SHE WAS FOUND?
IT'S WRATHUM, YOU KNOW, THE HEAD DUDE, 'CAUSE-
DON'T BE RIDICULOUS.
CONSIDERING HE APPOINTED BOTH THOSE COUNCIL MEMBERS, WOODRUE WRATHUM IS THE LEAST LIKELY SUSPECT.
HE'S PRAYING THE REST OF THE COUNCIL ACCEPTS HIS NEW APPOINTMENT. IF NOT, HE LOSES THE MAJORITY AND STOCKBROOK WILL BE VOTED COUNCIL HEAD.
BUT WHO WILL HE...?
THANK YOU, COUNCILMAN WRATHUM.
I'D LIKE TO BEGIN BY EXPRESSING MY UTMOST RESPECT FOR THE ESTEEMED PROFESSOR CRUMRIN. I DEEPLY REGRET THAT THESE MATTERS HAVE CAUSED HIM SO MUCH PERSONAL TURMOIL.
SUDDENLY, ALL BECAME SICKENINGLY CLEAR.

THEY CAN'T—

COURTNEY, ALOYSIUS CAN'T STAND *ALONE* AGAINST THE WHOLE *COVEN.*

THEY'RE GOING TO *KILL* HIM! HE DIDN'T DO ANYTHING!

DON'T YOU SEE? I ALL KNOW THAT.

IT DOESN'T *MATTER* WHO CAST THE CURSE, WHAT *MATTERS* IS THAT THEY HAVE AN *EXCUSE* TO *PUNISH* YOUR FRIEND *SKARROW* FOR STEALING MADAM *HARKEN* AWAY, AND TO *PUNISH* HERMIA FOR CHOOSING A *NIGHT THING* OVER THE *COVEN.*

AT!?!

IT'S ONE THING FOR A MAN LIKE YOUR *UNCLE* TO WITHDRAW INTO SOLITUDE, BUT A WOMAN LIKE *HERMIA—* UNFORGIVABLE.

WHY?

FOR *STARTERS,* HERMIA BELONGED TO AN IMPORTANT *MAN!*

HER *FATHER* WAS THE HEAD OF THE *COUNCIL* BEFORE *WRATHUM.* HE'D PROMISED HER TO *MARRY...*

WELL IT'S *TOO LONG* A *STORY.*

SHE SIMPLY DIDN'T *WANT* THE LIFE *CHOSEN* FOR HER, SO SHE *WALKED* AWAY.

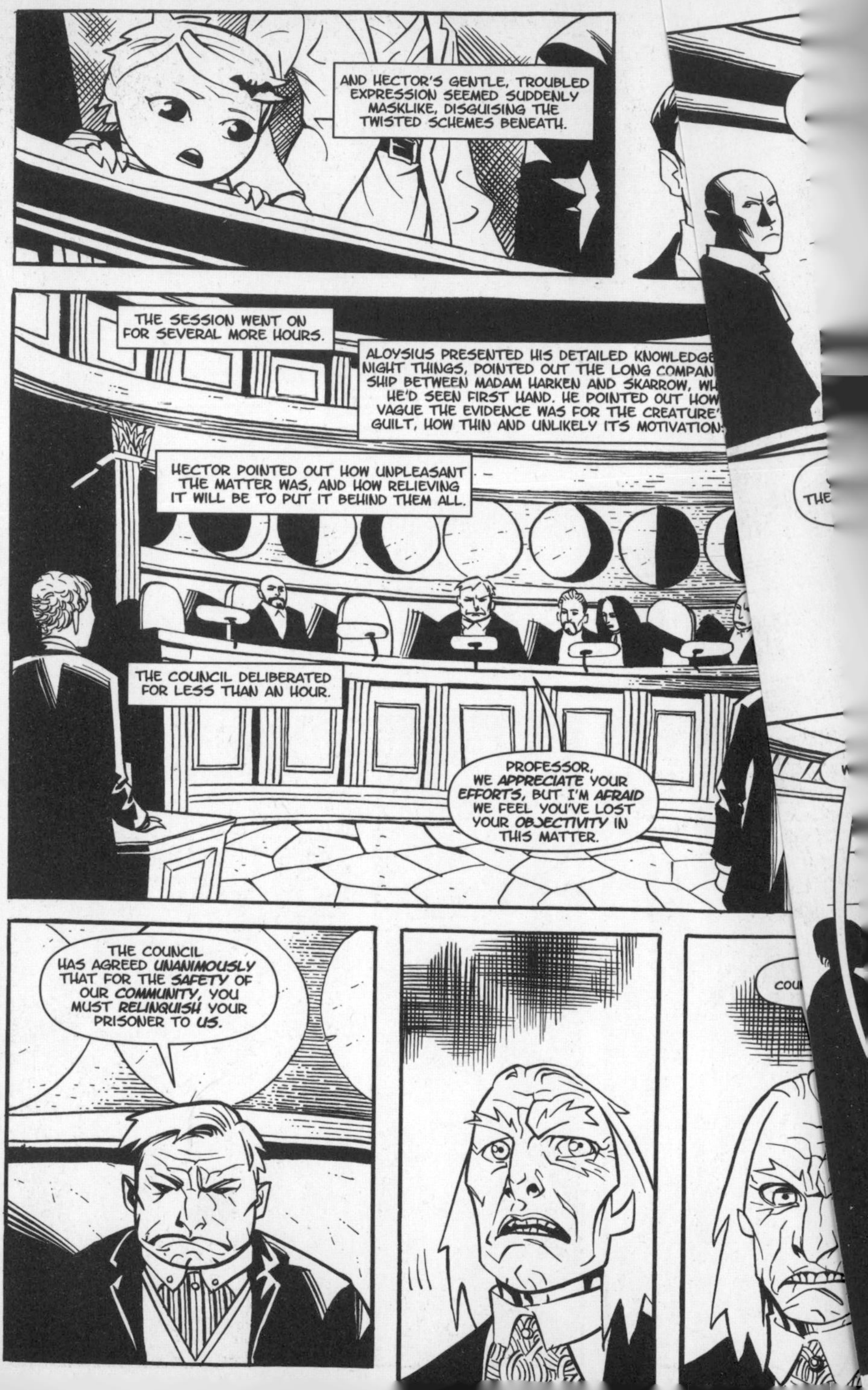
AND HECTOR'S GENTLE, TROUBLED EXPRESSION SEEMED SUDDENLY MASKLIKE, DISGUISING THE TWISTED SCHEMES BENEATH.
THE SESSION WENT ON FOR SEVERAL MORE HOURS.
ALOYSIUS PRESENTED HIS DETAILED KNOWLEDGE NIGHT THINGS, POINTED OUT THE LONG COMPAN SHIP BETWEEN MADAM HARKEN AND SKARROW, WH HE'D SEEN FIRST HAND. HE POINTED OUT HOW VAGUE THE EVIDENCE WAS FOR THE CREATURE' GUILT, HOW THIN AND UNLIKELY ITS MOTIVATION
HECTOR POINTED OUT HOW UNPLEASANT THE MATTER WAS, AND HOW RELIEVING IT WILL BE TO PUT IT BEHIND THEM ALL.
THE COUNCIL DELIBERATED FOR LESS THAN AN HOUR.
PROFESSOR, WE APPRECIATE YOUR EFFORTS, BUT I'M AFRAID WE FEEL YOU'VE LOST YOUR OBJECTIVITY IN THIS MATTER.
THE COUNCIL HAS AGREED UNANIMOUSLY THAT FOR THE SAFETY OF OUR COMMUNITY, YOU MUST RELINQUISH YOUR PRISONER TO US.

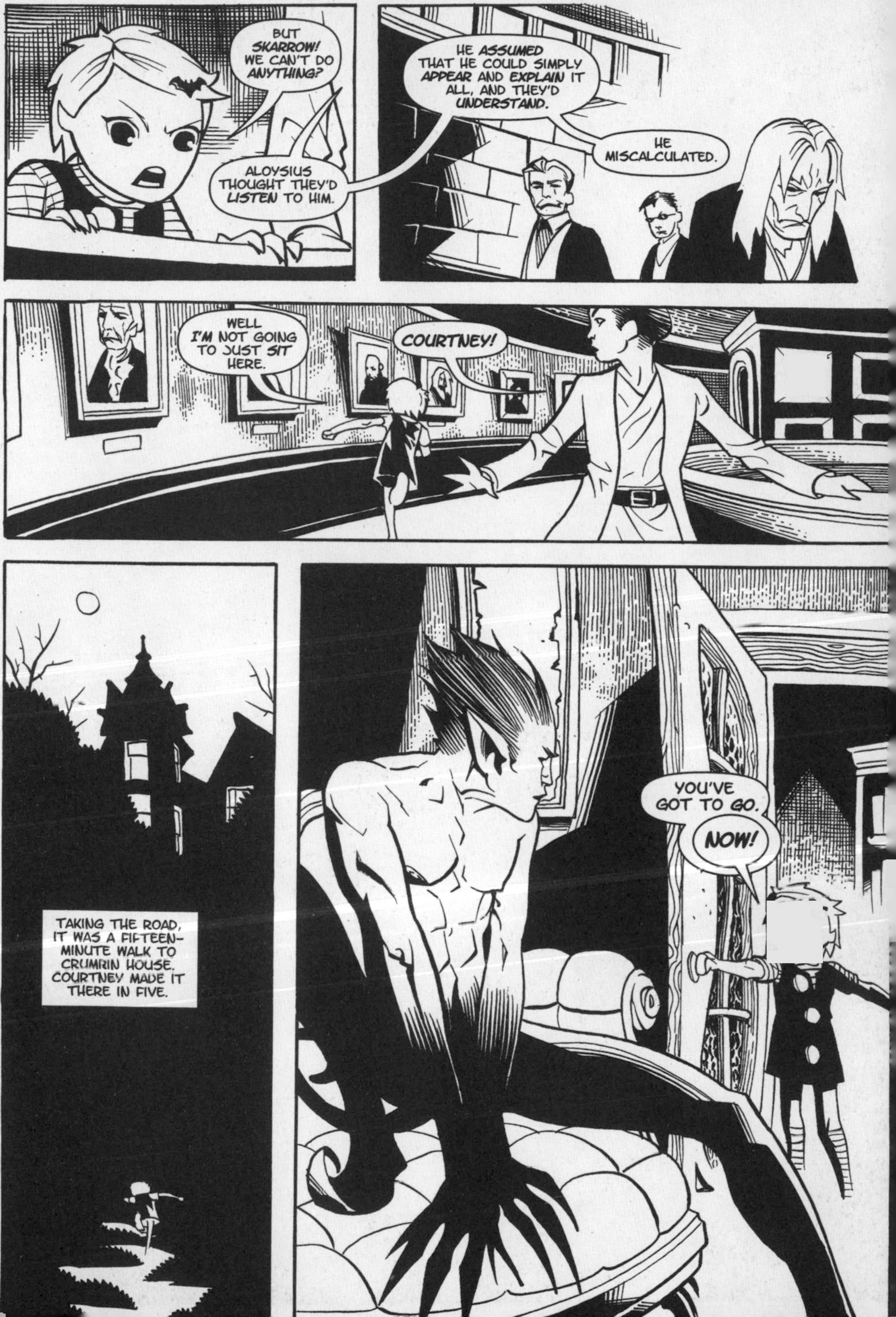
BUT SKARROW! WE CAN'T DO ANYTHING?
ALOYSIUS THOUGHT THEY'D LISTEN TO HIM.
HE ASSUMED THAT HE COULD SIMPLY APPEAR AND EXPLAIN IT ALL, AND THEY'D UNDERSTAND.
HE MISCALCULATED.
WELL I'M NOT GOING TO JUST SIT HERE.
COURTNEY!
TAKING THE ROAD, IT WAS A FIFTEEN-MINUTE WALK TO CRUMRIN HOUSE. COURTNEY MADE IT THERE IN FIVE.
YOU'VE GOT TO GO.
NOW!

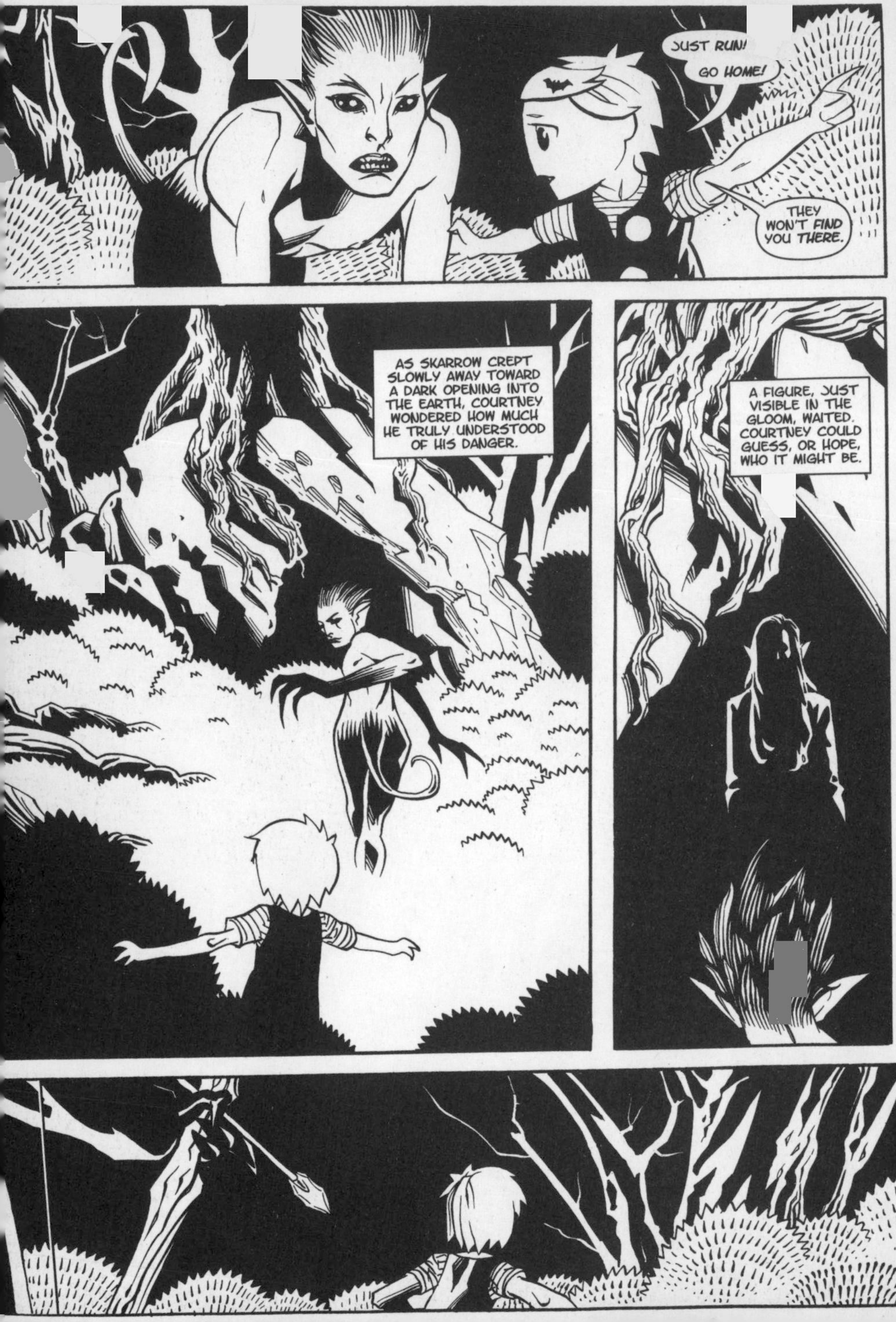
JUST RUN!
GO HOME!
THEY WON'T FIND YOU THERE.
AS SKARROW CREPT SLOWLY AWAY TOWARD A DARK OPENING INTO THE EARTH, COURTNEY WONDERED HOW MUCH HE TRULY UNDERSTOOD OF HIS DANGER.
A FIGURE, JUST VISIBLE IN THE GLOOM, WAITED. COURTNEY COULD GUESS, OR HOPE, WHO IT MIGHT BE.

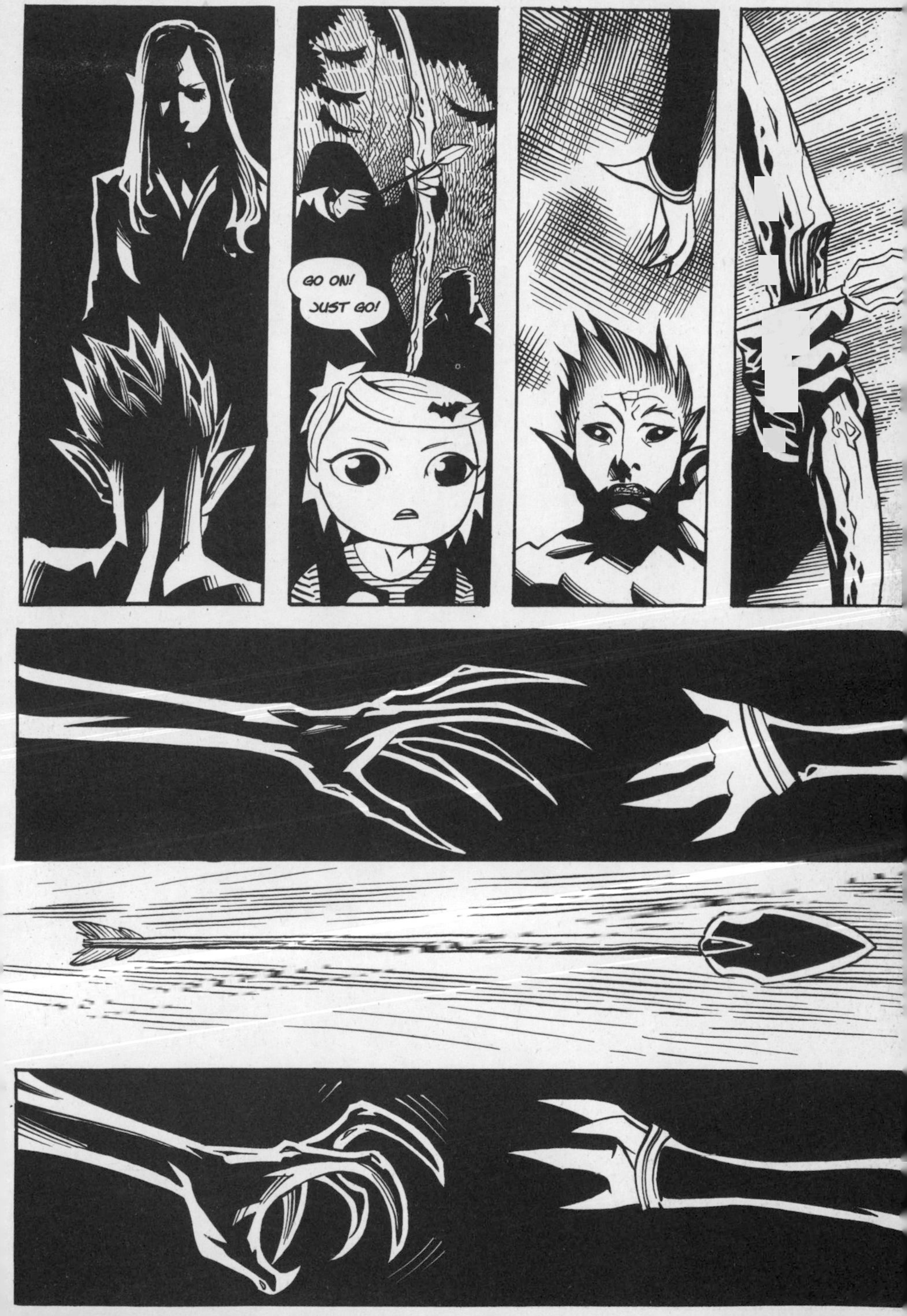
GO ON! JUST GO!

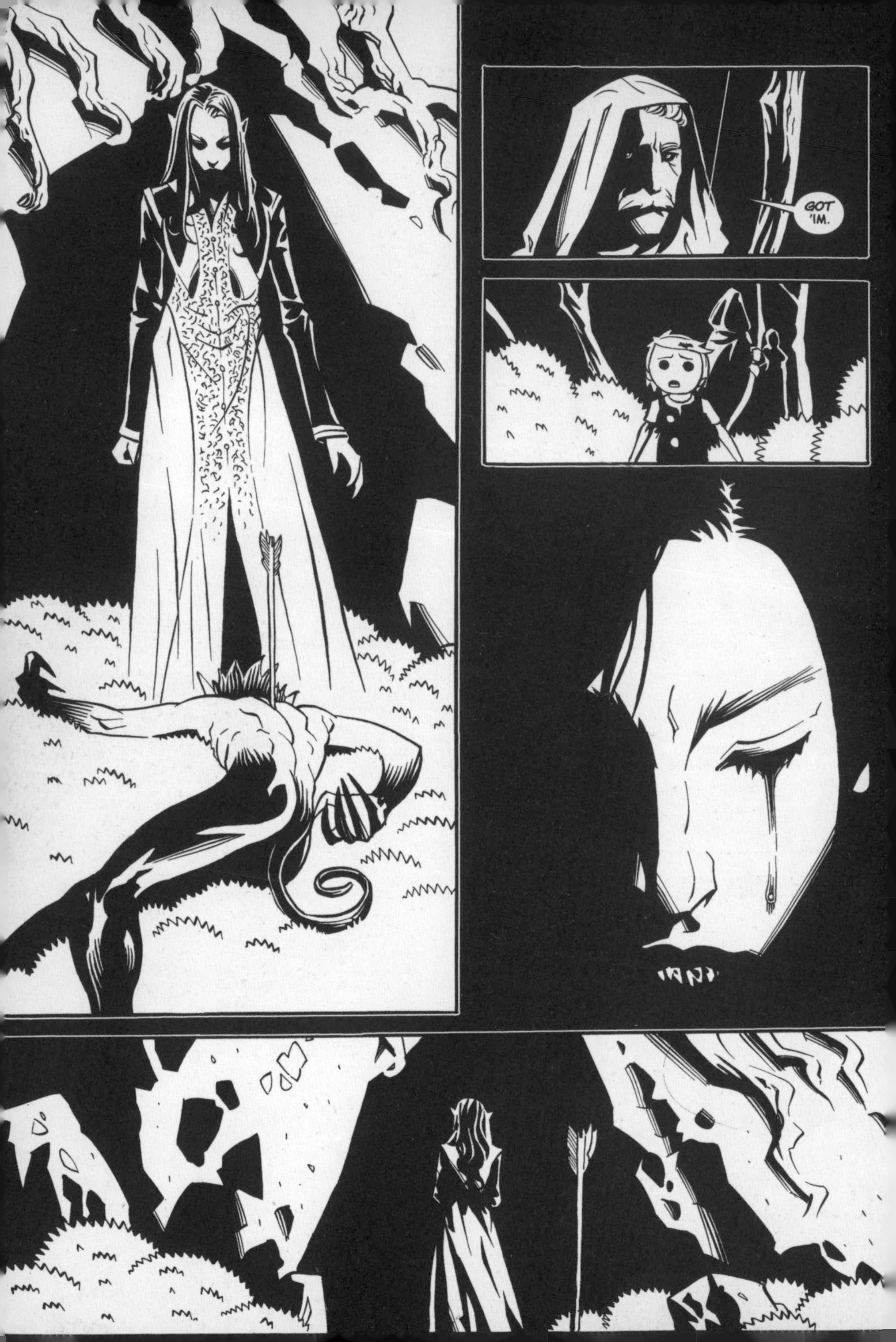
GOT 'IM.

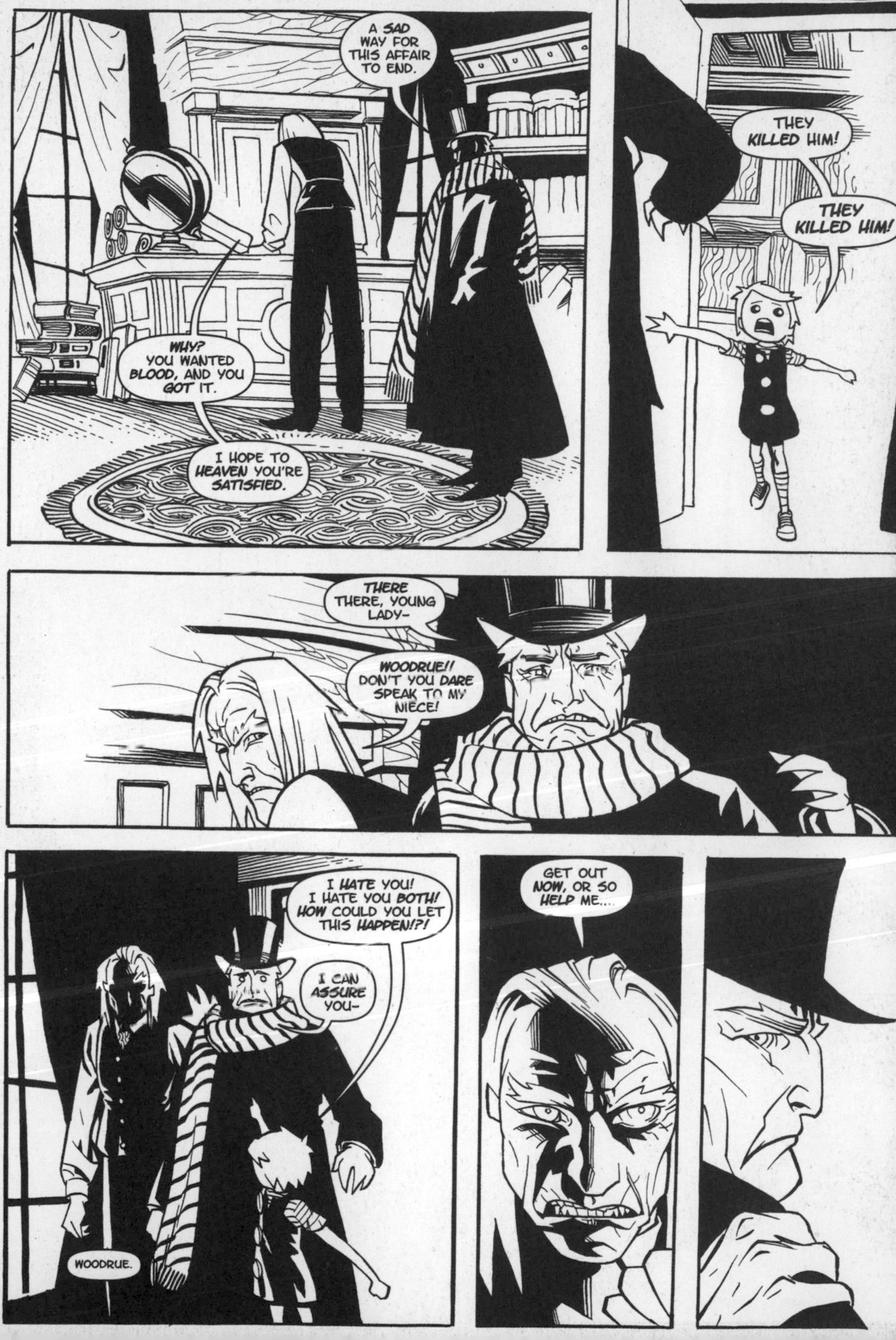
A SAD WAY FOR THIS AFFAIR TO END.
WHY? YOU WANTED BLOOD, AND YOU GOT IT.
I HOPE TO HEAVEN YOU'RE SATISFIED.
THEY KILLED HIM!
THEY KILLED HIM!
THERE THERE, YOUNG LADY-
WOODRUE!! DON'T YOU DARE SPEAK TO MY NIECE!
I HATE YOU! I HATE YOU BOTH! HOW COULD YOU LET THIS HAPPEN!?!
I CAN ASSURE YOU-
WOODRUE.
GET OUT NOW, OR SO HELP ME....

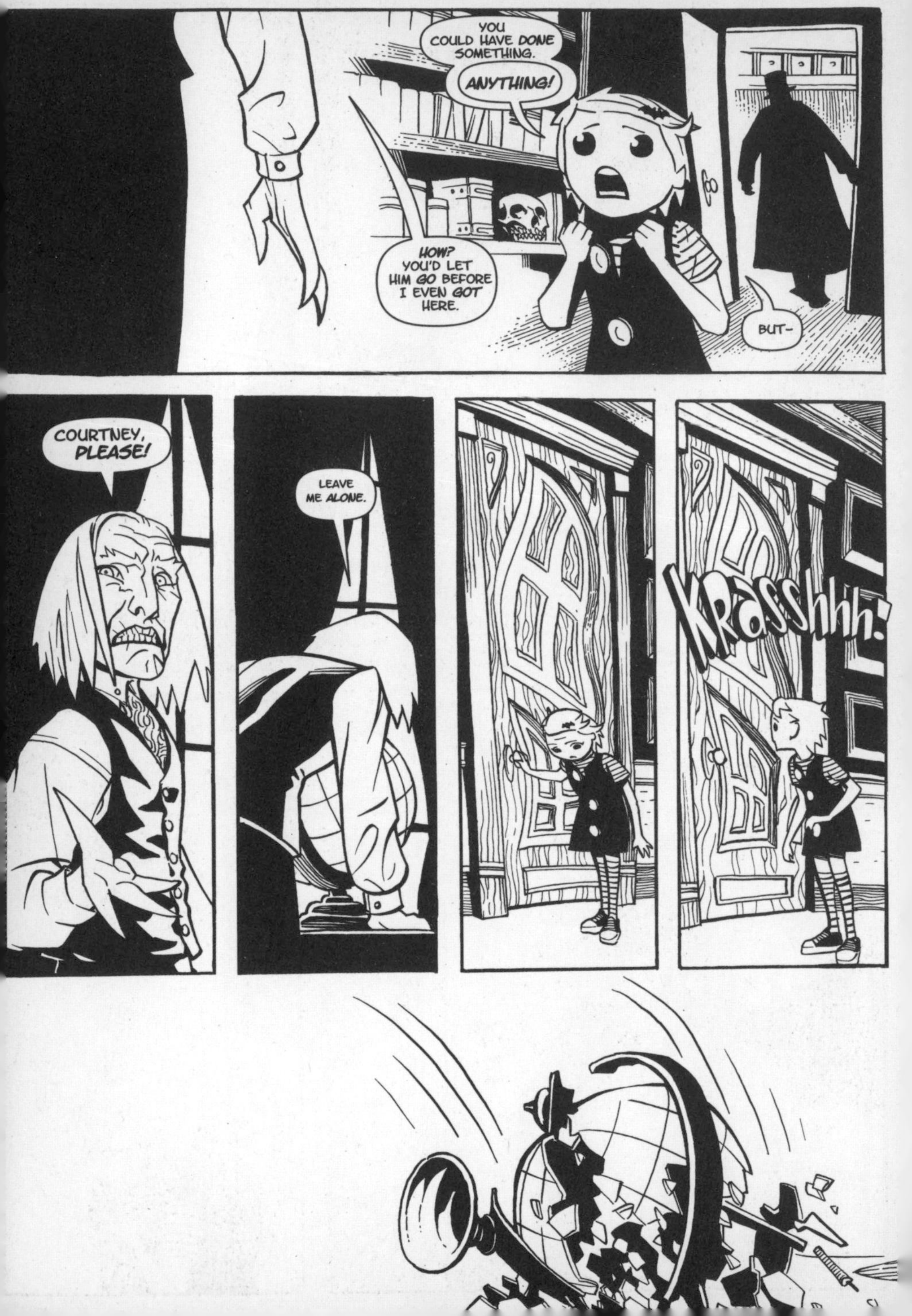
YOU COULD HAVE DONE SOMETHING.
ANYTHING!
HOW? YOU'D LET HIM GO BEFORE I EVEN GOT HERE.
BUT-
COURTNEY, PLEASE!
LEAVE ME ALONE.
KRASSHHH!

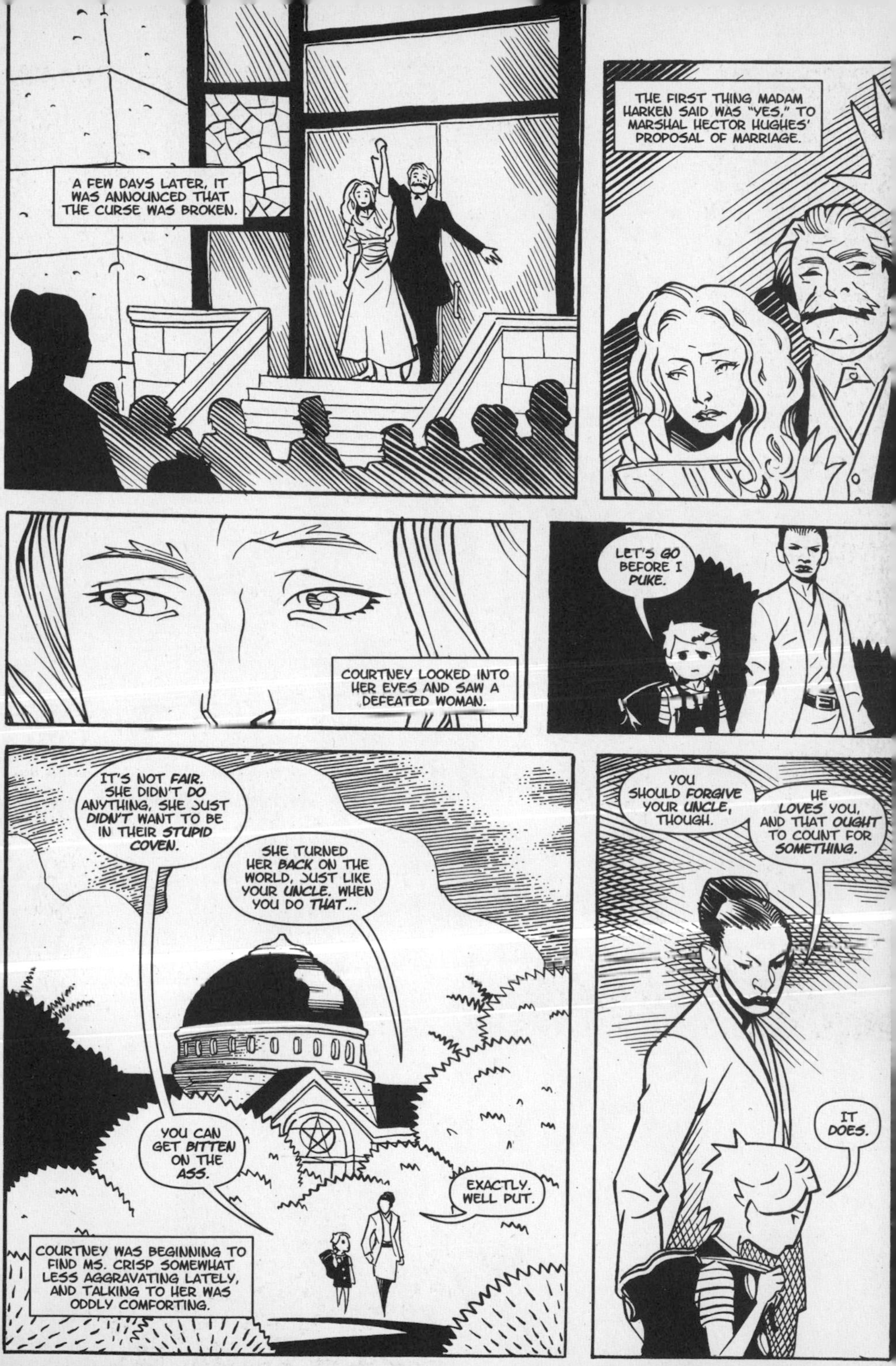
A FEW DAYS LATER, IT WAS ANNOUNCED THAT THE CURSE WAS BROKEN.
THE FIRST THING MADAM HARKEN SAID WAS "YES," TO MARSHAL HECTOR HUGHES' PROPOSAL OF MARRIAGE.
COURTNEY LOOKED INTO HER EYES AND SAW A DEFEATED WOMAN.
LET'S GO BEFORE I PUKE.
IT'S NOT FAIR. SHE DIDN'T DO ANYTHING, SHE JUST DIDN'T WANT TO BE IN THEIR STUPID COVEN.
SHE TURNED HER BACK ON THE WORLD, JUST LIKE YOUR UNCLE. WHEN YOU DO THAT...
YOU CAN GET BITTEN ON THE ASS.
EXACTLY. WELL PUT.
COURTNEY WAS BEGINNING TO FIND MS. CRISP SOMEWHAT LESS AGGRAVATING LATELY, AND TALKING TO HER WAS ODDLY COMFORTING.
YOU SHOULD FORGIVE YOUR UNCLE, THOUGH.
HE LOVES YOU, AND THAT OUGHT TO COUNT FOR SOMETHING.
IT DOES.

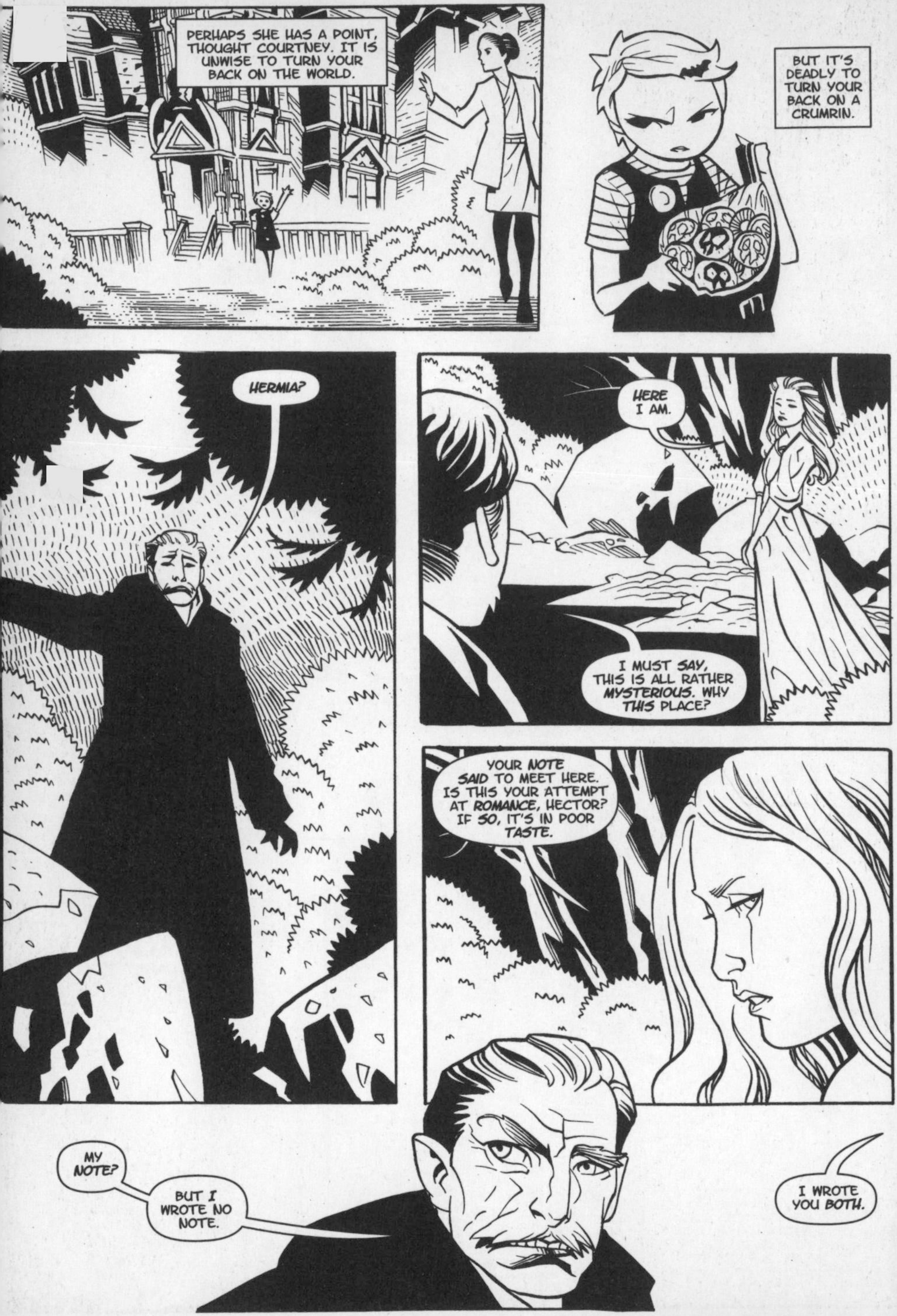
PERHAPS SHE HAS A POINT, THOUGHT COURTNEY. IT IS UNWISE TO TURN YOUR BACK ON THE WORLD.
BUT IT'S DEADLY TO TURN YOUR BACK ON A CRUMRIN.
HERMIA?
HERE I AM.
I MUST SAY, THIS IS ALL RATHER MYSTERIOUS. WHY THIS PLACE?
YOUR NOTE SAID TO MEET HERE. IS THIS YOUR ATTEMPT AT ROMANCE, HECTOR? IF SO, IT'S IN POOR TASTE.
MY NOTE?
BUT I WROTE NO NOTE.
I WROTE YOU BOTH.

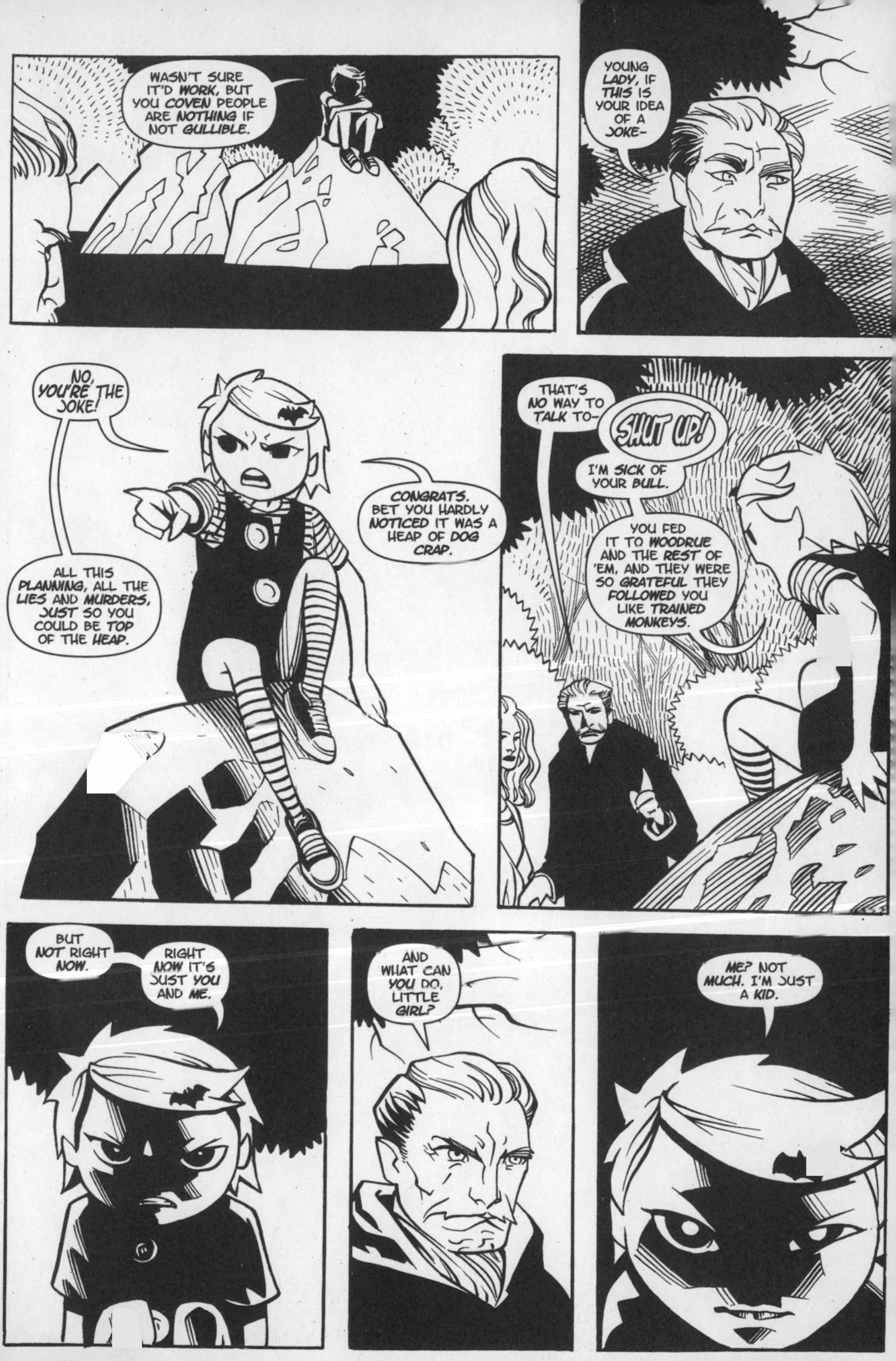
WASN'T SURE IT'D WORK, BUT YOU COVEN PEOPLE ARE NOTHING IF NOT GULLIBLE.
YOUNG LADY, IF THIS IS YOUR IDEA OF A JOKE-
NO, YOU'RE THE JOKE!
ALL THIS PLANNING, ALL THE LIES AND MURDERS, JUST SO YOU COULD BE TOP OF THE HEAP.
CONGRATS. BET YOU HARDLY NOTICED IT WAS A HEAP OF DOG CRAP.
THAT'S NO WAY TO TALK TO-
SHUT UP!
I'M SICK OF YOUR BULL.
YOU FED IT TO WOODRUE AND THE REST OF 'EM, AND THEY WERE SO GRATEFUL THEY FOLLOWED YOU LIKE TRAINED MONKEYS.
BUT NOT RIGHT NOW.
RIGHT NOW IT'S JUST YOU AND ME.
AND WHAT CAN YOU DO, LITTLE GIRL?
ME? NOT MUCH. I'M JUST A KID.

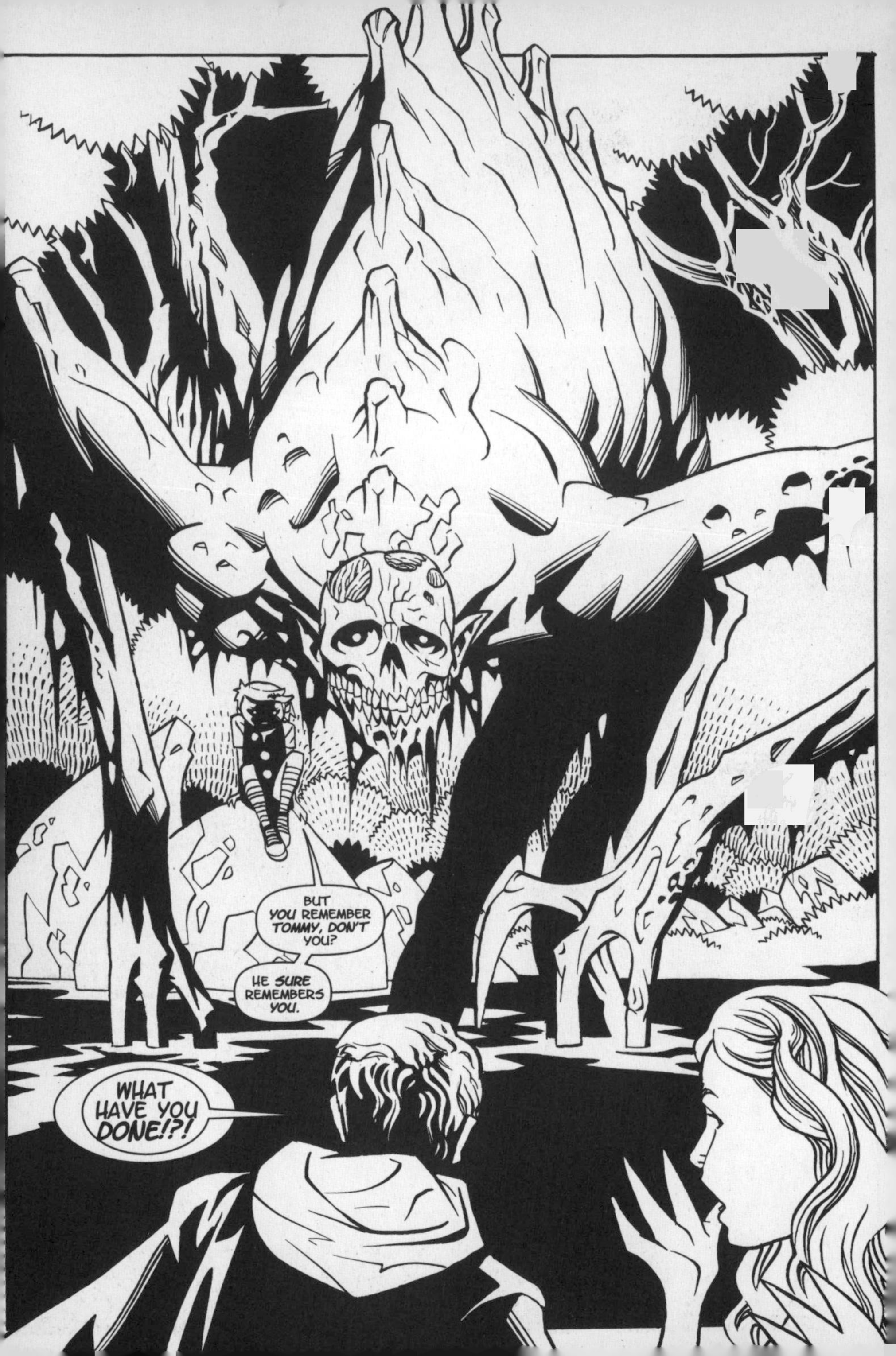
BUT YOU REMEMBER TOMMY, DON'T YOU?
HE SURE REMEMBERS YOU.
WHAT HAVE YOU DONE!?!

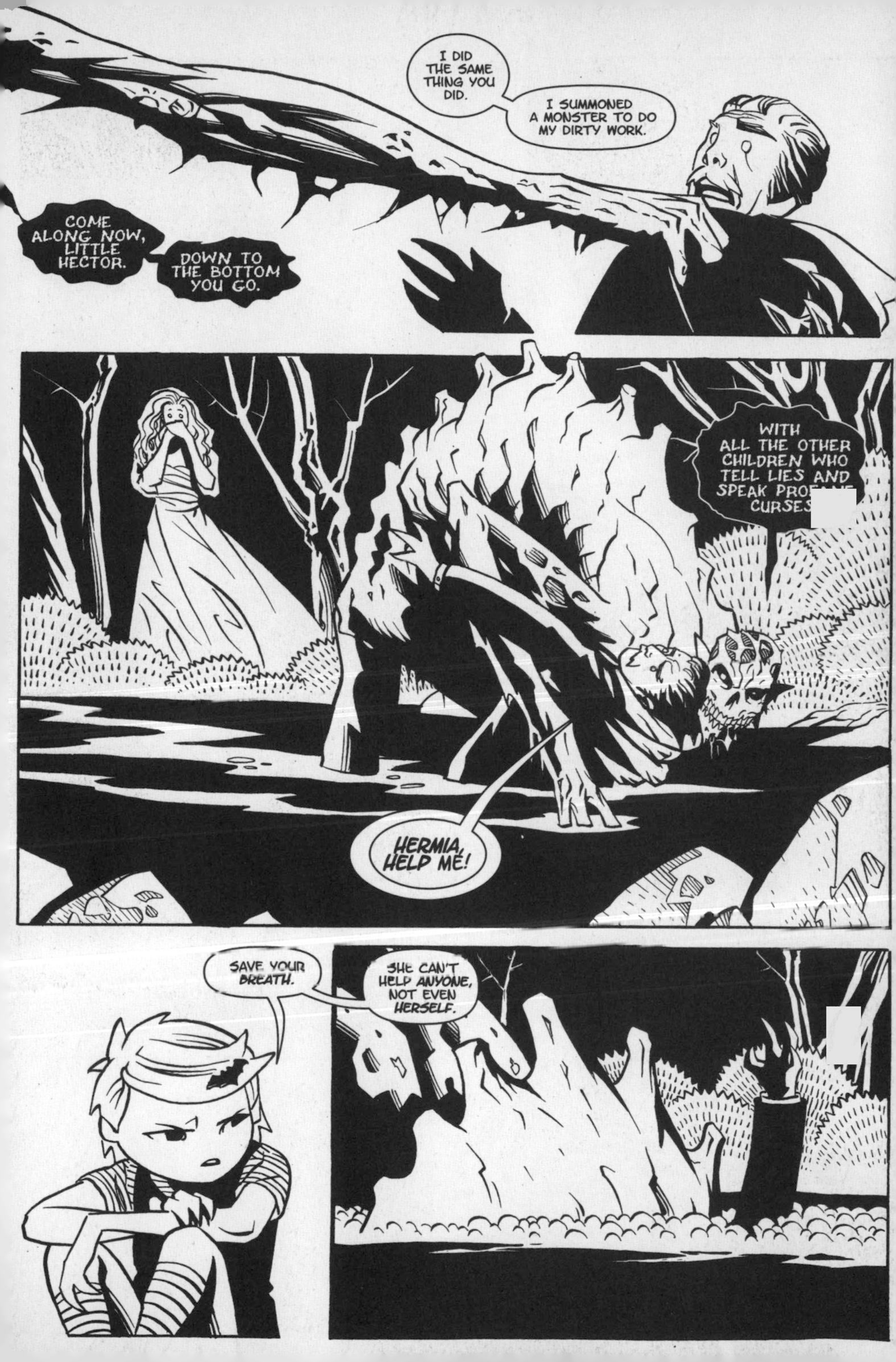
I DID THE SAME THING YOU DID.
I SUMMONED A MONSTER TO DO MY DIRTY WORK.
COME ALONG NOW, LITTLE HECTOR.
DOWN TO THE BOTTOM YOU GO.
WITH ALL THE OTHER CHILDREN WHO TELL LIES AND SPEAK PROF CURSES
HERMIA, HELP ME!
SAVE YOUR BREATH.
SHE CAN'T HELP ANYONE, NOT EVEN HERSELF.

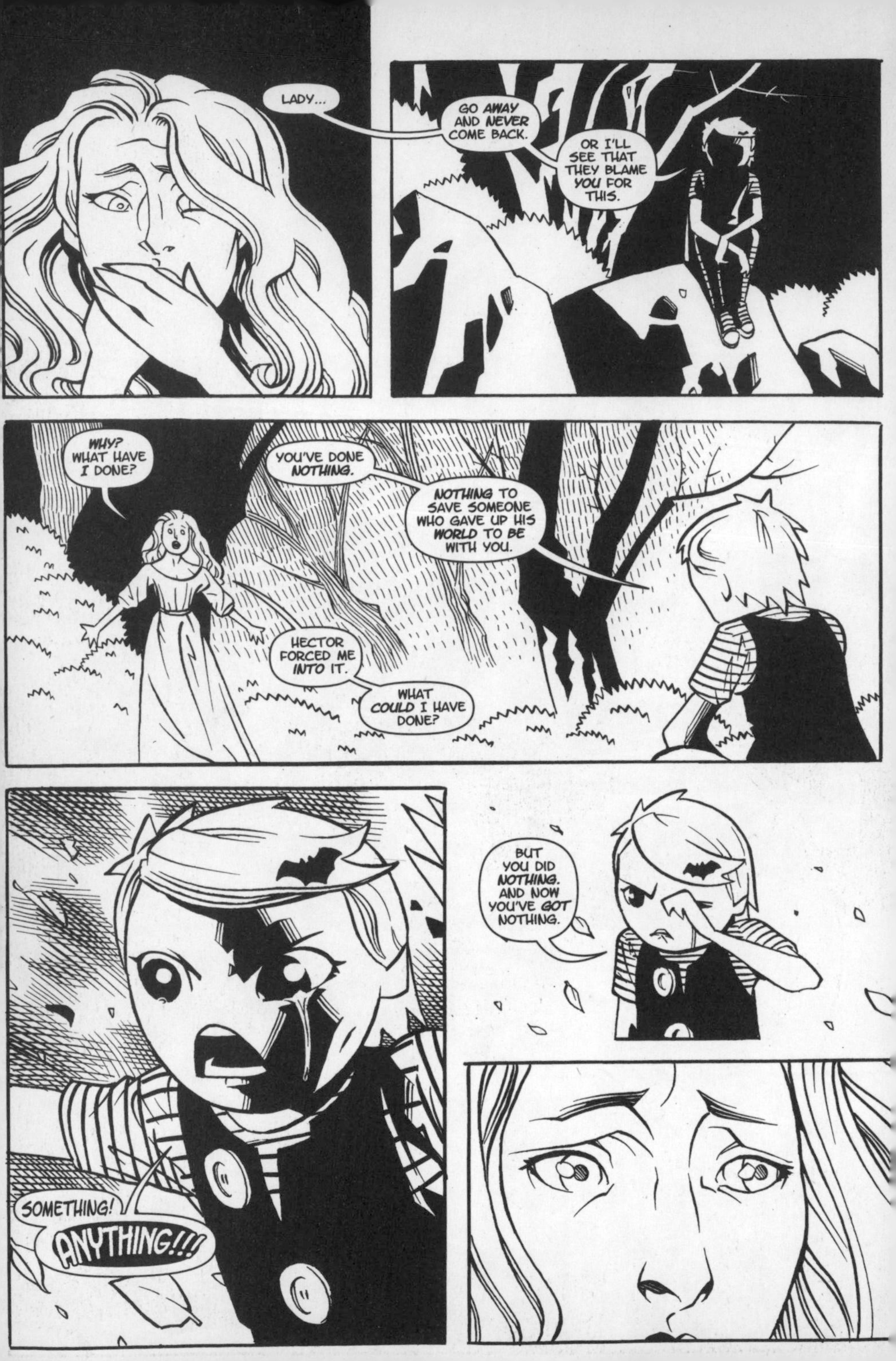
LADY...
GO AWAY AND NEVER COME BACK.
OR I'LL SEE THAT THEY BLAME YOU FOR THIS.
WHY? WHAT HAVE I DONE?
YOU'VE DONE NOTHING.
NOTHING TO SAVE SOMEONE WHO GAVE UP HIS WORLD TO BE WITH YOU.
HECTOR FORCED ME INTO IT.
WHAT COULD I HAVE DONE?
SOMETHING!
ANYTHING!!!
BUT YOU DID NOTHING. AND NOW YOU'VE GOT NOTHING.

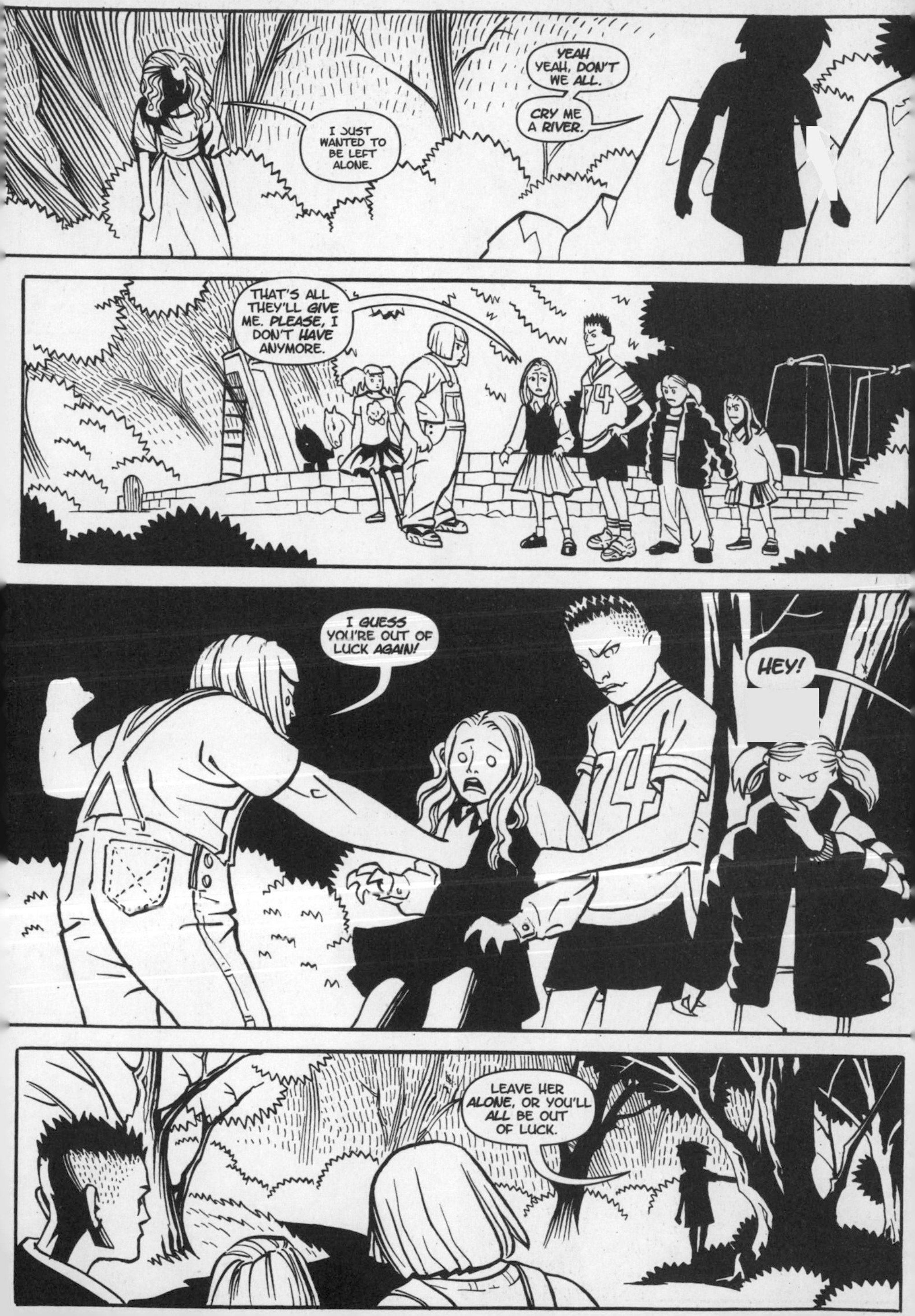
I JUST WANTED TO BE LEFT ALONE.
YEAH YEAH, DON'T WE ALL.
CRY ME A RIVER.
THAT'S ALL THEY'LL GIVE ME. PLEASE, I DON'T HAVE ANYMORE.
I GUESS YOU'RE OUT OF LUCK AGAIN!
HEY!
LEAVE HER ALONE, OR YOU'LL ALL BE OUT OF LUCK.

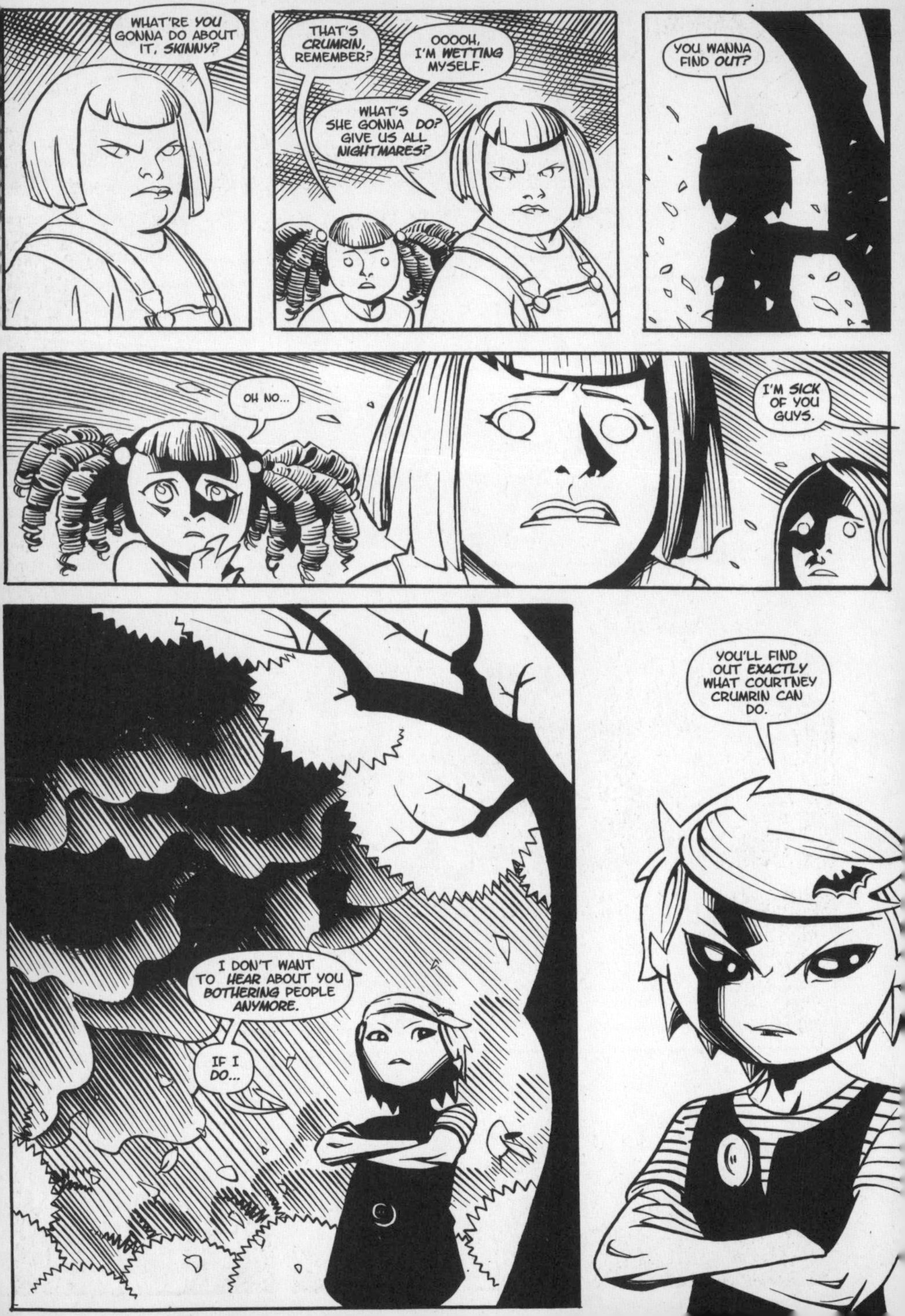
WHAT'RE YOU GONNA DO ABOUT IT, SKINNY?
THAT'S CRUMRIN, REMEMBER?
OOOOH, I'M WETTING MYSELF.
WHAT'S SHE GONNA DO? GIVE US ALL NIGHTMARES?
YOU WANNA FIND OUT?
OH NO...
I'M SICK OF YOU GUYS.
I DON'T WANT TO HEAR ABOUT YOU BOTHERING PEOPLE ANYMORE.
IF I DO...
YOU'LL FIND OUT EXACTLY WHAT COURTNEY CRUMRIN CAN DO.

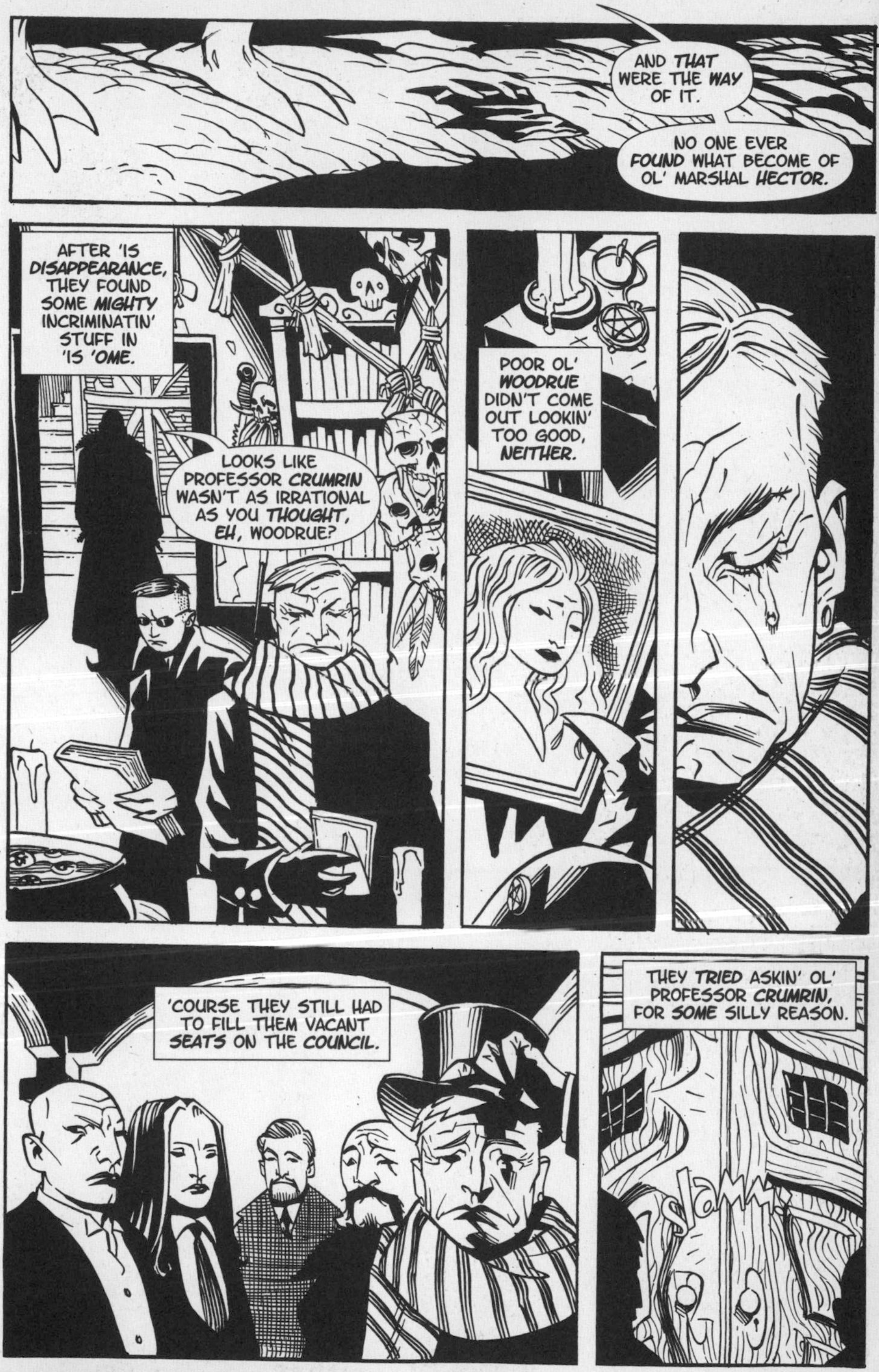

AND THAT WERE THE WAY OF IT.
NO ONE EVER FOUND WHAT BECOME OF OL' MARSHAL HECTOR.
AFTER 'IS DISAPPEARANCE, THEY FOUND SOME MIGHTY INCRIMINATIN' STUFF IN 'IS 'OME.
LOOKS LIKE PROFESSOR CRUMRIN WASN'T AS IRRATIONAL AS YOU THOUGHT, EH, WOODRUE?
POOR OL' WOODRUE DIDN'T COME OUT LOOKIN' TOO GOOD, NEITHER.
'COURSE THEY STILL HAD TO FILL THEM VACANT SEATS ON THE COUNCIL.
THEY TRIED ASKIN' OL' PROFESSOR CRUMRIN, FOR SOME SILLY REASON.
slamm!

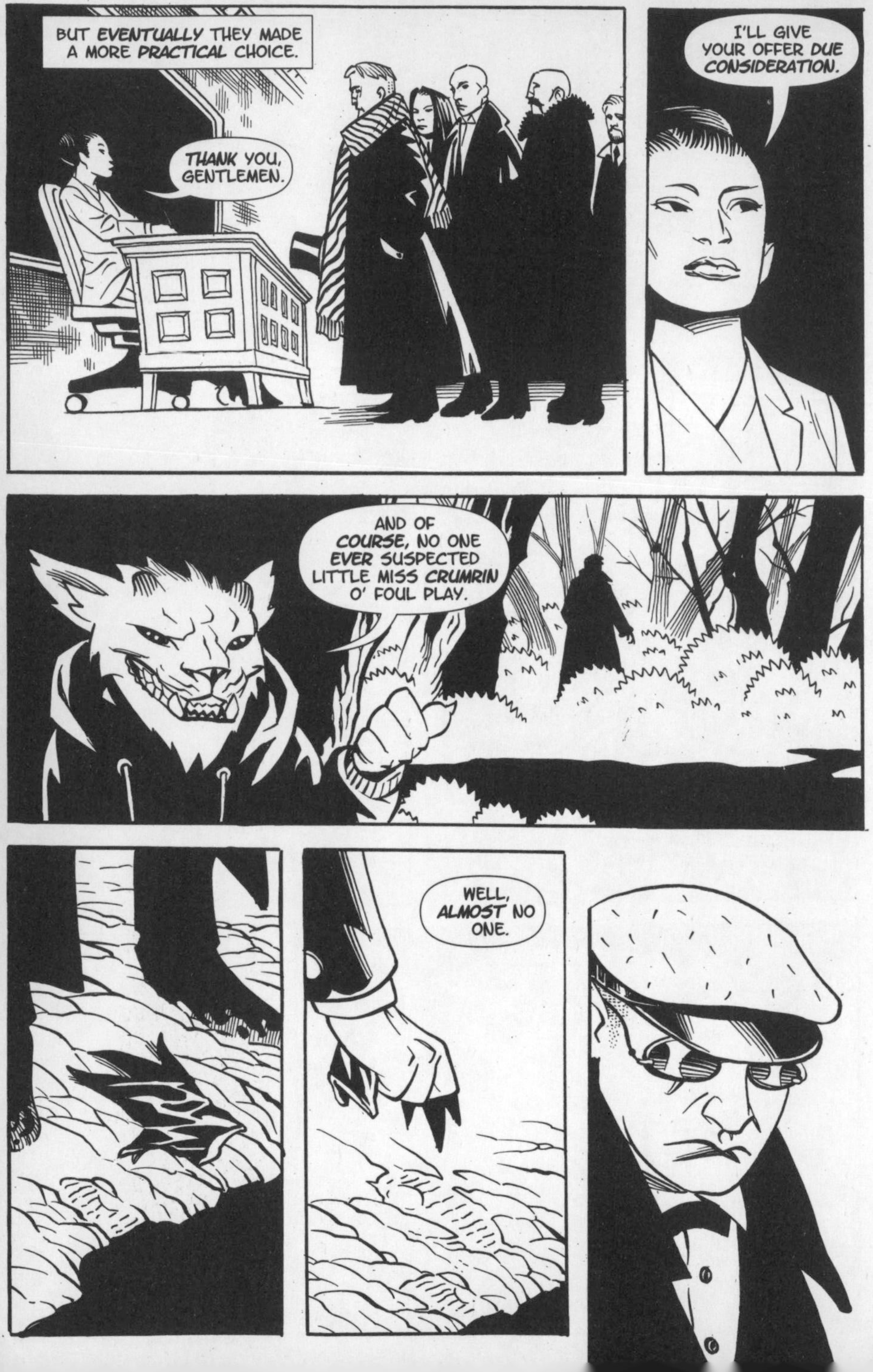
BUT EVENTUALLY THEY MADE A MORE PRACTICAL CHOICE.
THANK YOU, GENTLEMEN.
I'LL GIVE YOUR OFFER DUE CONSIDERATION.
AND OF COURSE, NO ONE EVER SUSPECTED LITTLE MISS CRUMRIN O' FOUL PLAY.
WELL, ALMOST NO ONE.

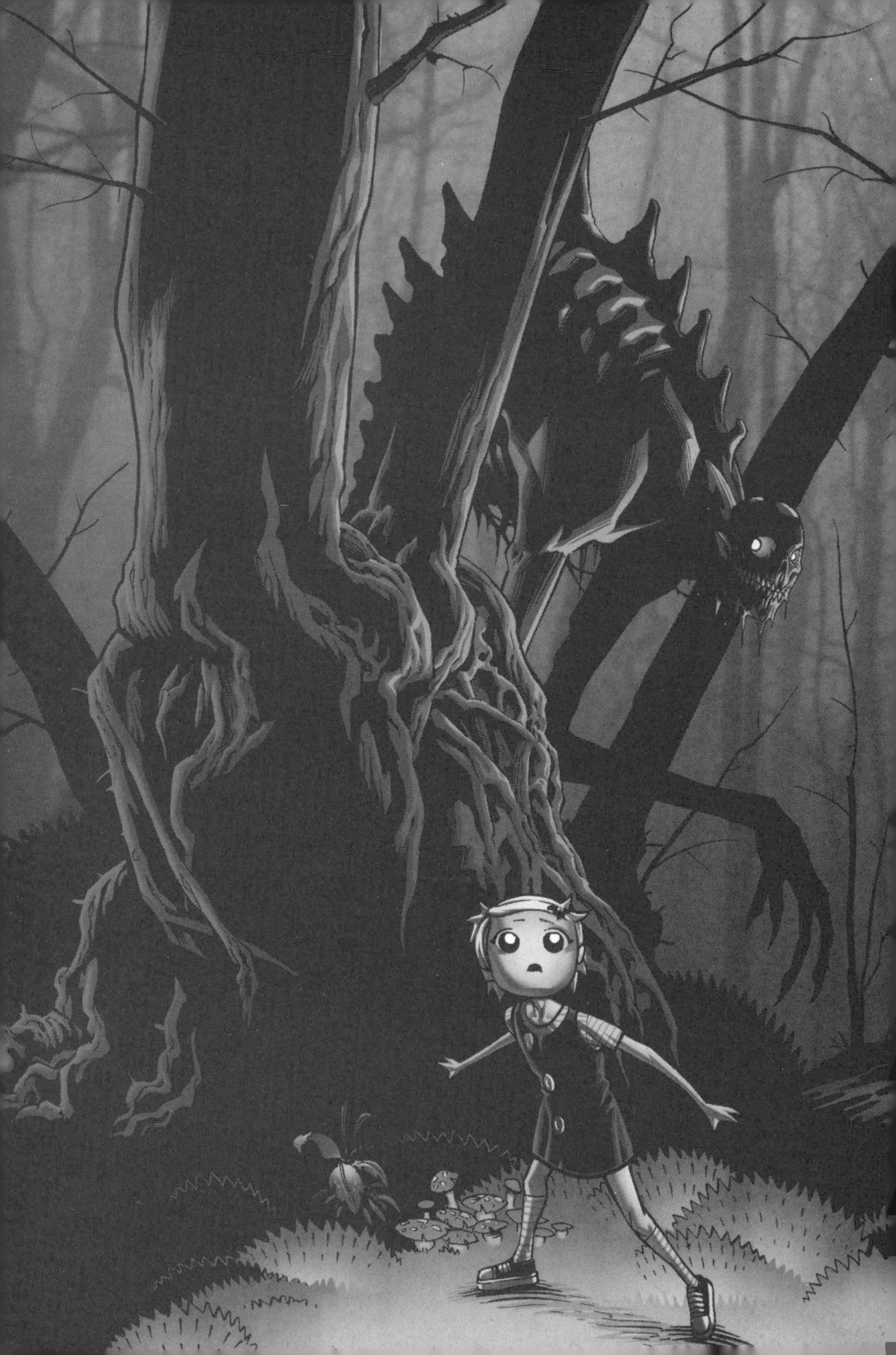

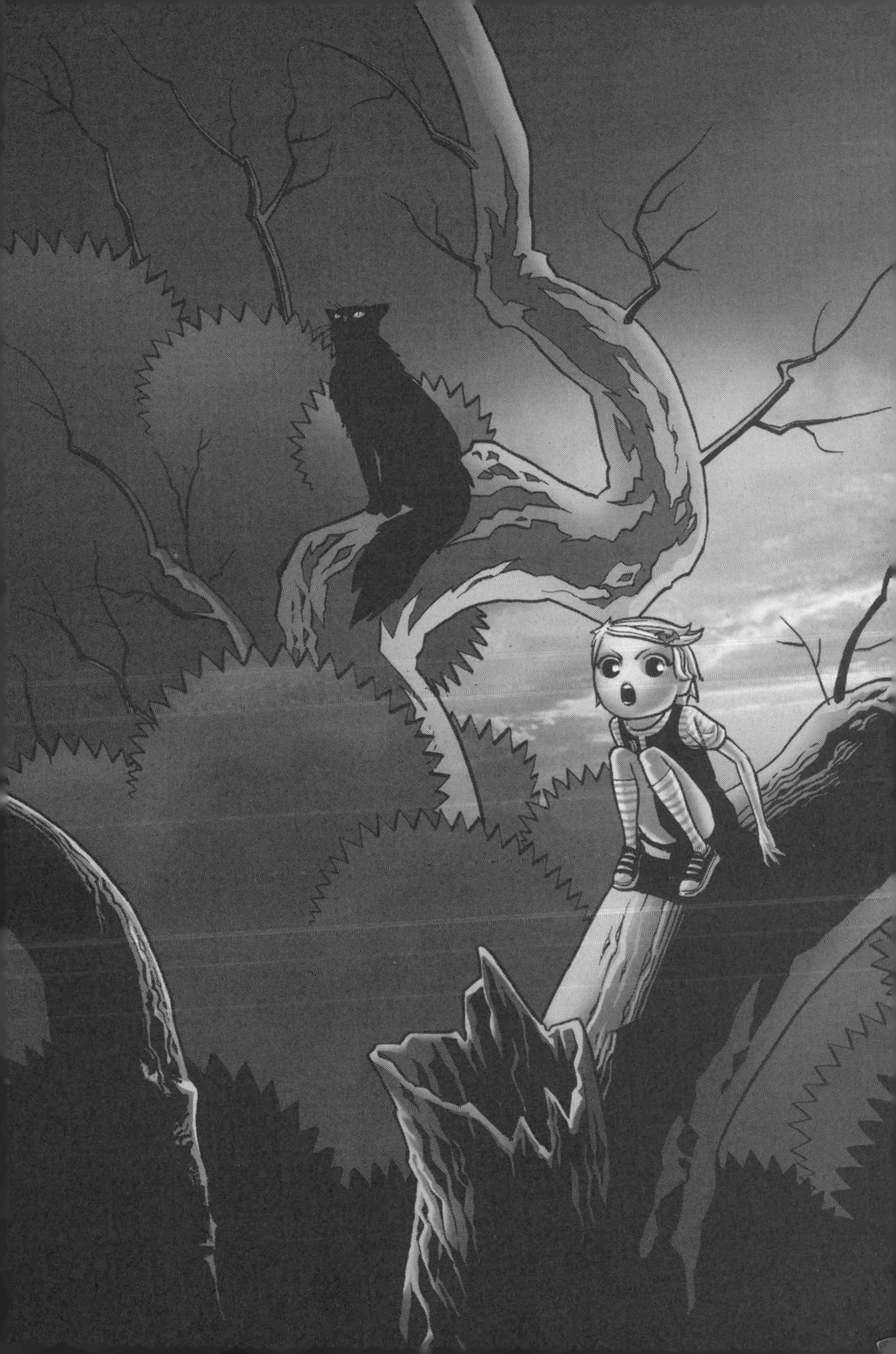

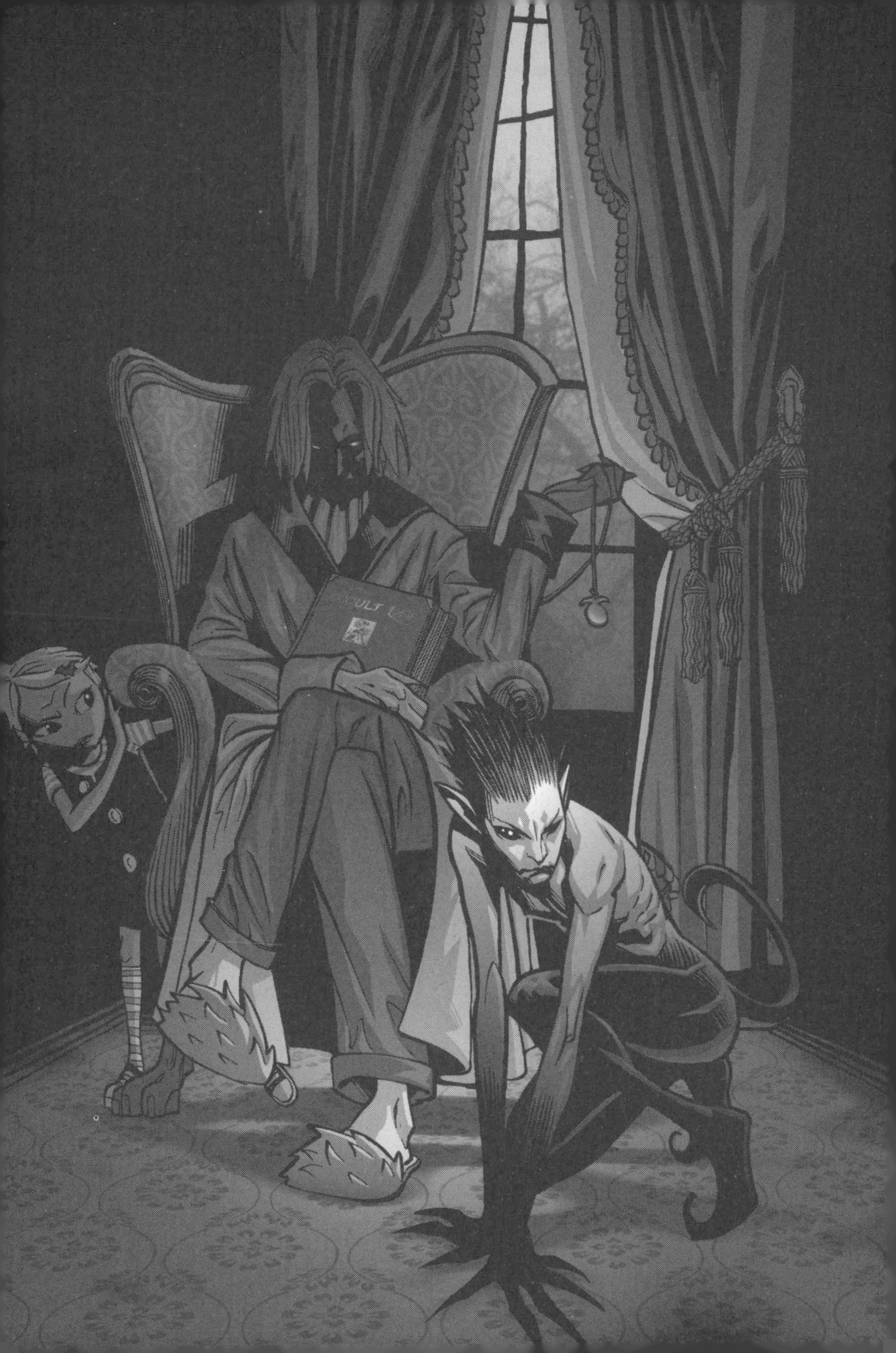

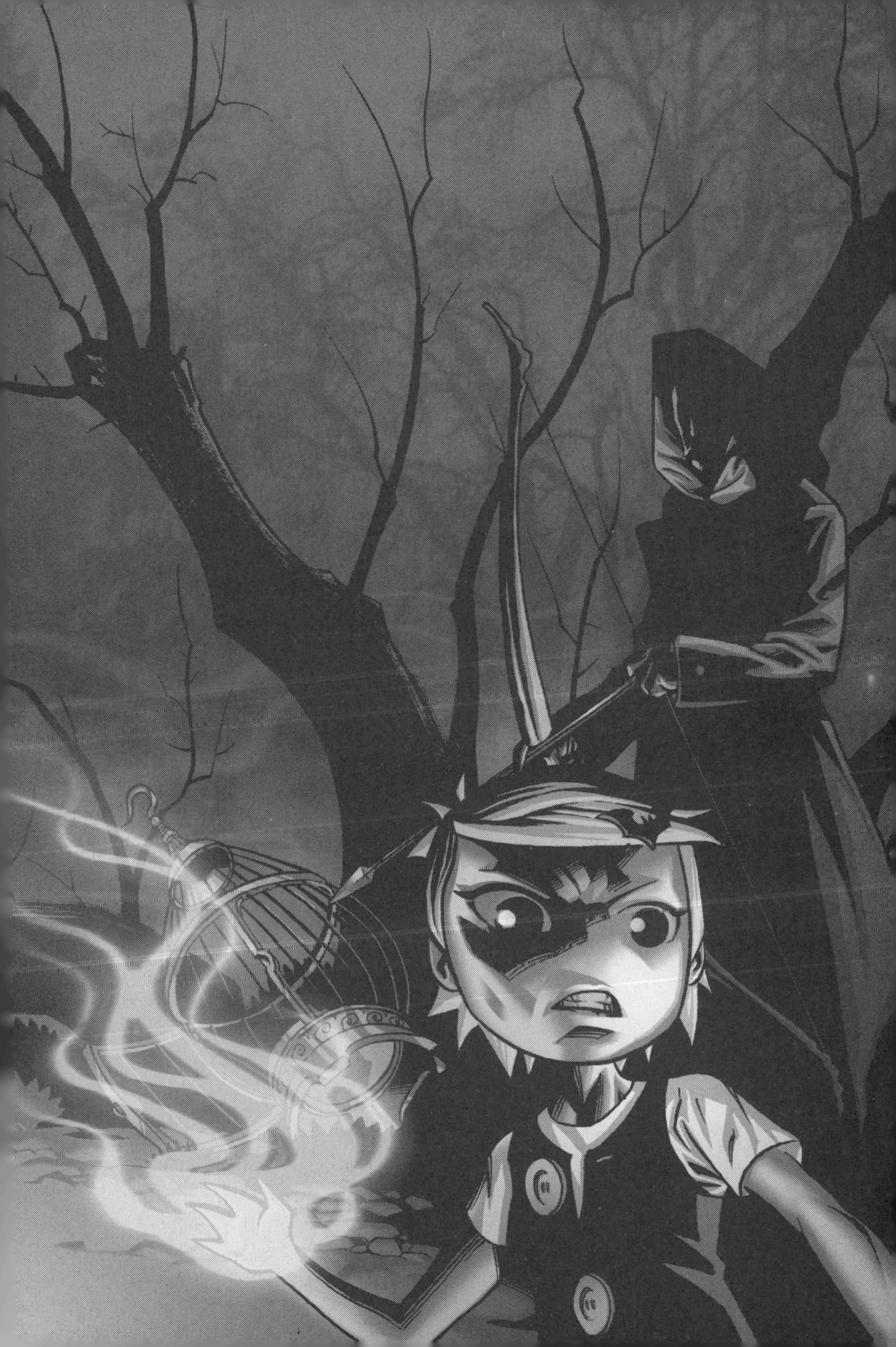

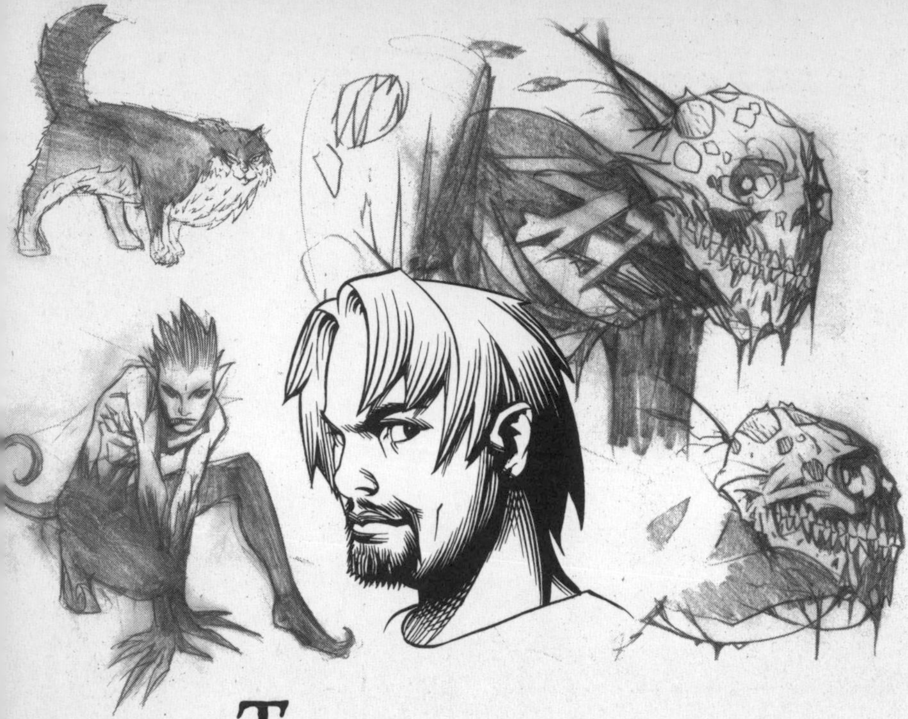

Ted Naifeh's first love is comics. Since the age of eighteen he's worked as a professional artist on a variety of genres ranging from horror to western to science fiction and fantasy. *Courtney Crumrin* represents his first published writing, and has been surprisingly well received. The original mini-series, *Courtney Crumrin and the Night Things*, was nominated for an Eisner award for best limited series in 2003.

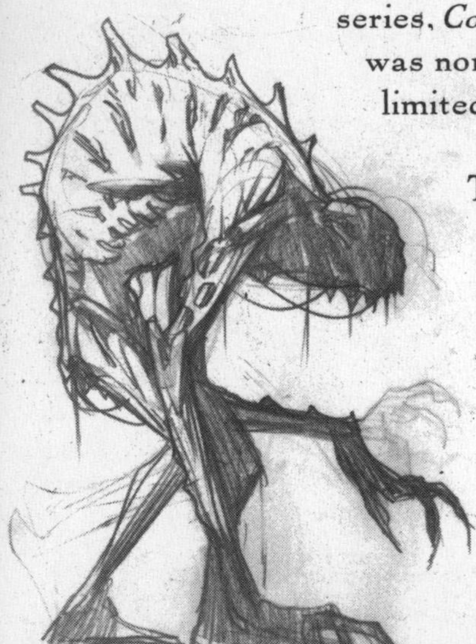

Ted is also the co-creator of comics such as the goth romance *Gloom Cookie* and the groundbreaking *How Loathsome*. He is currently starting to work on the third Courtney Crumrin tale.

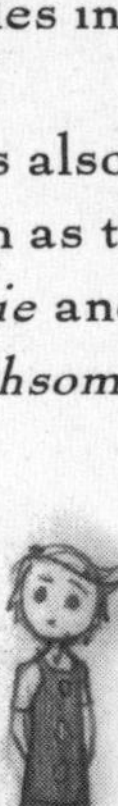

Ted Naifeh resides in San Francisco, city of night things.

More great books from Oni Press:

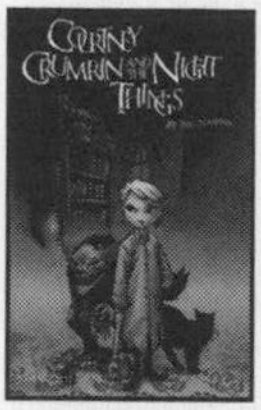

Courtney Crumrin
and the Night Things
by Ted Naifeh
128 pages
black-&-white interiors
$9.95 U.S.
ISBN 1-929998-60-0

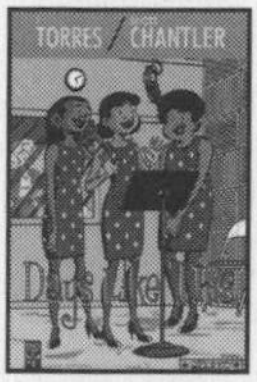
TORRES / CHANTLER

Days Like This
by J. Torres
& Scott Chantler
88 pages
black-&-white interiors
$8.95 U.S.
ISBN 1-929998-48-1

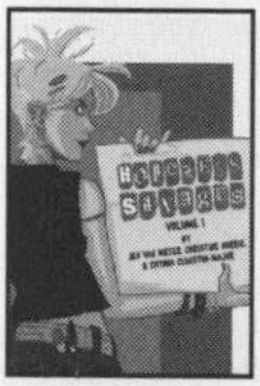

Hopeless Savages Vol. 1
by Jen Van Meter
Christine Norrie
& Chynna Clugston-Major
136 pages
black-&-white interiors
$11.95 U.S.
ISBN 1-929998-75-9

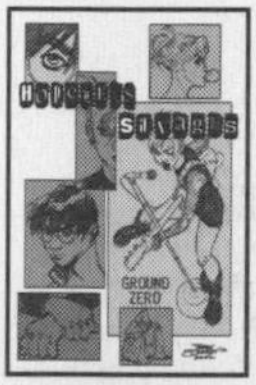

Hopeless Savages
Vol. 2: Ground Zero
by Jen Van Meter & Bryan O'Malley
w/ Clugston-Major, Norrie, & Watson
128 pages
black-&-white interiors
$11.95 U.S.
ISBN 1-0200008-52-X

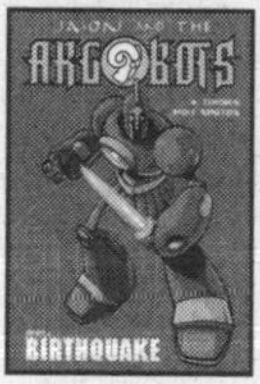
ARGOBOTS
BIRTHQUAKE

Jason and the Argobots
Vol. 1: Birthquake
by J. Torres & Mike Norton
112 pages
black-&-white interiors
$11.95 U.S.
ISBN 1-929998-55-4

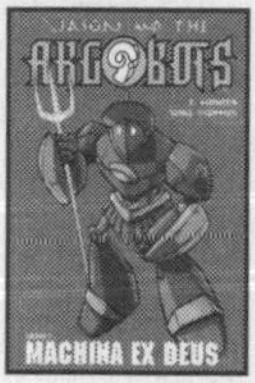
ARGOBOTS
MACHINA EX DEUS

Jason and the Argobots
Vol. 2: Machina Ex Deus
by J. Torres & Mike Norton
104 pages
black-&-white interiors
$11.95 U.S.
ISBN 1-929998-56-2

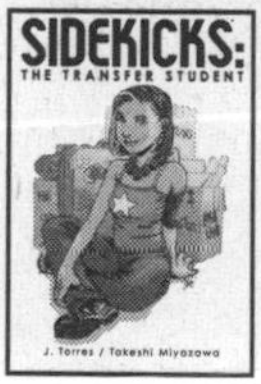
SIDEKICKS:
THE TRANSFER STUDENT
J. Torres / Takeshi Miyazawa

Sidekicks Vol. 1:
The Transfer Student
by J. Torres & Takeshi Miyazawa
144 pages
black-&-white interiors
$11.95 U.S.
ISBN 1-929998-76-7

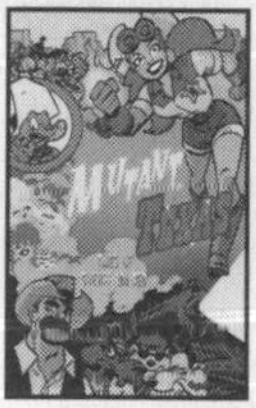

Mutant Texas:
Tales of Ida Red
by Paul Dini & J. Bone
128 pages
black-&-white interiors
$11.95 U.S.
ISBN 1-929998-53-8

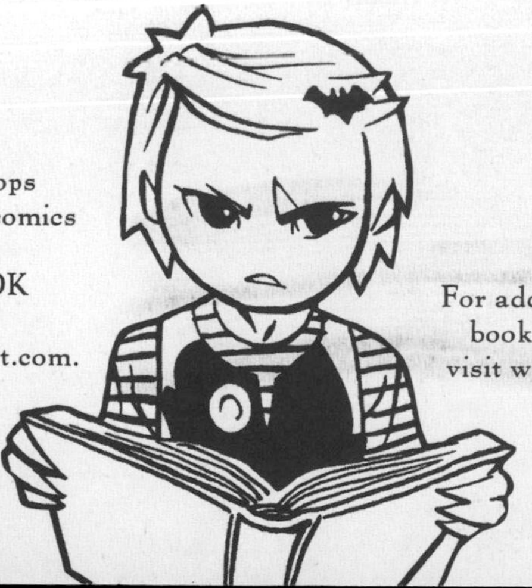

Available at
www.onipress.com
and finer comics shops
everywhere. For a comics
store near you, call
1-888-COMIC-BOOK
or visit
www.the-master-list.com.

For additional Oni Press
books and information
visit www.onipress.com.

[redacted]

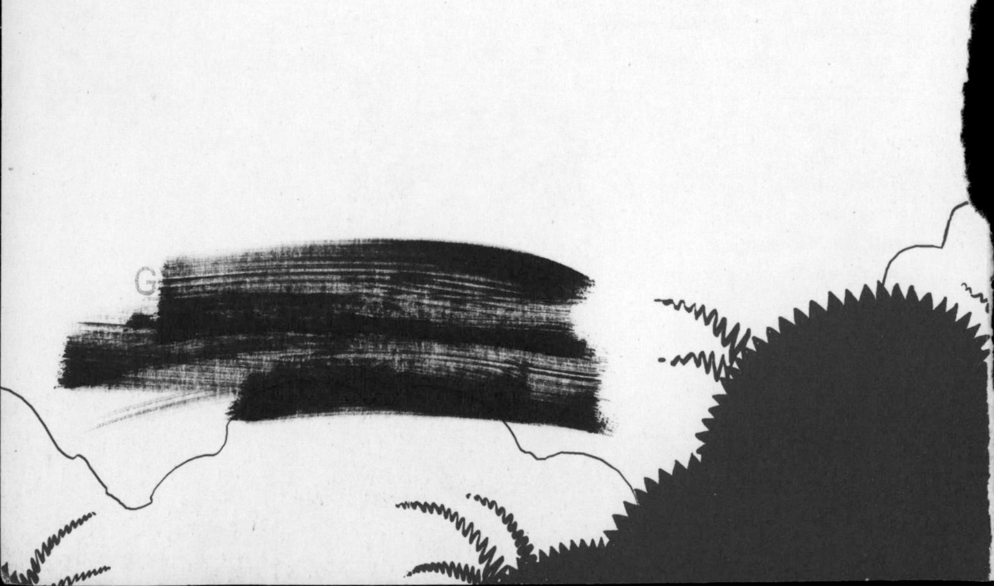